D1087813

Praise for the novels of

'Read on, adventure fans.'
**NEW YORK TIMES**

'A rich, compelling look back in time [to]
when history and myth intermingled.'
**SAN FRANCISCO CHRONICLE**

'Only a handful of 20th century writers tantalize
our senses as well as Smith. A rare author who
wields a razor-sharp sword of craftsmanship.'
**TULSA WORLD**

'He paces his tale as swiftly as he can with
swordplay aplenty and killing strokes that come
like lightning out of a sunny blue sky.'
**KIRKUS REVIEWS**

'Best Historical Novelist – I say Wilbur Smith, with his
swashbuckling novels of Africa. The bodices rip and the
blood flows. You can get lost in Wilbur Smith and
misplace all of August.'
**STEPHEN KING**

'Action is the name of Wilbur Smith's game
and he is the master.'
**WASHINGTON POST**

'Smith manages to serve up adventure, history
and melodrama in one thrilling package that
will be eagerly devoured by series fans.'
**PUBLISHERS WEEKLY**

'This well-crafted novel is full
of adventure, tension, and intrigue.'
**LIBRARY JOURNAL**

'Life-threatening dangers loom around
every turn, leaving the reader breathless . . .
An incredibly exciting and satisfying read.'
**CHATTANOOGA FREE PRESS**

'When it comes to writing the adventure novel,
Wilbur Smith is the master; a 21st century
H. Rider Haggard.'
**VANITY FAIR**

**Wilbur Smith** was born in Central Africa in 1933. He became a full-time writer in 1964 following the success of *When the Lion Feeds*, and has since published over forty global best-sellers, including the Courtney Series, the Ballantyne Series, the Egyptian Series, the Hector Cross Series and many successful standalone novels, all meticulously researched on his numerous expeditions worldwide. A worldwide phenomenon, his reader-ship built up over fifty-five years of writing, establishing him as one of the most successful and impressive brand authors in the world.

The establishment of the Wilbur & Niso Smith Foundation in 2015 cemented Wilbur's passion for empowering writers, promoting literacy and advancing adventure writing as a genre. The foundation's flagship program is the Wilbur Smith Adventure Writing Prize.

Wilbur Smith passed away peacefully at home in 2021 with his wife, Niso, by his side, leaving behind him a rich treasure-trove of novels and stories that will delight readers for years to come.

For all the latest information on Wilbur Smith's writing visit www.wilbursmithbooks.com or facebook.com/WilburSmith.

**Mark Chadbourn** is a *Sunday Times* bestselling author of historical fiction novels about the Anglo-Saxon warrior Hereward, published under his pseudonym James Wilde. His *Age of Misrule* books, under his own name, have been translated into many languages. As a screenwriter, he's written for the BBC and is currently developing a series for Lionsgate and several of the streaming networks. He began his career as a journalist reporting from the world's hotspots.

# WILBUR SMITH

WITH
## MARK CHADBOURN

# TITANS OF WAR

ZAFFRE

This is a work of fiction. Names, places, events and incidents are either
the products of the authors' imaginations or used fictitiously. Any resemblance
to actual persons, living or dead, or actual events is purely coincidental.

Copyright © Orion Mintaka (UK) Ltd. 2022
Author photo © Hendre Louw

All rights reserved, including the right of reproduction in
whole or in part in any form.
First published in the United States of America in 2022 by Zaffre,
an imprint of Bonnier Books UK

Typeset by IDSUK (Data Connection) Ltd
Printed in Great Britain by Clays Ltd, Elcograf S.p.A.

10 9 8 7 6 5 4 3 2 1

Hardcover ISBN: 978–1–8387–7908–5
Canadian paperback ISBN: 978–1–8387–7910–8
Digital ISBN: 978–1–8387–7909–2

For information, contact
251 Park Avenue South, Floor 12, New York, New York 10010
www.bonnierbooks.co.uk

MIX
Paper from
responsible sources
FSC
www.fsc.org
FSC® C018072

*For my love*

*MOKHINISO*

*Spirits of Genghis Khan and Omar Khayyam reincarnated*
*in a moon as lucent as a perfect pearl*

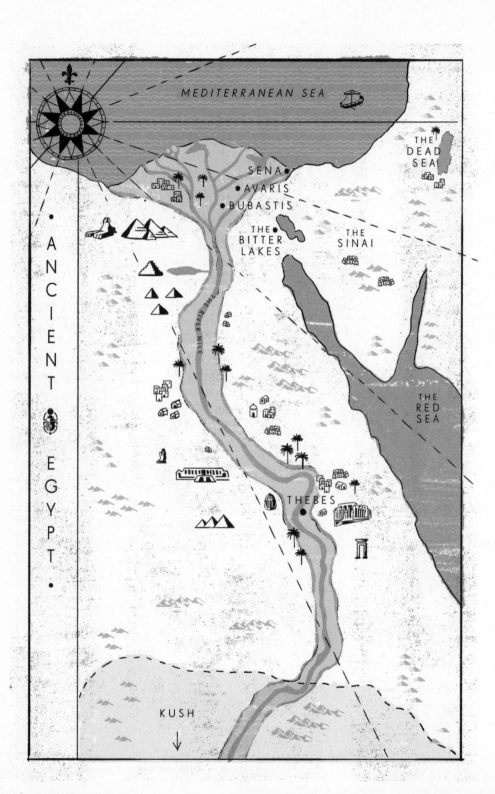

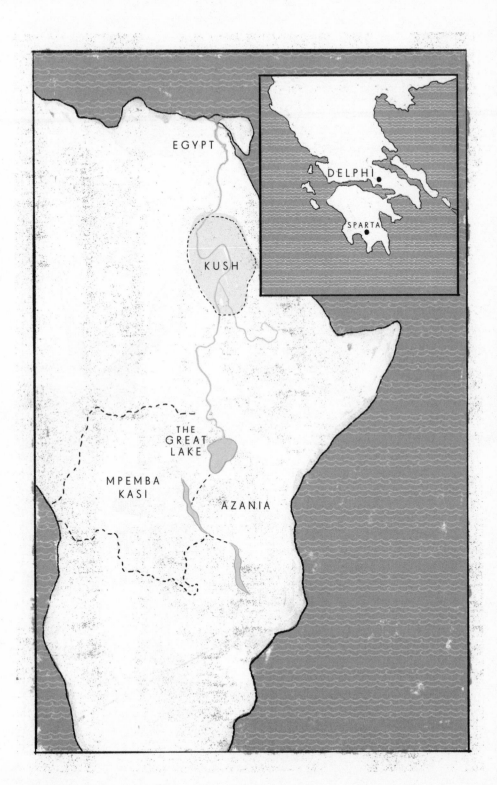

# EGYPT

The two men crept along the edge of the moonlit barley field. Sweat trickled down their taut bare backs. Fingers were tightened around the hilts of bronze swords and their eyes darted. Along the horizon a red glow wavered from the blazing farms littering the lush Nile Valley, and a warm desert wind whipped sheets of smoke across the stars. The men choked on the reek of burning, their ears ringing with the cries of the dying which shredded the stillness like the howls of wild cats. This was grim work, but they were ready.

They were a mismatched pair. Piay was tall and muscular with a strong jawline, high cheekbones and dark eyes that turned the heads of the women who served the Pharaoh. Hannu, his assistant, walked with a limp. He was squat, with a thatch of black hair covering his body, and a jagged scar carved down his left cheek to an unkempt black beard. As he looked around, he glowered with eyes like hot coals.

'Go much further and you will not return,' Hannu grunted as they halted to search the way ahead. 'The Hyksos swarm across this land like rats at harvest time.'

'Courage, my friend,' said Piay. 'Faint hearts will not drive these invaders back to their distant home.'

Hannu snorted. 'Courage. If that was all it took, we would have been victorious fifty years gone, when they first came here. See how courage helps when you've got one of their beasts thundering towards you and a crescent sword hacking off the heads of your friends.'

Piay jabbed a finger. 'We have a job to do.'

'Aye. But not at the cost of our necks. "Get as close as you can," Taita said.'

'And we can get closer! I will not return to my master empty-handed.'

Piay glanced back at the six soldiers who had been sent to accompany them on this spying mission. They were young, their blades wavering in their hands as they crouched, waiting for an order. So many of the experienced soldiers had been killed in the fighting that they were recruiting boys who a short while ago had been working in their fathers' fields.

Piay peered into the dark ahead. What were the barbarians planning to do next? That was the question he needed to answer.

This interminable war had been rolling back and forth along the valley of Mother Nile for nigh on half a century. The barbarians had superior numbers – what appeared to be an endless supply of the best fighting men in the world. They had the greater weapons – those cruel swords and bows that were three times as powerful as any in Egyptian hands. Most importantly, they had those damnable beasts that so terrified Hannu – the horses, powerful and well trained, able to pull gleaming chariots from which each warrior could loose a hundred arrows as they advanced.

Many had lost hope that Egypt would ever be free. But not his master. Taita the Wise, the Pharaoh's mage and counsellor, insisted that a moment would come when they could drive the Hyksos out once and for all. They had to watch and wait. Taita had sent his agents out time and again to learn the valuable information that would turn the tide of battle. And every time, those spies had failed.

Piay felt his chest harden. Not him. He was the best of them all. He would succeed. He glanced at the white kilt he wore, embroidered with the yellow orb of Ra's fiery chariot. It was his most prized possession, a present from Taita on the day he had finished his studies, and each time he had worn it, he had experienced good fortune. This was his moment. Glory awaited him.

'You asked me to tell you if your confidence swelled your head to the point where it might burst,' Hannu cautioned. 'It is happening now.'

A terrible scream tore through the night and Hannu stiffened. Piay flinched. His soldiers' faces were as bloodless as if they had seen the dead return from their tombs.

Piay would not show fear. These men depended on him to lead them into this blood-soaked territory. The Hyksos had advanced again, reclaiming land they had been driven from only two years before. They were showing no mercy to anyone they encountered. To save themselves, the farmers would follow the orders of their new masters. They always did.

Hannu's gaze skittered across the dark fields. He wasn't scared, Piay knew – he was never afraid. The instincts he'd honed in battle during his former life as a soldier were coming to the fore.

Piay remembered stumbling across Hannu begging on a dusty street in Thebes. His ruined leg, hacked in some battle, meant he could no longer be a member of the elite Blue Crocodile Guards. Many thought he was useless, with no future. But Piay had seen something in this fierce little man that day, in his incisive stare and his contempt for well-educated strangers. He was also knowledgeable and wise, two things that an even wiser man valued. Piay had hired him as an assistant, an occasional advisor, servant and diplomat.

Hannu took it upon himself to keep Piay's feet upon the ground.

'I admit I sometimes let my confidence get the better of me,' said Piay.

'And your mouth.'

Piay tightened his lips. 'I am a spy of great renown, foremost in all skills—'

'Except humility.'

'. . . trained in the arts of war and peace, by the great Taita himself, but I defer to your knowledge of blood-soaked battle-fields and the smell of defeat.'

Hannu narrowed his eyes.

'We will continue with caution. And at the first sign of trouble we will retreat. Is that fair?'

Hannu grunted again. His assent wasn't convincing.

Piay raised his hand and snapped his fingers forward. Away they went, deeper into enemy territory.

Laughter split the air across the swaying crops. Piay could smell the heavy musk of the barbarians' beasts. The horse had once been unknown in Egypt, so he had been told. But that was long before he had been born.

Taita had told him the story of when the Hyksos had first swept like a storm upon the backs of their mounts. Taita had witnessed this fearsome sight himself, so he said, and if that were true then Taita must have been blessed by the gods, for he looked barely older than Piay.

Piay heard the beasts snort and stamp their hooves. They were close but not close enough.

They'd known of these strange barbarian people from the distant east, the Hyksos, for many years, Taita had said. They came from a mountainous land and had once been farmers until they learned the way of the crescent sword and the bow. When their small bands had started to move into the Sinai and along the fringes of the Nile, the Hyksos had been considered little more than an irritant, raiding caravans and turquoise mines and isolated settlements.

In those days, who could have guessed they had designs upon Egypt itself?

But their king had been planning for a long time. Reports reached Thebes of a vast army bearing down upon this civilised land. The Red Pretender, that false pharaoh in the Lower Kingdom, with all his forces, had been crushed as if he were nothing. And then the Hyksos had turned their attention to the south, to the Upper Kingdom.

The Hyksos wanted it all.

In Thebes, the Pharaoh heard these tales of blood and destruction from the north and dug deep into his coffers to repel any invasion. New galleys were built and the army was marched along the banks of the Nile to destroy these arrogant intruders. Even after hearing what had been wrought upon the Red Pretender, the Pharaoh still drank deeply of the heady brew of the myth of Egyptian supremacy.

Taita had trembled when he recounted how the great Egyptian army had been routed in just one day, and his master was not a man given to displays of emotion. Galleys sank in flames and the Hyksos drove the remnants of the once proud force south, harrying them at every opportunity. It had turned from battle to mere sport.

Since that day, Egypt had known endless war and bloodshed and death. Fifty years of it. After Thebes had fallen for the first time, Taita had fled south with the current Pharaoh. The great king had only been a boy then. After a stay in the lands beyond the cataracts, Taita had returned with renewed vigour to drive the enemy out of the City of a Hundred Gates and back towards the Lower Kingdom. But the Hyksos never relented, pressing ever onwards, recapturing land lost only to lose it again. And under Taita's guidance the brave resistance had continued. But over time the Egyptian army became diminished, the chance of reclaiming the land of their birth beginning to fade like the morning mist.

Now they had reached a time of desperation.

Smoke swept across the fields from the farmstead blazing nearby, the roar of the flames combining with the laughter of whoever was gathered out of sight.

Piay pushed the flat of his hand down and the men behind dropped lower. He slipped forwards below the level of the swaying barley, sensing Hannu at his back.

The laughter was louder, and he could hear the guttural notes of that strange barbarian tongue.

On the edge of an irrigation channel, Piay dropped to his belly and slid forwards like a serpent. The steady heartbeat of the shadoof rolled out as the water wheel turned, plunging the bucket on the pole into the water, then swinging it back up with the counterweight.

Ahead, the flames of a campfire rose towards the stars. A constellation of sparks drifted on the night breeze. Around the burning sods of animal dung and straw, six barbarians lounged in their leather caps and breastplates, gnawing on what looked like strips of cured meat. Their crescent-shaped swords were sheathed, their bows set aside. They were not expecting any attack. Why would they? They were masters here.

One of the barbarians picked through a pile of swords, amulets and rings – booty taken from dead Egyptian soldiers.

Piay blinked away tears as the smoke stung his eyes, and when his vision cleared he glimpsed another figure on the edge of the circle of wavering amber light. This man was hunched over, but when he raised his head the dancing flames picked out blood caking the edge of his mouth and his left eye. Bruises mottled his skin. An Egyptian soldier, a captive, beaten for information on what remained of the fleeing force.

Piay felt anger simmer in his breast. One of the barbarians heaved himself up and sauntered over to the captive. Squatting beside the bloodied man, the Hyksos warrior grunted something in the captive's ear. It must have been in the Egyptian tongue, for the soldier shook his head. The Hyksos warrior cuffed the brave Egyptian round the ears and laughed as he returned to the fire. The others chuckled and fell back to their conversation.

Piay studied the group, looking for any signs of weakness. His attention settled on one he sensed was the leader of the band. The captain sat apart from the others and rarely joined in with their chatter. His back was as straight as a rod, his chin held high. Above his black bristles, his skin was scarred with the marks of the pox. His eyes moved slowly and sullenly across the dark countryside beyond the firelight. Piay felt a power rolling off him like the rippling waves of heat that rose from the baked desert sands.

This was a dangerous man, he was sure. He would be the greatest threat.

Piay steeled himself. Here was a situation that would bring him all the glory of which he had ever dreamed. The band was small. The element of surprise would allow them to counter any superior battle skills these seasoned warriors might possess. This was a fight they could win easily. They could not leave an Egyptian in the hands of such barbarians. Who knew what terrible things he would be forced to endure before they took his life?

What secrets had the captive overheard? Piay could bring back valuable information. Perhaps even to turn the tide of battle.

Piay beckoned his men to crawl up behind him. Their faces were taut, their eyes widened. They were anxious, but they would obey his orders to the last.

Hannu came up beside him and whispered, 'Now's not the time for an attack, we've not scouted the surrounding land.'

'We don't have the time,' Piay breathed. 'We act now. The longer we wait, the more chance we might be discovered. And then we would be slaughtered.'

Piay knew he had brought them to the point of no return. He could almost hear Taita's praise ringing in his ears.

Piay noticed the captain had taken himself further away. He was sitting cross-legged on the edge of the circle of firelight, looking up at the stars with his lips moving as if he was praying. He dipped into a leather pouch that hung at his waist.

Piay levelled his left hand to signal for his men to wait.

The captain unfurled his fingers to reveal a handful of small flowers. The petals were dark and Piay shivered when he recognised their distinct shape. The blue lotus. He had heard it called the Dream Flower, sacred to Ra, for it rose from the waters of the Nile at first light and disappeared as the sun fell. The priests of the temples had drunk it in a brew from the days of antiquity, for it allowed them to contact the gods themselves. Some said it transported the *Ka* to the afterlife to learn secret knowledge before returning to the land of men. Others, that it filled those who consumed it with supernatural powers.

'Wait,' Piay whispered. 'The blue lotus will suck their leader into dreams and visions. Then our advantage will be greater still.'

The other barbarians laughed and chewed and tossed more sods on to the fire, sending golden sparks cascading towards the heavens. The captive's head nodded on to his chest. For him all hope was gone – he had resigned himself to death.

The captain let his eyes drift to the stars, and the full moon, and gradually his lids weighed down.

Easing up his sword, Piay pushed himself onto his haunches and uttered 'Now.'

The Egyptian band surged forwards. Blood-curdling screeches rang out across the lush fields.

Piay bounded ahead. He was strong and fast, and the memories flooded through him of all those lessons with a sword from when he had been barely old enough to lift one: sweating under a hot sun, parrying and thrusting and moving with the grace of a temple dancer until all of it became second nature. He told everyone he was the best swordsman in all Egypt. Few argued.

By the time he could feel the bloom from the heat of the campfire, the barbarians were on their feet and fumbling to draw their curved blades. Except the captain, who remained cross-legged, drifting in whatever netherworld the blue lotus had imprisoned him.

Piay darted in front of the first Hyksos warrior. As his opponent swung his weapon to hack, Piay rammed his blade through flesh and bone to the heart. He wrenched his sword free and spun to confront the next opponent.

But all the other Hyksos warriors were engaged. Hannu swung his weapon with the strength of a man twice his size. One Egyptian soldier reeled from a deep gash on his upper arm, but he would survive.

Piay leaped to the captive. The man looked up with wide eyes, scarcely believing what he was seeing.

'You came for me,' he croaked.

'Remember to tell your friends who it was that saved your life. My name is Piay.'

'Piay.'

His name sounded from behind him in little more than an exhalation, almost lost beneath the hissing of the fire. He turned and saw the captain's eyes begin to focus as he dragged himself out of his trance.

Piay sawed at the strips of hide that bound the captive's wrists. He pulled the man to his feet.

'Away,' Piay said. 'We will guide you home when we are done here.'

'Piay.' The captain's voice was stronger now.

Piay moved round. Levelling his sword, he said, 'You have been defeated by better men. You can keep your life if you flee. Tell the others like you that Egypt will never be vanquished.'

The captain eased himself up to his full height, a head taller than Piay, without a hint of bewilderment from the blue lotuses he had consumed. A grey fire seemed to flicker in his eyes. The captain's unkempt black hair was bound with strips of hide on which hung small bones that clacked together in a macabre music of death every time he moved his head. He drew his lips into a wolfish grin.

Piay had seen many Hyksos in his time, but none like this. He saw the swirls of intricate tattoos along the captain's arms, symbols which seemed to tell a story.

'I see you,' the captain breathed. 'Your god Anubis stands at your shoulder.'

The captain peered past him with that strange, implacable stare, as if something lurked in the shadows.

'Flee,' Piay said as the battle raged behind him. 'My patience is not endless. This is the last time I will show mercy.'

'I have walked along the shores of the black ocean to the very edge of the afterlife,' the captain continued, as if he had not heard Piay's words. 'I have heard the whispers of the gods.'

He drew his own blade. The reflected firelight glinted along it in amber ripples as he waved it in front of Piay.

If the liquor of the blue lotus still coursed through his veins, it did not diminish his potency. The movements of the blade were precise, the skill of a master swordsman.

'My name is Sakir,' the captain said in a rumbling voice. 'Known by many as the Red Hawk, by others as He Who Walks With the Gods. Of all the Hyksos you could have chosen to make an enemy, you have found the worst. I do not fear death. I embrace it. And now that you have stirred me from my dreams, I will bring that death to you.'

Piay laughed. 'You think highly of yourself. But you are just another filthy invader trampling across the glory that is Egypt. You are a passing shadow on this land and soon you will be gone.'

Sakir pushed two fingers in his mouth and blasted out a long whistle.

Piay glanced at the fighting barbarians, trying to comprehend what their captain was signalling to them. They seemed unmoved, still attacking in the same chaotic manner. Suddenly Sakir swung his sword in an arc with such strength it could have cleaved Piay in two had not Piay swept up his own blade and, with a delicate flick of his wrist, positioned the weapon at an angle to deflect his enemy's strike.

Sakir hacked again, driving forwards. Piay danced back. He felt his concentration narrow. The Hyksos captain was as good as he'd said.

They moved around the campfire. Piay's nostrils sucked in the drifting smoke and his eyes stung with tears. Sakir appeared unmoved. He was barely blinking. Their blades sang into the night.

Sweat drenched Piay's back and soaked into his kilt. He forced a grin to hide his unease. He had never faced an opponent as skilled as this warrior. They were evenly matched.

*I will not be defeated*, he told himself. *I am the best swordsman in all Egypt.*

Piay kicked at the campfire. A burning sod flew up and hit Sakir's thigh. Not a wince crossed the captain's face. It was as if he could feel no pain.

There was a sound like distant thunder. An instant later Piay heard cries ring out.

Hyksos riders pounded along the track towards them. The whistle blast had not been intended for the barbarians engaged in that furious battle. Sakir had summoned reinforcements.

Piay felt his stomach knot. Hannu had been right – he had been too confident. He should have scouted the area before launching his attack.

Dropping, he spun on his left hand and swung one foot in an arc. Sakir's legs flew out from under him and he crashed to the ground. Piay threw himself forwards. He stamped his foot on the wrist of his opponent's sword-arm and rammed the barbarian's head down. The left side of Sakir's face crunched into the hot embers. This time he howled. The stink of searing flesh filled the air.

Piay darted away. 'Come!' he yelled to his men.

Hooking one hand under the Egyptian captive's arm, he dragged him away.

He glanced back and horror flooded him. The Hyksos warriors had fallen upon the rest of the scouting band. Hooves shattered skulls. Swords cleaved through necks and chests. The screams of the dying spiked deep into his heart.

Piay felt someone slam into him and he pitched into the shadows of an irrigation ditch. Snatching a gulp of air, he plunged into cold black water. Two other figures splashed beside him. One was the Egyptian soldier, the other Hannu.

His assistant grabbed him and whispered, 'Ahead, as fast as you can, but quietly. This has bought us a little time, but that is all.'

Piay grasped the arm of the former captive and together they half-swam, half-waded away from the rolling thunder of hoof beats circling the area.

'I will come for you, Piay!' Sakir's voice boomed through the night. 'Run as fast as you can, run for days and weeks and months. But there will come a time when you turn and I will be there and then your life will be over!'

As he pushed through the cold water, Piay's mood darkened. The faces of the young men he had commanded floated into his mind. Barely more than boys, innocent, trusting in him. He had failed them.

Could he ever make amends? Piay felt the murk of the ditch seep into him and close around his heart.

Hannu pulled at his arm and pointed. Ahead, caught in silver glints of moonlight, writhing rats swam away from them. Where the steep bank had partially collapsed, they scrambled up the black earth into the field beyond.

'Follow them,' Hannu breathed.

Piay dug his fingers into the soft mud and hauled himself up the side of the irrigation ditch. At the top, he dragged the battered soldier up behind him, and then Hannu. For a moment their eyes met, and Piay communicated a silent look of thanks for his accomplice's quick thinking at the campfire.

The bellows of the roaming Hyksos warriors thundered as they searched for their prey. A moment later a roar rang out.

'They've seen us,' Hannu gasped. 'Into the fields.'

Piay and the two men scrambled into the golden sea of barley, keeping low. Their passage opened up a channel through the crop that would be visible in the moonlight, but what choice did they have? Piay pushed on, zigzagging until they were far from where they had been seen.

Piay threw himself on his belly. The soldier and Hannu collapsed beside him. As his breathing subsided, Piay strained to listen. In the distance, hoof beats thrummed off the tracks that criss-crossed the fertile land beside the Nile, and the call and response of the barbarians echoed.

'Let us be away,' the soldier said. 'My wounds are burning—'

Piay clamped a hand on the man's mouth and pressed a finger to his lips. His instincts told him they were not yet free.

Piay sensed the sharp reek of smoke. An instant later, a dim crackling became a low roar, rising in intensity.

Hannu understood.

'They are burning the fields.'

Piay looked back towards the irrigation ditch. Smoke swirled above a crimson line glowing in the night. The flames licked up and raced across the field with gathering speed.

The soldier cried out. Scrabbling to his feet, he lurched away. Hannu threw himself at the escaping man like a bull, knocking him to the ground again.

'We must flee!' the man cried.

'That's what they want,' Hannu spat. 'They'll be waiting for us on the other side.'

'We can't stay here.'

Piay glanced one way, then the other, as he found his bearings, then beckoned for the two men to follow him parallel to the line of fire.

'Are you mad?' the soldier cried.

'Most likely,' Hannu grunted.

Piay sprinted, ignoring the blaze rushing towards them. The flames leaped as high as his chest, and his ears ached from their hungry roar. Whipped up by the wind, the choking smoke swallowed them so that he could no longer see the way ahead.

When his lungs began to sear from the hot air, Piay felt hope begain to ebb. But the wind gusted, the smoke cleared and a black expanse opened up.

'Here!' he called.

The canal ran straight and true from the Nile, taking the life-giving water deep into the fertile countryside. The blaze scorched Piay's flesh. He choked on thick smoke. But his step never faltered as he dived off the edge of the canal. When he thrust his head up from the chill depths, he heard the two men entering behind him.

'This time your gamble paid off,' Hannu said.

He shook the water from his beard like a dog. In the midst of danger, Hannu was the level-headed and wise seasoned warrior, but Piay could see he had now reverted to his usual sharp-tongued self.

With the flames crackling above their heads, they dragged themselves along the edge of the canal and when they reached a floodgate, they hauled themselves out of the water.

At the top, Piay glanced back. Silhouetted against that infernal glow a figure stood, as rigid as one of the temple statues. Though it was too dark to tell for sure, Piay was convinced it was Sakir, and that the Hyksos warrior was staring directly at him.

The rushes along the banks of the Nile rustled in the breeze. Breathing in the dank scents of the river, Piay tentatively made his way along the papyrus beds, fearful of disturbing any resting crocodiles. When he was a boy, he'd seen one of those monstrous beasts swallow a child whole. Life was filled with lessons, his master Taita said, and he had taken this one to heart.

Hannu whistled from further along the track. He had located the skiffs they'd hidden when they had arrived on the eastern bank earlier that night.

The skiff was small enough for one man to row, the hull constructed from rolls of papyrus reeds bound tightly together. Astern, a filthy linen sheet was tied across a frame to shelter from the sun during the day.

Piay crawled beneath the shelter and lay with his hands behind his head. The rescued soldier collapsed in the prow. Hannu lowered himself on to the bench and grasped the oars. He showed no sign of exhaustion. All those years in the Blue Crocodile Guards had given him a hardy disposition.

Once they were in mid-stream, Piay allowed himself to relax and stopped glancing back at the eastern bank. But the memory of the Hyksos captain silhouetted against the fire had burned its way into his mind. He saw it even when he closed his eyes.

'Tell me, my friend,' he called to the soldier, 'why did the Hyksos take you captive instead of killing you on the battlefield?'

The soldier levered himself up on his elbows.

'The barbarians are planning an attack on Thebes. They wanted to know the strength of our army – if we could defend the City of a Hundred Gates. I told them . . .' His voice broke. 'I told them nothing.'

'You are a brave man. You'll be well rewarded when we return.'

Piay leaned back so he could watch the milky river of stars that mirrored the Nile in the heavens. An attack on Thebes! This was the kind of information that Taita had dispatched him into the enemy's territory to find.

And yet he could not revel in the success of his mission. Six lost lives weighed upon his soul. Six *Kas* forever denied the afterlife.

It was his error of judgement, his reckless gambling, that had led them into danger. He would never be able to forget the toll of his own failings. Bowing his head, he muttered a prayer for his lost men. It was not enough.

After a while, Piay felt he could not stare into the darkness inside himself any longer.

'The captain of the Hyksos band will have to explain to his generals how he lost a valuable captive. That will teach him not to be so arrogant.'

The soldier stirred. 'I would not want Sakir for an enemy.'

'Why do you say that?'

'He is crazed. His own men fear him. He has given himself fully to the dreams of the blue lotus. The barbarians whispered that he has walked with the gods and they have given him powers beyond mortal men.'

Piay laughed. 'What do you say, Hannu?'

'I remember digging a grave for an enemy who said he walked with the gods,' said Hannu. 'Two or three of them, if truth be told.'

'Mock all you want,' the soldier said. 'But I looked into his eyes, and I heard what his men said about him when he was not present. Trust me, he will never forgive you for what you did this night. His heart burns—'

'And his face,' Hannu interjected.

'His heart burns with hatred and that will fuel him. He will not relent until he has his revenge.'

'Let him come,' Piay said with a waft of his hand. 'I'm no stranger to enemies who bear a grudge. If he thinks he can slit my throat in the middle of the Egyptian army, then I will bow to his greater skills.'

The conversation drifted into silence until there was only the gentle splash of the dipping oars and the lapping of the river currents against the hull. In the stillness, Piay drifted with his own memories. In his life, the fighting was all he had known. His master Taita always spoke fondly of the great age of peace before the Hyksos came, when there was music and art and trade and learning. But even then the Pharaoh had been at war with the Red Pretender, the false pharaoh who had seized the Lower Kingdom.

Now, though, no one knew peace, only periods of great tension punctuated by fierce battles as one side or the other tried to gain an advantage. The Hyksos coveted all Egypt and perhaps far beyond its boundaries, too. Taita, the master tactician, knew that if the barbarians were allowed time to occupy the entire land it would be nigh on impossible to uproot them. They were clever, those barbarians, quickly getting the people on their side. Daily life was rarely disrupted for the conquered. The people were allowed to govern themselves, or given the illusion of governing, with the Hyksos generals standing in the shadows directing and taking their share of taxes.

The people only wanted peace and the chance to live under the eyes of the gods. That left Taita's war council with few options.

Yes, Taita was Piay's master, but he had also been like a father to him. Piay closed his eyes and tried to summon up the faces of his parents, but they hung, as always, in shadow. He'd seen only five spring floods of Mother Nile when they'd brought him to Taita. They'd begged the Pharaoh's wisest advisor to teach their son so he could claim a good life for himself, one free of the hardship they had endured in the disputed territory where the Hyksos continually raided.

He remembered crying as they walked away that night, or thought he did, but from then on his days had been a whirl of learning under his eunuch master. Taita had a dagger-sharp mind and did not suffer fools. But he was kind and quick to praise when it was merited. Piay had come to love him, and his life had been immeasurably better than anything his parents could have offered, surrounded as he was by all the riches of the court and the most beautiful women in all Egypt.

But he had earned it. He recalled the sting of pain when Taita had lashed his rush switch on the back of his hand every time he got an answer wrong or failed to wield his sword with the necessary expertise. More than anything, Piay had wanted to make Taita proud, and in that he had succeeded time and again.

But how would he explain the lives he had lost and the miseries he had inflicted on the men's families? A lesser man would pretend he had played no part in it. That the gods had decided upon the outcome. But he could not lie to Taita. Honour was more important than gold – that was how he had been raised. He would take his punishment even if it destroyed him in the eyes of his master. And how devastating that would be. For as long as he could remember, he had only ever wanted Taita's approval.

Piay felt his heart sink, but he would not allow his guilt to show to Hannu or any others. Confidence in all things was the rule he lived by. Weakness was for lesser men.

In the abiding dark of the far bank, lights glimmered among the swaying date palms silhouetted against the starry sky. They had returned alive. And now he would face his judgement.

The tent billowed in the night breeze and the ropes cracked. Inside, shadows swooped across the cloth from the dancing flame of the lamp. Piay took in the sweet scent of the olive oil as he watched his master pace. Piay thought back to that first night when he had been introduced to Taita and it was true – the eunuch didn't seem to have aged a day in the intervening years. He was tall and handsome, his lips full, and his eyes were bright lanterns of intelligence, searching, incisive. He was a slave who had risen far above that role, from helping raise Princess Lostris to guiding the destiny of Egypt. Tonight he was wearing a robe of white silk studded with jewels in the shape of a falcon, the wings outstretched across his chest.

Piay felt awe rise up inside him as he stared at his master. Many had spoken of a strange, almost supernatural power that seemed to burn within Taita, as hot as the fiercest forge. Now Piay could feel it for himself. In the half-light, sparks swirled in his master's eyes and when Taita levelled his gaze, Piay fought the urge to sink to his knees.

'There was never any doubt the Hyksos would try to retake Thebes,' his master said, almost to himself. Taita had questioned the freed soldier for more than an hour and now the former captive had been sent away to have his belly filled and his wounds tended. 'To possess the City of a Hundred Gates, the jewel in Egypt's crown, has long been their greatest desire. They have never forgotten how they took the city in a storm of blood and swords soon after they first invaded our land. They know the value of that prize.'

'But we did not know the barbarians were planning to attack Thebes so soon,' Piay said. 'With this knowledge we have bought ourselves some time to prepare our defences.'

Taita shook his head. Piay watched his master's face cloud as he remembered.

'When the Hyksos army crushed our own in one bloody day and swept up the Nile, we had no choice but to flee. I was there alongside my Queen Lostris, and her son, the Pharaoh, and the brave general Tanus. Our tattered army would have been wiped out if we'd stayed to defend Thebes that day. As if it were yesterday, I recall standing astern in the royal galley and looking back as the City of a Hundred Gates vanished into the heat haze. My eyes filled with tears and my heart ached for what we had lost. But there was nothing we could have done. We escaped beyond the cataracts, to Kush, and licked our wounds. Finally we were strong enough to return and we retook Thebes. That day my heart soared. We vowed never to let the city fall into the hands of our enemy again. But now . . .' His voice trailed away as he stared through the tent flap into the night.

Piay plucked a ripe fig from the bowl, tossed it in the air and caught it. Ripping it open, he swallowed a mouthful of the sweet flesh and drank deep of the refreshing juices. When he'd wiped his chin with the back of his hand, he saw Taita was staring at him. His master's eyes were hard and Piay sensed the condemnation that was to come.

'I will not try to make excuses for the lives I lost this night,' Piay said. 'I should have scouted the area. I should have listened to Hannu and proceeded with caution.'

'You were reckless. You have always been reckless. Too sure of your abilities.'

'I know my own worth, that is all.'

Taita wagged a finger at him. 'I saw it in you that night your father delivered you to me. Yes, even then. You had little respect. You spoke without being asked. And you told anyone who would listen how great you were and what a remarkable destiny would be yours. Two doors awaited you, one marked Glory, the other Destruction. And I remember thinking that if you passed through the door of destruction, it would be by your own choice.'

Piay felt a flicker of irritation. His pride had been stung. Yes, he had made a mistake this night. But he did not deserve to be damned so totally in this way.

'Have I not been a good student? Your best student? Have I not learned every lesson you taught me?'

Taita sniffed. 'In the early days I feared you were an imbecile who would never learn a thing. But now it's true – you know all that I can teach of the arts of peace and war. You are the greatest of all spies. And yet I feel sorry for you, Piay.'

'Why?'

'Because you have not known hardship.'

'Surely that can only be to my benefit.'

'A man cannot learn who he truly is until he has suffered. You are an unformed thing, balancing on the brink of great-ness, wavering on the edge of an abyss of failure. The door to glory or the door to destruction.'

'And you say I need to suffer to find glory?' Piay fought to keep the note of incredulity out of his voice. If truth were told, he was still afraid of that switch lashed across the back of the hand. He winced. Even now, even as a great hero of Egypt.

'You need to be taught humility. And to listen to your fellow man. A wise man knows when to act and when to take advice.'

'Listen to Hannu? He'll be holding that door to destruction wide open.'

'Since I took you under my guidance, your life has been one of privilege. The finest robes, made by the greatest craftsmen, encrusted with jewels upon the softest Syrian silk. Your belly has never known hunger. Indeed, you have drunk the richest wine and partaken of dishes crafted with the skills of artists, meals laid before the Pharaoh himself. And all that privilege, and all that fame, has served only to swell your head.'

'This is true. For all the constant fighting, life has been good. In the darkest hours, one must seize the bright moments when one can. You taught me that.'

'A good student does not hear only what he wants to hear.'

Taita glided back to the tent flap and sniffed the air. He was searching for any trace of smoke from the burning that was always left in the Hyksos' wake. His master had allowed himself to become over-burdened with the worries of war. That could be the only explanation for his sour tone.

'I ask again,' Piay said. 'You would like to see me suffer more? More than I have this night?'

'No good man wishes hardship upon another. But you will never know your true worth until you have been shaped by travails upon the hard road of life.'

Piay lounged along a bench, grinning. It was a show, of course. He was incapable of revealing to the world how deeply any matter affected him, something that Hannu had pointed out time and again. But Taita and all those at court had expectations of his strength, his skill and his charm, and he was determined to live up to them. Anything else would be to admit weakness. Inside, though, his mind's eye tormented him with each twisted expression on the faces of the men who had followed him – trusted him – as the blades fell.

'What now for me?' He heard the hollowness in his voice.

Taita looked up into the smoky reaches of the tent. When he spoke, each word came gently, as if chosen with the utmost care.

'You are of no use to me here.'

Piay flinched.

'These wounds you bear after this night will continue to eat their way deep into the heart of you, and there they will fester. I have seen this many times.'

'Then my service is over.'

'At your best, you are too valuable to waste, Piay. And you may yet have much to offer. But you must learn who you are first. You must prove to yourself that you can overcome any challenge. Only then will you regain your confidence, and see it tempered by experience and humility.'

Taita stroked his chin. A plan seemed to be forming, and when he next looked at Piay his eyes twinkled.

Piay tried to show a contrite face. Was he not still the greatest spy in all Egypt? He would not see himself tossed aside so easily, not even by such an exalted man as Taita.

'I can make amends. Give me any challenge, no matter how dangerous. I will prove to you my worth.' As if he had not proved it a thousand times over.

A ghost of a smile flashed across his master's lips, or perhaps he had imagined it, for there was nothing to smile about in his demand.

'Our survival here hangs by a thread,' said Taita. 'Our army is depleted. We have too few horses to match the relentless cavalry of the Hyksos. Any hope for victory is draining away by the day. All that stands in our favour is that so far we have managed to shield our weakness from our enemy. But if the Hyksos decide to come for us in any number, we will be crushed.'

'But now we know their plans to attack Thebes—'

'We do not have the numbers to defend Thebes. It will fall as surely as the morning follows night.'

'What then? Retreat beyond the Second Cataract once again?'

'We will have no choice but to attempt to retake Thebes. And we will be defeated, and that will be the end of the glory that is Egypt. Unless . . .'

Piay narrowed his eyes. He knew that tone. His master's great brain was burning white-hot. A plan was forming.

'Unless we can find an ally.'

'Who will ally with us? We have traded with all the world and we have many friends in foreign lands. But friends who will send an army to stand against the might that is the Hyksos?'

'It is a difficult task, perhaps an impossible one. But I entrust it to you.'

'To me? But if I fail . . .?'

'Then all is lost.'

Piay felt his head swim, and when it cleared he realised Taita was staring at him in a strange manner, a look that he could not divine. Yet he had the certain feeling that his master had guided him to this moment.

'A desperate man can achieve great things,' his master pressed in a quiet voice. 'A man with nothing to lose will walk farther, climb higher, risk everything – including his own life – to find the prize that will bring him redemption. And you have nothing to lose, Piay. If you fail in this task, do not return. There will be no place for you here. Indeed, there may be nothing for you to return to.'

'But where will I go? West? Only desert wanderers and murderous Libyans live there and they will not see any gain in sending men to fight the Hyksos. South, to Kush? Would the king beyond the cataracts ever help us?'

'To the lands north of the great sea. To Mycenae,' Taita said without a moment's thought. 'We have strong ties to the city states, through trade, through the exchange of knowledge with our wise men. The Mycenaeans are much like us. An ancient people, civilised, wealthy. And, most importantly, they have great armies, for those city states are always at one another's throats.'

'Mycenae? Do you wish me dead?' Piay pressed his palm against his forehead. 'I will have to travel through the heart of the Hyksos lands, find passage on a ship to cross the great sea through pirate-infested waters, traverse the war-torn lands between those city states . . . and then brave it all again on the return journey. Never mind negotiating with kings with little to offer them in return beyond gratitude and the promise of future riches.'

'Then we are done here—'

Piay held up his hand. 'Now that I mention it, those things are no real obstacles, not for a man like me. Consider it done. Make your plans for victory. The days of the Hyksos are already over. One thought – how should I convince the Myceneans? Even my own powerful debating skills may not be persuasive enough.'

Taita strode to a chest in the corner of the tent and delved into its contents. He pulled out something wrapped in cloth and handed it over. When Piay unwrapped the item, he gazed at a gleaming chunk of violet quartz.

'This is amethyst,' he said. 'I have never seen so much before.'

Taita folded his hands behind his back. 'That is only the smallest part of it. There is a secret mine, known only to a very few and certainly not the Hyksos, which is the purest source of this beautiful gemstone. The Myceneans prize amethyst highly. Offer this sample in your negotiations and promise the mine to whomever becomes our ally. When the Hyksos are defeated, all the riches are theirs.'

Piay stared into the violet depths of the crystal. Strange that Taita had such a sample on hand. But no matter.

'I will depart immediately, if I can be given a vessel to carry me along the river.'

Taita smiled fully this time, as if he had won some unspoken wager.

**P**iay swept out through the sprawling camp. In the east, a thin line of silver edged the horizon. Soon the Pharaoh's army would be waking, a new day of struggle ahead. There was no time to waste. The journey would be long and hard and there were many arrangements to be made.

He found Hannu sitting by embers of the campfire, gnawing on a knob of bread. His assistant eyed him as he approached in a manner that suggested he thought Piay was coming to wrestle the bread from his grasp.

'Did he whip you?' Hannu said, spitting crumbs.

'No, Taita did not whip me.'

'Why not?'

'Because I am not a child.'

Hannu sniffed in a manner that seemed to speak volumes. Piay looked at the other man. Perhaps it was his imagination.

'We have an important job to do,' Piay said.

'Another one?'

'More important than the last one.'

'Ah, I see. The reward of failure.'

'Things did not go as planned, that I admit,' Piay said, raising his gaze to the sunrise. 'But we learned the plans of the enemy, the very point of our foray this night. How can that be classed as failure? No, no, it may very well be that all our fortunes turn on what I have achieved.'

Hannu swallowed the last morsel and sighed.

'What's our punishment?'

'Our *reward*, my little friend, is the honour of being the saviours of Egypt.' Piay let his hand drop to the hilt of his sword. 'We are about to embark upon the greatest adventure of your life. Glory awaits you, Hannu. Glory awaits us both. Ready yourself to set out before the sun rises above the hills.'

**A** forest of masts reached across the harbour. Piay marvelled at the number of vessels moored along the wharf as Hannu rowed their skiff in to the side. There must have been more than a hundred, of all shapes and sizes. Many had travelled from along the length of the Nile, but others had strange designs of a kind Piay hadn't seen before and those could only have come from distant lands. Never had he seen so many crafts in one place.

But this was Avaris, and all life must pass through the city if business was to be conducted in the Hyksos lands.

Piay pulled himself out of the shelter at the rear of the skiff. Shielding his eyes against the bright morning sun, he surveyed the docks. They were swarming with sailors and merchants, but also Hyksos warriors with eyes as hard as stone, hands resting on the hilts of their crescent swords. This was the time of greatest danger. They would have to take extreme care from this moment on.

The barbarians had chosen their administrative centre well after the invasion. Deep in the delta where the Nile drifted eastwards, Avaris stood in a commanding position for trade coming from the great sea to the north, or for those Egyptians who wanted to take their wares to distant climes.

Piay studied the sprawling city beyond the walls. The Hyksos had been hard at work here. Scaffolding clung to several towering buildings. Masons heaved blocks of creamy stone into place. New homes for the burgeoning number of officials required to count the riches flowing into the coffers from all that trade and taxes on the now-conquered lands. A palace for the king? Most likely. And places for the generals to plot their campaigns against the Pharaoh.

In the smoky distance, he could make out a half-built temple reaching up above the surrounding rooftops. The Hyksos left no doubt who were the masters here. With such shows of grandeur, it was unsurprising that many Egyptians bowed their heads to their overlords.

Piay felt the bite of cold anger in his gut and imagined running from building to building with a flaming brand, burning the entire city and the legacy of the hated barbarians to the ground.

Piay crawled back beneath the shelter. The chance of him being recognised so far north and deep in Hyksos territory was slim, but Taita had taught him to take no chances when he was on a spying mission.

'The gods will challenge you when you least expect it,' his master had said. Like most of Taita's lessons, it had served him well.

As he fanned himself with a palm frond, Piay watched the array of vessels drift by. No stranger would ever guess there was a war being waged along the frontier. Life went on as it always had. The Hyksos kept their intrusion into the affairs of the people to a minimum, encouraging trade and prayer and learning so that few could tell any difference whether it was god-given pharaoh or barbarian king who ruled over them.

That made his task a little easier. He was well-versed in the art of blending in.

But the journey north had been tense to begin with. They'd left the camp at sunset the day following their rescue of the Egyptian soldier and sailed under cover of darkness to cross the frontier. Even so, flaming arrows had seared through the night from the bank every now and then, coursing past their skiff to sizzle in the water.

The boat given to them by Taita was larger than the one they had used to transport themselves across the river the previous night, but still small enough to be powered by the muscle of one man at oars. Hannu sweated under the blazing sun on the rowing bench. He didn't complain, and why should he? He had the easy task. Piay had to expend the powers of his mind to plot a path through dangerous territory with enemies on every side.

Once the sun had risen, it became easier to blend in. The Nile soon filled with vessels as far as the eye could see, from nimble skiffs to vast cargo ships low in the water, their holds filled with stone from the quarries. Sails cracked in the cooling breeze that swept along the valley from the Lower Kingdom, carrying the vessels towards Thebes in the south. Those travelling downstream towards Memphis took advantage of the powerful current pulling them towards the great sea.

Hannu heaved the skiff towards the wharf. He was naked, the mat of black hair covering his back glistening with sweat.

'Hyksos everywhere,' he muttered.

'All will be well as long as we do nothing to make them suspicious,' Piay said in a low voice, his eyes constantly searching along the quay. 'We are two papyrus traders, that is all.'

'Then keep your hands hidden. They are as smooth as a handmaiden's,' Hannu said. 'Anyone who sees them will know you've never done a day's work in your life.'

Once the skiff had drifted into the shadow of the wharf, Hannu jumped out and tied it up. Piay climbed the steps to where the multitude thronged. His ears ached from the din. Traders shouted over one another while they haggled. Sailors lounged on bales, singing and drinking beer and resting their aching arms. The prostitutes flashed their eyes and smiled with their red-painted lips at every passing man.

Piay stared at the strange races that had found their way to Avaris: men with thick black hair shaped like mushrooms and narrow eyes in round faces; others with skin the colour of ebony, wearing scarves piled high on their heads; olive-skinned travellers in long white robes; slave traders with waxed beards; others with skin as pale as milk. Their voices formed a cacophony of unfamiliar languages, sighing and singing and jabbering.

The air was thick with the scents of the spices being unloaded along the wharf. A new aroma tantalised his nose with each breath of wind.

Suddenly realising he had been gaping like a stranger, Piay clapped his hands and grinned in a show of a trader eager to do business. He looked around with purpose. After a moment, one of the tax collectors walked up – an Egyptian. Though a slight paunch hung over the waist of his kilt, he was slender, his muscles undeveloped, and he held his hands as if his wrists ended in dead fish. He carried his record scroll under his arm. The barbarians had no writing of their own, so they employed Egyptian scribes to maintain their records.

A Hyksos warrior prowled by, examining Piay to see if he was likely to be any trouble. Piay ignored the warrior's piercing gaze and focused his attention on the thin man.

'What is your business in Avaris?' The scribe's voice had a faint sibilance.

'Papyrus.' Piay gestured towards the skiff and the bales of papyrus that Taita had ordered to be prepared for them. 'We are transporting our wares to Sena.'

The scribe studied the skiff. Hannu kept his head down, pretending to rearrange the stack of bales.

'One bale,' the scribe said, turning back.

Piay hesitated, not sure if he should haggle or give up the tax without a complaint. Either one could draw suspicion if it was wrong. He glanced along the quayside, watching the other new arrivals being met by the tax collectors.

'I said one bale,' the scribe snapped.

'Very well,' Piay said, making his choice. 'But you will turn me into a beggar.' He shouted to Hannu, 'One bale!'

With a few swift strokes of his brush, the tax collector made his mark on his scroll. Piay felt a note of relief that he'd made the right decision. But as he finished his mark, the scribe added, 'Next time don't complain.' He looked pointedly from Piay to one of the patrolling barbarians.

Once Hannu had dragged the bale on to the side and the scribe had arranged for it to be taken away to the wharf ware-house, Piay leaned in and whispered to his companion, 'Stay here with our wares to protect them from thieves. I will replenish our supplies with some bread and dates from the city. Then we can be on our way.'

Hannu glanced around from under hooded brows.

'The sooner we're away from here, the better. I have a bad feeling about this place.'

With a small bale of papyrus on his shoulder for payment, Piay strode past the donkeys dragging laden carts from the docks into the city. The sun-bleached road was wide and paved with white limestone, but once he'd passed through the gate, the streets became narrower and offered some cooling shade from the heat of the day. The air around the warehouses near the wall was rich with sweet scents of cinnamon and olive oil. But as he pressed on, he breathed in the dank air of old, waterlogged buildings that he'd been told afflicted most of the cities in the delta. Beyond that, the oppressive reek of the middens from the poor quarter hung over all.

Leather-capped Hyksos riders clattered by from the garrison somewhere on the edge of the city, but here they were at ease, laughing and chattering as they passed. Gradually, Piay felt his shoulders loosen. The barbarians were confident in their rule. They expected no enemies here.

Many taverns lined the narrow street from the gate to serve the travellers who passed through the city every day. Selecting one that contained the fewest drunken sailors bellowing at each other, Piay slipped into the cool interior. The beaten-earth floor was covered with fresh rush mats. On stools and chairs along the walls, men sipped cups of beer, wine, palm brandy and some perfumed liquors which Piay didn't recognise, but which he presumed the Hyksos had brought from their distant homeland.

Once he'd haggled with the tavern owner, Piay took his supplies and a cup of beer to a stool near the door where he could watch the life of the city pass by. Avaris seemed at peace. Two priests wandered by in their pristine linen robes and white papyrus sandals, and slaves hurried to complete some urgent task for their masters and mistresses. Children chased one another, laughing. All as it would have been in Thebes.

Piay felt a pang of contempt for these Egyptians who had settled so easily into life under the yoke of their oppressors. While good men fought and died along the frontier to return Egypt to its past glory, these people cared for naught but themselves. Taita had advised him to find some compassion in his heart, for these were not warriors. They merely wanted to live their lives and care for their loved ones. But if all the people accepted the invaders with a shrug, Egypt would be lost without a battle being fought.

'Piay?'

He jolted at the sound of his name being called. Squinting into the bright sunlight on the other side of the street, he realised a woman was reaching out a hand towards him.

'Piay! It is you!'

The woman stepped forwards into the shade and he saw it was Meryt, still as beautiful as the last time he had seen her at the court in Thebes. Wrapped in a white sheath dress that made her glow in the sunlight, she was tall and slender, with a girl's tendency to smile quickly that belied her high status. He'd always loved that about her. Her blue-black wig gleamed and she had prepared herself with green malachite eye make-up that accentuated her almond-shaped eyes.

As she beamed at him, she suddenly seemed to remember where she was. She glanced at the handmaids clustering around her, peering into the depths of the tavern with curious expressions, and flapped her hands to usher them away. Once they were gone, she beckoned to Piay as she eased back into a shadowed side street.

Piay sauntered over, grinning. Meryt looked around to make sure they would not be overheard and then said, 'What are you doing in Avaris?'

'I am a simple trader,' Piay said with a bow.

'Of course. On the day the heavens collapse into the Nile.' Meryt laughed, hiding her mouth behind her hand. 'I know who you are and what you do, Piay. That sly master of yours has set you a task, I would wager.'

Piay pressed his finger to his lips.

For a moment their eyes danced together, summoning up warm memories of a stolen night in Piay's chamber after a long day drinking at the Pharaoh's banquet during the Festival of Tekh in the Season of Flood. Meryt had made no attempt to hide her attraction to him from the moment the first cup touched her lips.

'You vanished from the court,' Piay said. 'There one day, gone the next. Everyone thought you had been spirited away by a Hyksos war-band. I mourned for—'

'An hour? A day?' Meryt grinned. 'You flatter well, Piay, but every woman at court knew your reputation well. And many were prepared to tolerate it, if I remember.' She glanced past his shoulder, searching the street. 'But it was for the best. My husband suspected what we did together – he beat me with a cudgel the day after our tryst and left me black and blue. If we had stayed, he would have sought a punishment for adultery and that would not have ended well for either of us.'

Piay nodded. A thousand lashes for him; divorce – perhaps even death – for Meryt.

'It was a risk worth taking,' he said.

Her lashes fluttered at his compliment.

'And Lord Kranos decided his fortunes would be much improved by joining with the Hyksos,' Piay noted.

'My husband had been in secret discussions with the barbarians for a season. He would not betray the Pharaoh, or any of our friends, as the Hyksos wanted, but he saw no profit in continuing to fight. The barbarians were pleased that such a high-born Egyptian had bowed their head to them and they gave him the seventeenth nome to command.'

Hoof beats echoed along the main street from the gate and Meryt flinched. Pulling away from him, she whispered, 'We cannot be seen talking together, and the servants are such awful gossips.'

'This moment has been too short.'

Meryt smiled, the curve of her lips and the arch of her brow offering a promise.

'Meet me after dark, by the new temple,' she breathed before hurrying away.

Hannu lay under the shelter in the skiff in the steaming heat, flapping at buzzing flies. He watched Piay clamber down the stone steps and ease on to the rocking vessel.

'Took your time,' the former soldier grunted.

Piay dumped a papyrus-wrapped bundle and a clay jar beside his companion.

'Bread, olives, dates, honey cakes and beer. That should keep our bellies full until we reach Sena, with whatever we can catch on the way.'

Hannu heaved himself up on his elbows. 'Then we should be away.'

'Let's not be hasty.' Piay sprawled on the bales of papyrus. 'Take a while to rest your arms after all that rowing.'

Hannu narrowed his eyes. 'The current did most of the work. And while my heart is warmed that you keep my well-being in mind, it is a rare occurrence.'

Piay reached out his hands. 'There will be plenty of rowing to come. I hear the river meanders through the marshes.'

'And when do you see our departure?'

'Tonight, perhaps. Certainly before sunrise.'

'Cooler, then.'

'This is true.'

'More dangerous to navigate in the dark.'

'Also true. But cooler.'

Hannu nodded slowly, his gaze heavy. Piay sensed the suspicion, but he was not about to address it. His sullen assistant would no doubt try to talk him out of what lay ahead, and Meryt was too fine a prize to forgo.

When dusk fell, fires licked to life along the quayside. Sailors squatted around them, drinking beer and singing songs of the women they'd left behind. Piay left Hannu sucking on olives and tossing the stones into the water, and made his way into the city. Six Hyksos warriors huddled together by the gate, deep in conversation, but they paid him no attention as he drifted past the walls and the warehouses. Lamps were lit like fireflies everywhere he looked.

Here the songs were more peaceful, mothers crooning their babes to sleep or children chanting as they eked out the last of their play. The music was broken only by the calls of the prostitutes as they beckoned to any man that passed.

Piay picked his way through a maze of streets until the half-built temple loomed up against the starry sky. The air was sharp with stone dust. Blocks of masonry were scattered around next to the chisels and mallets the builders had downed when their day had ended.

The temple stood at the highest point in the city and as he looked around, Piay realised Avaris was much bigger than he had imagined. In the moonlight, he peered out over vast areas of construction work on the far side of the city, away from the river. The new buildings reached into the dark. If the Hyksos continued building at this rate, Avaris would soon be the largest city in the world; he was certain of it.

A hiss whispered out. Meryt was standing in the shadows beneath the scaffolding, beckoning. She wore a shawl pulled over her head – to hide her identity from any onlookers, he presumed – but he recognised that smile instantly. She grasped his hand and dragged him into the dusty interior of the temple.

The moon and the stars were framed overhead and the inside of the roofless temple was flooded with their pale light. It was still bare, little more than flagstones and half-constructed walls with plain granite columns spiking up, impossible to tell to which god it would be dedicated. But Piay knew the Hyksos worshipped Seth, the god of the deserts and war, chaos and storms, though by another name.

Meryt ripped off her shawl and grasped Piay's cheeks, dragging his face down so she could press her lips against his. He sank into the depths of that warm kiss. It had been too long since he had enjoyed the pleasure of a woman.

As he pulled back, he breathed in the sweet scent of myrrh in her Mendesian perfume. Her eyes sparkled with moonlight as she looked up at him.

'Your husband . . .'

'Thinks I am meeting with friends to discuss a banquet in his name. But the only banquet I wish to consume is here.' She traced cool fingers across Piay's bare chest, down to the waist of his kilt.

'Are there no men here in Avaris to entertain you?'

'Men, yes, but few as daring and eloquent and strong as you.'

Piay nodded. 'Understandable. I am one of a kind.' He leaned in and kissed her again, slipping his hand up to the nape of her neck. 'Your husband has treated you well since you left Thebes?'

'I doubt he has forgiven me, but he can tolerate me now that temptation is . . . was . . . no longer around. But his hatred for you has not diminished.' Meryt shivered at his touch. 'Besides, he is distracted by his new-found importance. The Hyksos lavish praise and riches on him, and in turn he tells the people the barbarians are their saviours from the cruel pharaoh in the Upper Kingdom.'

Piay felt his heart harden, but this was not the time to consider Lord Kranos' betrayal. There was entertainment aplenty to be had here. Piay pushed deeper into the kisses, easing his hands over Meryt's body. She responded to his touch, pressing hard against him. He felt the heat rise, her passion increasing with every beat of her heart. Piay floated in the warmth of the contact. For once, his guilt at the deaths he had caused drifted away.

'Stand back!'

At the command, Piay jolted away from Meryt. Kranos hovered in the doorway. Guards brandished spears behind him. He was a short man with a hooked nose and fat lips. How Meryt coped with that visage bearing down on her, Piay didn't know. The lord trembled with rage. His eyes burned and his mouth twisted with loathing.

'It seems my plans for the evening have changed,' Piay sighed.

He felt the need to mock the aristocrat, but he swallowed his instinct this once. Any swagger would not benefit him – not when he could see the extent of the seething emotions in the other man's face. Piay shuffled through explanations in his mind, not least because he owed it to Meryt to try to drain the poison from the confrontation, but every response seemed laughable.

The spear tips bristled and his hand unconsciously fell to where the hilt of his sword would have been. But he had left it behind. Any glimpse of such a prized item in Hyksos territory would have raised suspicions.

So, he stood defenceless, before a furious husband wanting to cause him harm. It was not as if he hadn't been in this position before.

'My Lord,' he began, 'I—'

'Silence!' Kranos raged. His lips pulled back from his yellowing teeth. 'Now there will be judgement.'

Meryt leaped forwards. Piay eased. She would argue his case, perhaps find some way out of this conundrum that he hadn't yet chanced upon.

'Kranos, my love!' Meryt cried. 'This man tricked me! He threatened to rape me!'

Piay sighed. The price to pay for being a lover. He cocked one eyebrow, but his mind raced to discover a way out. His life was now hanging by a thread, he could not deny that.

'Still your tongue.'

Kranos' voice was a low rumble. He knew his wife well enough, but she had given him something he could use to save face.

'He dared to lay a hand on my wife,' he said to his guards, 'and you heard what she said – he deceived her with the intention of raping her. Kill him!'

Kranos stepped aside and his guards surged in. Piay turned and raced into the depths of the temple. There would be no other way out, he knew that, but he had to buy himself time.

Leather soles rattled on the flagstones behind him. Piay looked around. The moon gave him light to see, but also denied him shadows in which to hide.

But then a shaft of buttery light circled a cedarwood scaffold. He looked up the towering structure and saw one of the stone blocks resting on the lofty platform, ready to be heaved into place on the half-built wall when the masons returned to their posts at first light.

Piay hurled himself up the ladder resting against the scaffold, like a monkey scrambling to reach the treetops. Cries rang out from the guards. Kranos' mocking laughter echoed before the lord boomed, 'See this coward, my wife. There is no escape for him, but still he runs like a frightened child. Face your punishment like a man, Piay!'

True, there was little dignity in fleeing, Piay thought, but he preferred his head still sitting upon his neck and his member nestled within his kilt.

Hauling himself up the rungs, Piay rolled on to the platform beside the block of masonry. For a moment, he caught his breath and then he peered over the edge at the dizzying drop. He felt his head spin. He preferred both feet on the ground, too.

He could feel a plan forming. Pressing his back against the half-completed wall, he braced his legs against the stone block and heaved. At first, he thought he would be too weak. But then he felt a faint movement in the scaffold and he strained again. The wooden structure shifted, rocked back. Again, he pushed until he caught the rhythm of the rocking motion. He forced all of his might into the soles of his feet and with one final shove, the scaffold teetered and fell away from the wall.

At the same time, Piay hooked an arm over the top of the half-built wall and dragged himself on top.

The block of masonry slid off the platform. Screams rang out from below as the guards suddenly grasped what he was attempting, and then the stone thundered into the ground with a crack like the heavens opening.

Piay didn't glance back to see the results of his action – the shouts and cries were enough to signify the mayhem. He crawled along the top of the wall, feeling the cooling breeze from the river dry the sweat on his back.

He muttered a prayer to the gods and glanced down the outside of the wall until he glimpsed more scaffolding. He grinned to himself. Yes, he supposed he had been reckless again, but this time the gods had been on his side.

Dropping to the platform, he scrambled down the ladder. As he leaped to the ground, a tumult echoed from within the temple.

'A spy!' Lord Kranos was bellowing. 'There is a spy loose in the city!'

Shouts boomed across Avaris, leaping from one mouth to the next as the alarm was carried far and wide. Piay raced on, his lungs burning. Was the entire city erupting in clamour? In the distance, he could hear the thunder of hoof beats as the Hyksos rushed from their garrison, and though he was certain it was his imagination, he felt he could hear a thousand swords singing as they were wrenched from their sheaths.

Perhaps he had thought too soon that the gods were on his side. Now he'd endangered his own life, and Hannu's, too.

He darted through the open city gates on to the wide road to the harbour. Where the guards were, he had no idea, though they were probably drunk or dozing. After all, who in their right mind would challenge the Hyksos in the place where they were at their strongest?

Piay allowed himself a moment of bitter humour, but the rising din at his back drove out all but thoughts of survival.

Along the quayside, the sailors were stirring around their fires. Their songs drained away as they puzzled over the cacophony erupting in the city.

Piay raced to the edge of the dock and looked into the dark where the skiff was moored. As his eyes adjusted to the gloom, he could make out Hannu sprawled across the bales, dozing. Piay shoved his fingers in the corners of his mouth and blasted a piercing whistle.

Hannu jerked up, flailing.

'What is it? What is wrong?' he shouted into the dark.

'Throw off the mooring!' Piay yelled. 'Make the skiff ready to go!'

'What have you done now?' Hannu grumbled.

'No time for that. Get out into the river. Don't wait for me. I'll get to you.'

Piay didn't wait to see if Hannu followed his command. He glanced through the gates and in the light of the torches along the wall he could see a group of Hyksos rushing towards him. The thunder of hoof beats drowned out all other noise. They would be on him in moments.

Chaos and confusion was going to be his only way out of this. His thoughts flashed back to the escape from Sakir, and he suddenly knew what he had to do.

Running to the first of the crackling fires along the quayside, Piay kicked out at the burning bricks of dung and straw. The sailors lurched out of their drunken warmth, shouting and cursing, as sparks cascaded around them. Embers flew over the edge of the wharf. Some sizzled into the water, but some would land on the vessels moored below.

He was racing to the next fire as a roar rose up from the sailors behind him. Glancing back, he saw smoke rising past the edge of the quay, and an amber glow. One of those papyrus skiffs was aflame.

Piay dashed up to the next fire and kicked the burning blocks over the side once more. In their drunken beer-haze, the sailors were barely aware of what he had done. That bought him some time.

But when he raced towards the third fire, the rivermen were on their feet, bellowing and shaking their fists. Deciding he had drained the last of his luck, Piay dropped back. But he had already achieved everything he had hoped for. A tide of panic washed along the harbour as the sailors milled about, thundering their impotence into the night.

A wall of fire licked up. Flames leaped from skiff to boat to wooden ship along the closely packed moorings. Bales of silk and papyrus sizzled, the perfect tinder for the inferno.

One riverman lumbered towards him in a fury. Piay thrust him aside, clouting him around the side of the head for good measure. Others began to turn towards him as word spread that he was the source of this disaster. Behind him, the Hyksos were out of the city, their horses pounding over the limestone paving towards the harbour.

Piay darted away from the gathering mob, towards the area the inferno had not yet reached. As his enemies bore down on him, he hurled himself off the quayside and landed in a skiff. The vessel rocked wildly, but Piay rolled, thrust back to his feet and then dived off the stern.

The chill black waters swamped him. Piay kicked out to stay beneath the surface, letting the current drag him. After a moment, he swam up. Treading water, he looked back at what he had wrought. Flames roared so high he could no longer see the walls of Avaris. Crosses blazed against the night sky as the masts sucked the fire up to the heavens. Wisps of burning sail-cloth fluttered on the breeze. Piay's ears rang with the din of that inferno, like an enormous beast awakening to fill its belly, and the throat-rending cries of the men surging along the quay-side. He blinked at the glare of the blinding light in the dark and could just make out the fleeting shadows of the barbarians riding back and forth. What could they do? He had shown them the might of a wakening Egypt. Another great victory.

The Hyksos would not forget the visit of Piay the Spy.

He craned his neck and shouted 'Hannu!'

A response rolled back across the water, and after a few more hails, Piay glimpsed the silhouette of the skiff. He struck out towards it and a moment later rough hands grasped him and heaved him over the side into the vessel.

Piay sprawled on to his back, laughing as exhilaration coursed through his body.

'What a night, eh, Hannu?' he roared. 'The tales they will tell of this. Piay the Great! One man who tweaked the beards of the mighty Hyksos!'

'I would wager they are telling tales now.' Hannu settled on to his bench and snatched up his oars. 'Of an enemy who dared venture into the heart of their land on a foray of some great importance. Of a spy whose name and face are now known to all. And of the fury. Aye, imagine that. Fury so great that this wanderer will never be forgiven and who will now have the entire might of the Hyksos empire hunting him down to the ends of the earth, like a rabid dog.'

Piay's grin faded. He watched the stars drift by overhead, and shrugged.

'Well, that is a problem for tomorrow.'

Hannu dipped his oars into the water and leaned into the first stroke. A tuneless whistle broke out as he laboured. Piay knew that sound. His companion only blew that note when he was worried.

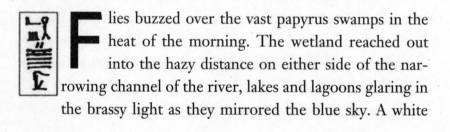 Flies buzzed over the vast papyrus swamps in the heat of the morning. The wetland reached out into the hazy distance on either side of the narrowing channel of the river, lakes and lagoons glaring in the brassy light as they mirrored the blue sky. A white

stork soared up from where it had been feeding, its huge wings beating. The air was thick with the reek of rotting vegetation and that black mud.

From the shade beneath the shelter, Piay squinted as he searched the waving rushes. Tomorrow had arrived and the problem seemed larger. That triumph was nothing more than a fading dream. Everywhere he looked he was seeing enemies. Hannu was right. The Hyksos would not rest now. He had a price on his head. He may well have put the entire assignment at risk. More, he could have thrown away the last chance they had to save his people.

'Was she worth it?' Hannu said, as if he could read Piay's thoughts.

'Meryt is a fine woman and her passion always runs hot.'

'As hot as that fire you lit along the harbour?'

'If you knew her, you would have found her hard to ignore.'

'Her husband will no doubt be thinking of you with as much passion, though of a different kind. I would imagine he's telling the Hyksos everything he knows about you. And of course we already informed the tax collector of our destination.'

'Then we'd better reach Sena before our pursuers. We have a head start. The current is strong. Row harder. Earn your keep.' Piay sighed. 'Why do you insist on finding a storm cloud in every sky?'

'When that storm cloud is a tempest, it's hard to ignore.'

Piay watched the stork glide across the papyrus beds, but his thoughts settled on the sensation of Meryt's skin beneath his fingertips.

'I often muse on the meaning of love, Hannu. I have never found it, as much as I enjoy the pleasures of a woman. The poets weave words of wonder about it. I have heard others speak of it as if they were lifted up to the gods. I think it is a myth. What say you, Hannu?'

'Love is real.'

'You've found it?'

'With my wife.'

Piay frowned. 'You never told me you had a wife.'

'You never asked.'

'What . . .? Where is she?'

'Dead. Killed by the Hyksos.'

Hannu leaned on the oars with steady strokes. He stared into the middle distance, past the shelter where Piay sprawled, seemingly seeing nothing, thinking nothing. But Piay sensed a change had come over him, so subtle it barely registered – a stiffness in the shoulders, perhaps.

'What happened?'

'While I was away harrying the barbarians with the Blue Crocodile Guards, she remained with her father and mother. She was in the fields one day at their farm when the Hyksos came. She died. They all died.'

'I am sorry to hear that.'

'What's done is done.'

'But still—'

'The captain of the Blue Crocodile Guards took pity on me. He ordered us to track down the war band responsible. We slaughtered them all. I plunged my own sword into the heart of the one who had ordered it.'

'Then there was justice. That must bring you some comfort.'

Hannu rowed, one stroke after another in perfect time. Eventually he said, 'That was the day I took the wound to my leg. I was no use to the Blue Crocodile Guards then.'

'I was surprised to find you begging. I thought the Blue Crocodile Guards looked after their own.'

Hannu said nothing. Piay watched him for a long moment, puzzling over the thoughts that might be running through his assistant's mind. Hannu was a mystery at the best of times.

Eventually he felt his eyelids droop and he drifted to the gentle splash of the oars.

Sena simmered under a blazing sun. The port nestled beyond the marshes, on the eastern extremes of the delta, caught between the bleak, unforgiving vastness of the Sinai and the cooling breeze blowing from the Uat-Ur sea – 'the Great Green', as it was known to all Egyptians.

Piay watched the expanse of rolling waves, as terrible in its own way as the great waste of the Sinai at its back. He felt trepidation as he imagined the voyage he would soon have to take across that gulf, and the tales he had heard of the dangers that beset travellers. His life would be in the hands of the gods.

Hannu grunted as he tied up the skiff on the muddy bank. His arms would be aching, Piay knew. The journey from Avaris had been relentless in a desperate attempt to stay ahead of the barbarians who would be pursuing them. He'd taken his own turns at the oars to give his assistant a rest, but Hannu had insisted on rowing harder and for longer. He was a good man to have on an adventure like this.

Piay peered upriver. There was no sign of that pursuit, but he knew not to let his guard down. The barbarians would reach Sena soon. He'd made the decision to leave the skiff here, away from any attention their arrival might bring at the busy river harbour. And if the gods were willing, they could collect it upon their return, hopefully with an army at their backs.

'What's the plan?' Hannu asked as they strode past the flax fields towards the city.

'Get on a ship. Cross the sea. Arrive in the land of the Mycaeneans.'

Hannu nodded. 'Good plan. Your master's lessons on strategy did not go amiss.'

'In situations like this, I've found it best to keep an open mind. The gods have a way of throwing obstacles into the path of a rigid thinker. A free mind leaves space for an agile response.'

Hannu was not convinced.

The streets of Sena throbbed with life. As he pushed his way through the crowd, Piay kept his head down. They could lose themselves among this multitude, two more strange faces in a sea of travellers from seemingly all over the world. He drank in the unfamiliar shape of features and skin colours and clothes, more disparate even than he had seen in Avaris. Sena was the gateway to lands untold – to Arabia in the east and those places from across the Uat-Ur that he had only heard described in Taita's stories.

Not far from the harbour, Piay slipped into a small temple to make a prayer to Khonsu, the god of the moon and all travellers. His feet whispered across the white marble floor under the watchful gaze of the shaven-headed priests. Endless numbers of Egyptian sailors drifted in to make their offerings, requesting fair weather and good winds for the journeys that were to come. He waited until he could approach the altar. The statue of the god loomed over it and Piay looked up at the falcon head and the mummy-wrapped body, the crook and the flail grasped in its hands. He had never seen fit to pray to Khonsu before and he hoped the god would forgive him.

Upon the marble altar, he laid a bundle of papyrus he had brought from the skiff and bowed his head.

'My Lord Khonsu, god of light in the night, keep me free from harm on my voyage across the Great Green,' he murmured. 'Be my pathfinder. Guide me to safe shores. Fill the sails with wind and keep my time upon the waves short.'

Piay's skin prickled at the unfamiliar sensation of unease. No adventure had ever daunted him, but he had never been upon the sea before, had never even seen that vast expanse of water. He did not like this feeling.

Once he'd ventured out from the cool interior into the baking heat of the day, he glimpsed Hannu hurrying through the crowd. Piay couldn't read the man's cold face at the best of times, but now he looked as if he had been carved from stone.

'What did you find?' Piay breathed as they bowed together close to the temple wall.

'I searched along the waterfront, as you requested,' Hannu said, 'and there is a ship sailing for Mycenae later this day. Whether you can persuade the captain to let you buy passage with our bales of papyrus is down to that silver tongue of yours. But you will need to take care doing it. The harbour is swarming with Hyksos.'

'Looking for us?'

Hannu nodded, his eyes darting. 'They wasted no time following our trail.'

'A small obstacle,' Piay said with a shrug. 'Once we are sailing out into the Great Green we will have nothing more to worry about.'

 Gulls wheeled across the blue sky and the white-tipped waves rolled in. From the shadows of a warehouse wall, Piay stared out across the azure sea, so awed by the sight of the expanse that he barely heard the din of haggling merchants and ship-masters yelling for their apprentices. Across the quayside, sweating men heaved bales of linen and flax and staggered under the weight of clay pots. One newly arrived vessel was disgorging the contents of its hold. Seamen lurched down the planks with what seemed to be tin and copper, no doubt from Anatolia, loading the valuable cargo into a succession of carts.

Hannu nudged him and jabbed a thumb. A gang of Hyksos warriors moved among the merchants and slaves, searching this way and that. They were dressed for battle in leather breast-plates, their swords swinging at their hips. As he watched their progress, Piay thought how many had been sent to hunt him down. He must have angered them indeed.

'Where is our ship?' Piay breathed.

Hannu pointed to where a vessel strained at its moorings on the swell.

Piay marvelled. The ship was larger than he had imagined, with a central mast on which a red-and-white-striped sail was furled. There was a platform at the front where the navigator stood, and at the rear a higher platform for the master of the steering oar. Rows of benches lined the decks for the oarsmen. From the depth of the vessel, Piay imagined a huge hold lay beneath them. The hull was constructed from large planks of cedarwood lashed together with woven straps. Reeds had been stuffed between them to seal the seams, and pitch had been painted across the lower part of the hull to make it watertight.

'That looks sturdy enough, I suppose,' Piay muttered.

Before Hannu could protest, Piay strode across the quayside, weaving among the flow of bodies. Keeping his head down, he looked from under his brows until there was a sufficient gap among the prowling barbarians, and then he hurried to the ship.

The captain was a short man with a hooked nose and half-lidded eyes that shifted with furtive movements. He introduced himself as Atmos.

'We would like to buy passage on your vessel,' Piay said as they stood by the plank to the ship. Hannu kept watch nearby.

Atmos looked him up and down. 'What can you offer?'

'We have a skiff filled with good quality papyrus. You will not be disappointed. Your men can fetch it from our boat and store it in a warehouse here, if that is to your liking.'

The captain showed an emotionless face, but his eyes flickered towards Hannu.

'What business do you have in Greece?'

'My own.'

'Keen to leave in a hurry, I see.'

'My business is pressing.' Piay hardened at the captain's questions. 'I'm offering a fair trade. Do we have an agreement, or should I find another captain willing to take us.'

Atmos fingered his chin, still watching Hannu.

'We have an agreement.'

Once Piay had given the details of where the skiff had been moored, he glanced along the vessels in the harbour. Bands of barbarians were searching each ship in turn. Cursing under his breath, he turned to the captain and said, 'We must make ready. When do you intend to sail?'

'When the sun has fallen to the tip of the mast.'

'We will return by then.'

'Make sure you do. If you are not here when we loose the moorings, I will not wait and I will not return your papyrus.'

He marched up the plank.

Piay beckoned to Hannu and they slipped across the quay to the shade of the warehouses.

'They know our only way out of here is across the sea,' Hannu grunted. 'They're not fools.'

'No, but we will still outwit them,' Piay replied in a confident voice.

There was no gain in pointing out to Hannu that he had not yet lighted upon a plan to evade those constantly searching bands.

As he watched, one of the barbarians strode up to where Atmos was overseeing the loading of his ship. The two men bowed their heads together in deep conversation. Piay stiffened, expecting heads to swivel in their direction, but after a moment the Hyksos warrior moved on to the next vessel.

In their ones and twos, the sailors made their way back to Atmos' ship. Most settled into their places upon the benches, but Piay watched two seamen take their position by the moorings. It would not be long until departure. Yet the Hyksos were everywhere, still questioning merchants and captains, watching any movement on board the vessels.

'Tell me again about that plan of yours,' Hannu said.

Piay looked around, his thoughts racing. His attention alighted on a slow procession of carts being dragged by donkeys to a vessel moored next to their intended ship. There, a line of sweating slaves hauled bolts of linen and tall jars off the back of the carts and passed them from hand to hand up on to the ship.

'Follow me,' Piay breathed.

Hurrying along the street to the last of the line of carts, he told Hannu to climb on to the back one and burrow among the contents. Piay clambered in behind Hannu. He tugged over them both a sheet of cloth that had been used to protect the contents from the elements. As the cart trundled out on to the wharf, Piay peered out of the rear at the passing crowd.

*How clever I am*, he thought. *We would never have been able to get past the horde of barbarians if not for my sharp wits.*

But as they reached the point where he could hear the waves against the hulls, a loud voice commanded the caravan to stop. The cart juddered to a halt. Piay glanced back. Hannu was gritting his teeth, fearing what was to come.

'They're here somewhere. I can smell them.'

Piay felt the hairs on his neck prickle. That voice sounded familiar. He sensed Hannu willing him to stay still, no doubt recognising that voice, too. An odd tinkling echoed when the breeze blew, another sound he had heard before. He should lie still as Hannu wanted, he knew, but he couldn't resist easing up the edge of the covering cloth to get a better view.

Sakir stood beside the cart with another barbarian. Above his beard, the marks of the pox now merged into a raw scarring from the burn Piay had inflicted on him. The tinkling came from the bones tied into his unkempt hair.

Piay stiffened. Sakir had called himself the Red Hawk, but it was his other name that forced itself into Piay's mind. *He Who Walks With the Gods*. Piay couldn't help but think that some supernatural force had brought the warrior across the vast distance. The Hyksos captain had promised he would gain vengeance on Piay, and Piay had dismissed it as the bragging of a deluded barbarian. Now, as he watched Sakir put his head back and sniff the air, almost as if he could smell Piay's musk, he felt a chill settle deep in his gut. The Red Hawk turned his head, levelling that sullen gaze on the faces of those who passed by, searching for the answer his instinct told him was close.

The barbarian rested one large hand on the edge of the cart. It rocked under his fingers. Piay caught his breath; it burned in his chest. Did Sakir know where they were hiding and was toying with them? Piay felt the chill grow as he anticipated the barbarian tearing off the sheet to expose them. He had no weapon to defend himself. He and Hannu would be hacked to pieces in a moment.

Sakir's fingers slipped under the sheet. Dirt caked the nails. The cart rocked once again.

Piay stared at that hand, unable to breathe. His thoughts tumbled over themselves. As he searched for a way out of their predicament, his gaze alighted on a brown shape as big as his palm nestled in the corner of the cart. A camel spider. Though it carried no venom, Piay had seen the wounds caused by one bite from those savage jaws.

Taking care not to rock the cart, Piay wrapped his scarf around his hand and pushed it towards the creature. The camel spider lunged and then scurried up the side of the cart. Whisking his bound hand this way and that, Piay herded it towards where Sakir's fingers lay.

When the camel spider jolted out from under the sheet, the Red Hawk snatched his hand away with a curse. That seemed to be enough to distract him. Piay heard Sakir step back a few paces and then he barked an order for the caravan to move on. Piay felt relief flood him. But they were not safe yet.

The cart rocked to a halt again and this time the sheet was ripped off. A slave gaped in shock when he saw the two men hiding among the merchandise. Piay pressed a finger to his lips and flashed a grin. It seemed to work, for the slave didn't cry out.

Piay eased out of the back of the cart and crawled around the side closest to the edge of the quay, where he was shielded from the view of any of the searching barbarians. Once Hannu had joined him, he scrambled along the line of carts.

At Atmos' ship, the sailors were about to draw up the plank. Piay scurried faster, waving to catch the men's eyes. They hesitated just long enough for him to hurry up the plank and throw himself on to the deck. Hannu landed beside him.

The barbarians continued to search the quayside. But the plank was already drawn up, the mooring lines thrown off, and the oarsmen were leaning into their strokes. They sang in full voice as they pulled the ship away from the port, drowning the clamour from dry land.

'See, Hannu, the plan worked,' Piay said.

Hannu sucked in a breath. 'I'll give you that this time. But, by the gods, we sailed close to a messy end.'

'Any escape is a good escape.'

Piay breathed in the salty sea air as he strode astern. Looking past the man at the steering oar, he watched the roaming barbarians along the edge of the quay.

One man stood like a statue, staring at the departing ship – Sakir, as he had done when they escaped the fire he had set in the fields. The Red Hawk had not seen them, or else he would have been summoning his men. But something about the vessel had arrested his attention.

'Run home, you barbarian dog,' Piay muttered. 'You have lost this fight.'

As the ship bobbed across the rolling waves, Sakir remained rigid, staring, and Piay felt the briefest hint of chill once again.

The firepot swung as the ship bucked on the swell. Sparks trailed in the dark and the red glow from the holes cut into the clay pot twisted shadows on the features of the man leaning on the steering oar. It was the only light in that vast expanse of water and night.

Limned in that faint crimson, the silhouette of Atmos prowled towards the stern. Though the wind gusted harder by the moment, somehow the captain kept his feet on the shifting deck. Piay watched him from his seat on the benches. Was that concern he had seen etched in those features as Atmos passed?

His own unease had mounted from the moment at sunset when the captain had ordered the sail to be furled. He'd noticed Atmos staring at the mountains of black clouds soaring up on the horizon before he made his decision. And as his command was uttered, the seasoned sailors around him had hunched over their oars with grim expressions.

Now their faces were lost to the darkness. Their singing had long since ceased and Piay sensed them sitting rigid.

Somewhere nearby, Hannu was perched on his bench. Piay wondered if his assistant was apprehensive, too.

Once again the ship soared up high, then crashed down into a trough. Piay's gorge rose and fell with it. He gripped the bench and muttered another prayer to Khonsu. Was this his punishment for leading his men to their deaths? Denied the afterlife in a watery grave?

How blessed he had felt not so long ago. When they'd escaped Sena by the skin of their teeth, he'd watched the Hyksos on the quayside receding into the hazy distance. He'd felt a rush of headiness as if he was drunk. The hated enemy had lost. Now he was safe and he could turn his mind to the challenges ahead. With the gulls screeching overhead and the sunlight turning the waves to diamonds, he imagined the glory that would be his when he returned to Taita at the head of a great army which could reclaim sacred Egypt for ever.

With a fair wind filling the sail, they'd skimmed across smooth waters under a clear sky the colour of sapphires. The sailors had sung raucous songs of drunkenness and fornication, and told tales of bravery and wonder that had been passed down from their ancestors. All had been well. Then, more than four days into their voyage and with the coast of Greece only a few hours away, a storm had blown in and suddenly Piay felt powerless. All his skills as a spy amounted to nothing in the face of the ocean's fury.

Lightning crackled at his back. The storm was bearing down on them fast. In the flash of white light, he glimpsed frozen moments: the desperate balers on their knees with their bowl-scoops, the seawater sluicing around them; rows of men gripping their oars for dear life, water streaming down their muscular backs; Hannu glancing back at him, his face graven.

The light winked out and he plunged into the dark of the deepest well. The ship rose again, then crashed down. Piay felt his stomach in turmoil.

A hand landed roughly on his shoulder. Atmos' head pressed close to his ear and he shouted above the howl of the gale, 'I need your help!' The captain tugged on Piay's arm.

Piay lurched to his feet, straining to keep his balance as the ship rolled. For a moment, he felt afraid that he would be washed over the side and lost, but he braced his leg against the benches until the ship righted.

Atmos grasped his wrist and dragged him on. Another flash of lightning burned an image of the captain stabbing a finger towards the stern. Piay peered past him, but the dark rushed in before he could see what was amiss.

Piay stumbled past the benches. Another bolt of lightning fizzed, and this time he glimpsed the helmsman fighting with the steering oar. The hull was straining against the force of the waves. Seawater crashed across the deck and washed around his ankles.

The ship rolled again. Piay pitched forwards. As he flailed to catch his balance, he sensed Atmos slip aside. The captain was a fleeting shadow half-caught in the thin glow from the firepot.

An arm snapped around Piay's neck, so tight he could barely breathe. He clawed at it, but his feet were sliding in the torrent on the deck and he could gain no purchase.

Atmos dragged him back, keeping him off balance. He felt the captain press his head close once again and this time he said, 'Sakir sends his greetings.'

No one would come to his aid. The crew were lost in the swelling darkness, their every attention fixed on the battle to save their lives.

In a shimmer of lightning, a bronze knife glinted in Piay's face. One quick release of the arm holding him, a slash across his throat, and he would be done for.

Piay's thoughts flew back to the Hyksos warrior talking to Atmos on the quayside at Sena. A reward must have been offered. Perhaps Sakir insisted a head be taken to prove the deed had been done.

Atmos' grip begain to loosen. Piay imagined the knife ready to cut into his flesh.

As the arm pulled away, he drove his heels down and threw all his weight into his shoulders. Atmos flew back on the slick planks, Piay with him. The captain roared as his back slammed into the side of the ship. A deluge crashed over them and Piay choked on a mouthful of brine.

Struggling for purchase, Piay pinned the captain against the rail with his weight. The boat pitched. More waves broke over them. The violent convulsions were growing stronger.

A fist crashed into the side of Piay's head and down he went. Seawater streamed over his face, up his nose, into his mouth. He choked, engulfed by the sensation that he was drowning. He kicked out again and again until by chance he struck his foot against what seemed like the captain's shin.

Lightning blasted almost overhead and there was Atmos bearing down on him, knife raised, his face twisted in fury. As the night rushed in, Piay rolled to one side. He sensed the blade slash down and felt it punch into the wood of the deck.

And then they were rolling in the foaming water, tearing at each other's flesh. Flickering images burned into Piay's mind with every burst of lightning: Atmos' lips pulled back from his teeth; black pebble eyes in a white sheet of a face; the knife stabbing; Piay's fingers raking the other man's features.

Instinct gripped him. Over and over they rolled in the deluge, but every time Piay tried to pin his opponent beneath him, the ship crashed across the waves and threw him away. Now the vessel seemed to be spinning in the force of those twisting currents.

Somehow Atmos flung himself on top of Piay, one hand rammed into his shoulder. Piay flailed without hope for that knife hand. White light flared again and this time he glimpsed Atmos' eyes widen with shock. Another face hovered behind the captain.

Hannu gripped the sides of the captain's head. In the sudden dark, Piay felt Atmos' head being rammed into the deck beside him. Once. Twice. Three times, with such force the boards jerked. The final blow ended with a crack and the captain's body slumped across him.

'Help me!' Hannu shouted.

Piay crawled out as his assistant dragged the body off him. Lurching upright, he felt around in the pitch dark until he gripped the corpse and helped Hannu press it against the ship's rail.

'Over the side!' Hannu bellowed.

Piay braced himself, fumbled for a grip, and with Hannu's aid he pitched Atmos into the roiling tumult.

A wave slammed against them with the force of a rockfall and Piay spun back. Gasping for breath, he felt Hannu stumble across him.

The hull was groaning almost as loudly as the roar of the elements. Piay felt a terrible dread.

A crack echoed and it sounded like the world splitting in two. A weight thundered into the deck with a terrible splintering, and the cries of the seamen rang out. The storm had shattered the mast.

Piay uttered a prayer. In the next lightning flare, he looked with horror on a scene of carnage. The fallen mast had shattered benches, pinned sailors beneath it and destroyed the side of the ship. The sail dragged in the mountainous waves, pulling the vessel down on one side.

The deck swung up almost vertical and Piay skidded down towards the black waves. He felt Hannu's weight against him, but then they were torn apart and he was falling.

The hull was rent in two. Piay plunged into the surging waters, shattered wood raining on him. The bitter-cold sea closed over his head.

Bodies swirled past him into the depths. Water flooded his nose and his mouth. In his mind's eye, he glimpsed Taita, who had been like a father to him and who now would never know what had happened to his son. He saw Hannu, whom he had saved from despair and who had saved his life in turn. And he fleetingly caught sight of the faces of the men he had failed, but those features were blurred and fading. There was no one else – no warm hands, no comfort, no love – and as the last of his breath burned in his lungs, he thought what an awful sadness that was.

Then there was only the blackness of the abyss.

The waves crashed to the beat of blood in Piay's head. He breathed in salt wind and the tang of seaweed. His face prickled from the heat of the sun.

As his thoughts swam up from the dark depths, his eyelids opened. Above him, gulls soared and dipped, shrieking their greeting. Like the drawing back of a shroud, the dullness in his mind slipped away until one realisation remained: he was alive.

Pushing himself up from the wet sand, he looked around at a beach rolling out into the distance. Shards of wood were scattered, and offshore the broken bones of the ship's hull floated on the swell. How close they must have been when that terrible storm tore their vessel apart.

He could scarcely believe it. The terrifying sensation of being sucked down into the gulf clawed at his mind. How had he made it to dry land? Only Khonsu could have brought him to safety. Those prayers in Sena had been heard.

Along the strand, a few sailors pulled themselves up and gazed about, as bewildered as he was. A few lay prone – alive or dead, he couldn't tell. Some bodies floated face down in the surf.

Staggering to his feet, Piay closed his eyes and turned his face to the sun. For one moment he let the joy of being alive course through him. After that close brush with death, he would be a different man, he told himself. He would not be reckless. Perhaps he would heed advice and even listen to Hannu's concerns.

The thought of his companion sparked sudden worry and he whirled, scanning the men pulling themselves up on shaking legs like children learning to walk.

Cupping his hands to his mouth, he yelled 'Hannu! Hannu!'

No reply came. He was surprised by his deep sadness at the thought that that irritable, sullen, disrespectful, acid-tongued assistant might not have survived. Throwing himself into a run, Piay called Hannu's name again. When a cry came back, he raced on until he saw a short figure standing with folded arms.

'You are alive!'

'No thanks to you.'

'Let us not grumble over our differences. We were lifted from a watery death by the hands of the gods. Our hearts beat in our chests and the fire still burns in our bellies. We are free to complete the great task we have been given, saved to become the saviours of Egypt. And complete it we will.' Piay was already planning the next step of the journey. 'And we no longer need to worry about the Hyksos.'

'You believe that to be true?'

Piay eyed his assistant. 'We have left them far behind, across the Great Green.'

'I have known men like Sakir. They are few and far between, that's true, but when I fought in the Blue Crocodile Guards we would encounter them from time to time. Most men are carried along in the current of life and deposited wherever the waters take them. But these men steer their own course. They have their own codes. They see the world in a different way from other men. They have a fire inside them that burns hot, and once they want something they will put their whole will into achieving it. Sakir will come and this will not be over until one of you lies dead.'

'You admire Sakir? Your words suggest you do.'

'I have learned many things in my hard life, but the one that guides me is this – you must take the measure of your enemy. You must understand them fully and treat them with respect. That is the only way to defeat them.'

Piay held out a hand. 'I have defeated Sakir twice—'

'You have escaped him twice.'

'You worry too much.'

Piay began to walk up the beach towards the green line of vegetation. He heard Hannu crunch behind him.

'Sakir will come to Mycenae, mark my words,' Hannu continued. 'He will find your trail. He knows where Atmos' ship was sailing. He will see the prints you make upon the earth. Death will come, and you will not hear it until it is upon you.'

'More gloom, Hannu,' Piay sighed. 'I sometimes wonder why I take you along with me.'

Hannu nodded. 'A part of you knows well enough. And one day you will admit it to yourself.'

In the verdant pastures, the air was rich with sweet and unfamiliar scents, and though the sun was hot, the wind that blew from the mountains in the west was cooling.

In citrus groves, they plucked oranges from branches heavy with fruit, tearing off the skin to eat the sweet, succulent contents. The juice refreshed them as much as any draught of water and the segments ended the rumbling in their bellies.

Piay knew well the lush valley of the Nile and the burning desert beyond – the black earth and the red earth that shaped their lives – but this land was different. Woods of oak spread out, deep and dark and cool. Streams tinkled over stones and a river ran by a well-used track. Olive groves dotted the countryside beside tracts of shrubland. Wild boar and red deer roamed. The bounty of the land was great, and it seemed to him that a man could live here merely upon what the gods provided.

He hoped the Mycenaean tongue that he had learned during his lessons with Taita would suffice to communicate with the inhabitants of this bountiful land. As they trekked, he tried to teach Hannu some words and phrases, though it would no doubt be like teaching a dog to read. But the little man managed to grasp some semblance of the teachings, even though he mangled every word that came back through his lips.

The farmers they met were suspicious at first, but softened when they discovered Piay and Hannu were travellers from a foreign land. Piay learned they were now in Lacedaemon. The farmers seemed to take to Hannu and laughed with him, only the gods knew why. Piay soon found these people had a tradition of giving aid to strangers, and they were offered gifts of flatbread and olives and a white cheese made from the milk of goats.

'This land is not like Egypt,' Piay said during one of his daily lessons to impart the information he had learned from Taita. 'The cities here are always at war with one another, and often for reasons that would puzzle civilised men like us. They take offence at the slightest thing, so we must watch our tongues.'

Hannu raised his eyebrow.

'If they are always at war, why would they spare fighting men to help us defeat the Hyksos?' he said. 'At least we have the sample of amethyst to persuade them.' When only silence followed his words, he glanced at Piay. 'You have the amethyst?'

'I lost it in the wreck.' Hannu's shoulders sagged and before he could speak, Piay gushed, 'We can still offer the amethyst mine. If my argument is strong enough, they will be persuaded.' His words sounded hollow, even to him. But they had to keep their spirits high. Failure was not a road they could ever contemplate. 'And I am formulating the argument even as we speak.'

'You know words and I know swords, so I will bow to your knowledge. But I would think it wise to have another plan. Just in case.'

Piay didn't answer. The truth was, there were times when he felt the burden of his task weighing him down. He was capable of it – of course he was – but there would always be things beyond his control. Some nights he woke in the early hours, his mind racing with doubts. So much was at stake. But he pushed those thoughts aside. What else could he do? He had to trust his own abilities. They had been given to him by the gods and they were great indeed.

He sensed Hannu drawing himself up for more questions and so he pursed his lips and whistled a jaunty tune, striding ahead.

The clash of swords rang through the gloom of the sweltering forest. Piay raised a hand to silence Hannu and strained to listen. They heard voices during lulls in the conflict.

'Trouble,' Hannu muttered. 'It would be wise to stay well away.'

'Or there may be someone in need. We should not turn our backs on them.'

Piay weighed his decision. He could not put the task Taita had set him at risk. But neither could he live with more scars on his conscience.

'It would not hurt to see what is amiss,' he decided.

Grasping a low branch, he hauled himself up a steep incline towards the sound of fighting. At the top, he looked down into a treeless bowl of grassland, soaked in the afternoon sun. A man was surrounded by five others, all of them jabbing spears at their prey.

The warrior at the centre of the circle turned slowly, levelling a bronze sword as he prepared for an attack from any quarter. But he was badly outnumbered and there was little hope of surviving this conflict. Yet Piay could not deny the warrior cut an imposing figure. He was tall and strong, an oak of a man. A bronze helmet covered his head to below his jawline, with a shadowed space around the eyes and a slit to the chin. A breast-plate of similar material glinted in the sun. A cape the colour of blood hung from his shoulders, and when he moved it swept in a manner that accentuated the strength and grace of a seasoned fighting man. On his left arm he sported a round wooden shield circled with bronze. A spear lay on the grass beyond the circle of opponents.

His enemies stabbed their spears and laughed, taunting him as they would a cornered boar. Their helmets were full-face masks with slits for the eyes and mouth, and a protrusion at the rear to protect the nape of the neck. They, too, wore bronze breastplates, but no capes, and they had leather kilts made from vertical strips to give them ease of movement in battle.

Piay took in the details in a moment.

*Different armies*, he thought. *The lone warrior must have been cut off from his men.*

Piay watched the taunting and felt his heart harden.

'Have you seen enough now?' Hannu hissed.

'Yes. We will help the lone warrior.'

Hannu's jaw clenched. 'We have no weapons. There are five of them.'

'This is a matter of honour, Hannu. Five against one is not honourable, not in war nor in peace, and not in the manner in which they are taunting that soldier.'

'Unless he . . .'

But Piay was already slipping around the trees. Trying not to draw attention to himself, Piay scrambled around the rim while keeping an eye on the battle. The five warriors seemed in no hurry to cut down their opponent. They danced back and forth, jabbing with their spears.

Piay's mind returned to that night his father and mother had abandoned him in Taita's care, as his thoughts did many times. He'd spent the night sobbing for the love that had been taken from him and the older boys had gathered around, mocking him. They had continued to bully him for seasons to come, until he had learned to master the fighting arts faster than them. And then they never bullied him again.

He threw himself down the steep incline with a roar. His heels skidded over the grass and he tumbled into a roll, landing on his feet near the bottom of the bowl. Letting his momentum carry him, Piay stooped and snatched up the fallen spear as he passed. The bronze tip shone as he swung it up. He glimpsed the six men who had gone rigid in surprise at this intrusion. He presented an odd sight: an Egyptian with a shaven head turning to black stubble, naked apart from sandals and a filthy white kilt sporting a gold design of Ra's orb.

He spun like one of the Pharaoh's dancers and whipped the haft of the spear up under the helmet of the nearest man. His arm jolted as the wood slammed into the jaw and the man went down hard.

That was the last of his element of surprise. The remaining four warriors hunched over their spears, waiting to strike. Now this was serious business. Piay could see they were seasoned in the scars that criss-crossed their torsos. The odds still favoured them.

'I don't know who you are, friend, but I welcome you.' The rich voice of the warrior in the crimson cloak was laced with sardonic humour.

Piay eased beside him, levelling his spear.

'This did not look like a fair fight.'

'Two against four is better.'

'Two against four for now.'

Their foes began to circle, preparing to make their move. Piay knew he had to act quickly or he and his new ally would be overwhelmed. Raising his hand in the air, he bellowed, 'Attack now!'

Those enemy warriors jerked and glanced around, suddenly fearful that they were the ones who would be overwhelmed. That instant of distraction was all Piay needed.

He lunged with his spear. As the tip came up, he glimpsed movement on the rim of the bowl. Hannu burst from the undergrowth. He thundered down the slope and before any of the warriors could turn he hurled himself into the back of the nearest man. Both slammed down hard. Hannu wrenched the spear from his opponent's hands, leaping up to spin the weapon round so the bronze tip was jammed against his fallen foe's back.

The warrior in the crimson cape threw his head back and laughed.

'I thought this day was over. Now there is more life in it, and me.'

Like a coiled cobra, he suddenly sprang into action. His sword flashed up, shattering the spear of the closest man to him, his cape billowing behind him as he lunged. His shield swept aside the remnants of the spear and his right arm blurred as he thrust his blade deep into the guts of his startled enemy. He wrenched upwards with such force he almost split the man in two.

Piay stared, awed by the skill and strength his new ally had shown. The warrior whisked his sword out in a red mist and danced back. His foe crumpled to the grass.

No doubt believing that Hannu was only the first of an attacking force, the two standing warriors scrambled up the bank and away. Hannu kicked his captive. The man jumped up and followed his comrades.

'Good as I am, I could not have done it without you. You have my gratitude.'

The soldier cleaned his sword on the kilt of the dead man and lifted off his helmet. Long hair tumbled to his shoulders, as black as a raven's wing but streaked with silver. Blue eyes sparkled with amusement. A web of lines circled them, and his cheeks were leathery from the elements. He was older than Piay had realised, yet as strong and powerful as a man a fraction of his age.

'My name is Mennias of Lacedaemon,' he said, reaching out a hand.

Piay took it. 'Piay of Egypt.'

Mennias looked him up and down. 'Aye, Egypt. I can see that. You are far from home.'

'I am an emissary from the Pharaoh. I have business with your king.'

The Spartan nodded, then turned to Hannu.

'And who is this little fellow?'

'Someone who will cut your balls off if you get on the wrong side of me,' Hannu growled.

'Well, I suppose they are at your height.' The Spartan laughed.

Hannu glowered, and Piay thought that if his assistant had had a blade he might well have done as he promised.

Piay balanced the spear on the palm of his hands and proffered it. Mennias took it with a nod.

'They could be back with reinforcements,' Piay said, looking in the direction of the vanished enemies.

'Aye. Corinthian bastards. We fought a skirmish on the banks of the river north of here. Cut off a few of my men, slaughtered them. Thought they'd have some sport with me.' Mennias ran his fingers through his hair, then pulled his helmet back on. 'If it's business with the king you have, it's my duty to deliver you to him.' He stepped away, then turned back. His eyes glinted in the shadowy depths. 'I owe you my life. I won't forget the risk you took this day for a stranger.'

Piay slipped behind the Spartan as he strode up the bank towards the north. Hannu fell in beside him.

'Big bastard,' Hannu grunted. 'Still, this is a day of wonders and we should celebrate it. You have made a friend instead of an enemy.'

The sun slipped behind the mountains until only a thin scarlet glow separated the deep ebony of the shadowed land and the star-sprinkled sky. Bats flitted among the branches of the woods, hunting midges.

Only the crunch of dry twigs underfoot broke the stillness. Piay thought they might as well be alone in all the world.

As they passed a twisted ancient oak, smoke drifted on the wind, more fragrant than the dung-fires of Egypt, and behind it floated the aromas of roasting meat. His mouth watered.

'Your camp?' he said.

Mennias nodded. 'The men would not have returned to the city until they found my body. No one is left behind as a feast for the ravens. That is the Spartan way.' He glanced at Hannu, who was a silhouette in the dying light. 'You were a soldier. I can see it in the way you hold yourself.'

Hannu grunted. 'A member of the Blue Crocodiles. The finest guards in all of Egypt.'

'The men will want to hear your tales of battle. You will be honoured.'

Piay watched Hannu cock his head, but his assistant said nothing.

As they crested a ridge and began to tramp down into a valley, Piay glimpsed lights flickering among the trees. His head was filled with the comforting scents and suddenly he realised how hungry and exhausted he was. The comforts of the court seemed a lifetime ago.

They hurried down the slope and out of the line of trees onto the bank of a winding river. The camp nestled into a bend, a jumble of tents around a fire. Lamps glowed like fireflies.

A sentry stepped out of the trees and swung a spear towards them, but only for a moment. When Mennias pulled off his helmet, the sentry gasped, 'General! You survived the skirmish.'

'Thanks to these good men.'

The sentry cupped one hand to his mouth and shouted 'Ho-lah!'

Piay glimpsed sudden movement in the camp as men stumbled out of tents and others hurried from the fire. They lined the perimeter, peering into the dark as they tried to identify the new arrivals.

'General,' Piay noted.

'You think my skills are not deserving of the title?' Mennias chuckled. 'Or that I am too old? All soldiers in Sparta serve until they have sixty summers behind them.'

As they marched towards the camp, an exclamation of recognition swelled into cheers that became a deafening outpouring. The men parted to let Mennias stride into the camp.

'Food for the general and his guests!' someone shouted.

Mennias paused to bow his head with a soldier who seemed to be one of his captains, no doubt to relate what had happened. Moments later they were seated around the campfire and slabs of quivering venison were thrust into their hands. Piay and Hannu tore into the meat as if they were starving beggars, the grease dribbling down their chins.

Once Mennias had finished issuing his commands, he squatted beside them.

'Our plan was to continue along the valley to drive out the Corinthian war band. But in our last battle, we shattered them and they are no longer a threat. Tomorrow we will return to Lacedaemon so you can deliver your message to King Hurotas. Sleep well, my friends. We march at dawn.'

The crimson capes swelled like a pool of blood spreading along the banks of the river. Sunlight spiked off bronze helmets and the ground throbbed with the beat of two hundred warriors marching in formation. Mennias strode at the head of the column. Beside him, Piay wiped the sweat from his brow. He was determined to show he could keep pace with these well-drilled soldiers. As a representative of the Pharaoh, it would not do to fall behind. But he already felt in awe of the strength and stamina of the Spartan army. With this force fighting alongside the might of the Pharaoh's soldiers, the Hyksos would be driven into the sea.

'Your friend seemed angry when I set him to ride in one of the supply carts,' Mennias said, 'but with his limp he would not be able to maintain the marching pace, and it is only what I would have done for any of our own wounded men.'

'Hannu is an angry man, that is true,' Piay replied. 'In fact, it is one of his favourite emotions, alongside irritation, annoyance and contempt for all men. But he is also a proud man.'

'Aye. That I understand. Fighting men find it hard to see the value in themselves when they lose their potency, for whatever reason. My men already revere him. The reputation of the fearsome Blue Crocodile Guards has spread even across the sea that separates us, and we still spin tales of your great general Tanus who once commanded it. I will find some way to let your friend know his worth.'

Piay wanted to say Hannu was his assistant, not his friend, but he bit his tongue. He was impressed by Mennias. The general seemed like a good-hearted man who understood honour and loyalty, those values which raised good men above the masses. If anyone could persuade King Hurotas to hear Piay's plea, it would be him.

A pair of swans glided along the river. Piay felt a bout of homesickness when he thought of a small carving of the bird that had been treasured by Taita. Swans were rare in Egypt, but artists were inspired by their elegance.

'It seems like there is much in common between our two peoples,' Piay began, laying the foundations for his argument to King Hurotas. 'But also many differences, I would presume. We could learn much from each other.'

'In times past we have had many wise and learned Egyptians travelling to our city, but few in recent days. Not since ...' Mennias caught himself before he mentioned the invasion of the Hyksos. It would not have been politic to discuss the fall of such a great power, Piay realised. A diplomat as well as a general. That was even better.

'Your soldiers would impress any general,' Piay flattered. 'I expect you strike fear into the hearts of your enemies, these ... Corinthians?'

Mennias' blue eyes continued to search the way ahead. He never rested.

'In Sparta, we are born to fight. All men are loyal soldiers – loyal to the king, loyal to our home. When seven summers have passed, boys begin their learning in the matters of war. They are taught how to fight with the sword and the spear, strategy and tactics. But a fighting man is more than just a weapon. We are taught to read, too, and to appreciate the arts and music. We learn honour and discipline and strength. This is the mark of a civilisation unmatched.'

'Except for Egypt.'

'Perhaps.'

'And the women?'

'Have more freedom than women anywhere. Educated as well as any man, with status in all eyes. This is the Spartan way.'

Piay thought about this, then said, 'If you're all soldiers, who works in the fields? Builds the homes?'

'Slaves.'

'And conducts trade?'

'We have traders and craftsmen, skilled workers from lands beyond. They are the dwellers around here, the *perioikoi*. Our weapons are shaped by them.'

Piay weighed how different this was from life in Egypt. Yet there could have been no better destination for his task than a land of warriors. Khonsu had smiled upon him once again.

L acedaemon sprawled on a green plain dotted with olive trees. The city shone like a beacon. As Piay emerged from the forest at the head of the column of warriors, he had to shield his eyes against the light reflecting off the limewash on the stone walls and the buildings sheltering behind them. This spectacle had clearly been foremost in the minds of the men who built this city. It said: here is a place of magnificence, a city that shines as brightly as the home of the gods itself.

Lacedaemon was not as big as Thebes and lacked those towering temples that took the breath of any new visitor to the City of a Hundred Gates. Yet though the citadel was still under construction, its scale dwarfed that of Avaris, as far as Piay could see. A thin pall of grey smoke drifted above the settlement, and flocks of birds swooped and cawed over the middens. The river they had been following through what Mennias called the Peloponnese curled around the western walls, and when Piay squinted against the glare he could make out a line of moored boats.

On the eastern side, outside the walls, the clay-brick shacks where the poor and the slaves lived reached out like a smudge of charcoal on the green plain. The smoke was thicker, the birds pillaged remorselessly, and when the wind changed Piay's nostrils flared at the reek of excrement and urine.

'Our city was named after the king's beloved wife,' Mennias said. 'It had other names in days long gone, but now, and always, it is Sparta.'

'He must adore his wife to give her name to such a city.'

'He adores his daughter, too. Her name is Serrena. She is, without a doubt, the most beautiful woman in all creation, like Aphrodite.' Mennias smiled. 'You may well be tempted by her charms. Take my advice. Do not be.'

As the column tramped across the plain, cries rang out from the watchers along the walls and the huge gate creaked open to admit them.

'This is the Gate of the Moon,' Mennias said, indicating the towering wooden door.

*How fitting that I should enter Lacedaemon here*, Piay thought. *A gate dedicated to Khonsu's moon. It is a sign of good fortune to come.*

Ahead, the street wound up to a palace that towered over the surrounding buildings. Grander homes of white-painted stone clustered around it, with pitched roofs and columns along the front. Here, separated from the vile odours of the poor quarter,

Piay breathed in the rich perfume of unfamiliar blooms arising from the gardens.

The garrison stood inside the gate, a square of low barracks and stores around a central courtyard. The aroma of baking bread drifted out from the kitchens.

As the soldiers trooped through the garrison gate, one of the supply carts at the rear of the column rumbled to a halt and Hannu levered himself out. He limped over to where Piay waited with Mennias.

'You are honoured guests,' the general said, looking from one to another. 'We will find you a place to live and some comforts until the king grants you an audience. For now . . . wait here.'

Mennias strode through the entrance to the garrison.

'You have found us a valuable friend,' Hannu said as he watched the general depart.

'If he has the ear of the king, our work here should be successful and quick.'

'Thebes may already have fallen to the Hyksos.'

'Then we will take it back.'

Hannu mused. 'The Spartans are a force to be reckoned with, no one could deny that. But the Hyksos horses – they are what separates victory from defeat. We have never found a way to counter that. On our journey I was told the Spartans know of horses, but they do not use them in warfare. They are still just men, on foot, before those powerful beasts and the chariots they pull.'

Hannu was right. Piay had wrestled with these same thoughts himself. But he wouldn't – couldn't – entertain the notion that only defeat awaited them back in Egypt.

When Mennias emerged from the garrison, he was carrying a bundle wrapped in cloth. He unfurled the wrapping to reveal two swords in leather scabbards. He presented one to Piay, the other to Hannu.

'No reward would ever be enough for saving my life,' he said. 'But this is a mark of the status that has been accorded you in Lacedaemon.'

Piay slid the sword half out of its scabbard and marvelled at the craftsmanship. The handle was bound with hide and studded with bronze pins. The polished blade gleamed in the sun and was engraved with a filigree of circular designs near the haft. Narrow at the hilt, it widened and then ended in a curved tip. Good for hacking, he noted.

'These are the finest blades in the world,' Mennias said. 'This style is called the *kopis*. Wear them with pride and all in Lacedaemon will know you are men to be respected.'

Hannu weighed the sword. 'Well balanced,' he said. He strapped the scabbard to his waist with the eagerness of a child with a new toy. 'I have felt naked without a weapon. Now the world is right again.'

'You honour us,' Piay said with a short bow. 'I will wear the *kopis* with pride when I stand before your King Hurotas and plead my case.'

The wind blasted across the waste, whipping up whirls of sand. The great pyramids of Giza soared up under the star-sprinkled sky and over them the full moon hung, white and bright and laden with the same mystery that suffused those age-old structures.

Piay craned his neck up to peer at the tip of the largest pyramid where that milky orb seemed to settle upon it. He felt such a wave of awe he crashed to his knees.

*Is this a premonition?* he thought.

The hairs on his neck tingled with a sense of anticipation and he continued to stare, waiting – for what, he did not know. Then, gradually, a vast silhouette formed, blocking out those twinkling constellations. The shadow took on shape and form, until the lambent rays of the moon illuminated a towering god.

Khonsu.

The traveller who marked the passage of time. Piay gaped, drinking in the appearance he had seen in temple after temple, the moon-disc suspended upon the head, the sidelock marking Khonsu as an heir of Osiris, the *was*-sceptre with the crook and the flail.

Piay tried to speak, but his mouth was as dry as the sands around him and no words would come.

Khonsu pointed the sceptre towards him and, though the god's lips did not move, Piay heard words ringing in his head.

'He is coming.'

The sceptre swept to the side, indicating figures on horseback thundering across the landscape. Though he could not discern any details, Piay somehow knew they were Hyksos. More, he realised the lead rider was Sakir.

As he stared, a red sun wavered behind Sakir and in the heat haze Piay could make out the flickering beast-headed figure of Seth.

The searing sun of the god of the desert and the cool moon. Seth and Khonsu.

But was Khonsu warning him about Sakir, or Seth? Whatever, Piay felt overwhelmed by the knowledge that this information he had been given was vastly important.

'Tell me more,' he called, but as the last word left his lips, the desert and the pyramids and the moon and the god rushed away from him.

Piay jolted from his sleep into a bed soaked with sweat. Even in the thin light of dawn, the intensity of that dream did not fade. The gods communicated with men in the visions of sleep – he had heard Taita say that time and again. Khonsu had spoken to him.

One thought remained above all others: there was no time to lose.

Piay paced the chamber, feeling his frustration mount. His lodgings were fine enough. The house was usually reserved for visiting dignitaries, and was clean and light. From the window, he could look out, past the large homes of the wealthy and important, to the palace. Yet he felt the weight of his dream-vision crushing down on him. The king was close, but he might as well have been three days' march away.

Cursing under his breath, Piay marched back to the low table at the foot of the bed where the slaves had left his morning meal of flatbread and cheese. Tearing off a morsel of the bread, he chewed slowly, but he had no appetite. It had been five days since he'd arrived in Lacedaemon, nearly four weeks since he'd departed Thebes. He feared what was unfolding in Egypt. He feared the arrival of Sakir and the disruption of all his plans. Why had the king still not agreed to an audience? Should he have brought some tribute, or was there some other strange custom that he hadn't yet discovered? Mennias had only said, 'The king will see you in time. Be patient and enjoy your comforts.'

But he couldn't be patient. What if Taita thought he had failed and decided to mount one final challenge on the advancing Hyksos – an attack that could only end with the destruction of the Egyptian forces due to the vast disparity in numbers?

That grand failure, those deaths, would be his failure. It would stain his soul forever.

He couldn't fault the kindness the Spartans had shown him and Hannu since their arrival. This house, and a chamber for Hannu, too, though Piay had suggested his assistant could sleep in the barracks with the soldiers. Silk tunics provided for him in the style the Spartans wore, while his filthy kilt had been taken away to be cleaned. Meals of venison and lamb and cheese and as much wine as he could drink. Every sign that he was respected. And yet still the king snubbed him, and in the process snubbed Egypt.

'There's something amiss.'

Hannu had appeared in the doorway. Thanks to the attention of the slaves who bathed him and smeared him with unguents, he was smelling sweeter than at any time since Piay had known him, and possibly than at any time in his life.

'Unless it pertains to the king or why the Spartan laundry is so inefficient, I do not wish to know.'

Hannu shrugged and turned to go.

'What is it?' Piay snapped.

'Mennias has taken a large number of soldiers outside the city walls. They've been herding the slaves out from their hovels as well.'

Piay thought for a moment, then said, 'Very well. There's nothing to be gained pacing the confines of this room like some captive beast. Let us investigate.'

The crowd swelled as the slaves wandered out of the collection of clay-brick huts on the eastern edge of the city. Some drifted out of the city gate, interrupted in the pursuit of their daily tasks. Piay frowned. What could so disrupt the day-to-day routines of Lacedaemon?

The Spartan soldiers watched the slaves like raptors. The soldiers' crimson capes flapped in the breeze, right hands resting on the hilts of their sheathed swords. They were perhaps a tenth of the number of the slaves.

'Some ritual?' Piay mused. 'Are they gathered to give thanks to their strange gods?'

Hannu scanned the soldiers and the slaves and said, 'Little joy in those faces.'

When the last of the slaves had taken their position, a silence descended on the gathering, broken only by the soughing of the wind along the walls.

Mennias strode to a circle of baked mud between the two sides where the grass had worn thin. The general beckoned to the ranks.

From the rear of the guard, two soldiers dragged a man – a slave by the looks of him. Bruises dappled his face. His mouth was twisted with fear. He had a mop of curly black hair, a strong jawline and a lithe body.

'Show me mercy!' he cried. 'I regret my crime. I will make amends.'

The words rolled out across the throng. No one moved; no one spoke. All eyes watched the captive as he was pulled to that circle of mud and thrown to his knees in front of Mennias. The slave looked up at the general with tear-flecked eyes.

'You have transgressed.' Mennias' voice echoed so that no one could be in any doubt what he was saying. 'You have strengthened your body and your mind. This is forbidden, as you and all here know. There is no mercy for such a crime. There can only be punishment.'

Piay stared, not quite sure what he was hearing. Could it be true that the slave was being punished for being strong and bright? Surely that would only increase his value.

Mennias drew his sword and swung it up high. In his panic, the captive tried to scramble to his feet. One of the soldiers who had delivered him whipped out his own sword and rammed the hilt against the side of the prisoner's head. The slave crashed down in a daze.

'Bare your neck,' Mennias growled. 'Resistance will only increase your suffering. Your death is decided. Make it a clean one.'

Piay shook his head. Death? This must be some kind of pretence for the benefit of the watching masses. What other explanation could there be?

The captive moaned, a terrible, juddering whine of anguish. The sound of a man who knew all hope had been extinguished. He arched his back, bowed his head and presented his neck for the blade.

Piay felt his heart beat faster. Mennias was drawing the emotion out of this performance like a master storyteller. At what point would he end it? When the edge of the blade hovered a finger's width above the flesh?

Piay searched the faces of those along the front of the crowd and saw no emotion. Whatever this display was, they had no doubt seen it before.

'Your fate has been written,' Mennias said in a clear, ringing voice, 'and this is your end.'

The sword slashed down. Piay was blinded by the light glinting off the blade, but then his ears rang with the sound of sharpened bronze hacking through flesh and bone. He watched the head bounce and roll before coming to the edge of the circle of baked mud, which he now knew could only be the space set aside for executions.

Piay reeled. Perhaps there was some aspect that, as a stranger, he was not understanding. He sensed Hannu stiffen at his side, and when he looked round he glimpsed a cold fury burning in his assistant's face. Piay had not seen the like before.

'Is this a land of savages?' Hannu said, his voice trembling. 'These Spartans are no better than the Hyksos. Worse, in fact, for those barbarians only kill in battle.'

'Let us wait before we pass judgement,' Piay cautioned under his breath. 'There may be much here in their customs that we do not understand.'

Yet Piay understood Hannu's contempt. They had slaves in Egypt. Who else would carry out the hard labour and mundane tasks of daily life? Captives of war; men and women who had fallen on hard times and sold themselves into slavery; others bought at the slave markets, transported from distant lands by the slavers. But while life was hard and they did not have their freedom, they were not mistreated. Masters had obligations. The slaves were fed and some even earned wages, and they were allowed to own personal property and conduct transactions. If they committed a crime, they would need to answer for it. But not like this.

Across the site of execution, the crowd began to drift away, back to their homes or to their labours. Their features were still blank and, while he had thought them emotionless, Piay reckoned they showed a grim acceptance of the world in which they existed.

'I would find out more about this,' Piay said.

He led the way to Mennias, who waited when he saw them coming.

'Not a task I relish, but a necessary one,' the general said as they drew close.

'Do I understand correctly?' Piay asked. 'His crime was that he was strong and clever? Would that not have made him a better slave?'

A boy handed the general a cloth to clean his sword. He wiped the gore off the blade as two soldiers dragged the headless corpse away.

'I would not expect strangers to understand our ways in Lacedaemon.' Mennias swept a hand towards the departing slaves. 'Our way of life here could not exist without the helots. They are captives, brought here from our victorious wars and from the surrounding land that we have conquered. They are our farmers, our servants, our nurses. They attend to our soldiers. Lacedaemon thrives because of them.'

'It is the same in Egypt,' Piay said.

'And yet not quite the same, I hear. The helots outnumber us. If we allowed ourselves to become weak, there would be the danger of an uprising. We must keep the slaves in their place. They must know their lack of worth. They must be afraid. We rule because we are strong. They serve because they are weak. This is the order of things. This is the Spartan way.'

Piay sensed Hannu simmering at his side. One wrong word could cause offence. Egypt needed the support of Lacedaemon.

'I have a task for you,' Piay said to Hannu. 'My kilt has not been returned since it was taken for cleaning and I am afraid it has been lost. It was a gift from my master, Taita, and I would not see it go astray. Find out what has happened to it.'

Hannu's eyes narrowed. He knew he was being dismissed for fear that he would cause trouble. But he turned and limped towards the gate.

Piay glanced at the smear of blood trailing from the execution site.

'You executed this man to send a message to the other slaves?' he said to Mennias.

'A message of strength. The helots know they cannot be too clever or too fit.'

Piay tried to swallow his contempt for the cruelty. Was this what it meant to indulge in diplomacy? There was a time, not so long ago, when he would have expressed his opinions freely and without hesitation. Hannu had cautioned him on it many times, and the gods knew how much trouble it had got him into when he was at court. Taita would be proud of him. His master had taught him the subtle ways needed to shape negotiations in your favour. He had never been able to put them into effect before. What an unpleasant task it was, but he thought he understood Taita a little more now.

'We have never had this problem in Egypt,' Piay began, adding in a light tone, 'so perhaps the problem may be the Spartans and not the slaves.'

Mennias cocked his head, unsure where this conversation was going.

'I suggest a wager,' Piay continued.

'A wager, you say?'

'If I take on a slave with some wits and strength and that slave stays true – does not run away, does not try to murder me in the night – then I would win.'

Mennias grinned. 'I like a good wager. And if you are prepared to risk your neck to prove your point, then who am I to stand in your way?'

'Then I will make the necessary arrangements,' Piay said, shaking the general's hand.

Bowing, he took his leave. He felt the plight of the helots weighing heavily upon him as he walked into the city, and he found himself looking into their faces as they went about their daily tasks. He had taken them for granted, imagining them as no different from the slaves of his home. Now he saw them in a new light.

'I will tolerate this no longer!' Piay raged.

He paced around the small garden at the rear of the house. Shafts of sunlight punched through the canopy of an oak tree and the sweet oily scent of laurel drifted around him.

Hannu furrowed his brow. He was standing in the shade of the high garden wall.

'The washerwomen said your kilt would be returned tomorrow, or the day after.'

'They said that four days ago.'

'You have plenty of clean tunics.'

'I want my kilt.'

'This is an important matter. No doubt about it. The Spartan laundry system is not what we have come to expect. Some might say arranging an audience with the king to petition for forces which could save all Egypt, never mind the Pharaoh, and our friends, and loved ones, and your master Taita, is a more important matter. But who am I to say? I am a simple soldier.'

'I need a slave to do the necessary work.' *And one to win my wager*, Piay thought.

'I am sure Mennias will provide you with one of the helots—'

'Not a Spartan slave. A slave like the ones we knew in Egypt.'

'We are not in Egypt.'

'I have spoken to one of the scribes. Slavers frequent Lacedaemon's seaport, a day's travel to the north. Perhaps I will find someone there who will provide for my needs. And then I will be free to give my full attention to arranging the audience with the king.'

Piay sensed Hannu scrutinising him, as if some deeper meaning lay behind this simple request.

'Do not try to change my mind,' Piay said, wagging a finger at his assistant. 'I have thought hard about this.'

'So I can see.' Hannu shrugged. 'Then it is decided. We will travel to this seaport with whatever Mennias thinks we need to buy a slave. I will make the arrangements.'

Piay and Hannu walked down a steep slope through shady woods where bees droned lazily. Finally Gythion revealed itself. The port huddled on a sheltered bay, the azure sea as still as a millpond. Seagoing trade-ships crowded the harbour, and out on the water others waited at anchor for a place to open up. Along the front, among the heavy flow of merchants and sailors, Piay smelled the suffocating tang of the fish sauce that the Spartans loved. The oily stew simmered in vats, the boys stirring as new carcasses from the latest catch were dumped in the liquor.

Finding a vantage point, Piay leaned on a warehouse wall in the shade. He watched the shards of light on the water while Hannu moved among the locals in search of information about the best slaver in the port. Piay's attention settled on the women passing by, and he enjoyed himself, summoning smiles and fluttering lashes. He showed the greatest attention to the ones with hair tumbling around their shoulders. During his short time in Lacedaemon, he'd learned that the women shaved their heads in preparation for marriage and kept their hair short after the ceremony, so it was easy to distinguish who had found a husband. But married couples lived apart as the men were contained in the barracks. He hadn't been able to resist smiling at some of the short-haired women as well. That is, until Hannu had cautioned him about raising the ire of another betrayed husband – as he had done in Avaris and Thebes – and bringing about the end of all they were trying to do.

Hannu returned and said, 'There are two slavers in port this day. One has sailed from Libya and has a reputation for being untrustworthy, with sickly, weak slaves. The other is from Phoenicia. His name is Hanbaal. He has travelled across the Great Green and has slaves from as far south as the kingdom of Kush. Like all slavers, he is quick with the knife and the sword and the whip, but I am told he will respect a strong hand in matters of business.' Hannu glanced around before adding in a whisper, 'And there is no love lost between the Phoenicians and the Hyksos, so you will not have to worry that he might spread the word to our enemies about an Egyptian buying a slave in Gythion.'

Piay nodded, pleased at his assistant's good work.

'Then Hanbaal is the man we need. Take me to the market.'

A small crowd had gathered around the slave market at the southern end of the harbour. Piay and Hannu pushed their way to the front through the wealthy Spartans. The slaver's block was a cube of rough-hewn stone on which the merchandise could be displayed to the potential buyers. To one side, the man Piay presumed was Hanbaal lounged in a wooden chair under a shelter of cloth stretched across poles to protect him from the heat of the midday sun. Piay studied the slaver's face, getting the measure of him. His eyes were dark and continually searching faces for the likeliest and richest buyer. His hooked nose hung over an oiled moustache and a beard that ended in a point. He wore white robes, as clean as if they had been freshly washed that day, cinched with a hide strip at the waist from which hung a leather scabbard containing a curved sword. In his left hand, he toyed with a whip of long hide strips, knotted at the ends, fastened to a wooden handle.

When Hanbaal seemed satisfied the crowd was large enough, he eased up from his chair and prowled the front of the crowd.

'Ready yourself, good Spartans, for here you find the finest slaves in all the world!' he called, with a sweep of his hand. 'Hard-working. Obedient. Silent. Plucked from the hot desert kingdoms from the south and tutored by my own hand aboard my ship. All know of Hanbaal of Phoenicia. All know my word is my bond, and my reputation is greater than any other master of slaves you will find in Gythion. Stake your claim without fear of disappointment.'

Hanbaal clapped his hands and two of his men brought out the first slave, a short man with a limp and a sagging belly. His hooded eyes were slow, his head bowed, his shoulders hunched. He levered himself up on to the block and stared at the ground as Hanbaal conducted his sale.

When the next three slaves were of similar appearance, Piay realised what was at play here. Hanbaal was a good salesman and knew his buyers well. What use offering strong slaves in Sparta? The need was for easily cowed workers who would never pose a threat.

This was not what he wanted. Piay stepped out from the crowd and strode towards the shelter, beckoning for Hanbaal to follow. Hannu stepped behind him.

'Is this the best you have?' Piay asked once the slaver had joined him.

Hanbaal made to speak, no doubt to protest that these were indeed the best slaves in all the world, when he paused and looked Piay up and down.

'You are Egyptian,' he said, taking in the shaven head and the eye make-up.

'I am, and we expect more than the Spartans, it seems.'

The slaver tugged on his oiled beard, his eyes sparkling.

'In my father's days the market in Egypt was strong. He was well rewarded. But then the Hyksos came. And they prefer to take what they want, rather than pay a fair price.'

'One day, perhaps sooner than you think, the barbarians will be driven from Egypt and you will have a good market again.'

Hanbaal seemed to like the sound of this. His lips slid back in a gap-toothed grin and he pressed his palms together and bowed.

'I will pray for those days. For now, what is it you require? I have many slaves to meet all tastes.'

Piay tapped his head. 'A slave with some wits. Someone I can trust to carry out tasks without being watched.'

Hanbaal nodded. 'A clever one, then. I would not be a good slaver if I did not warn you that there are always some troubles to accompany the benefits. These kinds of slaves may well come with a fast tongue, sometimes a sharp tongue. They do not always know their place and have to be shown it.'

'I am used to that,' Piay said without glancing at Hannu. 'And I require a slave who is strong. One who looks like they will survive a day's hard labour without collapsing to their knees.'

'Clever, and strong. Let me think.' Hanbaal clasped his hands and tapped his index fingers together. 'Yes, I have a slave who meets your requirements. But the price for such a fine specimen will be high.'

'We would expect nothing else,' Hannu said in a sardonically weary tone.

'General Mennias of Lacedaemon sends word that he will meet your price and will deliver full payment in good time,' Piay said.

Hanbaal cocked an eyebrow. 'General Mennias? Good. Very good. A fine man. Well respected.' The slaver raised a finger. 'Wait here. I will have my men bring the perfect slave for you.'

Hanbaal turned to his men and rattled off his commands in a strange tongue filled with clicks and odd throat noises, accompanied by a series of gesticulations. Two of the men hurried towards where the slave ship was moored, while another dragged out the next slave to the block. The slaver sat back in his chair, waiting while the market continued.

Piay sensed Hannu staring at him again and he looked round.

'If there is something you wish to say,' Piay snapped, 'then—'

'You made a good choice of the kind of slave you require,' Hannu said.

'What? No criticism?'

'If Hanbaal can find one who meets your requirements, I would wager General Mennias and the Spartans would perhaps see a sharp point on the end of your decision.'

Piay heard a surprising warmth in Hannu's voice – perhaps even respect. He realised he had not heard that tone before.

Piay looked away.

'No point, sharp or otherwise. I simply need a slave who meets my needs, that is all.'

He felt sure Hannu was giving him that familiar tight-lipped smile that said more than words, but he didn't look back to check.

When the men returned from the ship with a woman, Hanbaal jumped to his feet. She was a Nubian by the looks of it, with skin as dark as polished ebony. Hanbaal grabbed the woman's wrist and dragged her to where Piay and Hannu waited.

'This one is no good for a Spartan,' the slaver said. 'I would be surprised if she kept her head on her shoulders for a single day.'

The woman held Piay's gaze without blinking, and he sensed in it a silent vow that she would rather die than be cowed. He also saw a rare intelligence burning brightly there. With hair that was a mass of black curls, she was as tall as he was, and lithe.

He could see the muscles in her bare arms. Some experience of working hard, then. That was good. She was wearing a white dress to her mid-calves which Piay thought must once have been fine. The cloth looked to be delicate, and the hooped cut around her neck and the way it had been made to fit her curves suggested some workmanship. But now it was streaked with dirt and tattered along the bottom.

'What is your name?' he asked.

The woman stared into his eyes, her face expressionless, and he thought perhaps she did not understand him. But then she jolted from an unseen jab in the small of her back from Hanbaal.

'Myssa,' she said.

'This one has some learning,' Hanbaal said. 'She can speak your tongue and mine. She was taken from the kingdom of Kush. Some say she is a daughter of the king,' the slaver continued with a grin, spinning his tale to capture the imagination. 'Of that I cannot be certain, for she will not speak of her home or days gone by. Perhaps she is hiding her royal status, out of pride or because she fears it may draw the wrong kind of attention to her on the block.'

'Although that has not prevented you raising that question here,' Hannu noted.

Hanbaal held out both hands. 'I only pass on what I hear. But her learning will tell you she is a woman of status.' The slaver moved his hand up and down to indicate Myssa's physique. 'And strong, as you can see. It is said the daughters of Kush can throw a spear as far as any man.'

Piay found himself still staring into the woman's eyes, as if she were a cobra and he a mouse.

'Very well,' he said. 'This slave will be mine.'

Piay felt that he may well have created another problem for himself. But that was his nature, he had decided. One day he would learn those lessons that Taita had told him he would find on his travels. One day, but not this time.

The bright moon floated above the high branches. Piay stretched out on his back with his hands behind his head, watching the orb of Khonsu against the blue-black sky. Beside him, the fire crackled and spat. Hannu tossed more dry branches on it, sending up a shower of sparks. On the other side of the blaze, Myssa sat cross-legged, her back rigid. Did she never relax? Her hands were bound around the wrists with hide, at Hannu's insistence. He no doubt saw the same deep currents moving within her that Piay did.

Myssa stared into the flames, refusing to meet anyone's eye. Some would see humility in that – perhaps fear. Piay saw defiance tinged with contempt.

He'd expected Hannu to berate him in his usual sly manner for this detour. It was unnecessary, a distraction from the serious business he had been sent to conduct, no doubt about that. His assistant had said nothing, which was strange in itself. The truth was, he'd felt compelled to carry out this journey and he wasn't sure why. In Egypt, under Taita's tutelage, he'd never had a single doubt. Now there were times when he felt he didn't know himself at all and he felt troubled by that, as if he were losing his potency. It had started that night in the fields when he led his men to their untimely ends. If only he could forget that it had happened. Then he could be the Great Piay again. The master swordsman. The seasoned warrior. The spy who could do no wrong.

'You will be worked hard,' Hannu said to Myssa, 'but you will find life is better in the service of Piay than anything you experienced at the hands of Hanbaal.'

Piay didn't expect her to answer, but after a moment she looked up and fixed that cold gaze on Hannu.

'Better than my life in my home?'

'That life is gone,' Hannu said. 'It would be better for you if you forgot it.'

'And you are capable of forgetting your life?'

'I have forgotten many things.' Hannu jabbed a stick into the heart of the fire. 'And I would say I am better for it. Live in this moment. Think not of what yesterday held, or of what tomorrow might present to you.'

'Are you a wise man?' Myssa asked.

Piay chuckled. 'His wisdom was earned on the battlefield, caked in blood and choking on the reek of the dying.'

'The best wisdom,' Hannu said. 'You cannot know life until you see the light in a man's eyes go out.'

Myssa cocked her head, narrowing her eyes as she scrutinised her captor.

Piay frowned, too. There were times when Hannu seemed to have notions which might have been expressed by Taita.

'And you?' Myssa said, turning her attention to Piay. 'Where does your wisdom arise? On soft cushions and in perfumed gardens?'

This time Hannu chuckled.

'In Egypt, slaves only speak when they are spoken to,' Piay said.

'And what will you do if I speak out of turn? Beat me?'

'It is within my right.'

'Learn how to act quickly.' Hannu leaned back against an old oak tree. 'It will save you some hardship.'

Myssa cocked her head again. Now Piay could see she was doing it to taunt him.

'Yet I heard you ask Hanbaal for a clever slave. Why would you do that if you did not wish to hear the fruits of that cleverness?'

'I wish to hear it when I ask for it.'

Myssa nodded slowly. 'Now I understand. When you said "clever slave" you meant "obedient mute".'

Hanbaal had been right. Piay looked from Myssa to Hannu and back, and felt that he had indeed made life harder for himself.

As they tramped through the Gate of the Moon, Myssa craned her neck to study the temple, and the grand houses, and the palace, and the faces of the people who passed. This would be strange for her, Piay knew – so different from her home in Kush. Though he'd never travelled that far south along the Nile into Upper Nubia, Taita had told him of the land once known as Kerma. A searingly hot place, Taita had said, dusty and dry, where its people eked out a living as farmers and miners.

'If you are the daughter of a king, this will be a poor home for you,' Hannu said as he showed Myssa into the house. 'But for the rest of us it is comfortable enough. You have a room. You will be well fed. Do your work and life will be good. If you try to flee, you will be caught and your punishment will be great indeed.'

Myssa turned to Piay. 'What do you require of me?'

'The washerwomen of Lacedaemon are too slow, too inefficient—'

'I will wash your clothes.'

Piay felt surprised by the speed of her acquiescence. After her mood on the journey from the port, he'd expected more resistance.

'And the washerwomen have an item of clothing that is very valuable to me, a kilt. They keep saying they will return it—'

'I will bring it back to you.'

'You will soon find that the washerwomen of Lacedaemon answer to no one. Wait until you have been trapped in their labyrinth.'

Piay felt his frustration mount. This small matter should not be annoying him so much, and he knew if he had managed to secure an audience with King Hurotas he would not have become so obsessed with such trivial things.

A rolling thunder echoed in the dim distance. Myssa looked to the window and the sun shining across the rooftops.

'A storm is coming.'

Piay watched Hannu's body stiffen, but he was already feeling a prickle of unease at that familiar sound.

'Not thunder,' he said.

Hannu stared at him. 'Horses.'

Piay raced out of the house an instant ahead of his assistant, in time to see five riders sweep through the Gate of the Moon. The horses pounded up the street without slowing. Slaves and craftsmen who had ventured out to investigate the disturbance scrambled back to the shelter of the walls to avoid getting crushed under the hooves.

Messengers from one of the other cities, Piay hoped, but when he squinted into the brassy light, he could make out the leather caps and breastplates of the Hyksos. His dream – and Khonsu's warning – flooded back to him.

'You were right,' Piay said. 'They will never rest.'

'You have earned yourself a special place in their hearts,' Hannu replied.

The lead rider pulled his mount up and leaned down to one of the cowering slaves. A moment later, the slave pointed towards the palace and the riders lurched off once more. Piay tensed, waiting for the Hyksos to descend on his home, but instead the horses slowed to a canter and disappeared behind the larger stone houses.

'They're going to the palace,' Hannu muttered. 'Why?'

Piay peered towards the home of the king that he'd yearned to visit for several days now.

'To ask for permission to drag an Egyptian wretch away for punishment. They know the Spartans will not allow bloody retribution within the walls of their city.'

'Then we need to plead our own case.'

Pools of shadow were swelling in the streets as Piay and Hannu strode to the entrance to the palace, the Gate of Lions. The columns on either side towered four times Piay's height. The gate itself hung open. The Master of the Flame was already moving around the courtyard beyond, lighting the lamps along the walls. In the wavering light, Piay could see the king's personal guard standing sentry along the avenue to the interior, their spears erect at their sides, their crimson capes bright against the white walls.

From the edge of the courtyard, out of sight from the gate, Piay could hear the stamp of hooves and the whinnying of the horses. The Hyksos were already inside.

Piay marched up to the gate with the intention of striding through, but two guards stepped forwards and barred his way with their spears.

'I wish to speak with the king,' Piay insisted.

The guards said nothing.

'Hold.'

The command emanated from the growing darkness at their backs. Piay turned to see Mennias striding towards them.

Piay felt his irritation rising and he swallowed it as best he could, as Taita would have instructed.

'Why are we standing here in the dark while the barbarians are inside?'

'I understand your anger,' Mennias replied. 'You will get your chance to speak with the king tonight.'

'Why now? Why not when we first arrived in the city?'

The general looked up at the flickering lamps, choosing what he could say.

'The Hyksos sent a messenger ahead, saying that an Egyptian murderer and thief was coming to try to trick the king and perhaps take his life.'

'That makes little sense,' Piay snapped. 'Surely no one would believe such a thing.'

'The king is a cautious man, and a clever one. He wanted to hear both sides of the story before listening to your petition.'

'The Hyksos knew we were coming to try to find allies in the war with them,' Hannu grumbled.

'Of course they did. They are not fools. Why else would Piay, Taita's master spy, travel so far from the frontier?' Piay breathed in to calm himself. 'All we ask is a fair hearing.'

'And you will get it,' Mennias replied. 'The king is fond of Egypt. In his youth, he travelled along the Nile, to the City of a Hundred Gates, so he says. He tells many tales of the wonders he saw and the kindness of the people.'

'I did not know this.' Piay felt surprised by this information, but already he could feel his mind sniffing ahead, finding a path to use this to his advantage.

'One other thing,' Mennias cautioned. 'I know you and the Hyksos are bitter foes. So I will tell you what I am about to tell them – King Hurotas will not tolerate any bloodshed within the city walls. This is a peaceful place. And such things may well inflame the helots, and that we cannot have. Any transgression will be punished, regardless of your status as honoured guests.'

'Tell that to the barbarians.' The torchlight danced in Hannu's dark eyes. 'They are a murderous breed and they cannot be trusted.'

'The guards will take their swords before they enter the presence of the king, and yours too,' the general said. 'And I will have my men watch them carefully. My obligation is to you, do not forget that. I do not take my vow lightly. I have already put in a good word for you with the king and he will look on your request kindly, as courageous and honourable guests.'

Mennias raised a hand and the two guards stepped aside.

'Follow me,' he said.

Piay marvelled at the vast chamber. In the centre, four columns supporting the ceiling surrounded a reflecting pool. A shaft above it was open to the sky so that the waters would catch the rays of the sun and the moon. The surrounding floor was polished stone so that the light would seem to flow everywhere. The walls were covered with large mosaics of lions, deer and ships, and more tiles picked out interlocking designs of squares and circles across the ceiling. Gold and silver glinted in the torchlight, and the spicy scent of incense drifted through the air.

'Wait here,' Mennias said. 'The king will send for you when he is ready to hear your petition. I pray the gods will smile on you.'

The general strode away, the clatter of his leather soles echoing. Hannu looked around the room, his eyes wide.

'I have never seen such a place,' he said.

'There are riches here, yes,' Piay said. 'Let us hope there is wisdom, too.'

While Hannu peered into the depths of the reflecting pool, Piay paced the chamber, examining the mosaics. His mind was racing and he could not relax. Once again he had been too confident. He'd failed to suspect that the Hyksos might try to disrupt his plans. He should have known better.

'Hello.'

Piay turned to see two women standing in the doorway. They were looking him up and down as if he were some strange object whose function they could not quite understand. They were both tall, slim-waisted, with high cheekbones and almond eyes. Hair fell around their shoulders, one blonde, one black. Unmarried, then. Though they had both seen at least twenty summers, the one with blonde hair seemed slightly older, and her beauty was radiant. Her emerald eyes gleamed. She wore a dress the colour of the burning amber of the late sun. Fine gold wire was braided into a belt and more gold glimmered in a necklace. The younger of the two wore a dress the colour of a forest at twilight, with swirling ivy leaves embroidered down one side.

'My name is Piay.'

'The Egyptian we have heard about.' The blonde-haired one's lips twitched into a faint smile. Piay grinned back at her. 'This is my friend Tiasa,' she said. 'I am Serrena.'

Piay's grin tightened. 'The king's daughter.'

Serrena nodded.

Piay bowed. 'I am honoured.'

The two women glided over and circled, still scrutinising every piece of him. Piay settled into the attention. In his experience, the women at court were bored and always looking for distraction. He was happy to oblige without thinking too hard about the consequences.

'You have the body of a warrior,' Tiasa said, studying his arms.

'I have been known to wield a sword.'

Serrena held his gaze with a confidence that some might have considered brazen. Her thick lashes didn't flutter, like some of the women he encountered. Instead her eyes were as hard as jewels, challenging him, testing him. Here was someone who bowed to no man, he thought. He liked that.

'Why is a soldier visiting our city?' she asked.

'I am not a soldier.'

'What are you, then?'

'Many things. A man of learning. A man who seeks adventure in all things. A spy—'

'A spy?' Serrena pursed her lips. 'Of what use is a spy who announces his presence?'

'I am not spying on Lacedaemon. I am here to offer the hand of friendship.' Now Piay began to circle Serrena. She paused, allowing him to play his game. 'Would you accept my hand in friendship?'

'Are women so easily charmed in Egypt?'

'They are entertained by good conversation and wit, as all women are everywhere.'

'You are very sure in your abilities.'

'I know my worth, that is all.'

Serrena held his gaze for a long time. She seemed to be weighing whether he was an opportunity worth pursuing.

'I could tell you stories of life in Egypt, if you like,' Piay said. 'And perhaps if you enjoyed my tales, you could speak to your father to convince him of the rightness of my request.'

Was his tone light enough, his smile enticing but respectful? There was an opportunity here. If Hurotas had seen fit to name this city after his beloved wife, surely his daughter could sway him with a few honeyed words in his ear? And then once he had secured an agreement, perhaps he could see where her attentions might lead. He had never enjoyed the company of a daughter of a king.

As he flirted, Tiasa pushed between him and Serrena. Her jaw was set and her eyes had narrowed.

'Let me have this one,' she said, adding with a flinty tone, 'It is my turn. More than my turn.'

Serrena did not respond at first, but just as she finally appeared to reach her decision, Piay felt a hand clamp on his arm.

'If you will excuse me,' Hannu said to the two women, 'but I have pressing business I must discuss with my master before our audience with your father.'

'Have you lost your wits?' Hannu breathed as he tugged Piay away. 'Toying with the daughter of King Hurotas? That way leads to losing two things – whatever we hoped to gain by coming to this city, and then your head.'

'There is an opportunity here—'

'Aye, for what lies beneath your tunic. Sometimes it seems your brains hang below your waist.'

Piay glanced back and felt a pang of disappointment as he saw Serrena leaving with her friend.

'Life is hard and we all need comfort,' he said. 'You, me. Even them.'

'There are times for comfort and there are times when I need to save you from yourself.' Hannu gritted his teeth. 'Would that I had known the extent of my thankless task when I agreed to be your assistant.'

'Stop grumbling. I saved you from a life of misery. Some thanks would not go amiss.'

Mennias stepped out of the doorway on the other side of the reflecting pool, raised a hand and flexed his fingers. A moment later, Piay was walking beside him along a torchlit avenue to the king's residence. Hannu trailed behind.

'Has Hurotas spoken with the barbarians yet?' Piay asked.

'Not yet,' the general replied. 'At my request, he decided to hear your case first.'

'Will the king be receptive?'

'I cannot say. Hurotas is a wise man and he will weigh your request justly.'

Mennias ushered them into another large chamber. This one was as big as the waiting chamber and as ornately designed, with mosaics across the walls and ceiling, but it was darker. Only a few lamps had been lit and the shadows clustered in the corners. A fire crackled in the hearth, keeping the chill of the evening at bay. Guards stood in silence along the walls.

Hurotas stared into the fire with his hands behind his back. He was a broad-shouldered, muscular man, despite the grey hair Piay could see falling past his shoulders.

'Stay by the door,' Mennias murmured to Hannu. 'The king will hear only from your master.'

He took Piay's and Hannu's swords and handed them to one of the guards, then led Piay across the chamber to the king.

Hurotas turned as his guest approached, and Piay could see he had a thick grey beard and a skin that had a darker tone from the other Spartans. His eyes sparkled in the firelight and a smile played on his lips as he studied the new arrival.

'This is Piay of Egypt,' Mennias announced. 'Bow your head to the king of Sparta.'

Piay bowed, but he already felt a question burning in his mind.

'Leave us to speak, Mennias,' Hurotas said.

Once the general had retreated to stand near Hannu, Piay said, 'Forgive me, but . . . you have the look of an Egyptian about you.'

Hurotas' smile twitched. 'I have Egyptian blood in me, that is true.'

Piay nodded, hiding his surprise. He had heard many tales of the king of Sparta, but not this. But it could only make his task easier.

'Thirty years have passed since I last saw my homeland,' Hurotas continued.

'Again, I beg your forgiveness,' Piay said. 'The reputation of King Hurotas is known, but I had not heard of your heritage. I am surprised that was never spoken of.'

Hurotas' lips tightened into what Piay thought was a sly smile.

'Perhaps I was known by a different name then. Perhaps my wife was, too.'

'The queen of Lacedaemon is an Egyptian?' Piay could no longer hide his surprise. There were mysteries upon mysteries here.

The king beckoned and Piay followed him.

'Egyptians are not rare in Sparta,' Hurotas said as they walked. 'The admiral of my navy is one. He goes by the name of Hui. Have you heard of him?'

Piay frowned. He thought he had heard tell of such a person, perhaps in one of his master's long lectures about the past.

'He was a trusted friend of the great general Tanus, and he fought in the war when the Hyksos invaded.'

Hurotas came to a halt at a large and ancient wooden throne, carved with the heads of lions, and he sat in it, hanging one muscular leg over the armrest.

'As an Egyptian, you must feel anguish at the misery that the Hyksos have inflicted on Egypt,' Piay said. 'The battle has raged along the Nile for many years, but now the barbarians are planning an assault upon Thebes. The defenders of Egypt are sorely weakened and if the Hyksos are allowed to keep the city, Egypt may be lost for good.'

Hurotas snapped his fingers and one of the guards hurried out of the chamber.

'I keep my ears open to events in Egypt, but I am a King of Sparta now. I have much to concern me here – the constant harrying of the bastards in Corinth not the least of it.'

A slave hurried in with a flagon and two cups. He swilled red wine into both. Hurotas took one and offered the other to Piay. The wine was sweet and rich and refreshing after the long day.

'Tell me what you want,' Hurotas said.

'My master Taita bid me—'

'Taita?'

'You have heard of him?'

Hurotas stared into the shadows cloaking the corners of the ceiling.

'I may have.'

More games. What Hurotas was hiding, Piay didn't know, but matters were more pressing than uncovering the distant past.

'My master Taita leads the fight against the invaders in the name of the Pharaoh,' he continued. 'I speak in his name and on his authority. He has dispatched me to seek an ally—'

'Against the Hyksos?'

'An army to fight alongside us and drive the barbarians back into the sea.'

'And what gain is there to Sparta?' Hurotas watched Piay over the lip of his cup.

'I come in the spirit of fraternal bond. And now that I know you are an Egyptian, then we can both see that this is more than mere words. We have a bond, a blood-bond.'

'Do not overestimate my bond with Egypt. Yes, I love my homeland. But I left for a reason and I have not been back for thirty years.'

'I would not have come without more to offer. Amethyst. More of that violet gemstone than you have ever seen in your life. A mine, a secret mine, known only to a few. It will all be yours if you come to our aid.'

Hurotas nodded thoughtfully. 'Good. Good. I can see that would be a reasonable exchange. But how do I know this mine exists outside your imagination? How do I know that when I arrive in Egypt it will not mysteriously have vanished into the sand of ages?'

Piay felt his smile grow fixed. 'I was given a sample of the amethyst to persuade you of the quality of the mine's contents. But it was lost in the wreck of the ship carrying me across the Great Green. But you have my word—'

Hurotas shook his head. 'Then, in the matter of these nego-tiations, it is . . .'

He waved his fingers in the air. *Insubstantial. Worthless.* Piay felt the bite of frustration, but he forced himself to continue in a voluble manner.

'When the barbarians are gone, we will give you trade on more favourable terms than you could ever gain from the Hyksos. And we will be good allies in return. You are in a bitter fight with Corinth, and I am told wars with other cities come and go. With the might of Egypt beside you, those enemies would always know you have the upper hand.'

Hurotas swirled his wine around his cup. 'Or I could send men to fight with you and the Hyksos could destroy them all, and then Lacedaemon is weakened in the face of our enemies here. We have as much to lose as we have to gain.'

'With Sparta and Egypt together, the Hyksos could never win.'

Hurotas nodded. 'Perhaps. But you must understand – you are desperate. I would drive a hard bargain if we tried to reach an agreement.'

'Taita would expect no less.'

Hurotas threw back the last of his wine and tossed the cup aside. 'Very well. I will hear what the Hyksos have to say before reaching my decision.'

Piay held out his hands. 'What could the Hyksos say that would sway you?'

'That they would offer me more favourable trade terms than the Egyptians. That they have already conquered most of Egypt and they are close now to taking whatever remains. That your resistance has melted like the shadows at dawn and, however much you boast about the might of Pharaoh's army, you are too weakened to win. Why should I ally myself with a force facing certain defeat? That is what they will say to me.'

Piay felt the muscles in his shoulders tightening. This was proving harder than he had anticipated. Hurotas was no fool. To hold the throne of Sparta for thirty years – and as a foreigner, too – would require a man prepared to take hard decisions, someone not prone to sentimentality.

The king pointed a finger at Piay and drew a circle in the air.

'And they would make it clear – though they would not say it – that the Hyksos have crushed everyone they have ever confronted. No wise king would want them as an enemy.'

'And I would say that the Hyksos are a people that are as restless as their horses. They have no interest in Sparta today. Who is to say that will still stand tomorrow?'

Hurotas scrubbed a thumb along his chin, thinking. After a moment, he said, 'I see why Taita chose you as his assistant and his envoy. You have a quick mind, like your master. I admire that. I will think hard on all you have said. But do not expect me to decide quickly. These are weighty matters, with much at stake for Sparta.'

Piay bowed. 'I would expect no less. You have Egypt's gratitude for hearing my petition.'

Had he done enough? He couldn't be sure.

He was halfway to the door when Hurotas said, 'One other thing.'

Piay turned back. Hurotas levered himself from his throne and wandered to the fire.

'You have heard of the Oracle of Delphi?'

'Stories . . . whispers. Not enough to know if the Oracle is real or some wisp of imagination.'

'The Oracle is real. If I were in your place, with the survival of all I hold dear resting on what I can achieve, I would consult the Pythia – the Oracle.'

'And what could this Pythia tell me?'

'Everything. The gods whisper to her. She can pull aside the veil that hides days to come and tell what will be, or what might be if the right course is followed.'

Piay felt intrigued. Hurotas had spoken with the confidence of a man who had won many battles, but now his words were tinged with awe.

'Peasants consult the Oracle about what seeds to plant for a fruitful harvest. Kings leave the security of their thrones to ask her about the rise and fall of empires.'

'And her answers are true?'

'Let me tell you a tale of a young man travelling in a foreign land, far from his home. He had only his wits and his good right arm. That man heard tell of the Pythia from a farmer, while he laboured in the fields to earn a crust of bread to still the growling in his belly and to feed the woman he loved. With single-minded determination, that traveller set aside all else and made his way to Delphi to petition the Pythia for guidance. After a period of fasting, the Oracle disappeared into her sanctum where the gods spoke to her. When she returned, she recounted what they had said.'

Hurotas fell silent, staring into the crackling fire. This story seemed to consume him like the fire devouring the wood.

'What did she say?' Piay's words rustled through the stillness of the vast chamber.

'A riddle. A mystery. Words that twisted and turned and seemed to lead nowhere. The young wanderer was burning with rage. He had been tricked. But as he trudged away from the shrine, filled with gloom that the hours of his life had been wasted, those words crawled deeper into his mind, as the words of the gods are wont to do. Over and over he turned them, and with time they began to take shape, like a ship sailing out of the river mists. And then he could see what he had to – *had to* – do.' Hurotas stared at Piay and his eyes grew brighter. 'And now, against all the odds, that young man sits upon the throne of Sparta. I would not be here today if I had not heeded the Oracle of Delphi.'

Piay let these words settle on him.

'But why was the Oracle's message a riddle? Why not simply tell you what you should do?'

'Knowledge must be earned. Tell a man something and he will treat it lightly. He will forget parts over time. He will think it unimportant because it had come into his hands too easily. But point a man towards what he needs to know and let him fight to overcome the obstacles to achieve it, and that knowledge will burn in his brain to his dying day. He will be transformed by it.'

Piay thought back to the hot room where he had laboured over his studies and Taita had wandered around him with a switch to lash the back of his hands if he was lazy. He had grown frustrated at not being able to find the answer that Taita wanted, and his hand stung from the blows. Why could his master not simply tell him? And Taita had used those very same words that Hurotas had uttered: knowledge must be earned.

'You will be tested,' the king said. 'Some men never solve the riddle the gods have presented to them. Their lives disappear into the shadows. Only the sharpness of your mind will see you through this.'

Piay breathed in. He was ready for this challenge.

'While you reflect on your answer to my petition, I will consult the Oracle.'

'A wise choice.' Hurotas strode back to his throne. 'I will instruct Mennias to make the arrangements. It will take five days to journey to the Omphalos, the centre of the world, where the shrine of the Pythia stands on the slopes of Mount Parnassus. Two days for the Oracle to prepare to speak with the gods. And by the time you return, I, too, will have an answer for you.'

Piay bowed once more and turned to leave. But already he felt hot blood coursing through him at this new opportunity to learn his destiny. This was a last desperate chance to pluck victory from the defeat yawning all around him, and he would seize it with both hands.

'The king liked you,' Mennias said as he led Piay and Hannu along the avenue from the throne room. 'He would not have told just anyone to consult the Oracle.'

Piay strapped on his sword as he walked.

'I want to waste no more time. It's my intention to set off at first light.'

'I will arrange for supplies for the journey to be sent to you, and a horse, and one of my men will tell you what road to take. You need have no fear that you will be attacked, by men of Corinth or any others. The Oracle is revered and Delphi belongs to all men. Everyone in this land holds that truth in their heart.'

'Even so, I plan to keep one eye over my shoulder,' Hannu said. 'In my experience, the time to worry is when anyone says there's no need to worry.'

Ahead, two guards stepped out of the door to the chamber where Piay had been told to wait. Two figures strode behind them. Piay's hand fell to the hilt of his sword when he recognised the one who towered over the others: the Red Hawk.

Sakir's unwavering stare fixed on Piay as he was led along the avenue to the throne room. Mennias and Hannu fell silent, watching the approaching delegation. The only sound was the tinkle of the bones threaded into the Hyksos captain's hair.

Piay slid his blade partly out of its sheath. Mennias' fingers dropped onto the back of Piay's hand.

'Take no action here,' he breathed. 'You will not be harmed, and any trouble will reflect badly on you.'

The Red Hawk stepped closer, still staring. There was no rage in those eyes, no loathing, merely a chill emptiness, like staring deep into the night sky. Somehow that was more troubling than anything. The barbarian barely blinked, and when he did they were the slow, heavy movements of a lizard in the noon sun. That was the look of a man who had consumed the blue lotus, a dreamer who was hearing the whispers of the gods. Perhaps Sakir needed no Oracle to guide his hand. Perhaps he had already been shown the path to victory.

Mennias' fingers pressed harder. Piay breathed heavily and slid his sword back in the scabbard. Hannu stepped closer to him, ready to throw himself in front of his master if the two barbarians attacked.

Sakir slowed his step as the two parties crossed paths. The torchlight washed over the puckered pink flesh of the burns on his face. The bones in his hair clacked. Piay and Sakir came to a halt and they stared at each other across the avenue.

'Do you feel the cold breath upon your neck?' Sakir's voice was barely more than a whisper, but it seemed to resound off the stone walls of the palace.

Piay laughed. 'Have you not learned that you have met your match?'

'I told you I would follow you, to the ends of the earth if necessary. There can be only one outcome. I will hold open the door to the afterlife for you.'

Piay held out his hand. 'And yet you have failed time and again. In the fields where we met. In Sena, where I passed by under your nose, like a ghost. And the ship's captain you bribed to kill me now lies at the bottom of the deep.'

'Your end will come, when you least expect it.'

Mennias stepped forwards. 'It would not be in your interest to keep the king waiting.'

The general placed a hand on Piay's arm to urge him on. When they had reached the end of the avenue, Piay glanced back. Sakir was still watching him like the raptor that was his namesake.

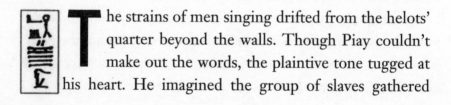The strains of men singing drifted from the helots' quarter beyond the walls. Though Piay couldn't make out the words, the plaintive tone tugged at his heart. He imagined the group of slaves gathered

around a hearth, recalling the songs that reminded them of lost homes, lost loves, yearning. They deserved more than the harsh treatment meted out to them at the hands of their masters.

That thought stayed with him when he walked into their home and Myssa was lighting the last of the lamps. The golden glow danced across her, igniting her dark eyes. She bowed awkwardly when she saw him. She seemed to have made some accommodation with her position since they had returned from Gythion. Perhaps – he hoped – it was because she had realised he was a fair master, one who was not unkind, and that her lot could be far worse.

'Get your rest as soon as you can,' he said. 'We are leaving Lacedaemon at first light on a long journey.'

'You're taking her with us?' Hannu said as if he was mad.

'She is our slave, our possession. It will be good to have an extra pair of hands to help out on the road.'

Myssa held her tongue. Perhaps she was learning there, too.

'I will make ready for the journey,' she said after a moment. 'But there is one thing I must show you.'

She slipped out of the chamber and when she returned she was holding a folded bundle of cloth. She shook it out and held it up. Piay saw that it was his kilt. The garment shone a pristine white in the lamplight, and the gold stitching on the lion's head design glimmered.

'You found it,' Piay said, amazed. He eyed Hannu. 'Within half a day of being asked to complete a task.'

Hannu shrugged and looked away.

Piay took the kilt and examined it. A warmth filled him. Here was his bond with Taita, whom he had not seen for a long time, and whom he might never see again – a prize from one of the few times his master had shown pride in his accomplishments.

'You have done well,' he said. 'I was right to take you into my employ. Yet I admit, when I saw you in the slave market I never imagined this level of efficiency. A slave who works this well is worth their weight in gold. What do you say, Hannu?'

'Anything that eases the great burden you place on me daily is of great value,' said Hannu.

As Piay folded his kilt, he thought he glimpsed a look shared between Hannu and Myssa – perhaps a smile – but when he looked up, they both showed only blank expressions.

P iay squatted at the base of a spreading plane tree and trickled water down his dry throat from his water skin. The breeze had dropped and the woods sweltered in the morning heat. For five days they had travelled the long, dusty road, through shaded olive groves and swaying fields of wheat. But now they were in the foothills and he could see the peak soaring up, grey and misty, to the north. That meant they were close to their destination – the place Mennias called the Mountain of the House of the God.

His eyes drifted to Myssa. Silhouetted against the glare of the sun, she faced the way they had come like a sentry. Her back was straight, her chin slightly raised, her eyes closed as she enjoyed the warmth on her skin. Not once had she complained since they had set out. Piay had ridden with Hannu behind him and Myssa had walked at their side. She'd kept pace without effort, her strength never flagging even at the end of a long day. But he was quickly learning she had other skills, too.

'Are we still on the right path?' he asked.

Myssa turned and nodded. 'From the position of the sun and the line of the trees' shadows, we are following the route General Mennias described.'

Quite how she had become so learned in the art of navigation, Piay did not know, but she was, without a doubt. At night she knew the positions of all the stars and where the moon would rise, far beyond his or Hannu's abilities. And that was the least of her skills, as far as Piay could see. She knew which roots and leaves were edible, even ones she had never seen before – how that could be, he could not begin to comprehend – and was wise in the ways of the beasts of the forest and the birds and fish. On any journey, Myssa would be a great boon. Piay was starting to understand how fortunate he had been in his choice of slave.

Hannu skidded down a dusty slope from where he'd been surveying the landscape. He mopped the sweat from his brow as he strode past their horse.

'No sign of those Hyksos bastards on our trail,' he said.

'I would have been surprised if they'd followed us from Lacedaemon,' Piay replied. 'Hurotas would not have told them we were travelling to consult with the Oracle, I am sure of that. But I will not be overconfident, not where the Red Hawk is involved.'

Hannu said nothing. He didn't need to. Piay looked over the treetops. He had made mistakes because of his overconfidence; he was aware of that now. But he would change, and when they returned to Egypt, Taita would see that change.

As they crested a hilltop, Piay looked down a grassy slope to a road running straight and true like a ribbon of gold unfurling among the green. The Sacred Way. A stream of travellers trekked towards the shrine. Poor farmers in mud-spattered tunics levered themselves along their wearying journey with gnarled staffs. Wealthy merchants rode or were drawn in carts, their fine robes of white and amber and sapphire revealing their high status. All of them raised their eyes to the hazy limestone crags of Mount Parnassus towering over Delphi, purple against the clear blue sky. They looked to the gods for guidance.

'So many of them,' Myssa muttered.

Hannu grunted. 'How long must we wait for the Oracle to hear our question? Weeks? Months?'

'King Hurotas has given us special dispensation,' Piay said. 'We will not wait long. Our matter is pressing.'

'All their matters are pressing, to them,' Myssa said. 'Life or death can depend on the planting of a seed.'

Piay eyed her. She possessed wisdom. Her gaze was fixed on the mountaintop, like those other supplicants. He admired the shape of her face, the beauty in the cheekbones, the dreamy look in her eyes.

Once they'd joined the trail of people on the Sacred Way, Piay slipped from the horse and walked beside Myssa. He sensed Hannu's eyes on him. He slowed his step so Hannu and the horse eased ahead. After a moment, Myssa fell in beside him.

'Is it true that you are the daughter of a king?' Piay asked.

'If I were, do you think I would have been so easily captured by a slaver?' Myssa searched the mountainside for their destination. 'My father is dead. My mother, too. I have nothing to return to. That is all that makes this life here bearable.'

'How did your father and mother die?'

'They were eaten by lions.'

Piay studied Myssa's face. She continued to look ahead.

'Is that true?'

'You will never know.'

This slave had some wit that set his own thoughts running. There would be no dull moments around Myssa if she enjoyed game-playing. He was used to this kind of back and forth with the women he entertained at court, but there was no flirtation here that he could see. Myssa seemed at ease around everyone, confident of her abilities, as he was.

'You should know that I will never treat you badly,' Piay said. 'You will never be free, like me, but it is said a slave in Egypt is better than a freeman in any other land.'

A smile flickered. 'Free? You are not free.'

Piay cocked his head. 'I am not a slave.'

'Can you change your profession? Can you leave your master? Can you travel across your land wherever your whims take you?'

'Of course not. No man or woman can do that. Except perhaps the Pharaoh.'

'You are not free, then.'

'I have as much freedom as any man of my status. More than most, thanks to my master.'

'We are both captives, you and I. I am the only one who recognises it.'

Piay snorted.

*What nonsense.*

His life was better than it would have been if he had been kept by his father and mother. He had everything he had ever dreamed of.

'One day you will see,' he said. 'When we return to Egypt.'

Swivelling on his horse, Hannu jabbed a finger ahead.

'There it is.'

Piay squinted, trying to pick out the detail of the shrine on the lofty slope. He glimpsed grey stone structures set hard against the mountainside, almost as if they had grown from the rock and soil itself. The hairs on the back of his neck prickled. Perhaps he was imagining it, but he was sure he could feel the presence of the gods. The air was heavy like the moments before a hot weather storm.

Hannu brought the horse to a halt and stared.

'What awaits us there?' he breathed, his words heavy with awe.

The three of them fell silent. The road had grown steep, winding a path around the mountainside. Piay studied the faces of those trekking down from the Oracle and their near-encounter with the gods.

To a man and woman, their features were drawn, eyes staring hard at the ground in front of them. No rush of excitement. No joy at a revelation that had changed the course of their lives. Was this all that waited those who petitioned the gods: bafflement and disappointment?

Piay pushed aside those thoughts. He would not yield to despair. He could not fail. This could be his only chance to return to Taita with some way to avert the destruction of Egypt.

Glimpses of the sacred precinct drifted in and out of view as the road twisted and turned, but then he stepped over an edge on to a flat area. The heaviness in the air was greater there, and for a moment Piay thought he might be crushed to his knees under the eyes of strange gods.

The road led into a complex of ancient, grey stone buildings, licked with moss and cracked by the elements. They were smaller than he had anticipated, mostly on one level with columns across the fronts. One seemed to be a temple, with those who wanted to consult the Oracle waiting to enter and make a sacrifice. The others looked like homes of the priesthood. And the priests were everywhere, with their shaved heads and white robes marked with the sign of the sun upon the chest in delicate yellow stitching.

One of the priests glided up, his hands clasped in front of him. He looked younger than Piay, perhaps with twenty summers behind him. He was short and slight, his eyes a pale blue. Hannu slipped from the horse and marched over to meet him. They spoke together for a moment and then Hannu wandered back.

'I have passed on the wishes of King Hurotas and promised that a suitable donation will be delivered in due time,' Hannu said. 'A powerful man can buy his way into the presence of the gods here as much as in Egypt.'

'This is not the time for sour words,' Piay cautioned.

Hannu shrugged. 'I am a fighting man. What do I know about anything? But they will provide us with some beast to sacrifice. And we will not have to wait.' His eyes darted around. 'And that is good. I do not know these gods. The sooner we are away from here, the better.'

'"In due time." They are very trusting,' Myssa mused. She took in the detail of the age-old buildings.

'Would anyone risk the wrath of the gods by failing to pay what is due?' Piay said. 'Then let us begin. I am ready to stand before this god of the sun they worship here.'

'Perhaps this god is the same as Ra, but called by a different name.'

'Perhaps.' Piay pondered on this spark of wisdom.

Ahead, those waiting to enter the sacred precinct lined up to bow their heads to a rock that came up to Piay's waist, sculpted like a beehive and carved to show a pattern of dia-mond shapes. The young priest beckoned and Piay walked towards the monument.

'What is this?' he asked.

'This is the Omphalos.' The priest's voice had a faint sibi-lance. 'Here, at Delphi, we are at the centre of the world and this stone is the world's navel. Bow to it. Show respect for this place where the heavens and earth meet.'

When his turn came, Piay bowed, and then the priest ushered him on before turning to Hannu and Myssa.

'You must wait here,' he said. 'Only those who would commune with the Oracle are allowed to enter.'

Hannu flinched. Piay put up a hand to calm him.

'I will return with the answer we need,' he said with confidence.

Piay looked back over the crags and valleys rolling down to the misty, verdant landscape. Shafts of sunlight came through the clouds that had drifted in, as if the gods were shining light upon this sacred place. He felt his heart lift after all the tribulations he had faced since he'd left the comforts of his home.

Piay stirred from a dreamless sleep. His body ached from a night lying on straw on a stone floor. Yet he felt strangely refreshed. Perhaps it was this place, though he couldn't understand why. The thin light of a silvery dawn broke through the doorway and he looked across a jumble of slumbering bodies – the others waiting to stand before the Oracle. Some would have many nights here.

Sitting up, Piay stretched. He'd been given a basic meal of flatbread, olives and white cheese the previous evening, but no wine, only a cup of sweet beer. His stomach was rumbling. Pushing himself up, he walked into the chill of the grey morning. The priests were already going about their business, moving from their homes to the temple to the storehouses. The comforting aroma of the day's bread was drifting from the kitchens.

Piay wandered until he found the young priest who had been assigned to him. The shaven-headed man had his arms folded around a weight of wood for the kitchen fires.

'Where can I find something to fill my belly?' Piay asked him.

The priest shook his head. 'Not a morsel shall pass your lips until you have had your audience with the Pythia.'

'How soon will that be?' Piay heard the grumbling note in his voice. Hunger always left him in a bad mood.

'Patience,' the priest said with a smile. 'I will come for you when the time is right.'

He walked away, whistling to himself.

Piay felt his frustration rise. He'd spent most of his time in this land waiting for something that never happened, it seemed, and he was sick of it. Time was short and too many people were relying on him.

Taking himself away to the quiet edge of the precinct, he kneeled in the shadows of the branches of an old oak and muttered a prayer to Khonsu. He had no offering to present, but he asked for safe passage through the day ahead. As he closed his eyes, he summoned the faces of the men who had died that night in the fields, as he did every day. He prayed that they would forgive him.

When he returned to the centre, the young priest was waiting for him. He reached out a hand. On his palm was a short bronze knife, highly polished with a curved blade.

'The hour has come,' he said. 'Your journey to enlightenment has begun.'

The priest led him into the cool confines of the temple. Apart from two other priests standing sentry in the gloom, the temple was empty at that hour. Incense hung in the air and lamps burned behind the altar so that the god's table appeared to glow with his power. But all around, the suffocating shadows pushed in amid the rising heat of the day.

Following the priest, Piay stepped up to a circular channel cut into the flagstones by the western wall. The priest pressed the knife into Piay's hand and said, 'Wait here.'

He vanished into the dark and returned soon after, dragging a goat. Once the beast was in the centre of the circle, the priest urged, 'Make your sacrifice. The lifeblood will open the way.'

Piay steeled himself. Men he could kill, but beasts made him squeamish. He slashed the short blade across the poor creature's throat. The blood spurted over his hand and his tunic and splashed into the circular channel, where it drained away. Once the goat's convulsions had ended, the priest eased the knife from his hand and led him out into the bright sun. Blinking, Piay felt disorientated, heady.

On the edge of the precinct, water sprang from the limestone of the mountainside and formed a small pool before streaming away and down.

'This is the Castalian Spring,' the priest said. 'Here you must purify yourself so you may stand before the eyes of the god untainted by the corruption of this world.'

Piay stripped off his tunic and stepped into the pool. His legs quickly grew numb from the cold. Under the gushing spring, he washed the blood from his hands and cleansed the dirt of the road from his body. Shivering, he stepped into the rays of the rising sun, closed his eyes and allowed himself to dry.

'It is time,' the priest murmured.

Once he had slipped his tunic back on, Piay strode behind the priest to the shrine – a circular domed building barely large enough to house fifty people. Columns supported the portico that ran around the dome, and the shrine had been painted white so it shone when the sun's rays struck it. Despite himself, Piay felt his heart beat faster as he neared it.

The priest stopped at the entrance and ushered Piay in. Piay stepped into a small hall well lit by a succession of tall windows. He expected to be struck down the moment he crossed the threshold into the domain of this god he did not worship.

A scribe stood beside an arched doorway. He was an austere man, with a face as hard as granite, hollow-cheeked and thin inside a heavy robe lavishly embroidered with coiled serpents rising open-mouthed to swallow the sun. His hair was silver. The scribe was holding an unfurled scroll on his left hand; his right was poised with his brush.

'Do not step forward. You must not enter the *adyton*,' he intoned. 'Ask your question.'

Piay frowned. Who was supposed to hear his petition? He peered through the doorway into the deep shadows beyond. Blinking, he realised someone else waited there. As his eyes became accustomed to the gloom, he watched the figure emerge from the surrounding dark.

The Pythia sat on a tripod above a fissure in the rough bed-rock of the mountain. Her heavy robes were maroon, edged with white and gold, and she had pulled a cowl over her head so her eyes remained lost to the shadows. She might as well have been carved from the rock itself, so unmoving was she, what little of her face he could see below the shade of the cowl expressionless. Her skin was pale, almost grey, and wrinkles were beginning to form around those rigid, bloodless lips.

'Ask your question,' the scribe repeated.

Piay steadied his heartbeat. He had thought long and hard about this question on the journey from Lacedaemon, weigh-ing each word until he felt certain the question would be pre-cise enough to elicit an answer from the gods.

In a clear voice, he asked, 'How can I save Egypt from its enemy?'

At first the Pythia did not move, nor did she respond. Piay wondered if she had heard his question, although he had said it loudly enough. Then she began to breathe deeply and faster with each passing breath until she was panting. As suddenly as she had started, she ended the inhalations with one long, juddering draught and her head flopped back.

*What am I seeing?* Piay wondered.

The Pythia sat motionless once again, her face turned towards the heavens. Then her lips trembled and words began to emerge.

Piay leaned forwards, straining to hear. The scribe scowled and held up a hand to warn Piay not to move from his place. The attendant moved closer to the doorway, listening. Piay caught fragments, but not all of what the Oracle was saying, but the scribe heard everything. Once the Pythia's low voice died away, the scribe wrote down the message from the gods with rapid brushstrokes on his scroll.

The scribe tore off the papyrus and handed it to Piay.

'Your question has been answered by the gods, and the answer is this – tame the beast that is both serpent and bull.'

Piay stared at the piece of papyrus. His thoughts circled, but he could find no answer to this riddle. It would come. He had to believe that. Given enough reflection, enough application of his great mind, it would come, as if he were dragging a carved block of stone from the mud of the Nile. This was the way it was meant to be. Knowledge had to be earned.

Piay peered back into the dark of the inner sanctum. The Pythia was sitting erect and unmoving once more. Could she see him, or were her eyes fixed on the realm of the gods?

The scribe flapped his hand to dismiss Piay and he stepped back out into the morning. The young priest was waiting, hands clasped.

'You have your answer?' he asked.

Piay nodded.

The priest tightened his smile, no doubt reading Piay's confused expression.

'You do not comprehend your answer. That is understand-able. The gods are testing you.'

'They are testing me well.'

Piay wished Taita was there. His master would know the solution to this conundrum, he was sure.

'You must take care,' the priest said. Piay thought he saw pity in the other man's face. 'It is your responsibility to interpret the message of the gods correctly. This is the path to wisdom that the gods have chosen for all men. If your answer is not wise, you will follow the road which ends in destruction.'

*The door to glory or the door to destruction* – that was what Taita had told him.

'I accept this gift of the gods and all that goes with it,' Piay said. 'I will choose the road wisely.'

Piay trudged down the Sacred Way beside Myssa. Hannu rode at their side. Now he could under-stand the taut features of those people he had seen returning from their audience with the Oracle.

Every one of them must have been tormented, strug-gling not only with the confounding riddle the Pythia had delivered, but also with the burden that reaching the wrong conclusion could lead to the end of their dreams – perhaps even to the end of their lives.

'The gods will not make it easy for mere men,' Hannu said. 'We have to prove ourselves worthy.'

'The answer is there to be found,' Piay replied. 'It is within our powers, or the gods would not have delivered it to us.'

Myssa's eyes shone. The riddle and its solving had excited her in ways Piay had not seen before. She had opened a flood of ideas even before they had begun the journey from the sacred precinct.

'We know the answer refers to a beast . . .' she began.

Piay shook his head before she continued. 'There is no beast that is both serpent and bull.'

Hannu shrugged. 'Perhaps there is one we have not yet discovered. In distant lands, they say dragons fly through the sky in the east, and to the south there are desert cats that speak with the voices of men.'

'And we should search the four corners of the earth until we find them?' Piay said. 'No. The gods would not give us an answer that relies on knowledge we do not have. Why would they torment us so?'

'Sport?' Hannu replied.

'Let us draw our attention first to the word "beast",' Myssa pressed. '"Tame the beast" and you will defeat the enemies of Egypt. But what kind of beast matches this description?'

'There is the beast,' Piay said, 'and there is what lies behind the beast. A man who is brave in battle is said to be a lion. A man who is cowardly or untrustworthy is a dog. Both are beasts. Both are men.'

'Then tame King Hurotas,' Hannu said. 'He has been a lion in battle. Tame him and he will become the ally you require.'

'But that only answers one part of it,' Myssa said. 'How is Hurotas at once like a bull and a serpent?'

'He has broad shoulders and he is strong like a bull,' Hannu said. 'And if beneath his tunic there lies a big—'

Piay eyed his assistant and Hannu fell silent.

'It is not Hurotas, I am sure of it,' Piay said. 'I know I have to convince him to become an ally. The gods would not tell me something I already know. Where is the wisdom in that?'

'We will find the answer,' said Myssa. 'The riddle tantalises, but a sharp mind will solve it.'

Piay felt pleased that he had bought a slave with such a mind, and that for once the burden would not be his alone.

'We have five days to find the answer before we are back in Lacedaemon.' Hannu pushed himself up on the horse's back so he could scan the land ahead. 'That should be more than enough time.'

When Lacedaemon rose on the plain beside the river, Piay felt his heart sink. On the long journey back, he had convinced himself that if he had not solved the riddle before he breathed in the woodsmoke hanging over the city, he never would. The three of them had talked all day and deep into the night until his head hurt. Myssa had dazzled him with strange notions, taking their search into areas he had not even imagined. Hannu, too, had offered extravagant thoughts that surprised him for a simple soldier. But in the end it was all for naught. They had come no closer to the answer.

'Do not be despondent,' Myssa said as she walked beside him while he rode. 'Though you have set this limit for yourself, this is not the end of it.'

'Where else can we find an answer if not in our own minds?' Piay felt surprised to hear the concern for him in her voice.

'The gods,' Hannu grunted from where he sat behind Piay. 'Khonsu has answered your call before. He could do so again.'

'You must not blame yourself,' Myssa pressed.

She reached out a reassuring hand to his thigh, then pulled it back as if it had been burned, recognising that she had crossed the boundary that lies between slave and master. Piay wished she had continued with her touch. He yearned for some human comfort to ease him.

When he glanced at her, she was muttering to herself with a furious intensity. Still trying to find the answer in the short time before they reached their destination, Piay thought. He was warmed by that.

They trekked across the plain until Piay could hear the din from the workshops. A hornet swooped from the sky and droned around them. Piay flapped his hand to drive it away but that only angered it more.

'It will leave us be when we pass through the Gate of the Moon,' Hannu muttered.

'The Gate of the Moon,' Myssa repeated. 'A name filled with beauty.'

'The moon is the mistress of mystery,' Hannu said.

Piay narrowed his eyes at his assistant's poetic turn.

'The moon is our guardian,' he added. 'We travel under Khonsu's gaze.'

'There are times in my life conducted under the light of the moon that burn brightly in my mind,' Hannu said, 'as if that light alone had fixed them in my head. Some of them I would not wish to remember, it's true. But others . . . those moments that fill the heart with joy, I am pleased to carry with me forever.' He paused, adding, 'The first time I kissed the woman who became my wife.'

Piay stirred the pot of his memories. He recalled saying farewell to his parents under the glow of the moon. He chose to say, 'The first time I met my master, Taita.'

Myssa cast her eyes down. From the tautness of her face, she was recalling some troubling incident. But then she nodded and forced a smile.

'Remember the moments that fill your heart with joy. Yes, that is good advice. There was a time . . .' Her words trailed away and her brow furrowed.

Piay glanced down at the quizzical tone in her voice. Some thought was working its way through her. Then her eyes opened and she stabbed a finger in the air.

'I have it!'

'You have what?' Piay asked.

'The answer!'

The hornet buzzed closer. Piay lashed at it, driving it away once more.

'By Ra's flaming chariot,' he said, 'tell me, before this thing drives me mad.'

Myssa clapped her hands, laughing. In that moment, Piay thought she seemed like the woman she had been before the slaver had dragged her away from her life.

'Hannu's words!' she said. 'My mind leaped back across the years to when I was a girl. I stood outside my father's house, watching the full moon shining in the sky above the trees. I heard a terrible sound blaring through the night – the cry of some huge beast. It filled me with terror and I ran to my father. He grabbed his spear and he raced into the night to protect me.'

Again the hornet attacked. This time Piay flapped at it half-heartedly. He was entranced by Myssa's story and her smile. As the furious hornet buzzed louder, the horse danced and Piay fought to keep the skittish beast under control.

'I stood in the door quaking as I peered into the dark,' Myssa continued, 'and after what seemed like an age I heard foot-steps approaching. My heart leaped with joy when I saw my father striding towards me, but I was puzzled. He was laughing because it was not some beast come to devour us. A merchant was bringing a present for the king of Kush along the road that ran near our house. A gift from a land beyond ours that would amaze and delight our ruler.'

'What gift?' Piay asked.

'An elephant!'

'An elephant?'

'That is the answer to the riddle. It has a body like a bull, broad and strong. And the serpent—'

'Is its trunk,' Piay said.

'. . . snaking out of its face.' Myssa beamed.

'If that is the god's advice, I don't think much of it,' said Hannu. 'How can taming an elephant help us save Egypt?'

At that instant, the furious hornet swooped again. The excitable horse reared up, pitching Piay and Hannu off its back. Piay crashed to the hard ground, the wind rushing out of him, and as he sat up he watched his mount galloping towards the city.

Hands on her knees, Myssa was laughing so hard she could barely catch her breath. Piay scowled, but then he was laughing with her.

Hannu rubbed his elbow. 'I have never had any love of horses. Let the Hyksos keep them.'

When Myssa was returning to the house and her chores, Piay felt his mood darken again. In the shadow of the city walls, he turned to Hannu and said, 'I will seek another audience with Hurotas. He must have an answer by now.'

'One way or another, our time in Lacedaemon is coming to an end. I'll make the preparations for our departure.'

'Think hard on the Oracle's message. Thanks to Myssa, we are close to the answer we need. I feel it in my bones. This may well be the last chance we have.'

Hannu shrugged. 'The gods will show us a way.'

'I would rather our fate was in our own hands.'

'The gods weave their webs and no man can see the strands until they unfurl around him,' Hannu said. 'But think about this – if Mennias had not executed that helot, you would not have felt the urge to travel to Gythion to buy a slave and so set an example to the Spartans. And if you had not gone to Gythion, but instead purchased one of the Spartan slaves, you would not have encountered Hanbaal and attended his market in the harbour. And so you would not have found Myssa. And without Myssa, you would never have begun to solve the riddle of the Oracle.'

Piay glanced along the street to where Myssa was disappearing into the stream of Spartans going about their daily business.

'Then our slave is a gift of the gods.'

Through the doorway of the palace hall, Piay watched the shadows lengthen, then pool until night cloaked the avenue beyond. He'd paced the chamber a hundred times, waiting for Hurotas to summon him to the throne room for his audience. Others had come and gone – scribes with arms filled with scrolls and grey-bearded foreign dignitaries. Now, as he peered at his reflection in the pool, he could feel his frustration mounting.

When he heard footsteps approaching, Piay looked up to see Mennias striding through the door. His face showed as little emotion as the bronze helmet crooked in his arm.

'Is the king ready to see me,' Piay asked, 'or must I wait here all night?'

'The king will not see you.'

Piay jumped to his feet, trying to hold back his anger.

'What have I done to offend him? When last we spoke, he did all he could to aid me.'

'You have not offended him.' Mennias' face softened as he walked over. 'There is no need for him to meet you. The king has asked me to pass on his decision. He will not agree to your request at this time.'

'How can this be? He is an Egyptian—'

'Hurotas did not make this choice lightly. His heart lies with you and the struggle you and your people face. But he must act in the interests of Sparta, and at this time those interests are best served by keeping a friendly relationship with the Hyksos.'

'You are afraid the barbarians will attack you.'

'We are afraid of no one.' Mennias paused, choosing his words. 'They are an unpredictable people, true, and their ambitions are great. We are already at war with Corinth, and any general will tell you it is not wise to divide our force for a battle on two fronts.' He held out both hands. 'And the trade we have with the Hyksos is too important to set aside, especially when there is no certainty that you will win.'

Piay simmered. 'I could go to Corinth.'

'Your answer will be the same everywhere you go. No one will wish to anger the Hyksos at this time.'

'Then you have damned us to defeat.'

Mennias dropped a hand on Piay's shoulder. 'This is not the news you wished to hear, I understand. But do not give in to despair. There is a way as yet undiscovered. And Hurotas has not ruled out offering aid at some time in days to come.'

'We need that help now.'

'The king's mind can be changed. I will press him myself, once again. The world will be better for both our peoples when Egypt is once again in the hands of its true ruler. But for now . . .'

Piay nodded. What point was there in arguing? With a heavy heart, he strode out into the night.

As Piay neared the gate, a figure separated from the shadows in the avenue. It was Serrena, the king's daughter. She was wearing a crimson sheath dress that matched the colour of the guards' capes.

'I heard you were visiting my father,' she said.

'Much good it did me.'

The hungry look in her eyes transported Piay back to the Pharaoh's court and the women he had dallied with there.

'Hurotas is like a young stallion. He needs a firm hand to guide him.'

'And you are that firm hand?'

'I could be.'

Piay weighed that unwavering stare, as hard and strong as any merchant negotiating an agreement.

'Spend some time with me in my chamber,' she continued. 'I would wager you are a man used to this kind of request. And, if you like, you can tell me what you need of my father and I will endeavour to deliver it to you.'

Piay would not normally have refused such an offer, with or without the promise of payment for what he wanted most in the world. Serrena was a striking woman, with her fine cheekbones and large eyes sparkling with intelligence, and her confidence was alluring. Yet he felt uninterested. He didn't know why. Instead, he was overcome with an urge to return to his house. Was it to find the full answer to the riddle?

He bowed and said, 'As entranced as I would be to spend an hour or two in your company, I have pressing business elsewhere.'

Serrena arched an eyebrow. She was clearly not used to having such an offer rejected. Yet Piay could see no anger in her face at the snub. Her lips curved into an intrigued smile. Was that respect he saw in her eyes? And when he recognised that it was, he realised there had been no respect before.

'Some other time, then,' she said. 'Perhaps I will have words with my father nonetheless.' She made to leave, but then her face darkened as if she had remembered something important. 'One other thing. The captain of the Hyksos delegation was asking after you earlier.'

'Sakir?'

'He wanted to know where you were staying. He said he wanted to pay you a visit.'

Piay felt as if a knife had been stabbed into his heart. His shock must have burned in his face, for Serrena's hand flew to her mouth and she recoiled.

And then he was racing away from her, through the gate and down the street to the house, praying that he would not be too late.

Piay crashed through the door. Myssa cowered by the lamp in the corner of the hall and he felt relief when he saw she was well. But his gaze fell on her hands pressed against her mouth and the fixed look in her wide eyes. He followed her stare to the stone floor. A trail of blood was smeared across the flagstones, leading into the night.

'Hannu,' he croaked.

Piay dashed into the night. In the lamplight, spatters of blood glistened. Not a life-ending amount, though. There was still hope.

Myssa came beside him, clutching at his hand.

'The barbarians burst into the house with their swords drawn, demanding you give yourself up.' She choked back emotion. 'Hannu was brave. He threw himself between me and them. To defend me. How furiously he fought. But there were too many of them. They cut him down.'

'He did not die?' Piay needed to be sure.

Myssa shook her head. 'A gash on his arm, one on his thigh, another on the side of his head.'

Piay breathed in a deep draught of cool air.

'The barbarians searched the house and when they found you were not here, they took Hannu.' Myssa's eyes gleamed with tears. 'The leader . . . Sakir . . . He said that I should tell you he will kill Hannu if you do not go to him. Slit his throat and throw his body in the river. "Time is short", he said. He will wait for a little while and if you do not come, he will end Hannu's life and leave Lacedaemon.'

Piay felt his fear for Hannu twist into a cold anger deep in his belly.

'Sakir said where I can find him?'

'The cistern.'

Piay knew the place. He'd marvelled at the engineering during his wanderings around Lacedaemon while he was waiting for his audience with Hurotas – a circular, domed stone structure housing a reservoir that supplied water to the city. It was fed by an aqueduct that ran to some clean source of the life-giving liquid in the nearby hills. In the dark of the cistern, Sakir could commit his murderous ambition away from prying eyes.

Myssa must have seen his intention in his eyes, for she gripped his wrist harder.

'Go to Mennias,' she pleaded. 'He has said there must be no blood shed on Lacedaemon's streets. He will send the army to free Hannu.'

'It may take too long to find him, I cannot take that risk. Imagine if Hannu was killed while I argued my case . . .'

'You will die!' Myssa exclaimed.

'And then you will be free.'

'That is not how I wish to earn my freedom.'

'I cannot abandon Hannu,' he murmured.

'No, *we* cannot abandon him – of course we can't.'

Piay eased his hand away and he looked along the trail of blood splashes disappearing into the dark.

'Farewell,' he said, hearing the note of finality in his voice.

And then he was running towards the eastern walls where the cistern stood.

The street wound away from the houses and the lamps and the sound of songs and stories told by hearths. As the silence pressed in, Piay prowled along an avenue of bay trees, breathing in their sweet scent with only the light of the moon to guide him. His fingers tightened around the hilt of his sword. He couldn't trust a man like Sakir to act with honour. The barbarian captain may have posted his men along this road so they could attack from the dark before he reached the destination. Nor could he trust Sakir that Hannu was still alive. He pushed that thought from his head.

The cistern loomed up, silhouetted against the spray of stars hanging over the Peloponnese. Beyond it, the impregnable walls of Lacedaemon towered. Piay cocked his head. All was as silent as the grave. He crept towards the door.

*Do not be reckless*, he warned himself. *For once, learn the lessons that the gods present to you, for the sake of Hannu's life.*

There were five barbarians. As good as he knew he was at swordplay, they would cut him down in an instant, as they had done with Hannu. His only hope was to be stealthy and hope the gods presented him with an opportunity to gain an advantage.

He knew there was little chance that he would survive this encounter. But he was ready. He had nothing in this world – no wife, no children. Would Taita grieve for him? He hoped that would be the case, but he could not be certain. He prayed that Hannu would reclaim his body and make the necessary preparations that would ensure the doors would be opened and his journey into the afterlife would be allowed. And perhaps Hannu could complete the task Taita had given him.

Piay pressed his ear to the door. The wood was cracked and blistered by the sun, age-old, and no doubt thick. He could hear nothing within.

Pushing his shoulder against the door, he eased it open. The wood groaned on the flagstones. He paused with an opening wide enough for his arm to reach in. Now the dim echo of voices whispered back, but there was no note of alarm in them.

Perhaps if the barbarian was confident in his victory, he might not have made the necessary preparations.

Piay leaned against the wood again. Sweat prickled his skin as the door opened a little more. When it was wide enough to squeeze through, he edged inside.

He breathed in dank air and the earthy aroma of wet stone. From deep in the dark, the voices droned on. One of those voices belonged to Sakir – he was sure of it.

Piay steadied himself against the wall as his eyes adjusted to the gloom. A faint glow was rising from below. The wall had been coated in shining plaster. He glimpsed a set of stone steps by his feet, leading down and curving around the inside of the wall.

Holding his sword up, he eased his way down the steps. As he descended, the glow grew brighter, the light shimmering along the slick plaster. No doubt the reflection off the water below.

The voices throbbed louder. Eventually he stepped on to the edge of a stone walkway where the shadows swelled. In the gulf ahead, a circle of golden light flickered. Two lamps had been set to mark a space in the gloom.

The reservoir was vast, extending out in all directions more than the circumference of the domed building above. The walkways criss-crossed each other and black water gleamed in the spaces among them. How deep that water was, he could not tell.

Dropping low, Piay crept forwards.

As he neared the orb of light, he picked out the details of the figures gathered there. He saw Hannu kneeling, looking up at his captors. Defiance burned in his assistant's face, even though blood caked his beard and stained his naked torso. His hands had been bound behind his back. No doubt the barbarians feared he would be a threat even in his wounded state. Hannu was a savage fighter who never gave up.

The Hyksos warriors stood around Hannu on an intersection in the walkways. Their crescent swords were sheathed. Sakir stared down at him.

When he spoke, his voice was a lazy whisper. The echoes floated back as if the gods were repeating his words. In his drawl, Piay heard the taint of the blue lotus.

'Many think I have been driven mad by my consumption of the dream flowers,' Sakir was saying. 'Perhaps I have. Any man who walks with the gods would be seen as mad by those who cannot break the shackles of this world.'

Piay felt a chill as he watched Sakir look around and smile at things that no one else could see.

'Perhaps one day the gods will keep you when you stroll by their side,' Hannu spat. 'Give me my sword and I will speed you there.'

Sakir prowled around him. 'If only you knew what they have shown me, little man, you would not be so rebellious. You would be humbled. Awed. My life was transformed that day I first ate the blue lotus. It was a dying priest who told me of the magic the flower contained. I left his body for the vultures and took the dream flowers from the pouch he carried. I swallowed them. Too many. I was swept away, and for a while I feared I might never return.'

Sakir looked into the dark above his head, as if he could see through it and the stone dome of the cistern to the very home of the gods.

'In my daze I wandered into the wilderness,' he continued. 'My throat was like the desert around me and I shook as if I was on the coldest mountaintop. Those vultures now circled over me. On I trudged, directionless, until I found myself in front of a towering rock curved like a talon. As I stood before it, I heard my name caught on the soughing desert wind. "Sakir," he half-sang. "Sakir."'

Piay was entranced by the tale the Hyksos captain was weaving with his strange, drifting voice.

'The orb of the sun sped down the sky, transforming from gold to crimson. The sands beneath my feet burned red. Red everywhere, as far as my eyes could see. And as I stared to the top of that rock, I saw a figure form out of the crimson light. I trembled in terror when I saw the jackal-like head and the cloven hooves.'

'Seth,' Hannu muttered.

'Aye. That is what your people call him. The God of the Desert, the God of Chaos. His eyes seared into me and I felt dread. I was being judged. My life hung in the balance. If the god so decided, I would be condemned to an eternity of torments. I looked up at that talon and the voice came to me again.

It said, "You are the Red Hawk. You will hunt your enemies and their blood will stain the sands." I would become a tool of Seth himself, enforcing his will upon this earth. Why do you think I have travelled half a world to destroy your master? Not simply to claim vengeance, although the fire burns within me. Seth has decreed that the Hyksos will rule over Egypt, for the Hyksos bow their heads to the god of the desert above all others. Your master works to end the rule of my people—'

'Piay is a threat to you,' Hannu interjected.

'A distraction. But he must not be allowed to succeed. Seth has tasked me with ensuring your master is crushed, his plans destroyed. And so Egypt will remain in the hands of the Hyksos.'

Piay thought back to Khonsu speaking to him in his dream, and he was swallowed by an overpowering vision of a war among the gods for the soul of Egypt itself. Was he then a tool of Khonsu, as Sakir worked for Seth?

'What happened after my encounter with Seth, I cannot tell,' the Red Hawk continued. 'But my men found me wandering the wilderness, deranged, raving. But I lived! And as the dawn came up the next day, I knew I had been chosen by Seth. I had been given my destiny.'

In that whispering voice, in the way he held his body, there was something inhuman that added to Sakir's terrifying demeanour. Perhaps he truly had been transformed by the blue lotus into something more than a man.

Piay crawled forwards, praying that the shadows would continue to cloak him. But Sakir turned his head and looked directly at him. Piay stiffened, knowing he had not made a sound that could have attracted the Hyksos warrior's attention; yet Sakir stared as if he could see through the dark, through Piay's skull and into his mind. Piay shuddered.

And yet Sakir did not move towards him.

'Seth has given me powers beyond that of men,' Sakir breathed. 'I am a warrior but I am also a prophet. I see things, little man. I see the days yet to come and the road to my destiny unfold across the baking desert sands. I can survive without food or water longer than any. I never tire. My thoughts run cold, even in the heat of battle. And I feel no pain. Perhaps it is true what my men believe – that I cannot die. What do you say to that?'

'I would happily put your notion to the test.'

Sakir smiled at Hannu. Even from that distance, Piay could see that dreamlike nature seemed to have lifted from him, as if Seth, for now, had departed. Once again he was merely the dangerous leader of a barbarian band.

'Your friend is too much of a coward to come to this place to confront me,' Sakir growled. 'I have seen his kind before. They swagger and they boast and they flounce like temple dancers. But when they are called on to put their necks on the line, they vanish like the morning mist.'

'Piay is no coward,' Hannu spat. 'But he is not a fool. He will not gamble his life for a wretch like me, not when he has work to do.'

Sakir laughed. 'Your hopes lie in ruins, little man. King Hurotas has already acceded to my request. The Spartan army will never become the ally of the Pharaoh, whatever feeble excuses Hurotas now makes. You will find no one to join forces with you. The Hyksos are too powerful, too feared. Too wealthy.'

If this news hit Hannu hard, he didn't show it. His chin still pushed up, those black eyes stared.

'One thing I have learned is that this world often grows dark, but there is always a flame of hope flickering somewhere.'

Sakir smiled. 'Not for you.'

The barbarian captain's sword sang as he drew it from its sheath. Streaks of lamplight flashed from the blade.

'I gave your master the time to come here to try to save you,' Sakir continued, 'whatever good it would do, but now this dance is over.'

Piay imagined that blade swinging down and Hannu's head bouncing off the walkway and into the water. There was no more time to waste.

Piay dragged the tip of his blade along the stone walkway. The grinding sound echoed off the walls.

Sakir froze; his sword swung to one side. His head snapped in the direction of the sound. Piay watched the barbarian's brow knit as he tried to decipher what he was hearing.

'Go,' he barked at the warrior nearest to him.

Still swathed in shadows, Piay sheathed his sword and eased over the edge of the walkway. As he lowered himself into the cold water, his entire body numbed. Pushing his fingers into a crack in the masonry, he hung against the wall, kicking gently to stay afloat.

In the dark, he would be invisible.

Piay closed his eyes as the warrior raced along the walkway. The steps slowed as the barbarian moved further from the light. Finally he was creeping along one step at a time, afraid he might plunge off the edge before his eyes adjusted to the dark.

The footsteps creaked closer.

The warrior would be staring ahead along the walkway, not looking down.

Closer.

Now Piay could smell the warrior's sweat, sense him looming above. Those leather soles tramped past him.

Piay lunged from the water and grabbed his enemy's ankle. Yanking with all his strength, he toppled the warrior off balance and dragged him over the edge. The barbarian cried out in shock before his head smashed against the edge of the stone walkway and dashed his wits away.

The echoes of the splash ebbed away until there was silence once more. Piay held the warrior under, allowing the water to flood the man's lungs. He unfurled his fingers and the body drifted away.

'Croyant!' Sakir called.

'He's fallen in the water,' one of the other warriors mocked.

Sakir whistled through his teeth and three sets of feet thundered along the walkway.

Piay pushed himself beneath the surface and swam. In the dark depths, the cold stabbed into his bones. At the next cross-walkway, he pulled himself on to the stone and rolled over to the water on the other side before he could be seen.

The calls and responses of the three warriors rang out as they searched in the dark, their tone growing more uneasy with each moment.

Piay swam on until the light shimmered across the water above him. When his fingers brushed the next walkway he raised his head. The sweet aroma of the oil in the lamps, mingling with the iron tang of Hannu's blood, wafted in the air.

Piay could see Sakir prowling to the edge of the circle of light, peering in the dark.

Stealth was still the best way. Piay slipped a short-bladed knife from his tunic and imagined slicing it across the Red Hawk's neck before his foe even realised he was there. Sakir had his back to him, and so, without hesitating, Piay pulled himself up on to the walkway, taking care not to splash the water. He gripped his knife tight and prowled forwards. There was just time to strike before the other Hyksos warriors returned.

He never made the slightest sound – he would have sworn to Khonsu that was true – but as Piay neared his enemy, Sakir stiffened as if he could sense Piay's presence. Turning, the Red Hawk looked Piay up and down, seemingly unsurprised to see his prey there, and showing only contempt for the appearance of this drowned rat.

'You came,' Sakir said.

Hannu wrenched his head round and scowled when he saw the man who would be his saviour.

'Why are you here?' he snarled.

'The thanks I get,' Piay replied.

'Perhaps you are not as cowardly as I imagined.' Sakir strode towards Piay. 'Though this show of courage is a futile gesture.'

Piay backed along the walkway, flexing the fingers of his left hand to beckon the Red Hawk on. His mind raced. He had lost the advantage of surprise and the knife in his hand seemed a feeble weapon when face to face with one so strong. As Piay considered tossing the knife aside and drawing his sword, Sakir sheathed his own blade. He pulled out his own short knife and rolled it in the fingers of his right hand.

'Let us meet on the same terms,' the Red Hawk said. 'Then we will see who is the greater. I will take your life, then set your friend free. I have no grudge against him. But this thing between us will only end with the death of one of us, and it will not be me. I cannot be killed.'

Piay felt the hairs on his neck prickle at the confidence in Sakir's words. He hunched forwards, balancing on the balls of his feet, ready for any strike.

'What, no boasts?' Sakir said, raising an eyebrow. 'Perhaps fear has stolen your tongue.'

'Let us end this,' Piay said.

Sakir was bigger, stronger, with a longer reach. This would not end well. Only one strategy might even out this contest, Piay thought.

With a roar, Piay hurled himself forwards. He dropped his head at the last, as the Red Hawk's knife slashed in an arc. Under the blade he went, slamming into his opponent with all the force he could muster.

Sakir flailed, knocked off balance, and the two of them plunged over the side of the walkway and deep into the chill water. Piay sucked in a breath of air just before the blackness closed over his head. He hoped it would be enough.

In a tangle of writhing arms and legs, down they went, both of them fighting to gain the upper hand. Piay gripped the wrist of Sakir's knife hand and stabbed and slashed in an unfocused attack of desperation. He felt the tip of his knife rip through flesh. Once it jammed deep into muscle. Sakir's own furious attack did not abate, as if he felt not a flicker of pain.

The last of his air burned in his lungs. How Sakir could continue to battle with such force, Piay did not know.

And then he felt his entire body wrenched round in the water. Sakir heaved, smashed Piay against the stone side of the pool. Piay's head cracked and his mouth jolted open. Water gushed in and all thoughts dashed aside as the sensation of drowning engulfed him.

Again Sakir smashed his head against the stone, and again, until Piay felt those huge hands push his shoulders down into the depths.

The terror of death rushed through him, but his attempts to claw himself free were pitiful.

Fighting against that terrible dread, one last desperate ploy flooded his mind. Piay slackened, letting his limbs go limp as if the life had already been expunged from him.

His trick worked. Sakir stopped fighting, and the next thing Piay knew was that his cold form was being rolled out on to the walkway.

Unable to contain himself any longer, Piay spewed out the water he had swallowed and heaved in juddering gasps of air.

When his vision cleared, he looked up at Sakir looming over him.

'Still alive, then,' the Red Hawk said. 'But not for long.'

Piay felt despair rush through him. Defeated. He had failed, and not only himself, but the Pharaoh and all of Egypt, too.

Suddenly a tumult erupted on the edge of Piay's senses. The Red Hawk wrenched himself round and stared into the dark. His men had returned and were hovering around Hannu, motionless.

'Lower your weapons!' a voice boomed.

Piay glimpsed rapid movement in the shadows and Mennias strode into the faint light, his cape swirling around him. Behind him a band of soldiers clattered, spears clutched across their chests.

'If anyone dares spill a drop of blood, I will take his head!' Mennias roared. 'Their standing be damned!'

Sakir eyed Piay with contempt.

Another figure hurried at the back of the Spartan Guard. It was Myssa. She must have raised the alarm when Piay had set off to confront Sakir. What other slave would have acted so independently? Now, perhaps, she had saved his life.

As the soldiers slit Hannu's bonds, Sakir showed a sly grin.

'There is no need for force here. This was mere entertainment between friends.' He eyed Piay. 'Is this not right?'

Piay said nothing.

Mennias stepped in front of the Hyksos captain.

'Your business in Lacedaemon is done. You will take your horses and leave immediately.'

Sakir glanced back at Piay one final time – a warning that this was not yet over – then he pushed his way through the band of soldiers and strode along the walkway into the dark with his men behind.

Sheathing his sword, Piay dashed to Hannu. Myssa kneeled beside him, examining his wounds.

'You have my thanks,' Piay said to her.

Myssa nodded. No other words were necessary.

Not so for Hannu.

'I am supposed to thank you for trying to throw your life away?'

Piay held out both hands. 'As you can see, I am still here.'

Hannu grunted. 'Any thanks must go to Myssa, it seems, and to the gods.'

Piay shrugged. 'Think that if you must. We both know the truth.'

He winked at Myssa and she grinned, but he knew in his own heart that his bravado was unwarranted. Sakir had beaten him. Next time he would have to be better.

Hannu winced as he stood.

'There was too much at stake. I am worthless. The Pharaoh . . . the fate of Egypt . . . all that hangs on you. And you risked throwing that away to save my neck.'

Piay walked off. 'All that is true. But if you were dead, I would have the burden of your work, and that can never be.'

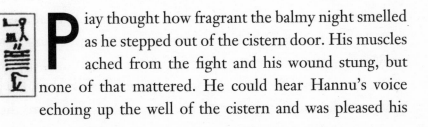 iay thought how fragrant the balmy night smelled as he stepped out of the cistern door. His muscles ached from the fight and his wound stung, but none of that mattered. He could hear Hannu's voice echoing up the well of the cistern and was pleased his

assistant's life had been saved and they had survived to fight another day. Despite their failure in Lacedaemon, there was still hope of a brighter tomorrow.

Ahead, a woman waited in the shadows of the bay trees. She was wrapped in a purple cloak edged with gold, a hood pulled over her head so her features were obscured. As she moved towards him, she slipped the hood off and he saw it was Serrena.

The king's daughter glanced around as if she was afraid of being seen, then whispered, 'Come with me.'

Serrena weaved a path across the city, avoiding the main thoroughfares. Whenever Piay tried to question her on their destination, she pressed a finger to her lips and urged him on.

Eventually the lamps of the River Gate glowed at the end of the broad street where goods were carted into the city. The gate hung open and the soldier guarding it turned away as they approached. Serrena must have prepared the way.

They continued beyond the walls, among the dank river smells and the smoke from the sailors' fires until they came to the largest barge moored there.

At the foot of the gangplank, she turned to him and smiled.

'I see something in you, Piay of Egypt, though I am not sure what. But I trust my heart in all things.' She nodded as she searched his face. 'There are many twists and turns in the road to destiny. Paths diverge and then they draw together. I feel we will see each other again one day, perhaps as allies in the great battles to come.'

Serrena swept a hand towards the gangplank. Piay smiled, baffled, but he acceded to her request and stepped on the creaking wood.

The benches of the oarsmen were deserted. Near the prow, Piay saw a lamp glimmering on the raised platform where the lookout watched the way ahead during voyages. In the light, a man peered up into the night sky, hands clasped behind his back. He was wearing the crimson cloak of the Spartan Guard, but no helmet covered the long grey hair that tumbled on to his shoulders.

Serrena must have wanted him to meet this man, whoever he was. Piay strode along the deck and climbed the steps to the platform.

Without turning to look at the new arrival, the man said, 'When I was a boy my father pointed out to me the Four Sons of Horus. They have been my guide ever since. However dark the world gets – however much strife and bloodshed – those four stars look down. Unchanging. Eternal. The troubles of men come and go, but the Four Sons of Horus will always be there to show us the way.' He indicated the milky constellation where four sparks glimmered. 'There. See?'

'The Four Sons of Horus,' Piay repeated. 'You are an Egyptian.'

The man turned. He had a long grey beard to match his hair and his crinkled face had been leathered by the elements. His eyes twinkled in the moonlight and Piay thought he saw a sly wit there.

'My home was Lahun, in the days before it fell during the Hyksos invasion. For many years now, I have called Lacedaemon my home. I am the admiral of King Hurotas' fleet. My name is Hui.'

'I know that name. You fought with the General Tanus against the barbarians and proved yourself in battle. Some say you taught Egyptians to ride the horse like the Hyksos. Taita speaks . . . of you.'

*Best not to say too much of what my master has said over the years,* Piay thought.

Hui chuckled. 'Taita and I had our differences, that's true. He thought me an unreliable boy, even after I killed the witch who threatened his Queen Lostris. I thought him an irritating curmudgeon, as much as I recognised his great wisdom and skill in many arts.'

'I will remember you to him when I return to Egypt.'

Hui's eyes widened. 'He still lives?'

'Taita looks as youthful as when I was a boy – some say as young as when the Hyksos first came.'

'A sorcerer, or blessed by the gods.' Hui shook his head in disbelief. 'Then I bow my head to him, for the years lie heavy on me. There are days when I am more ache than skin and bone.'

'Why am I here?' Piay asked.

Hui pointed to a stool and Piay sat. The admiral pulled up another stool and poured two cups of wine from a jug he had set against the rail.

'Serrena has told me about you and why you have journeyed to Lacedaemon. I would hear it from your own lips.'

Piay related the quest that Taita had sent him on and the response he had received from Hurotas. Hui sipped his wine and listened intently.

After Piay was done, Hui said, 'I have known Hurotas for a great many years. He is a good man. I would not have served him so faithfully if he were not. But as a good ruler of a good people, he has many demands placed upon him. He must put the needs of Lacedaemon first, whatever he feels about coming to the aid of the land of his birth.'

'That is the position that Mennias conveyed to me.'

'But Hurotas is a man of reason and he can be swayed by good arguments, over time. Particularly if he favours those making the arguments, like his beloved daughter, and the most courageous and highly commended admiral this land has ever seen.' Hui smiled. 'I am crafty. I have always been that way. And I have a silver tongue, even if I do say so myself. I will never forget my days in Egypt, nor my father whom I loved more than the world itself and who taught me the value of that place and its people. I vow to you now that I will do what I can to persuade the king to change his mind, and to send an army to help you crush the Hyksos. I cannot say I will succeed. But Hurotas will know that the Hyksos cannot be trusted, and whatever promises they make now will vanish like the light at sunset if they decide there is more value in taking Lacedaemon for their own. And a wise man will know it is better to defeat an enemy before they decide to be an enemy, rather than wait until the bodies pile up and the fields run red with blood.'

Piay raised his cup. 'You have my thanks.'

He didn't want to say that by the time Hui had been able to persuade Hurotas to change his mind, it might be too late.

'Now, tell me about this Sakir who was sent to sway the king,' Hui said. 'I have heard troubling things about him from Serrena.'

Between sips of wine, Piay told all he knew about the barbarian captain, from that first encounter in the fields beside the Nile to the confrontation in the cistern. As he spoke, Hui's face darkened.

'This is a bad business,' Hui said once Piay had finished.

'He is good with a sword, that's true,' Piay said. 'And fierce. And relentless. But he has not got the better of me yet. We are evenly matched.'

'You must not take him lightly.' Hui wagged a finger.

Piay was taken aback by the intensity he saw in the admiral's face.

'Those tales he told you about his abilities . . . they were not boasts. He may not have quite the skills he believes the gods have given him, but he is not like any other man. Not now.'

'How can you know?'

'He has consumed the blue lotus.' Hui splashed wine into both their cups. 'I have seen at first hand what terrible powers the dream flower can summon forth.'

Piay watched this seasoned warrior's hand tremble as he held his cup.

'It was long ago, before I truly knew how this world was and what monstrous things walk it. Before my father was murdered. Before I was betrayed by my own kin and condemned to a terrible fate.'

Piay thought how haunted Hui looked.

'My mother Isetnofret was a servant of Seth. My childhood friends whispered that she was a sorceress. How I laughed. The kind of things boys say when they're young and foolish and scared of their elders. But one night I spied her conducting a secret ritual at the pyramid in Lahun. I saw her consume the blue lotus as she made her vows to Seth and called the god into her life. I saw her sacrifice a river crocodile. And I saw her . . .'

Hui fell silent for a long moment.

When Hui glanced back, he looked hollowed out. 'Later I felt the full force of how the dream flower had the ability to transform. It is a conduit to the god themselves. My mother was a sorceress, yes. A sorceress with a power I had never imagined. She summoned my dead friend Kyky from the grave to torment me. She called Seth from his cold, dark home to witness my end. I saw him!' Hui's voice trailed away.

After a moment, Piay said, 'Yet she was not victorious.'

'No. She was not victorious. I killed her. My own mother. I killed her and left her in a pit of serpents. And in so doing I saved myself, and Queen Lostris, and Egypt itself.'

Piay nodded. 'Perhaps it is what lies in the heart that truly counts.'

'Perhaps. But I say one more time, do not think of this Sakir as a man.' Hui shook his cup at Piay. 'The blue lotus will have made him something more than a man. The god of the Hyksos stands behind him now. You face Seth, too, and all the terrible powers at his command. Beware, Piay.'

Piay nodded, remembering all that Sakir had said in the cistern. Could this be true? Was he now a part of some great struggle between the gods themselves?

Piay wound through the streets to the house. His thoughts had cooled after his conversation with Hui. What was the way forward? The shadows encroached on every side and he could no longer see the path. Was this the great Piay conquering all that lay before him that he had imagined since he was a child? The struggle was harder than he had ever presumed.

Laughter came from the golden haze in the house. What humour could there be in their desperate situation?

Piay stepped through the door and found Myssa laughing as she tended to Hannu's wounds. Hannu chuckled at some joke they had just shared. They looked up when he entered, sheepish like guilty children.

'We thought you had already left the city,' Myssa teased.

'I was doing the work we have been sent here to do,' Piay replied.

Hannu levered himself from the stool, wincing.

'I was bad-tempered when we spoke in the cistern. That was wrong of me. You have my thanks for risking your neck to try to rescue me.'

Piay nodded. 'No thanks are necessary. I only did what was right. And what you would have done for me.'

Myssa laughed. The two men stared at her.

'What is so amusing?' Piay demanded.

'The games the two of you play with each other!' Myssa replied.

Hannu scowled. 'Games?'

'You are friends! You bicker like husband and wife. You have great respect for each other, perhaps even love. Yet you act as if there is no love lost between you.'

Myssa laughed again when she saw the annoyed expressions on the two men's faces.

'Enough of this nonsense. We have plans to make.' Piay turned away to pour himself a cup of wine.

'It's true, then,' Hannu said. 'The king has denied our request for Lacedaemon to become our ally.'

Piay sipped on his wine. His thoughts were already racing ahead.

'There is no hope of changing his mind. I am as sure of that as any man can be. But we must not – cannot – give up.'

'Where do we go next?' Hannu poured himself some wine. 'Who else would send their army to fight alongside people they don't know and don't care about?'

Piay slumped on a large cushion in one corner. 'We must find an answer to that question, and fast, or all will be lost.'

Myssa slipped out and returned with some of the strips of cured and spiced meat that the Spartans liked so much. She handed one each to Piay and Hannu, and they chewed on them, despondent. She sat on another cushion and looked from one face to the other.

'You should be celebrating that you have survived a day of great challenges,' she said, 'not looking so glum.'

'It's hard to be filled with cheer when we are staring into the face of failure,' Piay said.

'Be brave,' Myssa chided. 'Not like that horse you rode today, which is frightened of the smallest thing and the largest.'

Hannu turned up his nose. 'We are not afraid—'

'Wait.' Piay felt something tug in his mind. 'What do you mean about the horse being frightened?'

'It was afraid of the hornet. That was why it threw you. The smallest thing that can do it little harm.'

Piay frowned. 'What are you trying to say?'

'I am talking about the largest. The elephant. Elephants terrify horses. Everyone knows that.'

Piay gaped. Myssa looked from him to Hannu, baffled.

'You did not know this?'

'No!'

Piay glanced at Hannu. The light of revelation was burning in his assistant's eyes, too. Hannu raised his face to the heavens.

'The answer to the Oracle's riddle.'

Myssa frowned. 'Are you playing games with me now? Explain what you mean.'

Piay clapped his hands together. 'The success of the Hyksos comes down to their mastery of the horse. They pull the chariots that have helped devastate our army. Any attack is conducted at the speed of the wind.'

'But if the horses are frightened, they are of no use,' Hannu said. 'They will not ride into battle. They will try to flee and take those barbarians with them.'

'"Tame the beast that is both serpent and bull",' Myssa mused.

'We need elephants,' Hannu said. 'And lots of them.'

Piay raised his cup high in a toast to Khonsu.

'Now how do we go about getting them?'

On the bright horizon, the crimson sail carved like a shark's fin through the azure waves towards the harbour. Piay watched its slow progress from the shade of one of the stores along the front. He'd waited for this moment for five days. He was ready.

Around him, Gythion throbbed with the daily life of a busy port. Carts trundled and slaves heaved bales, sweating in the afternoon sun. The aroma of baking bread battled in his nose with the sharp smell of that fish sauce that the Lacedaemonians favoured.

No one would have thought him an Egyptian traveller. His kilt was hidden beneath a tunic which he had smeared with the dust of the road so he wouldn't attract the attention of the merchants and beggars waiting for rich clients. A muddy-brown chlamys hanging from his shoulders kept his sword hidden. He'd pulled the floppy brim of his felt petasus low to throw shade across his features. To stray eyes, he was a Lacedaemonian, not worthy of attention.

Hannu leaned against the wall beside him and stared out to sea. He was dressed in the same manner, though he complained about being too hot in his cloak and tunic.

'Is that it?' Hannu breathed so low that no one passing could have heard.

'The sail is the right colour and this is the right day. Let us hope. I'm sick of waiting here.'

Piay felt his impatience as acutely as he had done during that period of his long-delayed audience with Hurotas. He was not a man who could rest on his heels when there was work to be done.

'No sign of those bastard Hyksos.' Hannu's eyes flitted along the moored ships creaking on the swell and the flow of men pounding up and down the gangplanks.

'Nothing from the west road?'

'Spoke to a beggar there. He'd not seen anyone riding into Gythion matching the description of those barbarians. Gave him some bread in reward and he cried.'

Hannu fell silent and Piay knew he must have been thinking about his own time as a beggar. Piay couldn't imagine that life – the hardship, the hunger. He'd never wanted for anything during his time under Taita's tutelage. If he was truthful, he'd never really thought of such suffering, nor how it could have affected Hannu.

'Good work,' Piay said.

Hannu eyed him at the unexpected praise. 'I won't rest until we're away from here.' Since their arrival, Hannu had roamed Gythion six times a day, once during the night, making sure Sakir and his band of murderous barbarians were not on their trail. 'Don't believe we've seen the last of them.'

'On that, I will never argue with you again. They defeated us in Sparta, with words and arguments, and for now I think they will be feeling pleased with themselves. That might give us some breathing space.'

The crimson sail cleaved through the water, drawing closer. Piay could see the ship beneath it – a strong, broad vessel, deep in the water with the contents of its hold.

Further along the front, Myssa moved effortlessly among the people of Gythion, flashing smiles and winning over passers-by with her cheerful conversation.

Hannu followed Piay's gaze.

'She puts on a brave face.'

'She is a brave woman.' Piay felt Hannu scrutinise him, but he didn't look round. 'She has a way about her that encourages people to tell her what she wants to know, and what we need to know. So it seems we are in her hands now. How strange this road the gods choose for us.'

'Aye. The slave has become the mistress, the world turned on its head.' Hannu shrugged. 'You will do well to hold on to her in the days to come.'

'If she chooses to flee, I won't hunt her down.'

Myssa drew his gaze, as she always seemed to do these days. Her elegance, her strength, the confident way she carried herself, the gleam of intelligence in her eyes.

When she came over, she threw off the mask she had been wearing for the strangers and showed a serious face.

'I have asked everyone without any luck. All rides on the plan you have dreamed up. There are no other choices.'

Piay nodded and turned his attention back to that crimson sail, but he had heard the note of disgust in Myssa's voice.

'Then let us pray that Khonsu smiles upon us. We have one chance. We cannot fail.'

The ship furled that blood-red sail and the oarsmen heaved it towards its berth. Once it had bumped against the dock, sailors leaped to the stone quay and tied it up. The gangplank clattered into place and the man Piay had been waiting for walked down. His dark eyes searched the crowd with a raptor's hunger.

Hanbaal looked confident and commanding. His pristine white robes shone and his moustache and pointed beard gleamed with fresh oil. His left hand twitched and the whip of long hide strips, knotted at the end, jumped. The Phoenician slaver was looking forward to another day's business.

When he stepped on to the quay, his men rushed down the gangplank and fanned out around him. Three sailors carried the poles and cloth with which they would construct the slaver's shelter. Others began to drag the sullen-faced captives out of the hold and, blinking, into the light, shoving them down the plank on to the dockside.

Hanbaal rested his hand on the hilt of his sword and looked around. Piay felt Myssa stiffen beside him. When he'd conjured up this plan, he hadn't considered how she might feel about it. Hanbaal had stolen her from her home, her family and everything she knew, stolen her freedom and made her a slave. And she had been transported for long days and nights in the suffocating heat and filthy reek of that hold, crushed in with all the other captives, surviving on whatever scraps the slaver chose to give her.

'I am sorry to put you through this,' Piay said to her.

Myssa jutted out her chin. Whatever she was feeling, she was not about to bare it. Piay felt only admiration for the courage she showed.

'There is nothing else to be done,' Myssa replied. 'This is the only way to follow the Oracle's guidance, so what point is there in complaining?'

Piay watched Hanbaal's eyes narrow when he saw them approaching. The slaver stood his ground, but he showed only a cold face.

'This slave is your property now,' he said once they stood in front of him. 'I warned you that her fire might prove too much. I cannot take her back.'

'I am not seeking to return her,' Piay said. 'She is all that I hoped for and more. I am pleased with our trade, Hanbaal.'

The slaver grinned, his shoulders relaxing. 'Ah, a satisfied customer. That is good. Then you have returned for more of the quality that only Hanbaal of Phoenicia can offer. We have many good slaves here today—'

Piay raised his hand to silence the slaver before he spun out his pitch.

'I require no more slaves, but I am here to offer you an arrangement which will make you very wealthy.'

Hanbaal's grin widened.

The evening was balmy and a cooling breeze drifted down from the woods of the Peloponnese. Piay felt lulled by the music of the quayside, the gentle lapping of the waves, the groaning of the ships and the creak of the taut mooring ropes. Sitting under Hanbaal's shelter, he watched the Keeper of the Flame light the torches along the front. A line of small fires reached into the dark. Sailors hunched around them, tearing off strips of cured meat and draining hides of beer, their grinning faces lit amber by the flames.

Hanbaal strode over from the direction of his ship. His auction had been another success. Every one of his slaves had been sold. Hanbaal had taken his rewards back to his vessel and stowed them away where his men could guard them.

'Business is good,' Piay said when the other man reached him.

'Business is always good in Lacedaemon. They need their slaves here more than most.'

The slaver was carrying a clay amphora and two cups. He settled into his wooden throne and poured the contents of the jar into the cups, handing one to Piay.

'And more business to come,' Hanbaal continued, 'if the gods smile on us and we find common cause.' He raised his cup. 'Let us drink to profitable friendship.'

Piay raised his cup in turn, then sipped the contents. The fiery liquid burned his throat. But once the drink had settled, a pleasing warmth rose up. The liquid had a comforting honey base, but there were red flakes of some kind of spice in it that gave it the heat.

Hanbaal nodded, pleased, when he saw Piay was happy to continue drinking.

'We are of the same mind. That is a good beginning. Now tell me what business is on your mind.'

'I want to hire your services.'

'My services?'

'Your ship.'

Piay felt the weight of the moment. Everything depended upon him convincing this man.

Hanbaal glanced towards his vessel, the mast silhouetted against the stars.

'I am a slaver. I seek out good slaves and sell them to the highest bidder. That is my business.'

'And you will have ample opportunity to conduct that business when you have agreed to what I propose.' Piay took another sip of the fiery liquid and leaned forwards, drawing Hanbaal into his confidence. 'I have more gold than you could ever see in your dreams, and it will be waiting for you at the end of the voyage we will take together.'

'I like what I hear. So far. Speak on.'

'I would like to hire you, your crew and your ship to transport me across the Great Green and then . . . beyond.'

'Beyond?'

'Southwards. Along the coast of Kush until we reach my destination.' *The land of the elephants.* 'You will be travelling there anyway in search of more slaves, is that not right?'

Hanbaal nodded. His stare never wavered. The thought of that mountain of gold had gripped him.

'So I will be paying you to do what you would have been doing anyway. I am not a man of business like you, but that seems like an offer that is impossible to turn down.'

'Perhaps.'

'Are you not interested?'

'I am a man of business, as you say, and in my long experience when a bargain seems too good to be true, it usually is. Where is the dark surprise? The little matter that you are not telling me that will one day be a big matter.'

'No surprise.'

*Apart from a bloodthirsty band of barbarians upon our trail.*

Hanbaal weighed this. He did not look convinced.

Piay smiled to try to soothe his doubts. He had always known that the slaver would be too seasoned in the matter of bargaining to be easily swayed by such a seemingly simple offer.

'The gold will be waiting for you in Thebes upon our return, and it will come from the coffers of the Pharaoh himself.'

'You speak for the Pharaoh?'

'I do. I was sent to Lacedaemon by his chief advisor, Taita.'

'I feel I have heard that name upon my travels. The eunuch?'

Piay nodded. 'My quest is of the utmost importance and the Pharaoh will pay any price to see it concluded in a successful manner. You will be amply rewarded for your efforts.'

'How do I know you speak for the Pharaoh?'

'I have been given the seal of approval of King Hurotas himself. We have already entered into negotiations.'

'And why do you wish to travel to the lands beyond Kush?'

'That is my business. For now.'

'This sounds like there will be danger ahead.'

'The more danger, the greater reward, you have my word on that. You do not seem to me like a whipped cur who will flee at the first sign of trouble. I would wager you have faced more than your share of danger on your voyages. There is nothing we might encounter that is beyond your vaunted skills.'

Hanbaal grinned at the flattery. 'The more I hear of this, the more I like it. Then tell me – what price do you offer for this great and dangerous work?'

'Your own weight in gold.'

The slaver's eyes widened. 'I have your word on that?'

'You do.'

Hanbaal thought for a moment and then raised his cup one final time.

'To business then, and a profitable arrangement. To calm seas and fair winds and full sails. Tomorrow we sail for Kush.'

The red sun burned on the eastern horizon. A ruddy road unfolded across the white-tipped waves of the Great Green and the ship slipped out of the harbour. Piay breathed in the rich scent of vegetation from the Peloponnesian woods as he watched Gythion fall away. His shoulders loosened. Even to the last, he'd expected to see the ghostly figure of Sakir emerge as the night's shadows ebbed.

The sailors boomed their rhythmic song as they heaved on the oars and then Hanbaal uttered his command. The crimson sail unfurled with a billowing as the wind filled it. The ship sped forwards, skimming across the swell, eastwards first, and then they would turn south, towards Egypt, towards Kush and – if the gods were kind – towards victory.

'I have never seen an elephant,' Hannu said as he stood at the rail beside Piay.

'Few have.'

'If they are as terrifying a beast as a horse, we will have difficulty taming them.'

'One day at a time,' Piay said. 'We have seen obstacles aplenty set before us and we have overcome them all.'

Piay glanced at Myssa, who was standing a little way away, looking across the heads of the crew. She was bundled in her thick woollen cloak against the ocean winds, upright and dignified, her gaze unflinching. He thought she looked like a queen surveying her subjects. Yet, for once, she was showing a cold face. He couldn't understand why. Even in the most difficult times she had always been bright, that joy for life shining from her like a lamp at twilight.

Piay saw she was watching a tall, muscular man move among the benches, exhorting members of the crew to various tasks. Piay had noticed him the moment he'd stepped on board. The man had a milky cast over his left eye and had lost part of his right ear and three teeth. He seemed to be Hanbaal's second in command. The slaver had settled on sumptuous cushions under a shelter of pristine cloth that matched his robes, and every now and again the white-eyed man would stride over to listen to the captain's demands before barking orders at the crew. If Piay remembered correctly, Hanbaal had called him Ragan.

He glanced back at Myssa's face and felt unsettled by the intensity he saw. Something unpleasant lay between them.

Piay strode over to her. As he neared, Myssa glanced at him and for the briefest instant the mask of her face slipped. He all but recoiled at what he saw there. Not fear at the memory of what she had endured on that vessel, nor despair that she was once again trapped within its confines, but a murderous rage that seethed as hot as a goldsmith's furnace. That intensity of emotion had been unglimpsed before, and Piay wondered how much else Myssa had been keeping from him. Perhaps deception was another of her skills.

'You do not need to fear these slavers,' Piay began. 'I will protect you.'

Myssa's eyes flashed. 'You will protect me? You think I need your protection, after all I have survived since I was taken from my home?'

Nor had he heard that flinty tone in her voice before. This was not some cowed slave or humble farmer's daughter. There was the crack of confidence there, perhaps haughtiness, the demeanour of someone aware of her own potency.

'I meant no disrespect. I only wish you to feel at ease while we take this voyage.'

'At ease? How can any slave be at ease?'

Piay puffed out his chest. 'In Egypt, we pride ourselves on treating our slaves well. We are a civilised people—'

Piay flinched at the look of withering contempt. This wound was raw and it had revealed another side of Myssa. He did not like to see this aspect of her.

'Not so long ago I was a free woman, with a family,' Myssa continued. 'I was valued by those who knew me, for who I was, not for the work I could do for a master. I had choices, and hopes, and dreams. Without those things, there is no ease. There is no peace.' She narrowed her eyes at him. 'Think how you would be if you had everything stolen from you and you were forced to bow your head to another.'

'I am an Egypt—'

'Yes, you are an Egyptian. One of the favoured people. You do not have to trouble yourself with such thoughts.' Myssa turned away and walked aft, but her words rolled back as hard as the stones of Thebes. 'If it was within my power, I would send this ship to the bottom and everyone who sails upon it.'

The firepot swung in the dark, tracing a red streak through the night. Piay watched it as he lay under his cloak and remembered their last voyage across the Great Green. That final moment of plunging into cliff-high waves still haunted him, but Khonsu had protected him that day and he prayed that the god would do so again. But he dreamed of feeling dry land under his feet and he was not too proud to admit it.

Hanbaal had offered them the chance to sleep in the hold away from the elements, as it was now empty of his precious cargo, but Myssa had recoiled at the suggestion. They had found a spot on the deck astern, next to the platform where the helmsman guided the steering oar. In truth, Piay, too, was happy not to take Hanbaal up on his suggestion. The hold was suffocatingly hot during the day and reeked of excrement and urine from its previous occupants. At night, sleep would never come easily down there, for the dark space was filled with the endless groans of the hull flexing against the swell. Now and then the balers would clamber down to drain out the seawater that leaked through gaps in the timbers. And then there were the rats.

*Oh, to be on dry land.*

Hannu snored. Nothing seemed to trouble his assistant. Myssa sat beside him. He could see her regal head silhouetted against the stars. Since she had glowed with the heat of her fury that day, she had barely said a word, and they had been at sea for three days. Her responses to his questions had been short, almost curt.

Perhaps she was dreaming of returning to her homeland. Perhaps she was plotting to escape the moment they reached Kush.

At noon on the fourth day, the lookout cried out and pointed across the sapphire waves. Hanbaal jumped from his cushions and strode to the rail. He peered out and then spun round, his face dark.

Piay stared into the distance where the lookout had indicated, but could see nothing. Hanbaal was striding among his men, barking orders. The sailors leaped from their tasks, snatching swords and billhooks and bronze axes from beneath their benches.

Piay caught Hanbaal's arm. 'What is wrong?'

The slaver's black eyes glittered and his lips pulled back from his teeth.

'A ship, coming this way.'

Piay's first thought was *Sakir*. Would his enemy hunt him down even here in the middle of the vast ocean?

'Most likely pirates,' Hanbaal continued. 'This part of the Great Green is rife with them. They attack the trade routes like wolves in the mountains, knowing they can plunder goods they can sell in the markets to the east, or the profits that have been made after trade has been completed.'

'Then you are fearful they will steal the gold in your hold?'

'I am fearful they will steal my life.'

Hanbaal yelled to the helmsman in his rolling Phoenician tongue and Piay felt the ship begin to turn.

'You plan to run?' he asked.

'Run or fight – neither choice is a good one. The pirates have smaller ships, faster. Staying close to land, they don't need a ship made to brave the harsh conditions in the middle of the ocean. And though my men will fight to the last, they are not the bloodthirsty rogues that these pirates are. Those cut-throats would gut their own mothers for a profit.' A thought seemed to strike him and he looked along the deck to where Myssa waited with Hannu. 'If they board us, slit the throat of your slave and throw her overboard. It will not matter to them if she is alive or dead.'

Piay felt sickened by what was hidden in the slaver's words, but he was surprised to hear compassion in the voice of this man who traded in human lives.

Piay pulled back his cloak to reveal his sword.

'I will fight beside you if it comes to that, as will Hannu. We both have some skill in battle.'

Hanbaal nodded. 'Good. I accept your offer.'

He whirled away, shouting more orders. Piay could see how drawn the faces of the sailors had become. Fear burned there.

Piay danced across the benches and jumped beside Hannu and Myssa. He pointed across the waves to a white sail cresting.

'Pirates,' he said. 'Hanbaal is trying to run, but they will likely catch us. Then we'll have to fight.'

Hannu nodded.

Piay turned to Myssa. 'I vow to do everything in my power to protect you.'

Myssa grimaced. 'I do not need you to protect me. Give me a weapon. I will fight.'

'You have fire in you,' Hannu began. 'But someone unused to battle can be as much of a danger to those standing alongside them as the enemy.'

'I have not fought with a sword, but I am well-versed with a spear, and a knife. Find me a weapon.'

Piay began to protest, but Hannu said, 'She knows her own mind. Let her have her own way. I'd wager that when the moment comes you will have little say in it anyway.'

'Very well,' Piay said, 'but I only ask that you stay back from the fighting and join the fray if we are desperate.'

'I will do what I see fit,' Myssa replied.

Piay managed to find Myssa a short-bladed knife. It would at least be some defence if the worst came. But he'd decided he would rather die than see her harmed in the way that Hanbaal had suggested.

The white sail drew closer. Hanbaal had been right. The other vessel was smaller and faster. It was only a matter of time.

Squinting into the glare, Piay saw the ship was low and narrow, the deck swarming with men. White water gushed past its prow. His mind flew back to those times he had watched the Hyksos chariots speed like the wind across the plains.

Gradually the faces of the pirates emerged from the haze. Mouths stretched wide, they roared their hunger for their prey. Their heads were shaven and their skin appeared to have the tawny tone of travellers he had seen from the Levant. Barbs of light glinted from swords stabbing the air.

When it became clear they would not be able to outrun the pirates, Hanbaal leaped on to a bench and grabbed one of the lines from the sail to steady himself. He thrust his crescent sword into the air and roared, 'Ready yourself, my men! We will fight as we have never fought before. These dogs cannot defeat us. They are a rabble, undisciplined and weak because of it. Not like you. Wait until they prepare to board, then turn the seas red!'

Piay looked at the rapt sailors. He had no idea if they had fought off attacks by pirates before, but these were not fighting men. But they were hardened by the brutal life at sea and the many raids they had conducted on the poorly armed communities where they rounded up the captives who would fill their hold. He could see fear in their eyes – they all knew the threat these Wolves of the Sea posed – but their defiance had hardened through their loyalty to Hanbaal.

The sailors thrust their own weapons in the air and bellowed their support for their captain. Then each man pulled up a circular shield from the rows strung across the side of the rail. The wood of each one was blistered by the sun, the central bronze plates discoloured, but they would serve. Piay grabbed two shields and handed one to Hannu. They strapped them to their left arms.

Hannu stripped off his tunic. The matted fur across his body was slick with sweat, but he could fight more easily unencumbered by clothes. Piay stripped down to his kilt and together the two of them squeezed into position along the rail.

The white-sailed ship rolled in like a storm and soon the roaring of the pirates boomed like thunder above the pounding of the waves. In contrast to that show of furious intent, Hanbaal's men stood in silence along the rails. Faces were graven, knuckles whitened against the weapons they clutched.

Hannu leaned over the rails, scowling as he surveyed the rabid enemy.

'After all the battles I've fought and the hardship I've endured, I'm not about to die at sea and have the afterlife denied me,' he growled. 'But how you're expected to fight with a sword across a gulf of water is beyond me.'

'We'll find out soon enough,' Piay said. 'But it's kill or be killed. That is the same on land or at sea.'

The pirate vessel swept in until it was skimming parallel with the slaver vessel. The water between churned white in the competing currents. On the ship opposite, the pirates balanced on the rail, brandishing their weapons. Three lines of them crowded on the deck.

The ships edged closer together.

Naked torsos rippled with tattoos, and the one who was clearly the captain of the pirates smirked on the platform astern. He swung his sword up and barked an order. The raucous show of strength designed to cow their enemies ceased. As one, the pirates dropped from the rail and crouched. For an instant there was only the rumble of the waves and the whine of the wind.

The line at the rear pulled themselves up tall and whirled slings around their heads.

Hanbaal thundered a command, just in time. His men swung their shields up in unison. Projectiles hurtled across the gulf – chunks of sharp-edged flint by the looks of it.

The stones thundered into the weather-beaten shields. Wood splintered. Piay lurched back on to his heels from the force of the impact.

One sailor floundered in raising his shield. The flint cracked against his skull, which spouted a glistening shower of blood. The man flew back, dead before he hit the deck.

Piay barely steadied himself before the next volley crashed down. Another man fell. One shield cracked in two. The sailor holding it dropped to his knees and crawled behind his comrades for shelter.

The attack was designed to soften them up, ready for the main assault.

'Stand firm!' Piay shouted. 'They will run out of stones soon enough.'

Hanbaal picked up his cry. The words seemed to work, for Piay sensed the trembling man next to him stiffen and draw his shoulders up.

After another wave of projectiles crashed, and then another, Piay peered over the rim of his shield and glimpsed the pirates at the rear hurl their slings away. The Wolves at the front bounded back on to the rail, bronze billhooks gripped in their left hands.

The pirate ship swept so close Piay feared they would crash and both vessels would plunge into the deep. But when he could almost smell the spicy sweat of their enemies, the pirate captain thundered a command and his men threw themselves across the void.

Piay was gripped by the terrible sight of those bloodthirsty cut-throats flying towards him, faces twisted in fury, mouths roaring their hatred. Along the slave ship, the billhooks bit into the wood of the rail, giving the boarders purchase so they could pull themselves over the side.

Instinctively, Piay hacked his sword down. The blade bit deep into the shoulder of a pirate hurtling towards him. The man screamed, flailing in mid-air. Before he could catch on to the ship, Piay wrenched his weapon free and the pirate plunged down into the chasm. The white water boiled pink.

On the edge of his vision, Piay caught sight of the chaos erupting along the side of the ship. Billhooks splintered into the rail, into shields, into forearms, shoulders and hands. In the deafening din of screams and battle cries, the pirates scrabbled to haul themselves up and over the side. If their vessel was boarded, it would all be over. These pirates were too fierce, more brutal than the men who stood against them.

'Shoulders against shields!' Piay shouted. 'Drive them back!'

Piay showed what he meant, slamming his shield into the face of a pirate clambering across in front of him. The bone-jarring impact stunned his enemy and down he went. The men around him followed his tactic and he sensed it run along the line.

'Keep standing your ground!' he boomed. 'We have the advantage!'

Yet it was not enough. The shields were poor quality and fell apart under a strong blow from a sword. Some of the slavers were so consumed with fear, they froze, gaping as the pirates tore into them. Others hurled themselves to hide under the benches. Piay could only imagine that fortune had been with them if they had encountered any pirates before.

Piay thrust his sword into the chest of another pirate pulling himself up on to the rail, and another who filled the gap an instant later. The waves of attackers seemed never-ending.

It was only a matter of time.

An axe smashed into his shield and he stumbled back under the impact. And then his attacker was over the rail and raining blows on him, driving him further back on to the benches. Shards of wood flew away from his shield until it crumbled into jagged slivers.

Piay tossed it aside and leaped on to a bench to gain the advantage of height. His opponent hurled himself on, hacking wildly. The bronze axe blurred.

Raising his sword high to draw his enemy into a strike, Piay leaned back as he slid into the space between the benches. He whipped his blade across the forearm of the pirate. The axe flew away from the wounded man's grip. As it clattered across the deck, Piay lunged. His sword ripped into his enemy's guts. Throwing himself up, he leaned his full weight into the hilt and drove the weapon deep.

Once he was sure the pirate was dead, Piay tore his sword free and darted to where Hannu clashed blades with a pirate almost twice his size. Piay rammed his blade under the attacker's ribcage, then let him fall on to the bodies that littered the deck around Hannu's feet.

Finally it seemed like the waves of pirates leaping from the other ship had ended. Spaces had opened up along the line. But fighting had erupted across the slave ship.

Piay whirled from fight to fight, giving support wherever he could, and he glimpsed Hannu doing the same.

In the melee, he lost all perspective. There was only hacking and thrusting and blood and death.

But then a keening cry rang out, loud enough to cut through the clamour of battle. Piay caught sight of two figures wrapped together on the stern platform of the pirate ship. He blinked, not quite sure what he was seeing.

The pirate captain stood rigid, his head pushed back and his throat bared. Behind him, one arm pressed tight against the captain's chest, the other hand holding a knife to his neck, was Myssa.

Piay felt a rush of terror that she had put herself in such danger. He could only imagine that in the confusion, she had thrown herself across the gap between the two ships and somehow caught the captain off guard.

Myssa ululated another high-pitched cry. This time more eyes were drawn to the source of the sound. The fury of the battle ebbed. Enemies stepped apart. Weapons drifted down.

The slavers were mesmerised by what they were seeing. But the pirates were gripped by the sight of their leader in peril. They knew any sudden movement on their part could cost him his life.

Piay watched Myssa's face, trying to read her intentions. Surely she'd call to the pirates to lay down their weapons in exchange for their captain's life. Time seemed to hang as her gaze moved across the pirates and the slavers staring at her.

With a swift flick, Myssa raked the blade across the pirate leader's throat. His men cried out in shock as the blood sprayed and their captain slumped to the boards.

The bloody blade floated to her side and she looked at the gathered men with disdain. She'd done what needed to be done. There could have been no benefit in keeping the pirate captain alive. His men might have retreated, but they would come back again until they had what they wanted. Myssa understood.

Hanbaal leaped on to the rail and commanded his men to seize the moment. The pirates were leaderless, their ship and their purpose lost. Any further fighting would be futile. Now they only had to pray for mercy.

One by one, their weapons clattered to the deck. Jeering, the slavers jabbed them with the tips of their swords to round them up. While a group kept watch on the captives, Hanbaal ordered others to leap across to the pirate vessel and search it for anything worth plundering.

Piay raced to the rail and held out his arms for Myssa to leap back. He held her tight.

'What were you thinking?' he breathed.

'I was thinking of victory.' Her eyes flashed. 'What were you thinking?'

Exhausted, Piay and Hannu slumped down by the helms-man's platform. Myssa crouched beside them, wiping her hands on the deck to clean the blood off.

Hannu eyed her. 'You wielded that knife with the skill of a seasoned member of the Blue Crocodile Guards. I'd wager there are things you are not telling us.'

Myssa stared at the streaks of blood on the planks, refusing to meet anyone's eye.

Piay glanced at Hannu. He knew his assistant's moods, and at that moment Hannu was like a dog with a bone.

'You can navigate by the stars and uncover tracks through lands you have never seen before. You know how to set traps, you know how to hunt. You are wise in the ways of the fruits of the land and the behaviour of beasts and birds. Who are you?'

'Who am I?' This time Myssa did look up and her eyes flashed. 'I am the hope of my village, the hope of all my people, and now that hope has been cruelly snatched away.'

Seeing Myssa's simmering emotion, Piay tapped Hannu's arm to urge him to stop pressing her. But Hannu wouldn't relent.

'Speak,' he said.

Myssa's voice was as cold as the dark depths of the Great Green.

'In my home, the king is advised by the one among all his people with the sharpest wits. They are chosen when they are a child, and from then on, they are taught all the knowledge of my people – of the stars and the land and the beasts. The knowledge of the mines and the farms. Other tongues. All the wisdom that the elders have amassed across their long lives. They are taught how to fight, to defend the king if needs must. Once chosen, they will guide the king, and through him the people. The prosperity and safety of the village depends upon them.'

'And you were chosen,' Piay said.

'And when I was stolen, I did not only lose my home and my people did not only lose a dutiful daughter. They lost everything. All their days yet to come . . .'

Myssa's voice trailed away and she turned her gaze back to the streaks of blood.

Piay felt his heart swell at her pain. He had never thought in any depth about her plight, and why would he? She was a slave. But now this matter would weigh heavily on him, he knew.

Piay glanced along the deck. Hanbaal strode around the ship, examining the wounded members of his crew to see which ones were capable of working. The pirates had cost him several men, but there were more than enough to get the ship to shore.

Hanbaal surveyed the huddled mass of surviving pirates. They were broken men, Piay could see. Their heads hung down, the fire in their bellies extinguished. They knew what their fate would be.

Hanbaal was not a man inclined to forget any sins against him. He ordered the pirate ship to be scuttled. Once it had been sent to the deep, he stood over his captives and told them they had a choice: die on the end of a sword, or leap into the ocean and drown. Most of the men knew what would be the easier death, and they shuffled to the rail and hurled themselves over the side. A few who were overcome with terror tried to struggle. They were cut down and tossed in after their crew-mates.

When he'd finished the grim work, Hanbaal ordered his men to take the ship back on course and then he strode over to where Piay, Hannu and Myssa waited.

'I told you she had too much fire for a slave,' he said, nodding towards Myssa. 'And this once I am pleased that I was right.' Hanbaal turned to Myssa and bowed. 'You have my gratitude, and that of all my crew. You showed courage this day, more courage than those black-hearted curs who attacked us.'

Myssa nodded, but she showed no warmth.

Hanbaal turned to Piay and Hannu. 'And you fought with courage, too. That has not gone unnoticed by my men, or by me.' He rubbed his hands together, grinning. 'We are friends now, and someone who has friends is rich indeed. Hanbaal the Phoenician is in your debt, and I am a man who can always be counted on to pay back what is owed.' He bowed, then added, 'For now, be prepared for the wonders that are to come upon our voyage – not the least of which is a ship that sails upon the land.'

Piay felt relief when he saw the ochre strip of shore emerging from the haze. The waters of the Nile were a joy to him, but if he could avoid sailing across the Great Green again, he would die a happy man.

At least for the rest of their voyage, they could sail within sight of dry land.

That vision seemed to cast its spell over everyone on board. Hanbaal strode the deck, beaming and clapping his hands as he urged his men on. Two more had died from their wounds since the pirate attack and several needed attention from a physician. Loyal to the last, Hanbaal had vowed to pay for their treatment, though whether it was a show to inspire undying loyalty in return, Piay was not sure. But the slaver would also need to find more sailors to replace those who had been lost.

The men settled on their benches and grasped their oars, their full-throated singing soaring high as they dipped the blades to draw the ship through the shallows. Piay heard joy, a musical prayer of thanks that they had been transported safely across the gulf.

Piay glimpsed a figure hunched over Myssa where she sat near the helmsman's platform. It was Ragan, Hanbaal's second in command. His mouth was close to her ear, whispering. Whatever he was saying, Myssa was not pleased.

Piay strode over. 'Is there something amiss?' he called.

Ragan stood up, grinning. His milky eye glistened in the sun.

'No troubles here. We are old friends, Myssa and me.' He walked away, whistling.

Piay crouched beside Myssa. 'Is there anything wrong?' he murmured. 'If Ragan is—'

'Nothing wrong.' There was a crack to her voice that hinted at the opposite.

Piay watched Ragan lean into conversation with Hanbaal. If Myssa didn't want to discuss this further, he wouldn't press the matter, but he would keep an eye on Ragan from now on.

The cooling sea breeze fell away as the ship steered along one of the narrow river channels and into the steaming heat of the delta. Piay breathed in the choking reek of rot from the vast papyrus swamps that reached out as far as the eye could see. Turtles sunned themselves on the islands that dotted the dank black pools, and the croaking of frogs was the only sound that broke the sweltering silence.

Piay sat beside Hannu and Myssa. Hannu was whittling a shard of wood from one of the shattered shields with the small knife he kept tucked in his kilt. He balanced the blade on his palm and glanced at Myssa.

'Have you killed before?' he asked.

Myssa's eyes flickered down. 'I have thought about it, many a time. But, no.'

'Then you should prepare yourself, for this is a burden that will take a while to slip from your shoulders.'

'I can see how that could be.' Myssa thought back to that moment when she had slit the pirate captain's throat.

'When boys join the army,' Hannu continued, 'they are brimful of the vigour of youth and can't wait for the first time they cut down an enemy in battle. Their captains warn them that there will be a cost. They never listen. Because, like in so many things, the learning comes in the experiencing. No one can imagine what anything will be truly like. In killing, there is a cost. Always. Even after your sword has tasted blood many a time. Taking a life should never be done lightly, even if that life belongs to the bitterest enemy, for it scars the soul.'

Piay heard the truth burning in Hannu's words and knew he was speaking from his own experience. And he was right. How many times had he tried to make light of the lives he had ended? Yet in the dark of the night they always haunted him.

'These are desperate times,' Myssa said. 'I did what I had to do.'

Piay understood. They were desperate times for all of them. Who would he have been if Egypt had not been convulsed with war for all his life? A scribe? A poet? A farmer? But those were the dreams of children and there was little point in dwelling on them.

Piay looked up to see Hanbaal hurrying along the ship towards them, his white robes swirling around his ankles.

'Quickly,' he said, his eyes darting. 'Move into the hold.'

'What's wrong?' Piay asked.

'There is a boat moored ahead. A Hyksos crew. Perhaps tax-men, perhaps not.' Hanbaal glanced over his shoulder. 'Bearing in mind your ... difficulties ... with the invaders, it's better you are not in plain sight should they decide to venture aboard.'

'You have our thanks.'

Piay pushed himself up. From ahead, he could hear the bar-barians hailing the ship.

'In the hold, go astern,' Hanbaal said. 'There you will find a heap of filthy sailcloth, for repairs at sea. Crawl beneath it.'

Hannu grunted. 'The last time we hid beneath a cloth we were almost discovered.'

'It is not the cloth that will hide you. The rats nest in that place. If they search the ship, the Hyksos will not look too hard there.'

Hannu blanched. 'Rats?'

Piay chuckled. 'You have fought the bloodiest battles against the most fearsome foes and you are frightened by vermin?'

'If you had been buried in a shallow grave with rats nibbling at your toes you might think differently.'

'You never told me that,' Piay said, frowning.

'You never asked.'

Myssa rested her slim fingers on Hannu's shoulders. Smiling, she said, 'Huddle up to me. I will stroke your brow and whisper soothing words. You will soon forget the rats are there.'

Piay felt surprised by a pang of jealousy at the kindness Myssa had shown Hannu – such an uncommon emotion for him, he wasn't even sure if he'd ever experienced it. Before he could consider it, they were hurrying across the deck and lowering themselves into the suffocating dark of the hold.

Once his eyes had accustomed to the gloom, Piay squeezed past the amphorae and baskets of supplies to where the sailcloth was heaped. He lifted one edge and watched the waves roll across the cloth as the rodents squirmed and scurried beneath it. Hannu clasped his hand to his mouth and for a moment Piay thought his assistant might vomit. But then Myssa was easing him under the cloth. Piay crawled in after them. A scaly ringed tail lashed his arm and claws scratched across the back of his hand, but then the movement stilled as he settled into place. His nostrils flared at the choking reek of vermin urine and he forced his breathing to stay calm.

Voices droned through the hold from the open hatch. In the dark, Piay strained to listen, ready to leap up to fight for his life. Hanbaal's voice was loud and clear and Piay realised the slaver was speaking so that they all could hear him.

From his tone, the Hyksos had already boarded the ship. Piay imagined the barbarians standing there, hands resting on the hilts of their crescent swords, sullen gazes sweeping across the deck. Had they heard tell of an Egyptian spy and his assistant? Had Sakir set his guards on all river routes into the interior?

Hanbaal was saying, 'We have had a profitable voyage and all our slaves have been sold across the Great Green. Now we go south, to Kush and beyond, to gain fresh supplies.' After a moment, he continued, 'I am a poor trader, as you can see, scrabbling to make a crust to feed myself and my men. This is a hard business. Little reward. But we keep going and pray to the gods that one day our fortunes will improve.'

Piay sensed movement beside him – a rat burrowing under the cloth, drawn by his musk. He stiffened, holding fast.

Hanbaal said, 'Yes, the hold is empty, as you can see if you look into the hatch. There is nothing down there but rats.' After another silence, he said with a note of reluctance, 'Yes, and what meagre profits we made from our voyage to the Peloponnese.'

The rat wriggled closer. Piay flinched as he felt its fur brush along his arm towards his shoulder.

'Taxes, you say?' Hanbaal boomed. 'We will pay our taxes when we travel along the Canal of the Pharaohs.' A pause, then, 'Ah. Taxes now, too, of course, of course.'

Piay could hear the strained tone in the slaver's voice; he was putting on a brave face, but this would irk him more than anything. Would he give up his passengers in return for keeping hold of his gold?

Piay moved his hand towards his sword and the rat clawed across his shoulder, nuzzling its nose and whiskers into his ears. He jerked his head before it could take a bite of him. The rodent twisted and rolled away, its tail lashing his face.

Piay heard movement in the hold. He clamped his hand on his sword hilt, ready for the sailcloth to be ripped off him. Instead, there was a rustling around the basket where Hanbaal kept his earnings and then the sounds receded. The slaver was paying his dues. Piay had misjudged him.

After what felt like an age in that sickening atmosphere with the constant squirming, Piay felt the ship begin to move. The barbarians must have departed with their booty. They were on their way south once more.

Piay pulled his way out from the hiding place. He flailed, trying to stay upright when Hannu scrambled past him as fast as any scurrying rat. In the middle of the hold, Hannu put his hands on his knees and dry-retched. He turned to Piay and stabbed a finger.

'Never again. I will take my chances with the barbarians. With an army of them!'

He stomped away and pulled himself into fresh air.

Piay threw his head back and laughed. He sensed Myssa slide next to him.

'Don't tease him,' she whispered.

'Sometimes I think my very purpose upon this world is to torment Hannu,' he chuckled. 'I keep him honest.'

'And he, you.'

After a moment's reflection, Piay nodded in agreement.

'And he keeps me honest, too.'

Hanbaal was waiting for them on deck.

'Now you have our gratitude,' Piay said.

'We must take care from this moment,' the slaver replied. 'The Hyksos were searching for two men – Egyptian spies, they said.' He fixed his gaze on Piay, but was politic enough not to probe further. 'But they had no expectation of finding them on a slaver ship, and so were easily bought off with a little gold. However, that tells me there will be plenty more questions asked between here and when we reach the Red Sea.'

'Whatever bribe you had to offer will be repaid in full once we reach Thebes.'

Hanbaal nodded. 'Very good, very good.' He grinned. 'But if there is danger ahead, and a great deal of it, then the price of our business must surely increase.'

An eagle swooped across the silver sky, its piping call ringing out over the date palms. Piay watched its passage, pleased to be out of the sticky papyrus swamps and into the Canal of the Pharaohs. How long ago this waterway had been built, he had no idea, but it had seen better days. The banks were crumbling and silt was heaped up in the shallows. There was little sign it had been dredged in recent days. But the air smelled fresher and he filled his lungs as he stood in the prow with the sailor who sounded the depths with his wooden pole.

Hanbaal's ship sailed along the centre of the channel where the water was deepest, moving steadily eastwards. The oars dipped and splashed, the lines creaked, the hull groaned, and the sailors sang along to the music of their vessel.

Piay searched the tracks running along either bank. Boys led donkeys laden with baskets and the farmers' wives carried bundles of washing to the water. But he could see no sign of the Hyksos. He wished he'd paid more attention in his classes with Taita. He had scant knowledge of this part of Egypt, or of how much the barbarians had intruded into the life of the local people.

Piay caught a distant sound drifting on the wind. As they sailed further on, it became a cacophony of voices – shouting, cheering, laughing – mingling with the thrum of drums, the blasts of trumpets and the strains of a lyre.

White walls and grand buildings shimmered in the heat haze ahead, their ghostly presence taking on substance as the ship sailed on until Piay realised he was staring at a city. Another canal plunged across the landscape and this city lay between the two channels. As they neared, both canals became filled with small boats, so many that it seemed he could walk from bank to bank without getting his feet wet. All were heading towards that gleaming city.

When Piay glanced over the rail, the occupants of some of those smaller vessels cheered and waved at him. He felt puzzled by this odd display – most Egyptians about their labours had more scowls than smiles. Yet many of these people were laughing and passing around a hide.

Piay heard footsteps and turned to see Hanbaal grinning at him.

'What is the meaning of this revelry?' Piay asked.

'A festival of some kind or other. They have so many here I can never recall which one is which. It seems to me they are excuses to get drunk for days on end. They love their wine, that I do know.'

Piay glanced back at the city walls and the flood of people approaching them.

'Where is this?'

'Your people know it as Per-Bast,' Hanbaal replied, 'but to us it is Bubastis, the City of Cats.'

'A festival?' Hannu said. 'I foresee disaster.'

He stood at the rail, watching Hanbaal's men tie up the ship at the wharf. The din from the city almost drowned out his voice.

'Why?' Myssa asked. 'It is only revelry.'

Hannu eyed Piay. 'Lakes of wine. Wild abandon. Women bored with their husbands. That is a rich brew, which in my experience leads to trouble.'

'We have no need to worry. And no need to discuss this *any more*,' Piay stressed.

Hannu shrugged. 'A thought, no more.'

Piay bristled at the implied criticism. But how could he blame Hannu? It was true. The man he had once been would have revelled in the opportunity to indulge himself in the pleasures of the festival, regardless of whatever dangers he might have got mixed up in. But he was no longer that man, he had come to believe. What man he was becoming, he was not yet sure. A better one, he hoped.

He looked out at the people thronging across the quayside towards the city gate. They were laughing, stumbling, throwing their arms around one another's shoulders. Some tried to kiss the women who passed and were brought up sharp by a glare or a torrent of abuse. Some women tried to kiss the men. He could see the joy in all this. He pushed aside those thoughts, telling himself to be disciplined. He caught Hannu glaring at him as if his assistant could read his mind.

'We will not be partaking of the pleasures of this festival,' Piay announced. 'We have work to do and serious business ahead.'

'One thing in our favour, there are not many Hyksos here,' Hannu said, scanning the crowds.

'Then we could venture into the city,' Myssa suggested. 'Just for a while? I have had my fill of this ship.'

Piay watched distaste shadow Myssa's face. For her, too many bad memories hung over the vessel.

'Then we shall creep out in disguise at sunset,' Piay said with a smile. 'Let us snatch a little joy on this long, hard road.'

The shadows had swallowed the far side of the canal, and flames danced across the water from the torches flaring into life above the city gates. The crowds along the quayside had thinned, with only the stragglers scrambling to get into the city for the festivities.

Piay pulled down the brim of his petasus and Hannu did the same. Myssa slid her cloak's hood over her head. No one would give a second glance to these travellers from foreign lands, Piay was sure.

As they marched down the gangplank, Piay nodded to Hanbaal. The slaver was sipping wine under his shelter, conversing with Ragan. They'd spent the hours since their arrival finding replacements for the sailors who had been killed by the pirates. By all accounts, it had been a successful exercise and the slaver had told Piay that they would be ready to sail at first light. That was good. The less time they spent in Hyksos territory, the better.

Piay led the way into the city, his ears ringing from the din beyond the walls. Crowds thronged along every street, shoulder to shoulder, drunken and singing and laughing. Myssa smiled as she watched the revellers. Piay felt pleased to see her happy.

Losing themselves in the multitude, they were carried along the streets. Ahead, music rang out through the tumult. On a square, a band of performers pounded drums and shook sistra. Hannu nodded his head to the beat, waving a finger to accompany the lilting strains of a harp and the piping of a flute. A boy danced in front of them, whirling and tumbling while his audience applauded.

Some merrymakers had passed out in the street. Those still standing stepped over the prone forms as they whirled through the bacchanal. Away from the torchlit main thoroughfares, the darkness of the side streets heaved with couples in congress. For this night there seemed to be no rules in Per-Bast.

Piay marvelled at the strangeness of this city, so different from Thebes in many ways. The land had been built up around the perimeter where the walls towered. From them, the streets swept down the shallow sides of a bowl to the centre where a great temple soared.

'There are cats everywhere, just like Hanbaal said,' Myssa observed.

Everywhere Piay glanced, felines ran through the streets or perched on walls or sped across the rooftops. The slaver had said there were as many cats as people in Per-Bast.

'This city is dedicated to the goddess Bast,' he said.

Myssa smiled. 'You have a goddess of cats?'

'The warrior lion goddess,' Hannu corrected. 'Protector of Lower Egypt, defender of the king and great Ra himself.'

*And the Eye of the Moon*, Piay thought. He liked the connection with Khonsu, who had offered so much protection during their travels.

'I think I will make an offering at her temple.'

Myssa crouched as a grey cat darted among the legs of the passers-by and strolled up to her.

'It understands us,' she said. 'Perhaps your god is listening.'

She reached out a hand and the cat brought its nose to her fingers before allowing her to scratch its head.

'That is a good sign in Per-Bast,' Hannu noted. 'The goddess has smiled on you.'

For the next hour they roamed the city, finding some relief among the eruption of joy. The festivities never dimmed. Piay began to wonder if they would continue all night, perhaps for days. He felt his shoulders gradually unknot when he realised there were no Hyksos anywhere he could see. This was not a city like Avaris, the centre of barbarian rule. Though Per-Bast was the capital of the eighteenth nome, it lay far from the Nile and the major trade routes, and was of lesser interest to the invaders. They would have their placemen in charge and would demand their dues as they did everywhere, but it seemed that any kind of military presence was considered a waste of resources. Perhaps they could sneak by beyond the view of Sakir.

'We should return to the ship,' Myssa said.

'First we must visit the temple to give prayer and make an offering for the voyage ahead,' Piay said.

Myssa shook her head, smiling. 'That is your god, not mine. I will go on ahead.'

She turned and disappeared into the crowd. The grey cat followed her.

Piay frowned. 'Will she be safe on her own?'

'Myssa has slit the throat of a pirate captain,' Hannu said. 'She can look after herself. Now, let's get this business done so I can rest before Hanbaal starts barking orders.'

They pushed through the crowd towards the temple. Like a beacon in the night, the towering structure gleamed in the light of a multitude of torches. The place of worship was vast, as big as the temple at the heart of Thebes. Two obelisks stood in front of towers which guarded the entrance. Piay craned his neck as he passed through the gate, which was at least four times his height. Inside was a courtyard with limestone columns lining porticos on either side, and beyond that was the entrance to the goddess's sacred place.

Within the hushed space, lamplight danced over more columns, these painted with the image of the goddess and marked with inscriptions of blessings. The ceiling was so lofty it was lost to the shadows. Piay breathed in an atmosphere rich with incense smouldering in bowls around the edge.

At the far end, the statue of Bast stared down at them. Behind it lay the goddess's home, where only her priests could enter. Piay looked up at the statue. Bast had the head of a lioness, fierce and protective of her cubs. In her left hand she clutched the ankh and in her right the sistrum. Barefooted, she was wrapped in a white sheath dress. Piay felt humbled under her gaze.

Through the doorway behind the statue, Piay glimpsed the priests conducting their nightly ritual. They were passing around a bowl containing the liquor of the blue lotus. Each shaven-headed man took a sip before passing it on. When they'd all drunk, they began a low, rumbling chant, praising the glory of the moon.

'Say your prayers,' Hannu breathed. 'I will keep watch.'

'There are no Hyksos here. You saw that.'

'The only time I will lower my guard is when we're back in Thebes.'

Hannu prowled away and stood looking out into the moonlit courtyard.

Piay stepped before the statue of Bast and lowered his head. He felt awe tingle up his spine.

'I pray for safe passage through the dangers that lie ahead,' he murmured. 'Protect me, O Bast, as the lioness protects those under her care in the wilderness. I pray, also, that I am not too late and that all my efforts have not been for naught. That Thebes is still free. That the Pharaoh and Taita still live.'

He stood in silent reflection on the troubles he had faced and what might be still to come. When he opened his eyes, his instinct prickled and he looked up to see the priests had emerged from their inner sanctum and were standing by the doorway, staring at him.

Piay felt his skin crawl. All of them were rigid, silent, looking at him with an intensity as if they could see deep inside him. Finally one of them walked over. His papyrus sandals whispered across the limestone floor. His pleated linen robe swayed around him as he came to a halt in front of Piay. The black make-up turned his eyes into the shadowed sockets of a skull. When the light shifted, Piay could see the fire of the blue lotus flickering in those orbs. The priest was in this world, but he was in the realm of the gods, too.

'Bast has a message for you,' the man whispered, so low that Piay had to strain to hear it.

The priest maintained that unsettling stare for a moment longer and then he said, 'He is coming. Seth has shown him the way.'

Piay felt a chill. 'Sakir?'

'He is coming.'

The priest turned and walked back to his fellows and the band trailed into the inner sanctum.

Piay stood for a while, his thoughts racing. He thought of Seth, and Khonsu, and his vision of the gods struggling over the soul of Egypt, and then he hurried to where Hannu was staring out into the night.

'What's wrong?' said Hannu.

'We have to return to the ship.'

Hannu couldn't understand this sudden urgency.

'Sakir is coming.'

Piay watched Hannu's eyes widen further and he looked back to the statue of Bast. He didn't ask any further questions. Perhaps he didn't want to know. A moment later, they were hurrying up the thronging streets towards the city gate.

When they reached the ship, a cat was yowling. The high-pitched cry tore through the stillness of the wharf.

Piay and Hannu bounced up the gangplank. The grey feline that had followed Myssa perched on a bench, head thrown back and making that terrible wailing. As they approached, the cat choked off its cry and stared at them. Green eyes flickered with the light of the moon.

Piay stared into those depths and felt an odd sensation creep over him.

'Where is Myssa?' he asked.

The deck was empty – they could see that in the light from the torches along the wall. Hannu peered into the hold. No one. They both ran back down the gangplank to the quayside. Piay felt his unease begin to shade into alarm.

Hanbaal sat upon his throne in front of a fire, sipping wine from a cup. His men lounged around other fires, most of them seemingly half-drunk.

'Myssa,' Piay called. 'Have you seen her?'

No one had.

'She is likely enjoying a brief moment of freedom,' Hanbaal said. 'Let her indulge herself for this one moment. She will be a better slave for it and work harder when she has had her time alone.'

Perhaps the slaver was right and Piay was being too anxious. He sat on the edge of the quay, listening to the jubilant sounds of the festivities. He felt oddly melancholic. Instead of joy, they reminded him of what he was missing – of life at the court and the comforts and happiness that went with it. There were times when he thought he might never experience them again.

'You know how much Myssa hates this ship.' Hannu's voice floated up beside him.

Piay felt his unease spike once more. If Hannu was still weighing Myssa's disappearance it meant he, too, was troubled. When their eyes met, Piay sensed the same question in his assistant's mind that he had been trying to keep at bay: could Sakir be here and have taken her?

Piay's stomach twisted. He felt more desperate than he ever could remember.

'We go back,' he said. 'Retrace our steps—'

A woman's cry shattered the stillness of the night. It came from beyond the quayside, somewhere along the track that edged the canal.

Piay raced towards the sound, Hannu at his heels. The beat of footsteps from other crew members echoed behind.

Away from the torchlight, he strained his eyes to pierce the dark. As he adjusted to the gloom, he picked out movement – two figures rolling around.

That cry again.

*Myssa!*

Ragan was gripping Myssa's wrists, trying to pin her down. Between laughter, he muttered words that Piay couldn't make out. Myssa writhed like a desert cat, her fingers hooked into claws. Her lips had pulled back from her teeth and she was snapping at Ragan, trying to tear off chunks of his flesh. He wrenched his head away to avoid the savage assault.

As Piay came closer, Myssa rammed a knee into the sailor's groin. Howling, he rolled over and clutched at his nether regions. Myssa scrambled to her feet, looming over him. Piay saw no fear in her face, only a furious loathing.

Snarling, Ragan heaved himself to his feet.

Piay pulled out his sword and jabbed the tip towards the chest of the sailor.

'Back,' he growled.

Ragan staggered and wiped his mouth with the back of his hand. He was trembling.

Myssa lunged, spitting at her attacker.

'This dog killed my father and the man I was to wed in front of my eyes,' she seethed. 'And he laughed as he did it, and mocked me.'

Ragan's milky eye glowed in the gloom.

'But that wasn't the end of the torment he wanted to inflict on me,' Myssa continued. 'Every night in that filthy, stinking hold, he attacked me, and every night I fought him off. You see that ragged ear? I took that, with these teeth. The missing teeth, the scars across his back and arms. All my work. He could not cow me. He could not beat me. And that defeat ate away at him.'

Piay felt hot anger consume him. No wonder Myssa loathed being aboard the ship. And now he could understand that simmering rage that had seemed to crackle between Myssa and Hanbaal's second in command every day as they crossed the Great Green.

'When we set sail, he told me it was not over,' Myssa spat. 'That he would take me if it was the last thing he did. He would punish me for my defiance and show me my true place in life.'

Ragan lunged for Myssa. She danced away from his grasp, eyes blazing. Piay felt that boiling fury bubble over. He pulled back his arm, ready to run Ragan through.

Before Piay could strike, a hand caught his arm. Piay turned and looked into the cold face of Hanbaal.

'Leave him be,' the slaver said.

'You heard what he has done – what he wants to do—'

'Leave him. He is my man.'

Hanbaal held Piay's stare. He was not about to back down.

Myssa stepped forwards and pressed her lips close to his ear.

'Walk away,' she breathed. 'There is too much at stake here. You need Hanbaal on your side.'

'You deserve—'

'Walk away.'

Myssa pressed her fingertips against Piay's chest and eased him back. A smile ghosted her lips – a little sad, he thought, but tinged with gratitude that he had stood up for her.

Piay glanced at Hannu. His assistant's face was filled with loathing for Ragan, but he held himself in check. His eyes flickered to Piay and he nodded.

'Leave him,' he said. 'The gods will deal with him.'

'If your man comes near Myssa,' Piay said to Hanbaal, 'if he lays a hand on her again . . . I will kill him.'

The slaver showed no emotion. Piay eased his arm around Myssa's shoulders and pushed through the crowd of sailors towards the ship.

'Why didn't you tell me? I could have protected you,' Piay said when the three of them had settled into their place next to the helmsman's platform.

'Once again, I do not need your protection,' Myssa replied. 'That is not the woman my father raised.'

Hannu grunted. 'Your father raised a fighter, no doubt about that. I can see why your village chose you.'

'You must be on your guard from now on,' Piay cautioned. 'Ragan is not a man to accept humiliation lightly. He will want his revenge and he will bide his time until he gets it.'

'I will take care, as I always do,' Myssa said.

'I'll also keep watch during the night,' Hannu said. 'I can't understand how Sakir could possibly have found us, but I'm not about to deny it.'

A grey shape floated along the deck towards them. Piay saw it was the cat again. A dead rat hung from its mouth. The feline dropped the rodent in front of Myssa, then raised its head to peer at her.

'You have a new friend,' Piay said.

Myssa scratched the cat's head and it purred.

'This one can join us on the voyage, I think. There are plenty of rats in the hold to keep his belly full.'

'And what will you call him?'

Myssa smiled as she held the cat's stare.

'I will call *her* Bast.'

Piay's eyelids opened at first light. Something had woken him. As he stirred, he realised it was the chatter of children on the quayside. He felt puzzled by the excited tones disturbing the quiet of that hour, and he pulled himself up to investigate.

A small group of boys was gathered on the edge of the quay, pointing at something floating in the canal.

As he stepped down the gangplank, Piay saw it was a body drifting. He grabbed one of the mooring poles and after a moment's struggle, hooked the clothes so he could heave the corpse over. Its throat had been cut.

Kneeling, he peered down at the remains. The flesh was pale and puckered from its time in the water. The eyes were open and staring up to the heavens. One of them had a milky cast.

When he glanced back, he saw Hanbaal standing by the prow, watching. The slaver still showed an impassive face, but a silent communication crackled between them. Justice had been done.

Hanbaal, as he had said, was a man who paid his dues.

By the time the sun was fully above the horizon, the mooring ropes had been thrown off and the oarsmen guided the ship into the canal. *Not a moment too soon*, Piay thought. It might have been the lingering unease from his encounter with the priests in the temple, but he felt something dark and dangerous was approaching.

As the heat of the day soared and the rising sun turned the canal into a ribbon of beaten gold, he watched Per-Bast fade into the haze behind them. Fields of wheat and cotton gave way to wilder land, and the date palms swaying in the breeze gradually vanished. The canal was less finished the further away from the city they rowed. In many areas it looked like work had not been carried out for decades. Ridged brown crocodiles basked in the sun on crumbling banks, watching their progress, and beyond them, vast sweeps of wild red lotus choked the edges.

Ahead, bands of bronze edged the silver sky, the highlands of the Sinai. Piay shielded his eyes against the glare, trying to imagine how Hanbaal planned to get to the Red Sea from the landlocked canal. As far as he knew, there was no waterway that provided access. But every time he asked, the slaver only tapped his nose and laughed.

The sweep of greenery of the fertile Nile Valley became intermittent smudges across the landscape and then faded completely, leaving only the vast inhospitable desert. The wind whipped up, blasting clouds of dust across the canal.

They encountered no other vessels as they voyaged east. The land was deserted. They could have been alone in the world, but Piay stood at the rail, searching the banks for any sign of movement.

'Hard to see how Sakir could gain on us,' Hannu muttered by his side. 'Unless he is already ahead and waiting.'

Neither of them expressed their fears to Myssa. Piay thought how much brighter she seemed with each passing day. Whether it was the death of Ragan, her tormentor, or that she was returning home, he did not know.

'Put your mind at rest,' she soothed as darkness fell and the moon painted a glimmering path along the water. 'Once you have the elephants under your command, the Hyksos will fall before your army. I believe this to be true.'

Piay felt touched by her words. After all she had suffered, she had no reason to care about his success. And yet she did care; he could see it in her eyes. She was a mystery to him, and he could feel himself wanting to understand the secrets of her mind more with each passing day.

On the morning of the third day out of Per-Bast, the ship sailed through a narrow valley between two areas of highland. On the other side a great lake shimmered into the hazy distance where the foothills of the bleak Sinai rose up. The surface was like a polished bronze mirror reflecting the blue sky, the water so still Piay imagined he could walk across it to the far side.

'The Bitter Lakes are as salty as any sea,' Hanbaal said, looking out towards the south. His restless eyes were always searching for other ships, for enemies or opportunities. 'We are nearing the end of the first leg of our voyage.'

With the crimson sail unfurled, the ship skimmed across the lake to the south. As they neared the edge, Piay scanned the band of ochre rocks and billowing dunes baking in the heat.

With a frown, he said, 'I can see no waterway. Where do we go from here?'

Laughter rippled out among the crew. Hanbaal showed a sly grin.

'You have never seen a ship sail on land?'

When Piay questioned him further, the slaver only chuckled and moved among his men, shouting commands. A few dropped into the hold and handed up coils of hide ropes. Other sailors dragged them into heaps along the deck.

Once the sail had been furled, the helmsman and the oarsmen guided the ship towards the lake shore. Piay made out a track leading from the water's edge between two towering heaps of rocks. The trail plunged straight and true across the desert towards the horizon.

Piay expected the crew to put down the anchor offshore. Instead, they let the ship drift into the shallows until he felt the grinding of the hull against the bottom. The sailors hurried to lace the hide ropes across the rails on both sides and then threw the ends overboard. The men followed, splashing into the water. Piay leaned over the rail and watched them grab the ends of the ropes and wade up to the beach.

'From here we walk,' Hanbaal said.

Piay, Hannu and Myssa dropped into the shallows. Piay stared with bafflement as the sailors wrapped the ends of the hide ropes around themselves. The only man remaining on deck began to beat the ship's drum in a steady rhythm.

The sailors heaved as one. The ship moved forwards. The men rested when the drummer paused and then they heaved again. Gradually, the ship emerged from the lake, creeping up the gentle slope towards the track.

'This is madness,' Piay said. 'They plan to pull the vessel across the desert to the Red Sea?'

'Wait,' Myssa said, pointing. 'Look.'

Piay followed her direction and glimpsed ridges half-hidden in the sand. As he studied them, he realised they were logs, buried by the drifting dust. The track was a wooden road.

He stared in amazement as the ship rose from the water on to the track. Step by step, the sailors dragged it on, over the crest between the two towers.

Hanbaal stepped beside Piay, Hannu and Myssa.

'Every vessel that sails this way is hauled by its men across dry land until water is once again reached. The track was laid long ago. Long before my father's time and his father's father, so I am told.'

'I cannot believe my eyes,' Myssa gushed.

'The work is hard,' Hanbaal continued, 'but the distance is short enough to make the effort worthwhile. One day, if the gods are willing, whoever rules Egypt will complete the Canal of the Pharaohs and my voyages between the lands along the Great Green and the coast to the south will become like a dream. For now, this is all we have.'

'How long will it take?' Piay asked.

'This is the narrowest stretch of land between the Bitter Lakes and the Red Sea. Our trek will take four days. We break only for short periods of sleep and to eat.' The slaver shielded his eyes, staring across the wasteland. 'But then we will have open sea ahead of us and a fair wind at our backs. And your destination will be in reach.'

Under the searing sun, Hanbaal's men heaved on the ropes and the ship creaked towards the south. Under the cool eye of Khonsu in the desert night, they strained every sinew. The vessel sailed across the dunes, its voyage made a little easier by the logs almost hidden beneath the shifting sands.

Piay marvelled at the sight. Never would he have thought to see such a thing, and he was sure he would never forget it. The drummer kept the men in time. Hanbaal prowled alongside them, but they were all diligent. They knew what was expected of them and they hauled their burden without complaint.

And then, on the fourth day, the setting sun illuminated the sea ahead and the sailors cheered and drew on the last of their reserves. The ship slid down into the shallows for the next leg. For Kush, for elephants, for the hope of Egypt.

Piay closed his eyes. The cool breeze wafted across his face, refreshing after so many days enduring the baking heat along the edge of the Sinai. He felt comforted to know the shore of Nubia lay close enough to identify the boats of the fishermen dragged up on the beach. No terror of being adrift in the great gulf here. Dry land was close enough to swim to.

A moment of peace.

His thoughts went back to that magical vision of the ship sailing across the dunes while he, Hannu and Myssa walked. The land journey had been gruelling for the men, sweating and straining in the heat of the day and the chill of the night. But they were used to this toil.

When he opened his eyes, he noticed Myssa at the rail, staring at the streak of ochre land. Bast snaked around her legs, purring.

'You are thinking of your home,' Piay said when he joined her.

Myssa nodded, showing no emotion. 'Kush is there, beyond the horizon.'

Piay couldn't imagine what it would be like to be stolen from everything he knew and dragged into servitude. Myssa was not an Egyptian, he knew that, and this was the way of the world. But he'd found this preying on his mind ever since she had unburdened herself about her plight. He'd thought about what he should do, and he'd reached a conclusion. He felt surprised by how much that pained him.

'You've been a great help in this quest,' he began, searching for the right words. 'We would not be on this path to success if you hadn't found the answer to the Oracle's riddle. And let us not forget, we would likely all be a feast for the fish if you had not shown courage during the attack by the pirates.'

Myssa searched his face.

'I have decided that once you have guided us to the land of the elephants, you will be rewarded.'

'Rewarded?'

'I will grant you your freedom.'

Myssa glanced back to the shoreline. 'You will allow me to return home?'

'That is my intention.'

When she looked at him, tears rimmed her eyes. Piay sensed her urge to throw her arms around him, to thank him, but she resisted. That would not be a seemly display.

Myssa bit her lip. 'I have a confession.'

'Speak.'

'I deceived you. All the aid I gave you was merely to get back home. Once we reached Kush, my plan was to flee once we stopped to take on water. Never would I have ventured back on this foul ship if that hope had not burned bright at the end of the voyage.'

Piay nodded. 'I understand.'

'You do not feel betrayed?'

'If I was in your position, I would have done the same. My offer still stands.'

'Then let me visit my village first, so they know I yet live. That will give them hope in what will be a dark time. Then I will return to them when you have found your elephants.'

'Very well. I will speak to Hanbaal.'

Piay turned away, only to find Hannu standing in silence behind him, listening to the conversation.

'What are you doing there like a desert cat stalking its prey?' Piay snapped.

Hannu smiled.

'What?' Piay couldn't control the crack in his voice.

'Nothing.'

An odd light glowed in Hannu's eyes. Piay thought it might have been respect.

'You are an infuriating little man.'

**M**yssa's eyes sparkled as she hurried along the road from the small beach where they had drawn up the rowing boat. Piay could see her untrammelled joy in every movement of her body and in the glow in her face.

'Not far now,' she gushed.

Myssa's village lay just inland, which had made it an easy target for Hanbaal's slavers. Piay couldn't imagine the terror those people had felt as they went about their daily tasks when a horde of cut-throats and rogues burst into their midst, cutting down any who resisted.

Many had fled to escape capture, Myssa had said, but she had been too slow, rooted when she saw people she knew and loved hacked down before her eyes.

'Hanbaal was wise to remain on board the ship with his men,' Hannu grunted as they hurried behind Myssa. 'I'd wager the village warriors wouldn't take too kindly to seeing them again.'

But Piay's attention was fixed on Myssa. He found her jubilation infectious, and he was overcome with his own joy at seeing her so happy.

But as Myssa crested a ridge, Piay watched her slow, her limbs growing heavy, until she came to a halt. Her chin sagged on to her chest.

'This does not bode well,' Hannu breathed.

Piay strode to Myssa's side and looked out across the dusty land stretching to a row of low brown hills in the distance. The plain was devoid of life. The bones of a village jabbed up among scrubby yellow grass, but some of the walls of the circular clay-brick huts had collapsed, and here and there the roofs of leaf and mud had fallen in. No smoke from the hearth-fires smeared the blue sky. No children gambolled. No cattle lowed. The only movement was whirls of dust whipped up by the wind.

Myssa sucked in a juddering breath, then pushed her chin up and trudged down the slope to the ghost of her home. Piay and Hannu followed at a respectful distance.

As they neared, Piay could see it was clear the village had simply been abandoned. Myssa drifted among the houses, glancing into dark doorways, but everything of value had been taken. She came to a halt at a row of graves on the edge of the settlement and there she stood for a long while with her head bowed.

When she finally turned back to Piay and Hannu, her face twisted as despair and anger fought inside her.

'This is the consequence of my capture,' she snarled. 'Once my people lost the receptacle of their knowledge – once the king lost the guidance of a wise advisor – the sun went down upon them. Hope would have drifted away. I know that, because my teachers impressed on me the absolute importance of my role from the very first day of my lessons.'

'Where could they have gone?' Hannu asked.

'Perhaps the crops failed. Perhaps the king was killed in a raid . . .' Myssa's words dried up. She swallowed. 'Some have died.' She nodded towards the graves. 'All that matters is that my people have gone. I have nothing.'

Piay felt his heart ache for her. The light that had always seemed to shine out of her had been extinguished.

'You will always have a place with us,' he murmured. 'I promise you that.'

For a while, they stood in the deserted village, listening to the soughing of the wind as Myssa mourned all that she had lost. Then, when she seemed drained of all emotion, she some-how found it within her to push her head up and lead the way back to the ship.

Piay felt impressed by the dignity he saw there. And while he grieved for her loss, a part of him felt pleased that she would still be at his side.

One day later, as they sped along the coast, a cry rang across the deck from the lookout.

'This does not bode well,' Hannu muttered. When Hanbaal stalked towards them his face was like thunder.

'We are being pursued,' he said. 'At least that is the only conclusion I can come to.'

Piay peered astern. 'More pirates?'

'A squadron of ships – five, perhaps six. The lookout has seen the sails. Big ships. Warships. We would never see their kind. Not along this route.'

Piay could not yet see those sails, but the lookout's eyes were used to seeing across great distances.

'Why would a squadron of warships be chasing down a lowly slaver?' Hanbaal's stare was piercing. 'You promised me no trouble.'

'Perhaps a little trouble.'

'The price of this voyage rises by the moment.' Hanbaal sim-mered, yet his anger was not as great as Piay expected. Perhaps he could see more gold for his coffers. As Hanbaal walked away, he wagged a finger at Piay. 'You and I, we need to have words sooner or later.'

Myssa watched the slaver urging his crew into action with wild gesticulations.

'What if Hanbaal gives us up to save his own neck?'

'Hanbaal would sell his own mother if the price was right,' Piay replied. 'That, we knew. We will have to make sure the gold we offer outweighs all other considerations.'

'There will come a time when he weighs tomorrow's promises against the hard truths of today,' Hannu noted.

'That is a thought for another day. For now, let us reflect on the fact that the Hyksos have sent a squadron of soldiers just for me.' Trying to make light, he added, 'If that is not a mark of my greatness, I can imagine no other.'

'You are a tall man now,' Hannu grumbled. 'In a little while you may be wishing you were a far smaller one.'

Piay stared into the cat's eyes. He felt oddly troubled by what he saw flickering in their emerald depths. Was that intelligence? Surely not. Yet what he saw there left him in no doubt that this was like no feline he had ever encountered.

Bast held his gaze a moment longer and then looked away with what Piay thought was insouciance.

*What a fool I am*, he decided, silently cursing himself. This life at sea was driving him slowly insane.

He was sitting cross-legged on the deck, out of the blast of the sea breeze. For three days, the warships of the barbarians had chased them along the coast of Nubia. Hanbaal had shown skill as a seasoned captain, using the currents to their advantage so that they not only kept the pace of the enemy at their backs, but even pulled ahead. On they'd raced, through the narrow strait, with Arabia looming in the east, and into the dangerous wide waters. If the gods were kind, they could lose the warships and reach their destination without further conflict.

He saw Myssa staring at him, a faint smile on her lips, the first time he had seen one since she had left her village. She walked over and said, 'Bast likes you.'

'The sentiment is not returned.'

'You do not like cats?'

'I don't like that one. It troubles me.'

Myssa laughed silently. 'That is because she sees your deepest secrets.'

'I have no secrets. I am a simple man.'

Myssa laughed loudly this time. Piay felt relieved that she was once again becoming her own self, though he knew that pain would still remain deep in her heart.

Hannu stalked across the deck towards them from the prow. He was scowling.

Piay sighed. 'Clearly it is time for him to torment me again. Is a little peace and quiet too much to ask?'

'What's wrong?' Myssa asked when Hannu reached them.

He turned and pointed. Piay looked past his finger to a grey smudge on the horizon.

'Storm's brewing,' Hannu said. 'Brace yourself.'

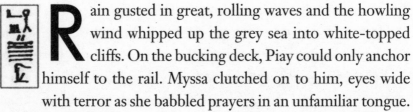 Rain gusted in great, rolling waves and the howling wind whipped up the grey sea into white-topped cliffs. On the bucking deck, Piay could only anchor himself to the rail. Myssa clutched on to him, eyes wide with terror as she babbled prayers in an unfamiliar tongue.

The storm had slowed them. Though the Hyksos ships were invisible in the tempest, Piay felt sure they were there, drawing closer. And Sakir would be on the lead vessel, riding those other waves of the blue lotus dreams with Seth looming over him.

The ship crashed down from the crest of the swell and a wave swept across the deck. Myssa screamed and Piay pulled her tighter. When he wiped the brine from his eyes, he glimpsed Hanbaal lurching across the benches to the starboard rail and peering out into the murk.

Piay beckoned for Hannu to take care of Myssa and he staggered down the rolling deck to the slaver.

'We know the currents here better than anyone!' Hanbaal bellowed above the howl of the wind. 'If the Hyksos are not used to these waters, we have an advantage.' He grabbed Piay's arm and pointed into the rain haze. 'There is a reef out there. Rocks as sharp as a lion's teeth that can tear through a hull. The currents will drag the unwise on to them.'

'What is your plan?' Piay shouted back.

'The reef is marked on our charts. On past voyages we have given it a wide berth for fear we would get dragged on to the rocks by the currents. We can skirt that reef now – as close as we dare . . . Draw in the barbarian ships and leave it to the gods to decide if they live or die. This is our only hope. One miscalculation and we will be on the bottom.'

'What other choice do we have?'

'None. My knowledge of the currents aided us, but still they drew closer. We must seize this moment.'

Hanbaal spun back to his men. Whatever he told them, Piay could see faces twist in confusion, but the sailors obeyed their captain without question.

The ship slowed and began to twist on the currents.

'Starboard, hard!' Hanbaal shouted.

The helmsman leaned on the steering oar. Slowly the ship began to turn in the direction of the reef.

Piay scrambled back to Hannu and Myssa.

'Brace yourselves!' he shouted.

Myssa stared, her mouth widening.

'Put your faith in Hanbaal,' Piay said to her. 'There is no better captain in my mind. If anyone can deliver us from the barbarians, it is him.'

*And if he fails, we will be swallowed by the ocean and in no position to complain.*

His words seemed to calm Myssa and she forced a smile and nodded. Hannu was more suspicious.

'Why are we heading towards the shore?'

'We have stopped running.'

Before Hannu could question him further, Piay staggered to the rail beside the helmsman's platform and stared into the blasting rain. For a while there was only the heaving sea and the deck rolling beneath his feet. But then he glimpsed movement in the grey curtain astern. Shadows slowly hardened.

The Hyksos warships rushed out of the haze, growing more distinct as they neared. One ship. Three. Six. The squadron was sailing in formation in the shape of a spearhead. They were disciplined, as he would expect from such a band of warriors. But were they ready for the confusion and chaos that was to come?

Piay watched the grand vessels ride the swell. Soon he glimpsed the barbarians on deck. Perhaps he was imagining it, but he was sure he could see them punch their fists into the air and roar their jubilation when they saw their prey before them.

Hanbaal was allowing his vessel to twist and turn in the current as if his men had lost control of it. The Hyksos would be thinking the ship was damaged, perhaps taking on water.

*Closer*, Piay thought. *Closer.*

The warships bore down on Hanbaal's vessel. In the prow of the one at the head of the spear-tip, a figure stood erect on the platform holding the rail. Piay squinted into the gale. He couldn't make out the features, but he was certain it was Sakir. The warrior seemed unmoved by the tumult, as calm as if he had been sailing across the Bitter Lakes.

Hanbaal was roaring his commands. The helmsman leaned harder still on the steering pole, and as the crew pushed into their oars, the ship began to turn and gather speed. Piay felt the vessel beneath him straining against the fierce currents.

Onwards the Hyksos came. After such a long pursuit, they would be giddy with the thought that their prey was almost in their grasp. That would make them reckless. Piay hoped; he prayed.

The slaver ship skimmed across the waves towards the hidden reef.

Piay wiped away the rain blinding him and peered into the churning water below. His heart leaped into his throat as the ship dipped and then twisted towards port. Hanbaal was asking much of his crew, and his vessel. How easy would it be for the claws of the ocean to rend the ship apart.

So violent now was the shaking that Piay gripped on for dear life. The vessel rolled hard. The water rushed up towards him as the deck pitched at a dizzying angle. His feet lifted off the boards.

Somewhere a sailor screamed. The man flashed past Piay and plunged into the cruel sea, sucked beneath the surface in an instant. Another man spun by, cracking his skull on the rail as he turned head over heels and disappeared into the waves.

Piay screwed his eyes shut tight. Brine sprayed across his face and he felt a surge of dread that the vessel was going to crash onto its side.

But then he sensed a shift in the forces dragging him down. The ship's timbers moaned as the vessel began to swing back on to its keel. Gathering pace, it crashed back down.

Piay jerked his eyes open. A line of jagged teeth stabbed from the water – the grey tip of the reef Hanbaal had identified.

A terrible grinding rolled out. The hull was dragging against the submerged rocks. Piay gasped, waiting for the moment when those vicious fangs ripped open the ship. The grinding rumbled louder, the vessel juddering.

Then Piay felt himself jolted forwards as if the ship had broken free of an invisible bond. The grinding vanished and the vessel surged away from the rocks.

Piay unfurled his grip and staggered back. So close had they come to disaster, only the gods could have saved them. He muttered a prayer to Bast, and then one to Khonsu for good measure, that they would be carried to safety.

He heard a terrible rending sound; one of the Hyksos ships careered across the reef. Piay watched as the fate they had narrowly avoided unfolded for the Hyksos before his eyes. The hull ripped apart, timbers shattering into flying shards. The grey water gushed into the hole. The deck spun up. The screams of sailors whipped on the gale as they pitched over the side into the boiling sea. Those furious currents wrenched at the wounded vessel until they ripped the bones asunder. The vessel crumbled, the mast swinging down into the gulf until it slid beneath the surface.

Piay watched men flailing in the heaving swell, gripped by terror. One by one the waves dashed them against the rocks or sucked them to the depths.

Two other Hyksos warships swept out of the haze of rain. The captain on the one nearest the reef must have been aware of what had happened to the first vessel. The ship banked at a steep angle as the helmsman fought with the steering oar to move the ship away from the rocks. Yet in the desperation of that action, the captain had only served to propel his craft into the path of the second warship.

There was no time to take evasive action and the currents were too strong for adjustments.

For an instant Piay forgot these were his enemies. A deep chill engulfed him as he watched the relentless passage of the two warships. They smashed together, the impact shattering both hulls. The sailors swarmed on the decks, but what could any of them do now? For a moment the two vessels seemed to be locked in a wild dance. They whirled together and then crashed in unison against the reef, as sailors were swept into the ocean.

Piay watched until the last man was lost and there was only the roiling sea.

Hanbaal showed no sentiment. He leaped from bench to bench, somehow keeping his feet on the bucking deck as he ordered his men to their tasks.

Piay stared aft. Timbers and sailcloth swirled across the swell. Of the other three ships, there was no sign. The gods had been merciless and those terrible seas had claimed all their enemies. He felt the rare taste of relief. Sakir was surely now a feast for the fish – for if not, he would still be hunting down his prey. The pursuit was done. They were free to carve out their own destiny.

He glimpsed Hanbaal gazing at the drifting debris. Searching, weighing. Then his eyes locked on Piay's and his lips curled into a triumphant grin.

 Sunlight jewelled the waves and spun gold along the length of shore. Now the tempest had blown itself out, Piay watched this unfamiliar land reveal itself, wondering what mysteries and dangers lay beyond the limits of his vision. He could still barely believe they had escaped with their lives.

All around, weary sailors collapsed across their oars. They'd fought against the storm and turbulent ocean for most of the day until they'd reached calmer seas. But now the skies were blue and the wind had dropped, and Hanbaal had ordered the ship to be taken in closer to land.

The slaver strode up.

'You are still sure you wish to go ashore?'

'This is the land of the elephants, yes?'

'Azania, they call it. There are elephants here, aye. Everywhere, deep into the south. I have even heard tell of a kingdom which has gained its power from warriors trained to ride on the backs of those great beasts.'

Piay felt a surge of hope. That was all he needed if he was to return to Egypt: an army of fighting men who rode on elephants – more than a match for the Hyksos horses.

Piay sensed unease as Hanbaal scrutinised the shoreline.

'What do you see?'

'There are dangers everywhere. But perhaps more for us than you.' The slaver stroked his oiled beard. 'We visited this land on one of our recent trips. But I make it a rule never to revisit one of our slaving grounds in quick succession.'

'I imagine you are not given a warm welcome.'

'This is business – the consequence of trade is not always favourable.'

'You don't have to venture on land. Anchor here and let us use the rowing boat. One man to deliver us to the shore. We will be back before you know it.'

Hanbaal nodded. 'And once you have your elephants, then we can discuss my gold.'

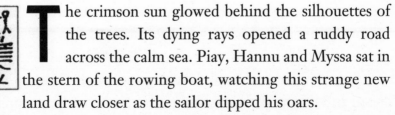

**T**he crimson sun glowed behind the silhouettes of the trees. Its dying rays opened a ruddy road across the calm sea. Piay, Hannu and Myssa sat in the stern of the rowing boat, watching this strange new land draw closer as the sailor dipped his oars.

'You can speak the tongue of the people here?' Piay asked.

Myssa shrugged. 'Some. Kush has close ties with many of the great kingdoms and the tribes that roam these lands. Trade always makes friends.'

'Sometimes enemies,' Hannu sniffed. 'If they think we are slavers, the next time Hanbaal comes he will find our heads on spikes as a warning.'

'I am trusting Myssa to guide us through any negotiations,' Piay said.

She glanced towards him, but he couldn't read her face in the growing dusk.

Once they reached the shore, they splashed into the shallows and strode up the beach. The sailor wasted no time in rowing back towards the ship.

As they stared at the dark line of trees, Piay felt a prickle of apprehension. Though it might have been better to wait on the ship until daybreak, they would be less likely to be seen as night fell, and they would be able to get the lie of the land before confronting the local people.

Even at that hour, it was steamy. They skirted a mangrove creek and moved into the shade under the coconut palms that lined the beach.

When the last of the sun ebbed, the darkness swallowed them, but enough moonlight broke through the canopy to illuminate the way ahead. They pushed through the thickening vegetation. They'd barely ventured more than a spear's throw when a cry rang out: *was-way-wah*, high-pitched and plaintive.

Hannu stiffened. 'Is that . . . a baby crying?'

'There may be a settlement ahead,' Piay breathed.

He eased his way past a plant with giant fronds. The cry came again, and again. Was it moving around them? Piay couldn't be sure, but he felt unsettled nonetheless. Now it didn't sound like any baby's cry. Hannu must have thought the same, for he dropped lower, his eyes darting.

Finally that bawling echoed ahead of them. Piay's breath burned in his chest. He watched Myssa creep forwards and press down a frond with the tips of her fingers. Beyond was a moonlit clearing.

An instant later Myssa beckoned them. Piay peered at a strange creature throwing back its head to issue that baby cry. Clinging to a branch was a bundle of fur, smaller than a monkey, with huge round eyes. It glared at them and scampered up to the high branches.

Hannu laughed. 'What a strange place this is.'

On they went, less troubled by the odd noises that emanated from the forest. After a while, Hannu dropped to his haunches and scraped his fingers across the ground.

'A trail,' he said. 'Made by men.'

Further on, the trail met a wide road rutted from the passage of carts. They trekked along it until they came to the edge of the trees. Ahead was a vast plain, silvered by the moonlight. Piay glanced up to the milky river of stars across the vault of the night. He remembered Hui talking about the Four Sons of Horus and he searched the sky until he found them. He felt comforted that they were there, watching over him so far from home.

In the distance mountains rose, silhouetted against the sky, and closer, Piay could make out a fire flickering. A jumble of huts nestled on the grassland and Piay thought he could hear the drone of voices. A musky aroma drifted in the air, no doubt from whatever beasts they kept.

Piay nodded, pleased. 'We will venture there at first light.'

The flames licked up from the dry branches. Hannu leaned back from lighting the fire and handed around the *dhourra* cake – the ship's dry biscuits – from the pouch at his waist. After delving into the forest, they'd nestled in a small hollow surrounded by snaking tree roots. Piay had been wary of any fire, but Myssa had warned him of the wild beasts that might be stalking among the trees – lions, she had said, and wild boar that could tear a man apart with their tusks. They had decided to take a risk to keep predators at bay.

As Piay and Hannu gnawed on their biscuits, Myssa eyed them. Piay noticed her look of curiosity.

'What is wrong?' he asked.

'The two of you have been friends for so long—'

'Hannu is my assistant,' Piay interrupted.

Myssa grinned. 'You have known each other for a long time. We can agree on that. Yet it seems to me that there are times when you barely know each other at all.'

'What is there to know?' Hannu shrugged.

Myssa said, 'Tell me what you think is your greatest skill.'

'I am good in a fight, that is certain,' Hannu mused. 'But . . . I would say my greatest skill is that I can see into a man's heart.'

Piay snorted. 'You think you are some kind of mage, now?'

Hannu was unruffled. 'I stare into the eyes and I see who that man is. What makes him. What troubles him. All is laid bare before me in an instant.'

'Ah. So that night in the field, you looked at Sakir and thought, "There is a murderous barbarian who wants to cut down good Egyptians,"' Piay mocked.

'I saw a man with an emptiness inside him who has been trying to fill it by any means possible.'

Piay shook his head.

'And you?' Myssa prompted. 'What is your greatest skill?'

'I am the best swordsman in all Egypt.' Piay folded his hands behind his head. 'And a great spy . . .' He winced at the sound of his familiar boasts. He added, 'I can sing. That is my greatest skill.'

'I didn't know you could sing,' Hannu said.

'You never asked.'

Myssa clapped her hands together. 'Let us hear you sing!'

Piay waved a dismissive hand, but she pressed and so he sat up and dug deep into his memory for a song. How long had it been since he'd given voice to those melodies he'd learned when he was younger? His thoughts returned to those nights after he'd endured a long day of Taita's tuition and the queen's handmaidens had gathered to hear him.

He closed his eyes, summoned a tune and let his voice soar. The song told of two lovers torn apart by war who fought their way back to be reunited, only to die before their hands ever touched again.

When the song ended, Piay was surprised to see Hannu with tears in his eyes. Myssa had her hands pressed against her cheeks, enraptured.

Hannu looked away. 'Aye . . . well . . . you're a better singer than you are a spy, I'll give you that.'

Piay grunted. 'In a different life, perhaps I would have given myself to music.'

'Would that have made you happy?' Myssa asked.

Piay reflected, then said, 'I think it would.'

Before anyone could utter another word, blood-curdling cries echoed from the dark. Figures swept down on them from all sides. Myssa shrieked. Piay lunged for his sword, but a spear shaft cracked down on to the back of his hand. The tip moved to his throat. He stiffened, knowing the slightest movement would result in his death.

A skull loomed over him with burning eyes. Piay realised he was staring into the face of one of the local men, the dark skin covered with crusted white mud so that it resembled a death's head. This warrior was naked to the waist, hard muscles gleaming in the firelight. He wore a plain kilt that had been dyed sapphire.

Hannu and Myssa both had spear-tips pressed against their necks. The remainder of the hunting band stood like sentinels, staring out into the night, no doubt searching for any other interlopers.

'Tell them we are friends,' Piay breathed.

Myssa began to babble in a tongue that Piay found strange. Her captor stared into her face, listening intently. When she was done, he uttered a few words in a voice drained of emotion.

Myssa's eyes widened and darted to Piay.

'He says you are slavers and you will be put to death at dawn.'

The hut sweltered like a baker's oven. Dust motes drifted in a shaft of sunlight, and through the open door Piay could see the grassy plains reaching out to the purple mountains in the distance. Dawn had come and gone. He prayed that was a good sign.

The hut was small and circular – a storehouse by the looks of it – the walls constructed from wood packed with the rich red mud of the land. Hannu slumped on the opposite side of their prison, staring sullenly at the view outside. Freedom was so close, but every time they approached the door, the guards outside jabbed them with spears until they retreated.

Despite the looming threat to their lives, Piay felt only one thought burning in his mind. Myssa had been taken before first light. He prayed she had not been harmed.

'It was a mistake to light the fire before we had a chance to study them,' Hannu grumbled.

'Perhaps they didn't like my song. No benefit in complaining now. We made our choice.'

'Eaten by lions or captured by a murderous band is no choice.'

The tramp of feet echoed. One of the guards stepped into the doorway and flicked the tip of his spear, urging Piay and Hannu to stand. They edged out into the bright morning.

At the centre of a spear-guard stood an older man in a lime green robe and a sash of the hide of some wild cat. He wore a headdress with a fan of white, pink and yellow feathers and his cheeks had been scarred with deep ornamental incisions. Their leader, Piay thought.

'Where is Myssa?' he blurted, knowing the elder would not understand him. 'If you have harmed her—'

As one, the warriors levelled their spears and hunched into an attacking posture. Piay bit off his angry words.

The leader looked Piay up and down, getting the measure of him. His cold gaze gave nothing away. Then he turned and walked away. The guard swarmed around Piay and Hannu, prodding them with spears to follow.

The leader appeared to be striding towards a lone acacia tree rising from the plain, oddly jarring in the featureless landscape. On top of its spindly silver trunk, the mushroom-shaped canopy offered some shade from the merciless sun.

As they neared, Piay glimpsed Myssa step out from behind the tree. He felt his heart leap to see she was alive.

'Have they harmed you?' Piay demanded when they reached the circle of shade. Myssa shook her head.

'Do as they say,' she said, 'and they will not hurt you.'

The leader strode past the tree and beyond Piay could see rows of graves, the sun-hardened red earth heaped over each one. The guard prodded Piay and Hannu up to the cemetery and as the leader turned to face them, Myssa stepped beside him.

The leader spoke in a deep, musical voice filled with authority and sadness. When he paused, Myssa said, 'His name is Dume and he is the chieftain of this clan. This is what he said.'

She began to translate the leader's words in a stumbling manner.

'Here lie those who fell under the swords of the slavers, cut down like barley beneath the scythe.' Myssa's eyes gleamed and Piay could see how she personally felt the suffering she was recounting. 'Since the lizard came from God to tell us that all men must die, we have prepared ourselves for that end. But not this way. Those who have left this world come to us in our dreams and tell us of their torment.'

Piay looked out across the graves, for the first time seeing the true cost of Hanbaal's business.

'Tell him we are not slavers,' he said.

'I have,' Myssa replied. 'That is why you are still alive.'

The leader spoke again, and Myssa translated: 'We live in peace here, at one with the sun and the wind and the grass and the rain. We farm. We sing. We give praise to God for all that is bestowed upon us. But then your slavers came. They took our women. Some of our strongest men. They killed those who tried to defend our people. We never harmed you. We only want friendship. No more. If you wish war, and death, so be it.'

When Myssa finished speaking, there was only the sighing of the wind across the plains.

'Tell him I do not speak for the slavers,' Piay began. 'I speak for the Pharaoh. I wish only friendship between Egypt and the . . .' He held out his hand for Myssa to respond.

'They call themselves "the people". *Abantu* in their tongue.'

'. . . only friendship with the Abantu. We mourn the loss of lives and when I return to the Pharaoh, I vow that amends will be made.'

Piay hoped he had said enough. He was bargaining for more than just his life. They would need to become friends, perhaps even partners in trade, if he was to get the elephants he needed.

'Will there be enough gold in Egypt to meet all the promises you have made?' Hannu breathed.

Piay silenced him with a glare.

Myssa bowed her head with the chieftain and when she was done conveying Piay's message, she said, 'Dume hears your words. But if you wish any friendship with the Abantu, you will need to prove you carry no evil in your hearts. Only time will tell that.'

Piay crouched in the long grass. The sun edged the western mountains and shadows streamed across the plains to pool in the hollows. The birdsong had spiralled into a cacophony as dusk crept in, punctuated by the jarring *gwaak, gwaak*, of a flitting bird with a brilliant purple plumage. It swooped across a cloud of pink flowers that filled the air with a perfume as sweet as honey.

Hannu had barely moved for the last hour, his eyes scanning the trees that lined the muddy lake.

Next to him, a tall young man squatted, balancing on his spear. Jabilo grinned easily, his good nature at odds with most of the other Abantu, who had treated Piay with suspicion as he tried to persuade the chieftain to trust him. Dume had at least allowed Piay and Hannu to reclaim their swords, but when Piay asked for aid in tracking down the elephants, the chieftain had only offered his youngest scout.

Jabilo had led them west at dawn, loping across the grasslands until more trees began to dot the landscape. The scout had followed trails, pausing to brush the crushed grass or sniff the air. Occasionally he chatted to them in his own tongue. Though Piay had no idea what he was saying, Jabilo seemed cheered by his own conversation, bursting into peals of laughter.

Finally they'd come to this watering hole, where Jabilo had flapped his hands until they realised he wanted them to hide.

Piay jolted from his reverie as a stork swooped down in a flapping of white feathers and settled gracefully on the edge of the lake.

'If we see these great beasts, what then?' Hannu asked. 'We three are supposed to round them up and lead them back?'

'We persuade Dume to help us. We will need to train them so they are obedient. I observed Taita among the few horses our army had at Thebes. It was not an easy task to make those creatures bend to the will. But elephants?'

'He will not help us. What gain is there for him? At best he tolerates us because of Myssa. Without her, we would be knocking on the gates of the afterlife.'

'We have to find some way to win him over,' Piay stressed. 'We cannot be defeated at this stage.'

Jabilo hissed and pressed a finger to his lips. The ground began to throb, like the heartbeat of the world itself, and from away in the trees came a blaring like a giant trumpet.

Piay felt a tingle of excitement. He'd heard so many tales of these great beasts from Myssa on their travels that he had conjured up a vision that surely could never exist. He sensed

Hannu tense. His assistant's hand went to his sword, as if that could do any good.

Staring through the clouds of midges dancing above the muddy water, Piay watched the branches of the trees begin to shake. Another blast of the trumpet. The ground rumbled more.

The first of the great beasts pushed itself past the swaying branches and lumbered to the water's edge. Piay's imagination had not been wrong! If anything, the elephant was more majestic than he had dreamed. It stood at least half the height of the mast on Hanbaal's ship. It was grey, and the skin looked so thick Piay doubted even an arrow could puncture it. The trunk snaked down, those huge ears twitching. Two cruel tusks curled out from the jaw, looking as if they could rip a man in two with one shake of the head.

Piay gasped as more of those beasts trailed out of the trees and squelched through the mud into the lake's edge. He marvelled as he watched those trunks suck up water and then whip up to spray the liquid across their backs.

The size of them. The power. Why, with an army of these elephants, the Hyksos would flee in terror the moment they appeared.

Piay grinned. The Oracle had been right: *Tame the beast that is both serpent and bull.* Here their hopes were enshrined. Here was victory guaranteed.

Beside him, Hannu gaped. 'How in the name of Ra are we going to train a beast like that?'

'Is there any way to persuade him?' Piay pleaded.

Myssa shook her head. She prowled around the campfire they had built on the edge of the settlement. 'I have begged Dume to help us. He listens to me with respect, but he sees no need to help you.'

'And without his help, there is no hope,' Hannu grunted. 'We cannot do this on our own.'

Only bursts of chittering from the woods and the lowing of the cattle broke the evening peace that lay across the settlement. The Abantu had retired to their huts and their families. Piay looked over the landscape, bright in the moonlight, but he felt only unease. He could feel that earlier hope already slipping away.

Two days had passed since they had wandered back from the watering hole and Piay had asked for an audience with Dume. He'd even called on Myssa to send Jabilo in to argue on their behalf, but the chieftain had dismissed the scout. Piay had offered gold and grain and jewels and linen. But Dume had merely wandered out of his hall to the acacia tree and jabbed a finger at the lines of graves. The chieftain knew they were not slavers, yet they were tainted by association with Hanbaal and his crew. In the end Piay had trekked into the woods on his own to be alone with his thoughts and conjure up a new plan, before returning to his companions.

Hannu tossed another dry branch on the fire.

'We could walk to another settlement to find someone who might help us.'

Piay shook his head. 'The legacy of the slavers is well known everywhere. The Abantu have only suspicion of strangers. And who can blame them . . .' His voice trailed off as he saw Myssa peering past his shoulder into the night. 'What is it?'

'Lights,' she said.

Hannu was already on his feet, striding to the edge of the fire's glow.

'Myssa is right. There. See?'

Piay squinted into the dark. He could see a constellation of lights drifting through the trees like fireflies.

Hannu whipped out his sword.

'Sakir has found us,' he growled. 'I knew we should not have rested in one place for so long.'

'We had no choice,' Myssa said.

Hannu shook his head. 'Is there to be no escape, ever?'

Piay rested a hand on his assistant's shoulder.

'Hold fast. We still do not know—'

'Who else could it be?' Hannu snapped.

The lights drifted closer and then broke out of the trees. Piay could see they were torches. He breathed in the sharp scent of pitch.

He could make out the shadowed shapes of a horde of men. They strode out of the trees and marched towards the settlement.

'They have drawn their swords,' Hannu said. 'We cannot defeat that many. My advice – run, and run fast.'

'Wait,' Myssa said, 'Those are not the ones you call the barbarians.'

The figure at the front of the band looked like a ghost in the gloom, his white robes giving off a faint glow.

'Hanbaal?' Hannu said.

Piay heard movement behind him. The Abantu were emerging from their huts. The men had snatched up their spears and their long oval shields. Dume's voice rumbled.

'The chieftain has ordered his warriors to defend the village,' Myssa translated.

Hanbaal held up his hand and brought his men to a halt.

'We have waited long enough!' he boomed.

'The madman,' Hannu growled. 'What is he doing?'

The Abantu warriors surged to the edge of the village and levelled their spears, bracing for an attack. Piay drew his sword and stepped past the spear-guard.

'Go back!' he shouted to Hanbaal.

'I have an empty hold and here is all I need to fill it,' the slaver called back. 'Your quest to find the elephants is doomed. I will never see the gold I was promised.'

'Go, or there will be a slaughter.'

Hanbaal laughed. 'Spears against swords and axes? The slaughter will not be on my side. I know that from experience. And once we are done, we will burn this village to the ground for daring to resist us.'

Piay looked along the line of bristling spears. He felt the weight in the air. Any moment now Dume would give the order to attack, and then there could be no good outcome.

He stabbed his sword towards Hanbaal. 'You will take some casualties, you know that. Perhaps even you.'

'Then let the chieftain spare thirty of his strongest men and we can avoid any battle.'

Piay could sense those Abantu warriors readying themselves.

'I have a better idea.'

'Speak.'

'Let you and I fight. The victor decides the course ahead.'

'No!' Myssa cried out at his back.

Hanbaal's lips curled into a grin. 'We have never fought, but you know I will defeat you. My sword is longer, my skills better. I have honed them in many fights across half the world.'

'Piay. Do not sacrifice yourself,' Myssa cried again.

'She's right,' Hannu growled. 'Don't take that risk.'

Piay turned to them. 'I have no choice. I cannot see these people slaughtered. Myssa, go to Dume. Tell him to hold his men back. Tell him what I plan to do.'

Myssa thrust her way through the warriors into the settlement.

Piay turned to Hanbaal. 'Let us make this quick. I have had a hard day and I am ready for my bed.'

'And I am fully rested and well fed,' Hanbaal said, his grin widening. 'So quick it will be.'

The slaver commanded his men to stand firm, then drew his crescent sword. He waved it from side to side, letting the torchlight dance along the edge.

Piay sighed. 'Are we performing to delight children? Enough play. Fight.'

With the flash of a striking cobra, Hanbaal lunged forwards. Piay gripped his sword tighter and hurled himself at his opponent.

The two blades clashed in a shower of sparks. Hanbaal was as good as he had boasted. His blade blurred, high then low, the light streaming off it. He fought in a manner Piay had not seen before, his feet flying like one of the temple dancers, his robe swirling as he circled to give more force to a hacking strike.

For a moment, Piay was wrong-footed by this agility, but he danced back when he saw Hanbaal begin to turn, then thrust as the slaver's blade sliced through thin air. This time Hanbaal was caught off guard. As he stumbled back, Piay hacked and sliced in a relentless assault. The swords clashed continually, but Piay was denying his opponent any chance to recover. And then he glimpsed his moment.

As Hanbaal swung his sword up in a half-hearted attempt to parry a strike, his left foot skidded in the dust. Piay jabbed his right foot, knocking the slaver's legs out from under him. As Hanbaal tumbled, Piay struck the sword from his hand with the flat of his blade, and when his opponent slammed to the ground, Piay leaped over him.

Piay held his sword to Hanbaal's throat. The slaver raised his trembling hands over his head and forced a smile.

'You have defeated me. There is no need to continue this battle any longer.'

'Perhaps I should finish you off,' Piay said, looking down the length of his blade, 'to make sure there is no more of this deceit in days to come.'

'No, no, I surrender!' Hanbaal cried. His voice carried across the rows of Abantu warriors and the entire settlement. 'Let me go back to my ship and I vow I will never return to this place again.'

'You will take no more slaves here ever again?' Piay said, so the Abantu could hear.

'No more slaves,' Hanbaal announced. 'You have my word.'

'Very well.' Piay stepped back and sheathed his sword.

As Hanbaal heaved himself to his feet, he looked at Piay and gave a sly grin.

'Was that a good enough show for your purposes?' he breathed.

Piay showed a faint smile in return. The plan he had conjured with the slaver earlier had worked as well as he had hoped.

'Do not forget, I meant what I said,' he murmured. 'You will never again capture any of these people. That is part of our deal.'

He felt relieved that he had also found a way to protect these kindly people from the slaver's machinations.

'Very good. Do not forget, more gold,' Hanbaal whispered with a wink as he stepped away. 'Much more gold. Twice my weight now.'

The Abantu warriors stepped back to allow Piay through. As he walked past them, he glanced into the faces of the silent sentinels and saw a new-found respect.

Myssa came out of the settlement and put her arms around his neck.

'I am pleased you are alive.' Her voice was unsteady.

Piay's heart beat faster at the feel of her body against his, at her embrace.

'You have courage,' she murmured, 'to risk your life for these people.'

'Your praise is undeserved,' Piay whispered. 'I will explain later.'

Myssa pulled back. Piay felt a pang of regret that he could no longer smell the perfume of her skin.

Hannu was waiting at the end of the line of warriors.

'Still alive, then,' he said.

'How could I die? You would be lost without me.'

Dume was waiting by the doorway of his hall, his crown of feathers upon his head. Myssa moved to the chieftain's side and spoke to him in the Abantu tongue. Dume stared into Piay's eyes as she talked.

When Myssa had finished, the chieftain began speaking. Myssa beamed as she translated.

'He says you have shown great courage and you have proven yourself a true friend of the Abantu. The Abantu will offer you the hand of friendship in return. They will help you capture the elephants, and train them, if that is possible.'

Piay bowed. 'I thank the chieftain for his generosity.'

He felt relief. His ploy had worked. He thought back to his excursion through the woods to the beach earlier that day, signalling until Hanbaal came across in the rowing boat and then negotiating his plan before returning. He hadn't told Hannu or Myssa. He didn't want to risk giving the game away. Nor did he want their conscience burdened if his scheme had gone wrong and ended in death.

As Piay walked away, Hannu slipped in beside him. His assistant breathed, 'Call that a fight? You could have cut Hanbaal to pieces before he'd even swung his blade. Some might say it was merely a good show for the Abantu.'

Piay said nothing.

Hannu nodded. 'A show for the Abantu,' he repeated. 'A clever and cunning show.'

He strode ahead, seeing no need to discuss the matter further.

T he plains sweltered under the midday sun. The wind had dropped on the grasslands and only the chirp of crickets broke the silence. Thirty Abantu warriors crouched in the bushes, faces crusted white as if for war, spears erect. None of them moved. Piay did not think there were enough men. But Dume had insisted thirty was the correct number and so they'd set off with this hunting band at first light.

'I say we stand back,' Hannu murmured. 'Let those who know what they're doing get their hands dirty.'

'On this occasion I am in full agreement,' Piay replied. 'Myssa made the right choice to remain in the village.'

An elephant trumpeted somewhere nearby and Hannu jumped.

'By the beak of Horus, I will be glad when this is over. Men I can fight. These great beasts will squash me like a scarab in my own dung.'

The ground trembled, and Piay felt the tremors grow stronger. The elephants were coming.

Piay stared towards the trees until he saw a grey mountain emerge in a shuddering of branches. It was a bull, bigger than any he had witnessed at the watering hole. This was what he wanted. Through Myssa, Dume had said the older elephants were better for war than the younger ones, less afraid, more easily trained to attack.

As the elephants came into view, Piay counted eight – some smaller males, females and young. For now, the plan was to capture only one and to learn how to train him.

When the bull was close, the Abantu warriors burst from their hiding place. Lowering their spears, they raced into a circle around their prey. The bull recognised the threat immediately. It spread its huge ears and raised its head and tusks high, thrashing its trunk from side to side.

Piay was relieved when he saw the other elephants cower back. If they'd chosen to attack as one, as he expected, they'd have crushed the Abantu in a moment.

The warriors at the rear jabbed the elephant with their spears, goading him. With a roar, the bull twisted towards the attackers. With the bull distracted, the warriors at the front tossed aside their spears and unfurled the ropes made of braided hide that had been coiled around their waists. Dume had said these were near-unbreakable. Piay couldn't believe that, not when faced with the power and fury of a cornered bull elephant.

The ropes had loops at the end, with knots that slid when the rope was pulled. The bravest of the warriors dashed forwards and caught the loop on one of the tusks, dragging it down until it was close to that thick grey skin. Another loop lashed around the second tusk.

The bull roared again, aware that it had been caught. Lurching forwards, the elephant dragged the two men holding the ropes. Though they strained and dug in their heels, they were powerless to stop it.

But then a third loop ensnared a tusk, and a fourth, and the bull's roars became more furious. Enraged, it ducked its head and lunged.

One warrior was too slow. As he fumbled with his rope, a tusk ripped through him. The man screamed as the bull wrenched up its head with the warrior still impaled on the tip. The warrior clutched at the tusk, trying to pull himself free. Still roaring, the beast flung its head from side to side. The man flew off, crashed into a bush and lay still.

The Abantu warriors dashed this way and that, confusing the beast. When it had grown dizzy, one of the hunters ran in front of it, dragging his rope. Another man grabbed the end of it and yanked it tight across the lower part of the elephant's front legs. Two more ropes were whipped across its legs and six warriors heaved.

Piay watched the elephant try to push forwards, but the ropes held the legs fast and it crashed down on its front. The Abantu were upon it in an instant, lashing ropes around its head. Warriors gripped the other ends of those ropes. In no time, the beast was secure and once it had been goaded back to its feet, the hunting party dragged on the ropes to hold it back and guide it.

Hannu folded his arms and nodded.

'Only one man dead. That went better than I expected.'

'A small step, but an important one,' Piay said. 'Now we know the elephants can be captured, the days of Hyksos rule are numbered.'

Piay watched Myssa sitting with the young Abantu warrior, Jabilo, in the shade of the acacia tree by the cemetery. How quick to smile she was, how gentle, how kind. Hanging on her every word, Jabilo bowed his head towards her, his face determined. After his journey across the plains with Piay and Hannu, the warrior wanted to learn the Egyptian tongue and Myssa had taken it upon herself to teach him.

As he studied Myssa, Piay wrestled with the strange emotions churning inside him. Was this love he felt? If it was, he was not sure he wanted it. At times he luxuriated in a warmth like the moment after waking before he left his bed. At other times he felt an ache as painful as hunger. How did others ever endure this?

Myssa clapped her hands when he strode over and said, 'Speak to Piay, Jabilo.'

The young warrior grinned. 'Hello, big man.'

Piay laughed. 'Hello, Jabilo.'

'He learns fast,' Myssa exclaimed. 'Soon he will be speaking as well as any Egyptian.'

The bull elephant's trumpeting blared from the pen on the far side of the settlement, followed by panicked shouts. Piay turned and ran towards it.

The journey back with the beast had been slow, but it had bowed to the will of the hunting band. For the last week, Hannu had overseen attempts to train the elephant with food and water, goads and ropes.

When Piay reached the pen, he glimpsed a group of Abantu gathered in a circle. Behind them, the bull threw its head back and bellowed.

Piay pushed his way through the men and women to find Hannu kneeling beside one of the Abantu warriors. The fallen man was writhing in agony.

Hannu looked up. 'His leg is broken. The beast hit him so hard he almost flew into the afterlife.'

Piay shook his head, puzzled. 'The elephant seems as wild as the day it was captured.'

'No change, not even a little.'

The Abantu lifted the injured man and carried him away for treatment. Hannu led Piay to the pen where more of the warriors ran around the elephant, using their spears to try to control it.

'Nothing we do works,' Hannu said. 'The bull is as stubborn as you are. I'm starting to think these elephants can't be trained.'

'There has to be a way.' Piay watched the roaring beast and the Abantu scattering to avoid its tusks. 'The Oracle said this was how we would defeat the Hyksos. And we have heard tales of how the elephants have been used in war.'

'Then we're not going about this training in the right way, that's all I can say. And the Abantu don't know any better.'

Piay felt his frustration rising. A season had passed since they had left home. How long would it take to break this creature's spirit? How long to capture and train enough elephants to take back to Egypt? For all he knew, the Hyksos might have already retaken Thebes, but he had to keep hoping, keep striving to meet the demands Taita had set for him.

'We must seek out another path,' he said. 'Let us talk to Dume.'

'There is nothing else that can be done,' Myssa said.

She glanced at the chieftain in his throne, waiting to see if he had more to say. His hall was ten times the size of the other homes in the settlement, and airy in the heat of the day. Old shields scarred by battle stood along one wall and sumptuous cloths dyed red and gold and green hung on the wood-and-clay walls.

Dume bowed his head in thought, the feathers in his crown swaying. When he looked up, his features softened. He spoke again, his voice barely a whisper, and Myssa translated.

'The Abantu do not have the skills to train the elephant,' she said. 'It has never been part of their way. They have tried, for you, to pay you back for your courage in defending the settlement. But this work is beyond them.'

Piay nodded. 'There are those who do have these skills, though. Does Dume know where they might be?'

Myssa asked the chieftain and then said, 'There is a kingdom to the south. A land of fierce warriors. They use the elephant in battle to crush their enemies.'

'Hanbaal spoke of this kingdom,' Piay said. 'If their war elephants are already trained, we could buy some and march them back to Egypt.'

'Dume says he can tell you how to find this kingdom' Myssa continued, 'but he fears they will not help you. The people there loathe strangers and keep their secrets close to their hearts.'

'There must be some way,' Piay pressed.

Dume stroked his chin as he thought. He seemed to reach some conclusion, for he looked up at Myssa and spoke for a while, making sure she understood every word. Myssa nodded and turned to Piay.

'This is how the Abantu will repay you for your courage – Dume will send his word that you are trustworthy and that these people should do all they can to heed your request.' She paused and added in her own words, 'This is a great gift. The Abantu are known far and wide and their word is trusted. The chieftain will stake his reputation on you. Remember this when you walk that land. If you fail, you will not only fail yourself and Egypt. You will fail the Abantu.'

Piay bowed. He felt the weight of this responsibility much more greatly than Myssa realised. He thought back to those lives lost when he had first encountered Sakir. He could not have another stain upon his soul.

'Offer the chieftain my eternal gratitude and let him know I understand what a gift this is,' Piay said. 'But how will he send his word with me?'

Once Myssa had the answer, she said, 'He will send Jabilo with you and he will speak on Dume's behalf. Jabilo admires you and will greatly enjoy the opportunity to learn at your feet and to see new places.'

Piay felt relief. Here at least was an opportunity.

'Then there is no time to lose,' he said. 'We must be away immediately.'

The sun was slipping towards the west by the time Jabilo had said goodbye to his family and friends. The young warrior squatted on the outskirts of the settlement, drawing patterns in the dust with the haft of his spear while Piay and Hannu stood with Myssa by the acacia tree.

'What is wrong?' Myssa could sense the strained atmosphere.

Piay stared up at the stars beginning to twinkle in the darkening sky. He had been turning this moment over in his mind for so long, yet he struggled to find the right words.

'This is where we must part company.' He kept his voice steady and showed no emotion. Inside, though, he felt as if he was sinking into cold water.

'Oh,' Myssa said, her eyes widening. 'But there is still so much to do.'

Piay took her hand. 'This is the right time and the right place.'

Myssa swallowed. 'You have not yet completed your quest.'

'You have been wise and loyal and brave. You have brought light into our lives. It is only right to say that I . . . that Hannu and I are in your gratitude, for we would not have advanced in our quest without your aid. You have earned your freedom and I must . . . grant it.'

Myssa's eyes gleamed in the last of the day's light. She seemed touched by his words, but there was a sadness there, too – a sadness he also felt. He would miss her company, her fierce intelligence, her wit.

'These are not your people,' Piay continued, 'and I cannot replace what you have lost. But I have seen you among them and you seem at home. Yes, I said there is always a place for you with me, and Hannu, and that is true. But I feel you could find some peace here and I want you to seize that opportunity, for peace is hard to come by in this world.'

'You are a good man,' she breathed.

A part of him had hoped she would reject his offer, but he knew that had been a futile dream. She had her own life in Kush, a chance to replace the one that had been stolen from her, and who would not want to return to that? If he had been in her place, he would wish to be back in Egypt, with Taita and the lavish life he had lived at court.

'You will find it easier to return to Kush from here, if that is what you decide,' Piay said. 'I think Dume would send two of his warriors to protect you on your journey.'

'I will ask him,' Myssa said.

Her lashes fluttered down. She opened her lips as if she was about to say something more, but no words came.

'Then let me say goodbye,' said Piay. 'Perhaps we will meet again some day on the long road of life.'

Myssa smiled. 'Perhaps we will.'

Piay turned and walked away. He imagined Myssa standing under the tree, watching him leave. He tried to consider what her expression might be, but he couldn't bring himself to look back.

Hannu stayed for a moment to say his own goodbyes and then he hurried to catch up.

For a moment they walked in silence towards where Jabilo waited.

'Myssa said I was a good man,' Piay said. 'You must have heard that.'

'Don't let it go to your head. You still have a lot to learn.' Hannu trudged on a few paces and then added in a softer tone, 'It will be hard for you, I know. But you did the right thing to let her go.'

Piay knew Hannu was right, but that didn't diminish the ache.

'Is this how you felt when the Hyksos took the life of your wife?'

For a while Hannu didn't respond. Then he said, 'A feeling that the light of the world has been extinguished and that there would be only darkness ahead? Aye.'

'I understand now why you left the care of the Blue Crocodile Guards and I found you that day sitting in the dust on the street. I understand many things now.'

'What's done is done. We can only move onwards.'

'You have some wisdom for a fighting man.' Piay sighed. 'Before we left, Taita said to me, "A man cannot learn who he truly is until he has suffered." I think I would rather live in ignorance.'

The two men strode towards the trees and as they passed Jabilo, he dropped in behind them.

n the ruddy light streaming through the trees, the night creatures began to stir and the shrieks and cries echoed to the high branches. Enveloped in those sounds, Piay stirred from his reflections. He tried to pick out the trail through the sea of darkness that was washing across the woods. If night had fully fallen by the time they reached the beach, they would light a fire to signal to Hanbaal to send the rowing boat ashore.

Jabilo had moved ahead of them to lead the way. He knew this forest well, and the barely visible trails that criss-crossed it. As the young warrior loped along the track, Piay watched him pause and sniff the air.

'What is wrong?' Piay asked.

'Men,' He twirled a finger in a circle. 'Here.'

'Hanbaal's crew, hunting for food?' Piay suggested to Hannu.

'Perhaps. They may be sick of fish by now.'

'Still, it would be wise not to draw attention to ourselves. Just in case.'

Hannu nodded. 'Agreed.'

Piay waved his hand up and down to signal to Jabilo that they were to keep low. The warrior understood and hunkered down. They pushed forwards again, as fast as they could in the growing dark. No one spoke.

Piay felt his senses catch fire. He strained to hear whatever it was that had alerted Jabilo, but the discord of the waking forest drowned out all else. His eyes darted, yet with the thickness of the vegetation and with the growing gloom it was impossible to see more than two spears' lengths on either side.

He felt unease begin to dig its talons into his gut. Would Hanbaal's men really be roaming through the forest in the deepening dark?

Jabilo prowled on, his speed increasing. He was unnerved, too.

Piay peered ahead. He thought he could see a hint of night sky through the trees and smell brine upon the breeze, clean and sharp after the heavy aromas of the sweating forest vegetation. They were close to the beach. Just a little longer.

A branch cracked behind them, loud enough to cut through the forest din.

Piay and Hannu whirled, both drawing their swords. Piay strained and thought he could hear running feet.

He flashed a glance at Hannu, who nodded, and they slipped off the path, hiding behind two cedar trees, one on either side of the trail. Jabilo darted behind a shrub with long, spiky leaves.

Piay pressed his back against the bark, feeling his heart thump. He tightened his grip on the hilt of his sword.

The light had almost faded.

The footsteps echoed clearly, thumping along the baked earth of the trail towards them. Piay held his breath, calculating the position of whoever was tracking them. When the sound of running feet was almost upon them, Piay leaped out of his hiding place and swung up his sword. Hannu bounded beside him at the same time.

A shriek rang out.

Piay blinked, at first not certain what he was seeing in the gloom.

Myssa was standing there, hands pressed to her mouth in shock. His sword wavered a finger's width from her breast. If he had mistimed his movement by even an instant, she would have plunged into his blade.

'Wh-what are you doing here?' he stammered.

Myssa let her hands fall away. 'I have made the decision to accompany you on your voyage. As a free woman.'

Piay could scarcely believe what he was hearing. He felt a foolish smile creep across his lips and he quickly pushed it aside.

'But your home—'

'My home will be there when I choose to return. Besides, you said how much I had contributed to your success on this road. It would be mean-spirited to deny you my help for the remainder of your quest.' Her eyes twinkled in the dying light.

Piay wanted to embrace her.

'Very well,' he said with a shrug, 'you are welcome to accompany us.'

Myssa grinned as if she could see through his pretence.

Smiling too, Hannu sheathed his sword.

'I'll feel safer now if we encounter any more pirate captains.'

Piay barely choked down his joy as he turned back to the path. Jabilo bounded ahead.

Soon the crashing of the waves on the shore could be heard through the trees and Piay caught glimpses of moonlight glinting on water. Then they were out of the forest's tropical heat and into the cooling sea breeze.

The rowing boat had been dragged up on to the sand just beyond the surf. Piay could see no sign of the oarsman, nor any other member of Hanbaal's crew.

'Perhaps they are here hunting, as we thought,' he began until he saw Jabilo, rigid as a statue, ahead of him.

As Piay crunched down the beach, Jabilo stepped aside, revealing what had gripped his attention.

A spike had been jammed into the sand – a branch, crudely and hastily whittled. Impaled on it was the head of the rowing boat oarsman, those sightless eyes staring up to the trees as a warning to any who dared approach.

Piay stared back for a moment and then he said, 'Sakir.'

Hannu backed down the beach, his restless gaze roaming along the line of trees. Piay grabbed Myssa's hand and pulled her towards the rowing boat, waving at Jabilo to hurry with them.

'Make haste,' Piay urged. 'We do not want to be caught with our backs to the sea.'

He'd convinced himself that Jabilo had been wrong about the men stalking through the forest around them – that it had only been Myssa's hurrying footsteps that he'd heard. He should have known better. How close had they come to being discovered? If the Hyksos had stumbled across them there, their lives would already be over, and, perhaps Myssa's, too.

As they scrambled through the sand to the rowing boat, Piay noticed Jabilo's eyes were wide with fear, and he glanced around as if some monstrous thing from Duat was about to descend on them. Though he was a warrior, it was unlikely he would have experienced the savagery of a man like Sakir.

Piay put a hand on his shoulder. 'All will be well,' he said.

Whether Jabilo understood his words, Piay didn't know, but the young warrior seemed reassured. He mimed pushing the rowing boat out and Piay nodded. Together they heaved it into the shallows.

Hannu walked backwards towards the water, keeping his eyes on the trees, until the cool surf was sluicing around his feet.

'Can't see any sign of them,' he muttered, 'but they're there. And if we're not quick, they'll see us and be on us.'

'Then stop grumbling and get in the boat,' Piay chided.

Hannu clambered in and offered a hand to help Myssa on board. Piay and Jabilo pushed the boat out until it floated easily and then they dragged themselves over the side. The bottom of the vessel was filled with fish. The hapless oarsman must have been foraging for food for Hanbaal's crew when the barbarians caught him.

Piay stared at that dark smudge of trees under the starry sky and wondered if Sakir was standing there, staring back. Hannu pulled on the oars.

'Will we ever be free of Sakir?' he said.

'You know what it will take to bring that about,' Hannu replied.

When the boat was finally rolling across the incoming waves towards the lamps of Hanbaal's ship, Piay relaxed a little. He glanced across the swell, but the rest of the ocean was dark. He felt his heart sink. He had convinced himself that the Hyksos' warships had been destroyed in the storm. But Sakir had clearly been following a strategy of stealth.

'Where have the barbarians moored their ships?' he asked.

Hannu grunted from his exertions. 'This coast is pitted with creeks. However many vessels he has left, all could be hidden away in any one of them while Sakir searches for us.'

Piay felt cool fingers on the back of his hand and realised it was Myssa.

'You have defeated Sakir before,' she whispered. 'You can do so again.'

Myssa left her fingers there and Piay did not pull his hand away.

n the lamplight washing across the deck of his ship, Hanbaal stood with his fists on his hips. He grinned as Piay pulled himself over the side.

'Where are the elephants?' he laughed.

'A discussion for another time,' Piay said. 'For now, we must be away from here as soon as possible. The Hyksos are close at hand.'

'Here?' The slaver's face darkened.

'They are on shore, hunting for us. Your man who took out this rowing boat is dead. It's only a matter of time before they come for this ship.'

Hanbaal cursed under his breath. He snapped an order to haul up the anchor and commanded his crew to prepare to sail.

Piay glimpsed Jabilo frowning as he watched the slaver move about the deck. No doubt he recognised him from the staged battle outside the settlement. He would have questions. But this was not the time.

Turning to Myssa, he said, 'I would wager Jabilo has not been on a vessel of this size – perhaps not on the open seas, either. He may be afraid as we voyage. Will you do what you can to soothe him?'

Myssa smiled. 'He will learn quickly enough. He is eager to see all this world has to offer.'

She ushered Jabilo towards the stern, where they squatted out of the way of the crew's labours. As they talked, Bast bounded up and slunk around Myssa, purring.

Piay slipped in beside Hannu at the rail as the ship sailed out of the bay. His assistant showed a gloomy face as he looked towards the shore.

'Time is running out for us,' Hannu said. 'With the Hyksos so close behind, once again we will be hard pressed to achieve what we want.'

Piay nodded. 'We can't keep running forever. Sooner or later we are going to have to take a stand.'

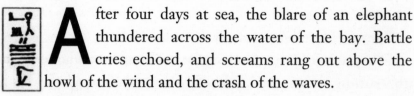

After four days at sea, the blare of an elephant thundered across the water of the bay. Battle cries echoed, and screams rang out above the howl of the wind and the crash of the waves.

Piay and Hannu leaped from their resting place and raced towards the prow. On the platform, Hanbaal frowned. He'd heard those sounds, too.

Across the deck, his men were returning to their benches, preparing to grab the oars to guide the ship out of the open water and into the sheltered bay. Hanbaal glanced back, no doubt wondering whether he should delay the order.

'Tell me those battle cries were not aimed at us,' the slaver said.

'How could they know we were coming?'

Piay shielded his eyes against the glare of the sun. He could make out a long line of trees, but the mysterious land beyond it hung in a haze.

Since leaving Azania, Hanbaal had forced a hard pace. They'd barely delayed to take on water, surviving on the fish that swarmed in those warm coastal waters. Of the Hyksos at their backs, they'd seen no sign, though Piay had long since given up hope of an escape. He'd been lured into a false sense of security when the ships went down on the reef, presuming that all the vessels had been lost. His enemies must have retreated to lick their wounds. And now Sakir was out there, somewhere, just over the horizon. They would never evade him. It was simply a matter of choosing when to fight.

Finally they'd closed in on this hot, steamy land where the Abantu said the kingdom that had mastered the war elephant was. Jabilo had passed on the knowledge Dume and the elders had communicated to him, and with his charts Hanbaal had calculated the most likely location.

But this was unknown territory to all of them. Hanbaal had never ventured this far south, and Jabilo had only fragmentary stories of the people who occupied this land.

Hanbaal turned to his crew and called, 'Furl the sail. Slow and steady.'

Without the wind in the sail, the ship's progress slowed and the drummer thumped his skins to set the pace. The oarsmen pulled to the beat.

The wind shifted direction and carried the screams across the water.

Hannu stared ahead. 'That is the sound of the dying. Once you have heard it, you never forget.'

Hanbaal moistened his lips. 'We may need to have another conversation about gold. In my mind's eye, I can now see three times my weight piled up and gleaming before me.'

'You will be well rewarded for whatever lies ahead,' Piay replied. He was prepared to empty the Pharaoh's coffers to achieve what they needed, and he knew Taita would back him.

As the ship skimmed the waves towards the bay, a thump reverberated off the hull, then another. Piay, Hanbaal and Hannu peered over the rail, afraid the vessel was plunging onto some hidden reef.

A body bobbed against the prow. An arrow protruded from the eye socket.

Piay studied it, taking in the streaks of white remaining on the face that suggested something akin to the Abantu war make-up. The muscular chest was bare, but a brown leather armour reached from his neck across his collar bones. Bands wrapped around the biceps, and from them trailed strips of long pale fur now sodden in the seawater.

Ahead more bodies littered the ocean, drifting with the currents.

Hanbaal raised his hand and the drumming stopped. The sailors leaned on their oars and the ship drifted in silence towards the shore. Arrows bristled from all of the floating bodies.

'I do not like the look of this,' Hanbaal murmured. 'We should turn back.'

'No,' Piay insisted. 'Keep going.'

The slaver hesitated and then raised his hand once more. The pounding of the drum rumbled, echoing the steady knocks of the bodies against the hull as the ship lurched forwards.

Hannu pointed to an upturned log-boat. A single oar floated nearby.

'Some kind of sea battle,' he said.

As they sailed into the mouth of the bay on calmer waters, the screams and the blaring of the elephants became punctuated with full-throated battle cries.

A battle was raging. Beyond the shallows, a multitude of log-boats dotted the blue water – two small navies in close combat. Eight men clustered in each boat. Arrows rained down from archers standing in the rear of the vessels. The shafts thumped into chests, limbs, heads. Some whistled by harmlessly, splashing into the swell or rattling into the wood of the boats. In the centre of the battle, opposing warriors hacked at each other with swords as their vessels rowed side by side. The waters ran pink.

Despite the fury of the conflict, Piay was fascinated by the fighting raging along the beach. Foot soldiers stabbed with spears and swords clashed. Two war elephants ripped through one army. They trampled warriors, gored others with their red-stained tusks. On their backs, riders urged them on into the throng.

Piay marvelled at the fury of those giant beasts. For the first time, he truly understood the Oracle's message. With these war elephants in the Pharaoh's army, the Hyksos horses would flee in terror. The barbarians' army would be routed.

Piay had barely dared hope that his quest would be a success, but he now felt a swell of exhilaration. If the gods were willing, he would soon be journeying back to Egypt where he would bask in his master Taita's praise.

Once they were in the bay, Hanbaal commanded his men to stop rowing. The crew dropped the anchor and the ship strained on the swell.

Piay watched the warriors in the boats observe the new arrival warily, no doubt each side fearing this was some ploy by their enemy. He wondered if they had ever even seen a vessel of this size. How terrifying must that be?

The deluge of arrows slowed, then stopped, the last few shafts fizzing into the water. As if on some unheard command, the log-boats rowed apart, one group disappearing around the edge of the bay. The warriors along the beach ground to a halt, staring, their weapons lowered to their sides. Then they, too, broke up, racing in opposite directions. The two war elephants lumbered on to a track through the trees and vanished.

In no time, the battle was over. Clouds of shrieking gulls swept in to feast on the remains.

'This is a bloody fight,' Hannu said as he looked across the field of bodies. 'And we're supposed to walk right into the middle of it?'

Soon after, the gulls soared into the blue sky with a thunderous beating of wings. Piay watched a knot of figures stride from the line of trees There were ten of them, coming to a halt halfway down the beach where they stared at the ship. Nine were warriors – towering men holding their spears in the crooks of their arms. They were dressed like the first corpse Piay had seen drifting in the waves, with the leather armour around the neck, bands trailing pale furs on the biceps, a studded belt from which hung a leather kilt cut into long flaps, and more pale fur hanging from straps around the shins.

At the centre of the group was a man with a tall head-dress constructed from a leather helmet from which sprouted multiple fans of brightly coloured feathers. He wore a long brown linen robe tied at one shoulder and what looked like a leopard skin thrown over it, like the *sem*-priests at the temple in Thebes, who mummified the corpses and chanted the incantations.

'They are waiting to greet us,' Myssa said.

'Or kill us,' Hannu added.

'We have no choice but to go ashore,' Piay noted. 'If they are the ones who commanded those magnificent war elephants, we must begin negotiations immediately.'

'I will accompany you,' Myssa said.

'It may be dangerous,' Piay said to her. 'You should stay here, where it is safe.'

Myssa cocked an eyebrow. 'I will accompany you.'

'But—'

'I am a free woman. I make my own decisions.'

'Don't waste your breath arguing,' Hannu grunted. 'Let's get on with it.'

'Good, good,' Hanbaal said, rubbing his hands. He showed a sly grin. 'The sooner you conduct your business, the sooner I can begin filling my coffers. Tell me who I should speak with in Thebes if you do not make it back alive.'

Piay slipped out of the rowing boat and strode through the surf. Hannu, Myssa and Jabilo kept close behind him.

They'd barely crunched on to the sand when Hannu whispered, 'They are not alone. The trees seethe with archers. They can cut us down in an instant.'

'I would expect no less.'

As they neared the group, Piay watched their eyes shift from him and Hannu to the more familiar figures of Jabilo and Myssa. That seemed to put them at ease, as he had intended.

Piay came to a halt two spears' lengths away from the welcoming party and bowed. He could see the one in the headdress was much older than the warriors, clearly a leader. His face was graven and his voice rumbled, low and unwelcoming. Myssa nodded, understanding; the dialect sounded to Piay like the tongue of the *abantu*.

'He says, "Leave here now. Or die."'

'Tell him we have been sent by the Pharaoh, the great king in the north, to discuss trade that will enrich such a powerful, exalted people.'

Myssa stumbled over the words a little. The leader of the group responded with only a few curt words.

'He says they do not trade with strangers.'

'We can become friends,' Piay pressed.

After another exchange, Myssa said, 'He says they are at war. Their king fights for the lives of the people of this land. They trust no one.'

Piay's mind raced. He could feel all they were hoping for slipping away.

'Tell him we may be able to help.'

Piay felt Hannu flinch beside him. As Myssa spoke, Piay watched a flicker of interest cross the other man's face.

'He will convey your offer to the king,' Myssa said. 'They will return to this place at first light to give their response.'

Piay bowed again. The one in the headdress offered a cold stare and led his men up the beach and into the trees.

The lamplight glinted in the eyes of Piay, Hannu and Myssa as they sat cross-legged. The warm night was filled with the sounds of the creaking ship and the lapping of the waves and the snoring of the sailors as they slept on their benches or in any space they could find across the deck.

Piay looked from one to the other. 'Tell me your thoughts.'

Hannu tapped his ear. 'Must have some water in there. It sounded like you were asking for guidance.'

Piay sighed.

Hannu turned to Myssa. 'Which cannot be true. Because Master Piay has never asked for advice in his life. And when it is freely given, he chooses to ignore it.'

Piay folded his arms. 'If you have nothing to offer—'

'I always have plenty to offer,' Hannu replied. 'If only you had ears to hear.'

'Piay is growing wise,' Myssa said, rubbing Bast's head. 'A wise man always listens to the wisdom of others before reaching his decision.'

In times past Piay would have bristled at Hannu's words, resenting the implication of weakness. But Myssa somehow had a way about her that soothed every situation.

Hannu said. 'My experience tells me it is never a good thing to push your way into other people's fights. These things are always more complicated than they seem at first.'

'And Hanbaal's crew are not fighting men,' Myssa said. 'He will not want you risking their necks, just so you can lay claim to some elephants.'

'You saw how the two sides fled when our ship arrived,' Piay said. 'It might be that we could frighten them into submission without unsheathing our blades.'

Hannu shrugged. 'Only if they don't care what they're fighting about. And if they didn't care, they wouldn't be fighting.'

'What, then?' Piay said. 'We cannot leave. We need those elephants.'

Myssa said, 'Your master trained you in the many arts of peace and war, yes?'

Piay nodded.

'Then if you do not wish for war, perhaps peace is the right course.'

Piay frowned. 'What do you mean?'

'Bring the two sides together. Help them find some common ground to avoid this bloodshed.'

'Hannu?'

'She has something. But you must go into this with open eyes. This will be a delicate situation and much will be hidden from us. There is plenty that could go wrong and we must be prepared for that outcome.'

'Still, I feel this is our best choice . . . perhaps our only choice.' Piay paused, 'Do you agree?'

Hannu nodded. 'I agree.'

The rain had come overnight, so hard and fast it seemed like it would never end. Still it fell. Piay breathed in the dank aroma of the sodden vegetation as he stood on the beach in the thin light of dawn.

Hannu, Myssa and Jabilo waited behind him. No one spoke.

Piay glimpsed movement in the shadows beneath the trees and the one in the headdress walked out with his band of warriors.

He raised a hand, and then spoke.

'He says we should go with him for an audience with the king,' Myssa said.

'Into the den of spears, then,' Hannu muttered.

The forest steamed as the heat rose. Moisture dripped from silky emerald leaves. Frogs croaked and birds swooped among the high branches, releasing whooping cries.

Piay, Hannu and Jabilo hung back as they trailed past pools of sunlight coming through the canopy, while Myssa eased her way into the confidences of the one with the headdress. She'd learned that his name was Omari and he was an advisor to the king, Chemue. He seemed to have little humour in him, though he warmed to Myssa's easy manner.

The track wound past shrubs with spiky pink flowers ripe with the aroma of honey, where gold and black butterflies fluttered, and through a swamp that filled the air with the reek of rot. They came to a wall of finely packed stone that was almost twice Piay's height. After the wooden huts of the Abantu, Piay felt surprised to see such a construction. The wall seemed ancient, the stones were weathered, and the trees clustered hard against it, almost as if it had pushed itself up out of the forest floor.

Omari led them through a gate into a sprawling city of narrow streets, the roads puddled and rutted with flies droning above the sticky mud. Shacks made of wood with roofs of leaves jumbled near the walls, but there were buildings of stone, too.

A mother with a baby at her breast stepped out of the house nearest the gate and stared at these strange visitors. Few travelled here from the lands around the Great Green, Piay presumed, and as they trudged through the mud, people ventured out to observe the new arrivals.

Once they'd left this crowded area, they stepped into a formal square, at the centre of which was a roughly hewn statue of an elephant. Beyond that was a grander stone building with two wings reaching out.

Two of the warriors waited at the entrance. Omari led the rest of the band under a shady portico into a smaller square with a pool at the centre. It was surrounded on every side by a covered walkway where the residents could stroll out of the heat of the sun.

Omari beckoned for them to follow him into a shadowy building. Soon they found themselves in a room with a wooden high-backed throne at the centre. On it sat the king. Chemue was a big, muscular man with scars from what must have been past battles on his cheeks. He was draped in the spotted pale fur and he also wore a headdress, the fan of feathers even more extravagant than the one Omari wore.

The king flexed his fingers and Myssa approached. As he spoke, he examined Piay and Hannu.

Myssa nodded and turned to the others. 'He knows I understand the tongue of these people and he is happy to use me as an intermediary in these discussions. The king wants to know what it is you wish to trade.'

Piay stepped forwards.

'Tell him spice, linen, papyrus ... weapons. Our swordsmiths are the best in the world.'

Chemue weighed this response.

'And what do you want that you do not already have?' Myssa asked on the king's behalf.

'Elephants. Trained elephants for war and men with the skill to ride them into battle. That is what this great kingdom is known for.'

The king beckoned Omari to the throne and they bowed their heads together in conversation for some time.

When they had finished their conversation, it was Omari who spoke. Myssa listened, then translated.

'A war is tearing our land ... our people ... apart. The forest runs red with blood and even women and children are put to the spear. How many lives will be lost before this is over? We cannot talk of trade while there is fighting and death.'

Piay nodded.

'Who is at war?' he asked.

Myssa listened, then said, 'The king is the rightful ruler of this land, a peaceful man beloved by his subjects. But his brother Temue has long coveted the throne and has promised riches to those who will join him in seizing power.'

*Warring brothers – a tale as old as time*, Piay thought.

'Tell them we will do what we can to help bring this war to an end,' he said. 'If we can put enough fear into Temue and his army, we may be able to bring them to talks to find some common ground. At the least, it will stop the fighting and the bloodshed.'

After Omari had discussed the matter with the king, he offered his response.

'If you help them, they will talk,' Myssa said. 'At this time they can say no more.'

'They're testing us,' Piay said. 'To see if they can trust us.'

'And who can blame them?' Hannu replied. 'Too much at stake to be trusting.'

'Tell them we will do what we can,' Piay said to Myssa. 'But ask them if we can see the war elephants. I want to learn what they have to offer.'

Piay breathed in the suffocating musk of the great beasts long before Omari led them to a vast stone-walled pen on the far side of the city. After climbing steps to the top of the wall, Piay looked down on ten of the elephants, using their trunks to snatch up bunches of leaves that three men tossed among them. They thrust the leaves into their mouths and chewed lazily.

'They look as good-natured as Bast,' Myssa noted.

'Aye,' Hannu replied. 'In my experience the most dangerous things do, until the time comes to reveal their true nature.'

'Ask how they train these beasts,' Piay said to Myssa.

Omari jabbed a finger towards the three men feeding the elephants.

'Those are the elephant riders, the keepers, the trainers,' Myssa translated. 'They are called Tumisi in this tongue and they are revered like . . .' She struggled to find the words and then said, 'Like our priests? Only a few families are Tumisi. The Tumiso is given an elephant when he is a boy and he is taught to train it by his family. They use only a hook, a long pole, and a short pole, though how they achieve so much with so little, Omari will not say. These are the secrets they keep and that knowledge is then passed from father to son. And over time, the boy and the elephant become . . . friends . . . perhaps brothers? They are joined together for life.'

Piay, frustrated, said, 'Then they cannot teach us to train our own elephants . . . and this is why we failed when we were with the Abantu.'

Myssa nodded. 'It takes time, it seems. A lifetime.'

Hannu grunted. 'Then we'll need these Tumisi to come with us. Will these people spare them if they are so rare and skilled?'

'We'll find a way,' Piay said.

Omari grinned – the first time his stone face had cracked. Myssa translated his words.

'He says you cannot imagine the power of the elephant until you see them in battle. Here they are calm. But when they charge an enemy, the ranks fall apart as if they were made of ash. Only terror comes from facing the elephant.'

The wind whipped across the deck and the lines sang. Hanbaal narrowed his eyes, his white robes swirling around him.

'Tell me again this will not cost me my ship or my crew.'

'You need have no worries,' Piay stressed. 'If the gods are kind, this will be done in no time, with no harm to anyone.'

The slaver looked from Piay to Hannu and then out to the edge of the bay, where Chemue's spies had warned that an attack would soon be materialising.

'If there is any damage done to my vessel or my crew, I will require full recompense.'

As Hanbaal stalked away across the deck to prepare his crew, Piay beckoned to Jabilo.

'You are ready?'

The Abantu warrior grinned. 'Ready, big man.'

Piay turned back to the bay and watched the rolling waves. After what seemed like an age, the first of the log-boats eased around the rocky outcropping to the south. Soon a multitude of the Temue vessels flooded in, paddles dipping as the rowers tried to seize the element of surprise, eight men in each. This time, under Piay's guidance, Chemue had not prepared a defence. The beach was deserted, the log-boats of Chemue's clan dragged up on the sand. To those new arrivals, the path seemed clear to the city where their hated enemy waited.

Piay raised his right hand. Hanbaal roared an order for the anchor to be raised and his oarsmen to begin their strokes. The drummer thumped his skins and the ship eased forwards, gathering speed.

Piay watched confusion turn to fear on the faces of those in the nearest log-boats. They had mounted an attack two days ago, and on that occasion Hanbaal's vessel had remained anchored and aloof from the strife.

The ship thrummed across the waves as it bore down on the log-boats. They were in formation, too tightly packed to manoeuvre. Some who could see disaster bearing down on them paddled faster, shifting their line.

One log-boat slammed into another. The first boat rolled, plunging the occupants into the water. The second log-boat careered into a third, setting off collision after collision until the navy milled in a confusion of upturned log-boats and flailing rowers.

Hanbaal's ship did not stop. The slaver yelled an order to the helmsman and the line of the vessel shifted to ensure it stayed in deeper water. Piay's plan was working well.

The ship ploughed into the outer edge of the log-boats. The small vessels shattered, overturned. Others plunged down as they were swamped. Yelling in terror, men leaped into the sea, attempting to swim to safety.

Jabilo hung over the rail and yelled, time and again, until his throat must have burned. Piay didn't understand the words, but he knew what he was saying: 'Ten more ships wait behind us. We are coming to destroy you. Surrender. Surrender.'

To add to his show, many of Hanbaal's crew rushed to the rail and thrust their swords into the air, roaring a battle cry.

Piay watched the boats at the rear of the tiny fleet turn and flee the way they had come. The mere size of Hanbaal's vessel had been more destructive than any pitched battle.

'That one!'

Hannu pointed over the rail at one of the log-boat rowers struggling to stay afloat in the water churning around the ship's keel. Three sailors tossed hide ropes into the turbulent sea until they had snagged the drowning man. Bracing themselves, they dragged him up the side of the ship and over the rail.

The rescued man collapsed on to the boards. When he raised his head, he trembled as he looked along the blades of the sailors who had captured him. Before the prisoner could panic, Jabilo squatted beside him and rested a comforting hand on the man's shoulder. Jabilo grinned, his words coming low and fast. It was a version of the message he had yelled to the fleeing log-boats in a tongue those warriors understood, a message that Piay with Myssa had taught him: 'We are merciful. We will spare your life. But you must tell your leader there is no hope left in this fight, for our force is too strong for you and we have allied with Chemue.'

Jabilo would tell the man to carry this message back to the rebel leader Temue, the king's brother, and urge him to meet with Chemue to find some common ground for peace. Piay hoped this would be enough.

Hanbaal yelled again and his men rushed to their benches, grasping their oars and heaving into perfectly timed strokes to pursue the surviving log-boats around the bay.

The men from the capsized log-boats clawed out of the water on to the broad beach. They barely had time to stagger to their feet when Chemue's army rushed out of the trees, screeching. The survivors of the confrontation on the water had nowhere to go, no weapons to defend themselves.

Chemue's men fell on them like vultures on a corpse in the desert, stabbing and tearing with their spears. The screams of the dying echoed across the bay. Those fleeing would be left in no doubt of the terrible costs of this defeat.

As the surf reddened, Piay looked away from the carnage. This was not his war, though he had now left his mark upon it. These were not his friends, nor his enemies, yet his actions had ended lives as surely as had his failings in the field that night beside the Nile. He felt queasy at the recognition that life was never as simple as he had once imagined.

Hanbaal's ship pursued the fleeing log-boats across the next bay and two beyond. By then the rowers were weakening from the strain of attempting to stay ahead. A few stood to loose arrows, but the shafts plunged harmlessly into the sea or rattled off the hull. Finally the log-boats swept in to shore.

As Hanbaal ordered the anchor to be lowered once again, Piay watched the escaping warriors race up the beach and into the trees, where Temue no doubt had his camp.

Piay glanced at Hannu. 'Now all we can do is wait.'

The moon hung over the water, limning the ship's mast with pale fire. From it, a silver road rolled out across the water and over the beach to where Piay crouched beside a tree festooned with pendulous yellow flowers. He whispered a prayer to Khonsu. All their plans turned on what was about to unfold, a plan as reckless as any Piay had attempted. This time he had convinced the others that they had little choice.

Hannu squatted beside him with Jabilo, both keeping watch in the dark of the forest to make sure they would not be discovered. They'd left the safety of the ship to hide here when dusk fell.

Piay nudged Hannu and his assistant looked round. The rowing boat was beginning its journey to shore, the spray from the oars glinting in the light. Piay could make out the silhouettes of two figures on board – the oarsman and the captive they had pulled from the sea. Despite Jabilo's words, he had been terrified that he would be executed for his part in the battle. Now, perhaps, he would be starting to feel some hope.

Once the rowing boat neared the shore, the captive threw himself into the water and raced up the beach. Piay could almost sense his jubilation.

As he bounded across the sand and vanished into the trees, Piay murmured 'Now.'

Jabilo darted away through the trees and Piay and Hannu scrambled to keep up. The young warrior was strong and fast, but also an excellent scout. If anyone could track the freed man through that forest, it was Jabilo.

The ghosts of the baobab trees blurred by on either side and moonlight shafted into pools of shimmering white among the shadows. Piay fixed his attention on Jabilo's pale soles as he raced ahead.

Finally Piay glimpsed firelight through the vegetation. Jabilo slowed his pace as they neared the camp, and they crawled among a tangled mass of tree roots to observe.

The freed man whooped as he ran, waving his arms above his head. A lookout stepped out of the dark with a levelled spear and recognised the man approaching. He cupped his hand to his mouth and called into the camp, then dragged the new arrival into the mass of men and women emerging from tents to investigate the disturbance.

'Temue will hear our message soon enough,' Piay said.

'They'll be afraid,' Hannu replied. 'They're ripe for the slaughter now Chemue has bought in new allies with vast ships that make their own fleet worthless. Should make them more likely to listen to sense. Or more dangerous.'

Piay watched the crowds swell around the man, to hear his tale and then follow him towards the fire. Once he was sure all those in the camp were distracted, Piay rested a hand on Jabilo's shoulder and nodded.

'Take no risks,' Piay said to him. 'At the first sign of danger—'

'He can't understand you,' Hannu said. 'You know that.'

Piay did, of course, but he needed to speak his mind.

'He knows the dangers,' Hannu added. 'He's made his choice.'

'He's young.'

'And so were you once. I'd wager you wouldn't listen to anyone telling you what to do. You knew better. We all did.' Hannu shrugged. 'This is how we learn. Failure teaches us to be better. Or we die.'

Piay looked deep into Jabilo's features, seeing the innocence there.

'I don't want him to die.'

'This is his choice. Not yours.'

Jabilo looked from one to the other and seemed to realise the conversation was over.

'Ready, big man,' he said.

He turned and loped away into the camp.

Jabilo could speak the language. He could easily pass for a member of this rebel army. But he was still little more than a boy, and not trained in the arts of spying, as Piay was.

Hannu clapped a hand on his shoulder.

'These are desperate times. We are all being forced to do things we normally would not do.'

For what seemed like an age, Piay leaned against the tree roots, straining to hear the faintest sound emanating from the camp. Dim voices hummed, occasionally shifting into the loud back and forth of a robust debate. But there were no shouts, no cries of alarm, and for that he thanked Khonsu.

When he began to relax, a figure loomed over him and he snatched for his sword. It was Jabilo. The Abantu warrior pressed a finger to his lips and beckoned them to follow.

Piay and Hannu crept close behind as Jabilo skirted the camp until he came to a fallen tree, the trunk sprouting cream-coloured fungi. A landmark, it seemed, for Jabilo then weaved a path through the small, patched tents and shelters of twisted branches and leaves.

Piay saw no movement nearby – everyone seemed to be gathered around the fire. Jabilo had done his job well.

Jablio raced up to a tent that was larger than the others. Glancing around, he lifted the flap so Piay and Hannu could slip inside.

Piay examined the sparse contents. The only light came from the red glow of the embers in a hearth enclosed by stones in the centre. The smoke twirled up through a hole in the roof of the tent. In the gloom, he spied a bed of leaves and grass, and a spear and shield. The man who would be king lived a frugal life, it seemed, or else this was the reality of a rebel leader fighting a long war.

Hannu drew his sword and let it hang by his side. He strained to hear any sounds. Piay slipped his own sword out of the sheath.

Jabilo peeked out through a gap in the tent. Soon he raised a hand and waggled his fingers. Piay and Hannu leaped to either side of the opening, pressing themselves as close to the cloth as possible. Jabilo backed to the other side of the hearth.

A woman stepped into the tent. Piay had not expected this. Her expression was flinty, her cold gaze that of a woman used to being obeyed. She was wearing a pale purple dress, tied at one shoulder, and a cloth of the same colour wrapped around her hair. A finely wrought necklace of what looked like gold gleamed at her throat.

A man pushed in behind her. This must be Temue, he thought. He was wearing a scarlet kilt and a fur sash, though no headdress of feathers. He was tall and strong like his brother, but his face lacked the hardness of Chemue.

The woman – perhaps Temue's wife – started when she saw Jabilo in the shadows beyond the twirl of smoke. Before she could call out, Piay and Hannu moved as one, swinging their swords up to the necks of the two new arrivals, pressing the edges into the skin so they wouldn't call out.

Temue and his companion understood their situation. They remained rigid, though the woman scowled.

Jabilo stepped forwards and began to speak. Piay translated it in his mind – they had gone over the words so many times.

'Nowhere is safe for you now. We are Chemue's new allies and we can come for you even here, in the heart of your camp. We have great ships. We have an army that dwarfs your own. We have swords – strong, bronze swords that can cleave a man in two.

There is no longer any point in fighting. You will be defeated. You will die, all of you. There is no more hope of victory.'

Piay watched despair creep across Temue's face as he listened to Jabilo's words. His chin fell and his shoulders sagged.

'The time now is for surrender, and talk. Chemue is a just king. He will spare those who have stood against him. Tomorrow, when the sun is at its highest, we will gather at his palace to end this war for good.'

For a moment, there was only silence, and then the woman blasted a fierce response. Temue shook his head. He whispered something and she stopped speaking, but defiance burned in her features.

'We take the king?' Hannu said.

'The woman,' Piay replied. It was a change of plan, but he saw the advantages. 'He'll come to the right conclusion to save his wife, if that's who she is. That will be better than trying to prod him with swords.'

Hannu removed his sword from Temue's neck and levelled it at his wife's breast. Temue flinched and made to move, but Piay wagged a finger at him.

Turning to Jabilo, Piay said, 'Tell him she will be kept safe. Safe. Do you know the word? Safe.'

Jabilo nodded and uttered a few words. Temue looked into Piay's face. What he saw must have reassured him, for he nodded.

'Good,' Piay said. 'And now we can claim our elephants. Our journey home begins soon.'

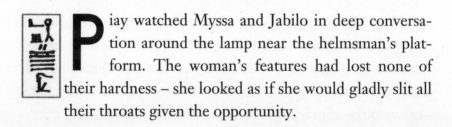 **P**iay watched Myssa and Jabilo in deep conversation around the lamp near the helmsman's platform. The woman's features had lost none of their hardness – she looked as if she would gladly slit all their throats given the opportunity.

'You were right about interfering in other people's wars,' Piay said to Hannu. 'It does not sit right with me. But at least we have brought peace. No more bloodshed, no more death.'

Hannu grunted, but revealed none of his thoughts.

Myssa joined them. *She looks serious*, Piay thought.

'What is wrong?' he asked.

'Things are not as we thought,' Myssa replied. 'Her name is Degba and she is the wife of Temue, as you thought. But Temue is fighting for a just cause. Chemue murdered their father to steal the crown, and he is a cruel ruler with much blood on his hands.'

'So she says,' Hannu said, unmoved.

Myssa shrugged. 'True. All causes are just to the ones fighting for them. But I feel the truth in her words, even if it is her truth.'

Hannu glanced at Piay. 'Do you trust this woman?'

'If there's one thing I've learned from you, it's not to trust anyone,' Piay replied. 'But if Chemue is as cruel as she says, his time will come. The gods will see to that.'

'Then we continue along this road?' Myssa said.

'We do what we do for the elephants, for the Pharaoh,' Piay said. 'This is the only way.'

The roar of the crowd lining the street resounded from the stone walls of the city. Men bellowed like forest beasts and the women ululated. Piay had never heard such a din.

Beside him, Degba stared into the middle distance as if she was oblivious to the outcry booming all around her. Yet when he glanced at her, Piay felt sure he could see tears brimming. A proud woman, a strong wife of a just man. But their time would come. There would be divine retribution.

Word of the arrival had spread rapidly. Piay squinted into the brassy light along the street and glimpsed the figures marching out of the shadows of the forest.

Head held high, Temue strode through the gates and into the city. Smiling, he locked eyes with Degba as if they were the only people in the world. Behind him, a guard of ten spear-warriors marched, not so many that the city defenders would think they were under attack, but enough to show that Temue was a leader who commanded respect and he was here of his own accord. Chemue's own spear-warriors stepped out of the shadows along the walls and followed.

When Temue reached Degba, he opened his arms and they embraced with a deep tenderness. Piay was moved when he saw the warmth of their touch, the way their heads bowed together.

Fingers brushed the back of his hand. He glanced at Myssa as she stared at the loving couple, and realised she was responding to the moment.

He looked at Hannu. His assistant's eyes were filled with tears as he watched the emotional reunion. Piay realised that his companion must be remembering his wife and the loving times they'd shared when she was alive.

When they pulled apart, Degba slipped by Temue's side and together they walked through the throng to the palace.

Piay, Hannu and Myssa stepped in behind the spear-warriors.

'I don't care how long it's going to take to march those elephants back to Thebes,' Hannu said. 'I am ready for good beer and a bellyful of honey cakes.'

The booming of the crowd died away as the procession moved into the peace of the palace. More of Chemue's spear-warriors lined the approach to the throne-room as a show of strength.

Inside, Chemue sat upright on his great wooden chair, his lips curled in a smile of victory. Omari stood beside him. The king paid no attention to the ones who had brought about his victory. He only had eyes for his brother.

Piay whispered to Myssa, 'Tell me what they say to each other.'

Temue looked up at his brother and spoke in a measured tone, free of emotion.

'He says he is here to surrender,' Myssa murmured. 'Chemue's new allies are too powerful. He will not see any of his followers sacrifice themselves for a lost cause.'

*A good man*, Piay thought. *A good leader.*

Chemue pushed his head back, haughty in victory. He spoke in an excitable voice and Myssa said, 'The king calls his brother weak, like their father. Doomed to failure from the beginning. The people deserve a leader who can protect them and guide them to greater glories.'

The king's smile faded and when he spoke, his voice was now low.

'You will always be a thorn in my side,' Myssa translated, 'as you were when we were young.'

Chemue leaned forwards in his throne.

'Kneel and bow your head to me, both of you.'

Temue's stare hardened, but he lowered himself to his knees. Degba remained standing, her face burning with defiance. Temue took her wrist, tugging her down. Trembling, Degba followed her husband.

The king leaned back in his throne and grinned. He nodded to Omari and the advisor uttered a single command.

A roar echoed and Chemue's warriors raced from the corner of the room. Temue's men gaped, not knowing what was happening as their opponents leaped on them like wolves. The spears stabbed and slashed in a frenzy, destroying those lives in an instant.

Piay reeled back from the carnage, dragging Myssa and Hannu with him. He could scarcely comprehend what was happening in front of his eyes.

When the bodies littered the ground, Chemue's spearguard turned on Temue and Degba, holding them fast as they kneeled. Temue raged at the betrayal, his words merging into a howl of fury.

Piay could see the cruelty was not over. He grabbed Hannu and Myssa to stop them interfering.

A tall man as big as a bull strode from the shadows, carrying an axe. Swinging it high, he hacked off Degba's head with a single stroke.

Temue stared in mute horror as it fell in front of him.

Hannu roared. Piay swung both arms around him and pinned him tight. His frantic flailing subsided, but Piay felt Hannu shaking with outrage.

Chemue walked over to Temue. Grabbing Degba's head by the hair, he swung it in front of his brother so that he could stare into those dead eyes, and then the king tossed the remains aside as if they were bones for his dog.

Temue began to sob.

The axe swung again.

In the burning heat of noon, Piay squatted in the square in front of the palace. Myssa stared into the middle distance. She hadn't spoken since they'd left the throne room. Did she blame him for these deaths?

No more than he blamed himself. This time he had not been reckless. He had planned thoroughly and seen everything through to a careful conclusion. But he had never imagined the blackness of Chemue's heart. He would not forget this lesson.

Hannu hunched nearby. The execution of Degba had affected him deeply. Hannu would not forget this either.

Piay saw Omari walking towards them. There was a lightness in the advisor's step that had not been there before.

When he joined them, Myssa translated his words.

'The long war is over and you have our gratitude for the part you played in it. You have earned our trust.'

'Then let us leave with the elephants,' Piay said. 'We have earned that, too.'

Once Myssa had spoken, Omari shook his head.

'We said only that once you had proven yourself, we would talk. And talk we will. The king has decided that the elephants will be yours. But first you must do one more thing.'

Piay swallowed the anger burning inside. After all that they had done, he could not throw it away now by opening his heart.

'Speak,' he said.

When she'd heard the response, Myssa said, 'Far north from here and to the west lies a land the Abantu call Mpemba Kasi. Beyond is a dangerous land of jungle and mountain and wild beasts. There can be found a bird with a plumage the colour of blood. Its feathers are prized more than anything. The mark of a king who can become a god. Bring those feathers back to us and you will have your elephants.'

The black clouds rolled towards the horizon. The winds sighed and the sun blazed. After a struggle against the elements so relentless that many on board thought it would never end, there was peace.

How long had they been trapped in that tempest? Piay lay on the sodden deck, unable to recall. An age, it seemed – days and nights of battling cliff-high waves and gales that threatened to snap the mast in two, rain that lashed like Hanbaal's whip and lightning that blasted the sky white. Day became night, an eternity of darkness. Every moment the crew felt death was standing with them. They fought for their lives, baling and steering, hoping to find a way through to calmer waters. Their biscuit was exhausted and eventually all their fresh water was gone. There seemed no hope. One sailor had thrown himself over the side rather than die parched and starved.

Men slumped across their oars or collapsed on their benches, arms thrown across their eyes. Every one was drained of vitality. If there was trouble ahead, Piay doubted any would have the strength to resist.

Hannu leaned on the rail. He had not been the same since they had left the Elephant Kingdom. All of them had been changed. The knowledge that they had another task to achieve before they could claim their rewards had sapped their resolve. Many of the crew had asked if this odyssey would end before their lives were over.

But it had hit Hannu the worst. Drained of humour, his features had hardened like a weather-blasted crag. The sheer cruelty of the executions ordered by Chemue, the injustice, had burned into Hannu's heart. He'd seen a deep love destroyed and he could think only of his own loss.

Myssa came to Piay's side. 'You should speak with Hannu, offer him comfort.'

After a moment's reflection, Piay replied, 'When the time is right. But I warn you, he will probably toss me over the side.'

Find the Scarlet Feather, Omari had told them, find it in the one place on earth where the bird nested. That place was so lonely, so dangerous, success seemed impossible.

At dusk they'd set sail into the south. After three days, the tempest struck.

But here they were, still breathing.

Piay saw Hanbaal clamber out from his shelter. His gaunt cheeks made him look ten years older.

But as he stepped across the deck, the brightness glowed in his face once more and he rubbed his hands. He beckoned Piay over.

'Can you feel it?' Hanbaal said. 'No, no, you can't. You are not a seafaring man. But the hull is straining, the ship pulling this way and that. We are at the point where the currents from the hot sea to the east crash against the currents from the cold sea to the west. We have done it. I have done it. You were right to press me to continue, my friend. From this day on the name of Hanbaal will be on the lips of all who voyage upon the waves.'

Piay shook his head, baffled.

Hanbaal went back to his shelter and returned with one of his charts. As he unfurled it on the bench, Piay glimpsed a black outline of the great land along whose coast they had been sailing.

'See, here is the Red Sea.' Hanbaal traced his finger along the edge. 'Here is Azania and the Elephant Kingdom.' He dragged his filthy nail around the tip of the huge land mass. 'And here we are, on the Coast of Storms. We have rounded the very edge of the world. When you persuaded me to continue, you told me this would be an achievement that would echo down the years. And you were right, my friend. Hanbaal the Phoenician is the first man to attempt this voyage. Other sailors said the storms would destroy anyone who attempted this passage. That there were monsters in the ocean that would tear our vessel apart. That it was impossible! But here we are.'

Hanbaal looked up to the sky, his eyes gleaming.

'Imagine,' he breathed, 'if I could sail all around this land. A full circle. I could establish the first trade route from east to west.'

'You deserve your pride in your achievement, Hanbaal,' Piay said. 'This will bring fame and even riches to you. See what you have gained by joining with me?'

Hanbaal clapped his hands again. 'Now, to shore, to take on food and water. And then onwards!'

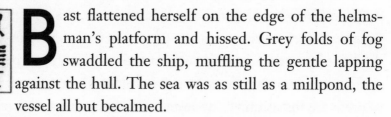 **B**ast flattened herself on the edge of the helmsman's platform and hissed. Grey folds of fog swaddled the ship, muffling the gentle lapping against the hull. The sea was as still as a millpond, the vessel all but becalmed.

'What's got her agitated?' Hannu grunted.

Myssa looked out into the suffocating cloud. 'She senses something.'

Piay felt unease. With neither sight nor sound of Sakir and the Hyksos since they'd left Azania, he'd started to believe that they might have lost their pursuers. Now he wondered.

The sailors hunched on their benches, their thoughts drifting with the currents. The ship had been trapped in this fog bank for hours. Hanbaal had made an offering to Yamm, his people's god of the sea, tossing into the swell one of the squares of linen he kept in the hold for such an occasion. Piay had prayed to Khonsu. So far their pleas had not been answered.

'You hear that?' one of the sailors said.

Heads raised across the benches.

For a while, only the gentle lapping could be heard.

Then a groan rumbled, the familiar complaint of boards flexing against the currents.

The sailors jumped from their benches and scrambled to the rail. Piay leaped beside them.

A faint moan drifted, deadened by the fog.

'Another ship's out there,' someone said. 'Mark my words.'

Piay's shoulders tightened. He breathed in the damp air, watching. The sheets of grey shifted and the noises rumbled closer. In the fog, a shadow appeared. The smudge darkened as it neared, taking on form.

'It's coming at us!' someone yelled.

The sailors snatched up the dock-poles and stabbed them over the side, waiting.

'Brace yourselves,' Hanbaal bellowed.

The ship emerged from the mist. He'd never seen a vessel like this. As big as Hanbaal's ship, it was arched like a bow, with a raised steering platform astern and an ornately carved prow in the form of a sea creature that appeared half fish and half man. Yet it appeared age-old. Mildew crawled across slimy wood and rot-holes peppered the blackened surfaces. The furled sail hung in filthy tatters. The deck was deserted.

'An abandoned hulk,' one of the sailors grunted.

'Aye, but why?' someone replied.

As the ship drifted towards them, the sailors with the dock-poles stood fast. The hull thumped against the tips of the poles and the men heaved it away.

Once contact had been avoided, Hanbaal ordered his men to anchor the other vessel to his with hide-ropes tied to billhooks.

'Let us see if there is anything in the hold worth looting,' the slaver said, 'though I suspect that is a slim hope.'

Piay sensed the sailors were uneasy. Did they fear a trap?

Once again Bast's hissing cut through the stillness.

Hanbaal leaped across to the other vessel, accompanied by ten men. Piay decided to join them and jumped from the rail. He felt the sodden boards of the strange vessel's deck give under his feet.

The sailors clustered around Hanbaal, eyes darting as if they expected an attack from any direction. The slaver ordered them to fan out and search the vessel. The men swept across the deck. Only one sailor edged towards the gaping entrance to the hold.

Piay saw a sword partially drawn from its scabbard. A half-eaten biscuit lying under a bench; not rotten or sodden from the elements, seeming as if it had been left only that morning. A bronze knife and a piece of whittled wood, the shaving curling from the last cut.

No sign of battle. No sign of storm damage. A sudden abandonment.

Piay felt uneasy. The atmosphere on the ship was oppressive, like the heaviness in the air before a storm.

'Why are your men so troubled?' he asked when he returned to Hanbaal.

'Sailors are superstitious. A life at sea is filled with dangers and the gods sometimes abandon us. Men carry their amulets and their totems and utter spells they have learned by heart. This is their daily existence in the face of ever-present death. And when they gather in the taverns after long voyages, tales are told and stories swapped. Accounts passed from mouth to mouth that may save lives some day out on the ocean.'

Piay watched Hanbaal's restless eyes as he searched the ship and thought he saw a hint of fear in there, too.

'One of those stories I have heard many times, across the lands to the east of the Great Green, in Mycenae, in Libya, throughout the Nile delta,' the slaver continued. 'It tells of a cursed ship that drifts the oceans, without any crew to guide it. A ship of the dead. Some claim to have seen it on the Great Green, in the Red Sea, far to the east, constantly travelling with the currents, never making landfall. Set foot upon its deck and you risk being dragged to the deep. Your spirit . . . your Ka . . . will be trapped on that ship until the end of all days, never knowing peace.'

'If you believe this to be that vessel, why are you here?'

Hanbaal grinned. 'I believe in nothing except good profit, and if there is gold left in the hold, then it is worth investigating.'

The fog pressed in on all sides so tightly they might as well have sailed out of the world and into another, one of shadows and mist.

A scream rang out.

Piay's hand flew to his sword. The sailor who had ventured into the hold was clawing his way out. His eyes bulged and his face was ashen. He screamed again, a blood-curdling sound that spiralled up into the air as if it had been issued by a madman.

Across the deck, the other crew members gaped in shock. The man pulled himself over the edge of the hold hatch and threw himself forwards, weaving wildly as he ran.

'What is it?' Hanbaal bellowed, his sword now in his hand.

The sailor's stare was as blank as if he had had his wits dashed from his head.

All eyes darted to that square black hole, waiting to see if anyone followed him out on to the deck. Piay felt his heart begin to thrum.

The crazed sailor raced across the deck to his own ship and threw himself towards safety, but he fell short of the rail on the other vessel and plunged into the void between the two ships.

Piay ran to the side, but the man had slipped beneath the surface without leaving even a bubble of air to mark his passing.

'Back to our ship!' Hanbaal yelled, whirling his sword above his head to urge his men to flee.

Piay leaped across the void and rolled across the deck. Hanbaal crashed down beside him, and the other sailors came, too, their eyes as wide with terror as their drowned comrade's.

Hanbaal climbed to his feet and barked, 'Away with it!'

The connecting ropes were cut free and the men with the dock-poles heaved until the two vessels began to drift apart.

Piay stared at that opening to the hold. For a moment, he thought he glimpsed movement in the dark, but nothing emerged into the light. Hanbaal slid in next to him, his cold gaze unwavering.

'What did he see down there?' Piay breathed.

'We will never know. And if you take my advice, you will not think upon it again.'

The rotting hulk drifted away, the edges of it blurring, and then the fog swallowed it as if it had never been there.

'It is a bad omen,' Hanbaal said. 'Whether it be for you, or me, or all of us, I cannot say.'

Sixty-five days passed as they sailed north along the coast of the great continent. The days were hot, occasionally broken by blustering storms that sent lightning crackling across the horizon. Piay watched the changing shoreline and accompanied the crew whenever they rowed in to take on water or barter with the locals for fresh provisions.

From time to time, their paths crossed with a great whale which seemed to be tracking them, but though the sailors grew fearful for their safety, the beast kept its distance.

Hanbaal pored over his charts, and on the sixty-sixth day he ordered the anchor to be dropped and pointed towards a land of thick forest and mist with purple mountains rising in the distance.

'There is our destination,' he said. 'The wild place beyond the land the Abantu call Mpemba Kasi. And it is here that we must part company.'

'How will we ever return to the Elephant Kingdom?' Piay protested.

Hanbaal looked towards the mysterious land of mists and mountains.

'There are tales of great rivers that carve through the interior, though I have never witnessed them myself. But they could offer you a quick passage back to Chemue.'

'I can offer you more gold.'

Piay felt frustration knotting his stomach. After coming so far, this was a great setback.

The slaver shook his head. 'Though I never thought I would utter these words, I am happy with the gold you have already promised me. And I will collect that when I am done. For now I see greater glory on the horizon.'

'What could be greater than gold?'

Hanbaal grinned. 'The name of Hanbaal the Phoenician shining through the ages, remembered as are kings and gods. I have already done what no man has done before, rounding the tip of this land, despite storms and currents that could tear a ship apart. It is my plan to continue sailing north, to see if it is possible to sail entirely around this vast land. Think about that. An achievement that has never been made by any humble sailor, one that will never be bettered.'

'There is no way I can persuade you to change your mind?'

'None, my friend. Great tales will be told of the time we have spent together and the adventures that we have had. But now it must come to an end.'

Piay gritted his teeth. Never would he have thought that the lure of glory would have been greater than that of gold for the slaver. But all men had their secret desires. He held out his hand and Hanbaal took it.

'Then we will meet again in Thebes over cups of fine wine,' Piay said.

Hanbaal laughed. 'And I will count my gold and the Pharaoh will weep!'

Turning to where Hannu, Myssa and Jabilo waited, Piay felt a surge of trepidation at the struggles lying ahead, which they would now have to face alone.

Cool surf lapped around Piay's ankles. Out in the bay, Hanbaal's crew rested ready for the journey to come. Soon, perhaps the next day, that crimson sail would be unfurled. How long had it been since he'd watched it drift into the port at Gythion? An age, it seemed.

Piay strode up the sand to where Hannu, Myssa and Jabilo waited with skins filled with water and a few meagre provisions. They would need to learn to forage for themselves as they journeyed into the interior.

'Just us now, then,' Hannu grunted.

Myssa held out her hands, making light of the situation. 'We can travel faster that way.'

Piay smiled. Her disposition always shone like Ra's orb, even in their darkest moments.

'You should have left that cat behind, though,' Hannu noted.

Bast slinked around Myssa's legs. 'I tried,' she said. 'It would have been better for her with a hold full of rats to keep her belly full. But she was having none of it.'

Piay looked towards the misty mountains rising above the rainforest, shaded in mauve and cerulean in the dying light.

'Omari said we would find the bird upon the slopes of the high land,' he said. 'That looks like a long trek through this inhospitable place.'

A roar rumbled across the treetops. Piay felt his spine tingle. He had never heard that sound before and couldn't imagine what beast had made it.

After a moment, Hannu said, 'Probably best to leave the start of our journey until morning.'

The salt-breeze whisked the crackling fire into a spiral of sparks. In the warm glow, Hannu snored on the sand with Bast curled next to him. Further along the beach, Jabilo hunched over his spear, his unmoving form silhouetted against the starlit sky.

There was peace, at least for a little while.

Piay sauntered up the beach with Myssa, his shoulder almost brushing her skin. He breathed in her natural perfume, a scent that somehow stilled the rapid beating of his heart and eased the tautness in his shoulders. A shiver of surprise rippled through him when he felt her fingers brush his hand once more. This time she slipped her hand in his and interlocked their fingers. A simple act of connection, yet Piay felt mesmerised by it. For all the hardship he had endured on the long road, if he had not left Thebes he would likely not have experienced this and, in doing so, become a better man.

Taita, as always, had been proven right.

In the sweltering atmosphere of damp vegetation on the edge of the forest, Piay leaned against the towering trunk of an iroko tree under the rustling canopy of dark green leaves. Myssa eased against him and his arms fell around her waist, folding into the small of her back. Her face filled his vision, her eyes glimmering, her smile broad.

'Don't wake the spirit-man,' she breathed.

'What do you mean?'

Myssa brushed the pale bark of the tree beside his head. 'The Yoruba people fear this tree. They say a spirit lives within the wood, and anyone who comes face to face with the iroko-man will be driven mad and then die.'

Piay pressed a finger against his lips.

Myssa held his gaze, looking deep inside him, perhaps seeing everything he had kept hidden from all others, even Taita. Leaning forwards, she kissed him, her lips soft against his, then harder.

Piay sank into that embrace. His thoughts rushed away in the warmth of the sensation and the rising tide of passion, and for a moment he felt overwhelmed. Nothing had prepared him for this swelling of his heart.

His fingers slipped into Myssa's lustrous hair, along the smooth skin at the nape of her neck, across the curves of her body, and down. He felt Myssa's fingers probing his chest, his waist, the taut muscles across his belly.

They tore away each other's clothes, luxuriating in skin upon skin. Piay was lost in that moment that seemed to stretch on forever. As they fell together, their lovemaking shifted from cool tenderness to heat.

When they were both spent, Piay held Myssa tight against him, feeling the rise and fall of her chest subside. But as he drowned in the soothing waters of what he could only believe was love, something he had never experienced before, he felt a corresponding chill. The cold spread into his limbs and his heart beat faster and panic throbbed on the edge of his perception.

Piay was unable to comprehend why he was feeling this way. The emotion was as strange to him as love, and he realised this must be fear – a deep and abiding dread. Why would he feel that way, now, in this special moment?

Then he locked eyes with Myssa and he knew that, in his moment of greatest joy, he had been damned. He had something to lose. He could no longer imagine a world without Myssa at his side. Terror had seeped into him alongside the love. Was this how it was for everyone? A bittersweet contract that exchanged his old life of simple pleasure for a new one of doubt and worry and greater joy?

Poor Hannu. Now he understood.

Myssa's smile faded and her hand went to his cheek.

'What is wrong?'

Piay didn't answer. He kissed her again, a kiss that seemed like it would never end.

When dawn streaked the sky, Jabilo turned to greet the sun. Hannu levered himself up on his arms and found himself staring into Bast's eyes. He muttered, 'This cat troubles me.'

Myssa laughed. 'She is speaking to you, Hannu. Can you not hear her words?'

Piay offered Hannu his hand, hauled his assistant to his feet and said, 'I think there is more to that cat, too. Probably wise not to examine it too closely.'

While Jabilo collected the provisions, Piay, Hannu and Myssa slung the water-hides over their shoulders. Hannu glowered at the dark clouds massing behind the purple mountains.

'We will not be short of water on this journey, I feel.'

'We should keep our spirits high,' Piay said. 'We are close to completing our task, closer than we have ever been. One feather, that is all we need. One feather and then Egypt beckons.'

'There is more to it than that.' Hannu tightened his jaw. 'You heard what Omari said. The Scarlet Feather gives power to whoever wears it in their headdress. To those people, Chemue will become like a god. Would you want a man like that to be a god?'

'Why does this trouble you?'

'An army will follow a god further than a man. They'll fight harder, risk their necks more. I wouldn't be surprised if Chemue decided to use this power to conquer.'

'This is not our problem,' Piay said.

'To spread his empire across the land, perhaps even to Azania. Perhaps even to Egypt itself.'

'We already have an enemy to defeat. Let us not concern ourselves with another one.'

'What lengths do you think a man like Chemue would go to? What slaughter?' Hannu shrugged. 'And we will give him the power to do it. All the misery he causes will be on us.'

'We have no choice.'

'Easily said.'

The air whined, ending with a thump. Piay looked towards the ocean, only to see a quivering arrow protruding from the sand.

Jabilo pointed out into the bay. Piay squinted against the glare off the water from the rising sun and, as his eyes adjusted, he felt the chill he had experienced the previous night creep into his bones once more.

Three warships stood at anchor close to Hanbaal's vessel. From them, rowing boats carved across the waters. In each one, archers holding the Hyksos' powerful recurved bow were nocking shafts to loose at them.

'Run!' Piay called.

After the wait and the worry, what they had all feared most had finally come to be.

Sakir was here.

'Only with Seth guiding him could Sakir find us.' Piay crashed through the palms. Sweat soaked his back from the suffocating heat under the verdant canopy.

Myssa scooped Bast into her arms as she hurried.

'And Seth speaks to him through the blue lotus.'

'Little matter the how,' Hannu said. 'Now there is only running, and hiding, and fighting for our lives.'

Piay glanced back at the rowing boats sweeping towards the beach. Three ships. Perhaps twenty crew to remain on board each one. That left perhaps one hundred pursuers, no doubt with enough scouts who could track their progress through even the densest forest.

'As long as they are chasing us, they have the upper hand,' Piay said. 'We need to make them afraid. A desert cat is never more dangerous than when it is cornered.'

At a mangrove swamp where the sandy soil gave way to pools of brackish water over which clouds of flies droned, Piay caught Jabilo's arm.

'We need you, my friend. Your skills. Only you can save us now.'

Jabilo grinned. 'Yes, big man.'

'Use your tracking skills to find us the most dangerous paths – the ones where the slightest slip could end your life, where the wild beasts roam, through the swamps and the high passes and the gorges where the white water rushes. And then we will put our faith in our own abilities, and in the gods to guide us.'

From Myssa's arms, the cat stared at him with unblinking green eyes.

'We will put our faith in Bast.'

On they fled, barely snatching moments of sleep. The world blurred in a haze of exhaustion, as they stumbled through the twilit world of emerald and shadow. Piay clawed his way past trees soaring up more than twenty-five times a man's height, clustering close on every side.

Jabilo found wild mushrooms for them to eat as they hurried on. They sprouted everywhere, strange growths with huge creamy folds or distended brown caps. The young warrior ripped up root vegetables for them to gnaw on, too. They were bitter and left an unpleasant aftertaste, but they filled their growling bellies.

Occasionally the cries of the Hyksos dogs rang out at their backs. Piay felt relief that their pursuers did not seem to be drawing closer. Their strategy must be to hound their prey to the point of collapse.

When the rain came, hard stones of water cascaded through the canopy, so thick and fast they could barely see more than three spear-lengths ahead of them. On it pounded, through the day and into the night until Piay could barely remember what it was like to be dry.

New streams gushed down channels, turning the ground into sucking marsh that hampered their progress.

As they stumbled past a swelling pool, Hannu grabbed Piay's arm and shouted above the roar, 'I do not like this! I cannot hear if those barbarian curs are close.'

Piay nodded. 'We need to shelter. At least this damnable rain should hide our tracks.'

'Take us to the high ground. I have a plan.'

ightning danced across the slate-grey sky. The thunder boomed and the rain drummed. Piay crouched on a narrow plateau on a blade of rock stabbing up through the forest canopy in the foothills of the mountains. Wiping the streaming water from his eyes, he squinted through the sheets until he saw Jabilo sprinting up the uneven path that curled around the precipitous cliff. Using his spear to balance himself, the Abantu warrior bounded with a grace and speed that belied the dangers of the winding track.

When he leaped on to the plateau, he hurried to Piay's side and ducked low.

'They are coming.'

'You left a clear sign pointing the way?'

'They will find us.'

Piay nodded. He peered over the lip of the plateau into the half-light. Hannu crawled beside him, streaked with rock dust and earth, his knuckles gashed, fingertips bleeding from his exertions.

'A good plan,' Piay said.

'A reckless one,' Hannu said. 'You have corrupted me.'

'Desperate times require desperate measures.'

Piay strained to look down the path. In the rumble of the squall he could hear nothing.

Silhouetted against a sky turned white by lightning, Myssa crawled over a rock from where she had been keeping watch. She waved furiously.

'Ready yourselves,' Piay said.

Hannu and Jabilo crawled along the plateau into the gloom.

Piay glimpsed movement along the narrow path. The Hyksos were feeling their way along the treacherous, rain-slick route.

When Myssa slid in next to him, Piay surprised her with a kiss, then he scrambled along the edge to where Hannu and Jabilo crouched. Myssa was just visible in the dim light – enough to see her signal.

'Start small,' Piay said. He grasped a rock as big as a coconut and lifted it to his waist.

For what seemed like an age, he braced himself, his gaze fixed on Myssa. She raised her arm. When she swept her hand down, Piay held the rock out over the edge and let it go.

In another flash of lightning, he watched the projectile hurtle towards the line of barbarians creeping along the ledge.

The rock hit the warrior who was behind the leader, shattering his skull. He flew off the path onto the treetops below. The man who was at the head of the column half-turned, lost his footing and pitched over after his comrade. His scream spiralled up.

Piay ducked back before he could be seen. Even above the rolling thunder, he could hear the cries of alarm echo down the line. The barbarians most likely believed they'd been victims of a random act of nature. They'd still be edging forwards, though more cautiously.

Piay glanced along the line of boulders and rocks that Hannu had rolled into place along the rim of the plateau and he nodded. Hannu and Jabilo raced along the line. At intervals, they pressed their backs against one of the boulders, dug their heels in and pushed. Once the stone began to trundle over the edge, they scrambled to the next one.

The rain of rock thundered down the cliff side. Piay leaned out to watch.

Mangled bodies flew into the abyss, turning amid the endless shower of stone and rain. Screams and cries of pain echoed around them. Piay couldn't tell how many of the Hyksos had been crushed, but he witnessed a good twenty die.

Here and there the boulders smashed the path. Voids appeared along the narrow track, making it impossible for any-one to climb to the plateau.

Hannu's plan had bought them some time.

Once all the stones had been used up, Jabilo bounded up with Hannu limping close behind.

'Good work,' Piay said above the thrumming of the down-pour.

Jabilo beamed. Even Hannu managed a smile.

'It won't be the end of it, but it will do for now.'

'And this won't be the end of it for us,' Piay replied. 'We will fight back whenever we can.'

Glancing over the edge of the precipice when a lightning flash lit the surroundings, Piay glimpsed a sole warrior staring back at him. It was Sakir, rigid, cold, unruffled by the mayhem.

Piay had hoped the Red Hawk would have been in the van-guard of the pursuit and been one of those blasted into the storm by the falling rocks. Perhaps his dark god Seth had warned him. Perhaps the instincts of a seasoned warrior had come into play. But Piay felt pleased that the Hyksos leader had seen him and knew who was the architect of this defeat inflicted upon him.

Their final battle would come. But for now, let Sakir carry with him the knowledge of who had bested him yet again.

The storm blew out in the early hours. By that time, Piay, Hannu and Myssa were trekking behind Jabilo on another path winding away from the plateau to higher ground. Three days later, without sign of pursuit, they had already climbed the low slopes of the mountains.

In the light of morning, Piay looked out over this inhospitable land from another plateau. Beyond the rainforest to the south and south-west, savannah stretched to the horizon. To the north, light glimmered off some great river that reached out across grasslands.

Piay glimpsed rivers flowing everywhere, just as Hanbaal had said. At least those waterways offered some hope of a faster voyage back to the Elephant Kingdom, rather than fighting their way through tracts of dense vegetation.

Ahead, the mountain range soared up, a brown slab of rock that seemed to climb to the heavens. From its reaches, the roar rumbled out that he had heard when they first set foot on this strange land. He felt disturbed by that sound. What was waiting for them?

Piay pushed through a wall of fronds and spiky leaves and paused to wipe the sweat from his brow. Was it his imagination, or was the dense forest beginning to thin out as they moved up the mountain slopes? He prayed that was so. The going had been hard and slow and not a moment had passed when he didn't fear the Hyksos closing at their backs.

'Hold!'

Jabilo crouched in an attacking posture, his spear levelled at Piay's back. The Abantu warrior's face hardened, his eyes growing half-lidded. Behind him, Myssa's hand flew to her mouth. At her feet, Bast arched her back and hissed.

Jabilo flicked the tip of his spear up and raised his eyes.

'Slow, big man. Slow.'

Piay craned his neck by degrees. A pair of moon-eyes stared at him. He stiffened as he took in the creature swaying a hand's breadth above his head.

'Bad poison, big man,' Jabilo breathed. 'One bite – dead.'

The tree cobra's sinuous body gleamed like the wet black earth along the banks of the Nile, the huge eyes seeming to glow in the small head. The lower part was coiled around a branch and the spiky tail lashed the air. That powerful cylindrical body was a good head or two longer than he was, he estimated.

These serpents were lightning-fast, Piay knew, and its venom was as lethal as Jabilo had said. The chance of escaping those fangs was slim.

The cobra's ebony hood flexed. It was preparing to strike.

Piay held his breath and began to retreat.

In a blur, the snake whipped forwards. Piay flung himself onto the ground, tensing for those fangs tearing into his flesh.

When he yanked his head back, he glimpsed the long body thrashing above him. The skull was impaled on the tip of Jabilo's spear. The tail coiled and lashed, not yet realising that it was already dead.

Piay felt his heart beating so hard he thought it was about to burst out of his chest. Eventually relief began to surface and he jumped to his feet and clasped Jabilo's arm.

'I owe you my life, my friend,' he said.

Jabilo lowered his eyes. His face tightened with a seriousness Piay hadn't seen in him before.

'What is wrong?' Piay asked.

'I would ask . . .' With a shake of his head, Jabilo held out his hands, unable to find the words to express himself.

'Let me.' Myssa stepped up. After a moment conversing with the Abantu warrior, she said to Piay, 'In the days since he left his village, Jabilo has seen wonders beyond his imagination.'

'And terrors too, I'd wager,' Piay said.

'Jabilo says you have opened his eyes to the world. His village . . . the simple life there . . . offers nothing for him in his days yet to come. His only family is his father who has beaten him since he was a boy.' Myssa reached out and rested a hand on Piay's arm. 'He wants to stay with you, to learn from you . . .'

'Me?' Piay couldn't understand this request at all.

'He calls you big man, but he is not talking about your stature. In the tongue of the Abantu it means "important man". "Good man."'

Piay glanced at Jabilo, who kept his eyes lowered.

'He wants to return to Egypt with you and to be your assistant.'

'But I already have Hannu—'

Piay bit off his words and studied Jabilo. He felt humbled by what had been said and undeserving in a way that he had never experienced before.

'He's been loyal,' Myssa whispered. 'And he saved your life.' She narrowed her eyes and Piay felt chastised.

If he examined his feelings, he was sure he would discover that he was afraid of the responsibility. Young men had depended on him that night in the fields and their trust had been misplaced. But here was a chance to make amends.

'Very well,' he said. 'Jabilo will become my new assistant and I will teach him all the arts of peace and war, as they were taught to me by Taita. It will keep Hannu on his toes to know he has a rival.'

Myssa smiled. 'I think Hannu will be relieved to no longer be the centre of your attention.'

When Myssa relayed his response to the Abantu warrior, Jabilo grinned and bowed his head several times. Piay squirmed with embarrassment. Hannu marched up from where he had been scouting ahead. He glanced at the serpent dangling from Jabilo's spear.

'Good. I have had my fill of mushrooms. Though some fish would have been better.' As he looked around, he sensed something had transpired. He dismissed his suspicion with a wave of his hand and added, 'While you were wasting your time talking, I have made an important discovery.'

Pools of brackish water shimmered among sickly trees and islands of yellow grass and sedge. Piay wrinkled his nose at the reek of rotting vegetation and mud. The swamp boiled in a large bowl covering most of this plateau, formed by the heavy rains streaming off the mountain.

Hannu crouched beside him, pointing across the bleak expanse.

'See those narrow tracks winding through the bog? One would think a war band would be able to pick their way through to reach the other side.'

'Slow going, no doubt, but – yes, a way, if treated with caution.'

Standing, Hannu kicked out his right leg and clods of black mud flew.

'Except they're not. Those tracks are like a desert mirage. They trick the eye into thinking they are solid ground. But out in the bog they become sucking mud covered with moss. One step on it and a man would be dragged to his death.'

'You are sure?'

'I stuck a branch in it and couldn't find the bottom.'

'Then there is no way forwards.'

Hannu shook his head. 'There's a way, around the edge. It's long and difficult and anyone tracking prey wouldn't waste their time going that way.'

Piay grinned. 'It seems you have done it again.'

Hannu folded his arms. 'I have my uses.'

Piay turned to Myssa. 'I have my first task for Jabilo as my new assistant.' He glanced at Hannu. 'There was no time to tell you.'

'Poor bastard,' Hannu said. 'He seemed to have such a happy life.'

'What would you have me tell him?' Myssa asked.

Piay pointed to where the ridges of mud and grass entered the swamp.

'Tell him to leave signs that make it appear we took those paths across the swamp. Flattened grass. Broken branches. Footprints in the mud. Do it with every one he finds, so the Hyksos will think we have tried to deceive them. I would think Sakir would send men along every one of them to save time.' He nodded. 'Now let us see how clever these barbarians are.'

Piay moistened his cracked lips with the water from his hide. Waves of heat crushed down as he perched on a rock on the track into the highlands that Jabilo had found. The air was sweeter and the trees had thinned the more they climbed, providing a clear view back along the way they had come.

The route around the swamp had been as hard as Hannu had suggested, the vegetation so thick that sometimes they had to use their swords to hack a path. But in the deadening heat of the afternoon, they broke through on to the rising slope and heaved their way up the mountainside.

The cry cut through the soaring birdsong. Another followed, and another – a cacophony of alarm, ringing across the mountainside from the bog below. Shouts of warning merged with screams as the panic spread.

Piay imagined the lines of barbarians weaving across the swamp, balanced on those narrow ridges of earth to avoid plunging into the pools of brown water and sucking mud. He could almost see their terror as man after man found the solid ground vanishing beneath their feet. Attempts to rescue those being sucked under would only have dragged others into the bog. Perhaps some tried to flee the way they had come, losing their footing or knocking some of their comrades to their deaths.

How many of their pursuers had been destroyed now? Perhaps half of them?

Piay turned to the others and said, 'Let us seek out the Scarlet Feather while the gods still favour us.'

A milky mist floated among the trees. Piay shivered. It had grown cold. The forest had thinned and patches of darkening sky were visible among the high branches. On the western horizon the sun burned low and shadows spread across the ground. Ahead, ivory clouds had gathered on the indigo peaks and were creeping down the slopes.

'Close now,' Piay said. 'This is the place where Omari said we would find the bird. At first light we'll begin our search.'

'Something troubles our young friend.' Myssa was watching Jabilo sweeping his fingers across the earth as he examined some trail invisible to the eyes of others.

'Sakir couldn't have got ahead of us,' Hannu said.

Before Piay could ask the Abantu warrior what he had found, a roar rumbled out among the trees.

Hannu halted, his eyes widening. They'd heard that troubling sound so many times, but never so close.

What creature could have caused that blood-curdling roar?

'Do we go back?' Myssa whispered.

'Whatever is there stands between us and the thing we need most,' Piay murmured. 'We have no choice but to go forwards.'

He pushed on into the drifting mist, hoping his advance would encourage the others to set aside their fears.

The pearly cloud thickened and soon he couldn't see more than a few trees ahead. The roar echoed again and was answered by another. How many of the beasts were there? As more voices chimed in, it seemed the hidden beasts were celebrating the setting of the sun and the night creeping in.

Piay drew his sword. He crept forwards, moving from tree to tree. The mist closed in around him. When he glanced back, Hannu, Myssa and Jabilo were ghosts. The roars rumbled out from every side, the cloud distorting the echoes so that it was impossible to tell the location of the beasts. It seemed an army of them lurked there.

The way ahead cleared as the mist drifted lower to the ground. Piay realised he was looking across a broad clearing where some trees had fallen. The cloud-topped mountain rose beyond.

In the centre of the space, the great beasts moved. Piay stared, mesmerised by their size and the power rippling through their muscular forms. They resembled monkeys – he'd seen enough of those in Thebes – but these were as big as he was, but broader of shoulder and chest. One powerful hand looked as if it could crush his skull, and when they bared their teeth he felt those huge jaws could eviscerate him in an instant. The black fur gleamed in the fading light and was long and thick, no doubt to keep them warm in the cold temperatures high up the mountain.

Piay counted ten adults and three infants in the clearing. The largest one was roaring into the dusk. As he prowled the space, he showed his dominance to the others.

Piay saw Hannu, Myssa and Jabilo gripped by the sight, their faces showing the awe and terror that he felt.

He waved his hand to one side and they moved deep into the trees away from the clearing, fearful that these creatures might pick up their scents and attack. Only when the roars echoed far away did Piay allow himself to breathe easily.

'If Sakir and his men stumble across that band, I don't fancy their chances,' Hannu said. 'Let us pray there are no more of them ahead.'

Hannu squatted on the edge of the plateau, keeping watch down the mountainside where the sun dappled the clouds drifting among the treetops. He'd grumbled about being excluded from the hunt, but he knew his limp would make him near-useless in their attempts to catch the bird.

The plateau matched the description that Omari had given Piay, with a brown rock the shape of a skull looming over it. But though they'd been searching since first light, they hadn't seen the distinctive birds anywhere. A dark grey head with a white band across the eyes, shading to a silvery grey across the chest and legs, had been how Omari had described it. But it was the scarlet tail feathers that caught the eye, like a flash of blood across the green of the forest canopy.

'I hear them,' Myssa said as she strode among the trees. 'That shriek that Omari told of. But they are shy.'

Piay felt his frustration growing. 'The longer we tarry here, the more likely Sakir will find us.'

'If he still lives.'

'He lives.'

Increasingly, Piay thought he could sense Sakir's presence, like a chill wind on a hot day, almost as if their spirits had become entwined during this long, bitter pursuit.

Jabilo bounded soundlessly among the trees. Here, even his fabled scouting skills could not help him.

'We are wasting our time,' Piay complained. 'Omari said there was an abundance of the scarlet-tailed birds on this plateau. Was he lying?'

'Perhaps Chemue didn't want to give up his war elephants.'

'And now they are laughing at the foolish Egyptian? If that is the case, I will be returning with my sword drawn.'

On they ranged through the trees as the sun slipped across the sky and the temperature dropped. Was Myssa right? Eventually Piay kneeled and muttered a prayer to the gods. Shortly afterwards, Jabilo jabbed a finger towards the treetops and whooped. A blur of scarlet flashed by.

Piay raced through the trees with the Abantu warrior close behind. False hope, it seemed, for wherever they roamed they could not find the bird again.

Piay trudged back to Myssa.

'I fear we may have to continue our hunt tomorrow,' he sighed, feeling a hollow in the pit of his stomach. One more day when Sakir could draw closer to them.

'Ask the cat.'

Hannu limped out of the trees.

'Ask the cat.' He pointed a finger towards Bast. The feline was licking her paw next to Myssa.

'Have you been out in the sun too long?' Piay said.

'That cat is like no cat I've ever seen. Somehow it keeps its belly full with the rats it catches in the forest when I haven't seen any vermin anywhere. And when you look in those eyes . . .' Hannu shook his head. 'Ask it.'

Piay rolled his eyes. *What is there to lose?*

'A prayer to the goddess, then, the protector of her cubs in desperate times.'

'Ask the cat,' Hannu repeated with a firm nod.

Myssa grinned and rolled on to her belly. As she muttered in her own tongue, the cat and the woman held each other's gaze and looked like they were communicating. When she was done, Myssa smiled.

'I have asked her,' she said in a light voice. 'We will see if she chooses to answer.'

Bast licked her paw and groomed herself and then slunk away into the undergrowth. Piay and the others followed. Round the trees she wandered, in seemingly random patterns.

*Searching for food*, Piay grumbled to himself, feeling like a fool.

Finally Bast ambled to an ebony tree and looked up to the low branches. Piay followed the cat's gaze. The grey bird with the scarlet tail was perched there, staring down at the feline.

Piay nodded to Jabilo and the agile Abantu warrior crept to the base of the tree and began to pull his way up. Piay's shoulders tightened. Surely the bird would take wing. Somehow, though, it didn't move, caught in Bast's gaze.

Jabilo pulled himself on to the branch as if he was weightless. He poised, no doubt expecting the bird to take flight, as did Piay, but it was rigid under Bast's unwavering stare. Lunging, Jabilo clamped both hands around the grey bird. Only then did it squawk and struggle, but it was too late. Jabilo yanked out one of the tail feathers.

'Take two!' Hannu called. 'Three.'

Jabilo shook his head and uttered a few words.

'What did he say?' Piay asked Myssa.

'He said these birds are sacred, and to take more than is needed will anger the gods.'

Jabilo unlocked his hands and the bird thrashed away to freedom.

Once he'd dropped to the ground, Jabilo handed over the prize. Piay held it up, impressed by the way the colour seemed to take on greater depth in the fading sunlight.

'All this for a feather,' he said.

'All this for elephants,' Hannu said.

'Offer Jabilo my thanks,' Piay said to Myssa. 'He has saved the day.'

'You tell him,' Myssa said with a twinkle in her eye.

In stuttering, short words, Piay managed to convey their gratitude. He clapped Jabilo on the shoulder and the young warrior beamed as if he'd just been made king.

Hannu shrugged. 'I can't believe you actually asked the cat.'

The light drained and the clouds rolled in from the mountaintop, obscuring the moon and stars. The birdsong faded and soon there were only the roars and hoots of the great apes. Piay leaned over the edge of the plateau where the land fell away in a steep slope and peered into the dark.

'We will break our necks if we try to descend in this gloom,' he said.

'We have no choice but to wait till first light,' Hannu agreed. 'The path Jabilo has found is dangerous enough in the day. At least it will lead us away from the route the barbarians are taking, so we don't have to worry about meeting them head-on.'

'We are fortunate to have Jabilo with us. I am not sure we would have made it this far without him.'

'The gods have smiled on us again.'

Piay felt reluctant to risk another night on the plateau, but as he stared into the murk he accepted Hannu was right: there was no choice. Somewhere ahead he could make out the rumble of rushing water. Jabilo said there was a gorge, with a fall and white water flowing to the south. They couldn't risk stumbling into that in the dark.

'We rest here, then, and you and I take it in turns to keep watch,' he said. 'Tomorrow we begin the long journey back.'

Piay perched on the twisted root of a mahogany tree. Hannu snored and Myssa and Jabilo slept peacefully. The dark was so deep, he felt he was floating.

Thebes seemed so far away, and the life he'd had then, and the man he'd thought he once was. In many ways he felt diminished, more wary, more reflective, more aware of his many and varied shortcomings. He thought that perhaps this was what Taita had wished for him. He had found wisdom, or at least he had placed his foot upon that never-ending road that led to wisdom.

In the dark, his eyes began to play tricks on him. The faces of his mother and father floated, indistinct, and the blurred features of the first woman he had ever kissed. He blinked, realising they weren't faces, but fireflies swirling among the trees.

Piay watched them dance, weaving their ritual ever closer.

He blinked again and felt cold creep down his spine. Not faces from his past, not fireflies. Torches.

The brands glimmered among the trees in a wide arc, sweeping towards him so fast it seemed that they were flying.

'Up!' he called, leaping to his feet.

Hannu scrambled to his feet in an instant. Jabilo offered a hand to Myssa to help her to her feet. She snatched up Bast and clutched him to her breast.

'What is wrong?' she gasped.

'The barbarians have found us.' Hannu watched those advancing lights. 'We must be away.'

'There is nowhere to run!' The Red Hawk's voice boomed in the night as if he had heard what Hannu had said. 'My men are guarding all ways off this plateau.'

Piay glanced down the slope behind him. They were trapped. Even if they dared to flee, Sakir would only close the circle until he had them in his grasp.

'I will kill your friend this time,' the Red Hawk taunted, 'and then the woman. And when you see you have lost everything, then I will take your life.'

Piay could not – would not – see Myssa or Hannu die.

'Take the feather,' Piay said, thrusting his pouch into Hannu's hands.

Hannu shook his head, realising what this act meant.

'No.'

'Take it!'

Piay jerked back, leaving Hannu no choice.

'There is still a way, down this slope—' Hannu began.

'Once Sakir has me, he will not care about you.'

Piay looked round at those torches rushing through the forest. He realised nothing mattered more than saving the lives of Myssa and Hannu.

Myssa grabbed him. 'Please,' she begged. 'Don't leave me now.'

'I'll take you with me if I have to knock the wits from your head,' Hannu snarled.

Piay lunged. Thrusting Hannu over the edge, he glimpsed one flash of his friend's startled face before he crashed down through the vegetation.

Myssa cried out.

'I am sorry,' Piay said before pushing Myssa off the plateau, too. He spun to Jabilo, who stared, wide-eyed, barely able to comprehend what he had seen. 'Protect them,' Piay snapped. 'That is your work now. Keep them safe.'

Jabilo hesitated, but only for a moment. He nodded his head and slid over the edge of the plateau.

And then Piay was racing away from the rim of the plateau, deeper into the forest. In the dark, he careered off tree trunks, winding himself, snarling his foot on a curling root and crashing to the ground, heaving himself back up and running again.

*This is the only way*, he told himself.

It didn't matter if he lived or died as long as Myssa and Hannu were safe. This sacrifice could only end in his death. But he was ready for it.

Piay caught sight of the torches floating through the trees, coming towards him. He bounded over a fallen tree at the last moment, stumbled and skidded across the ground. His head cracked against a trunk and he staggered to his feet, determined to keep moving.

Those brands seemed to be burning everywhere now, even in front of him. Piay searched for a path through them. Something hard clattered against the side of his head and he spun away.

When he'd shaken himself to his senses, Piay looked up and shadowy shapes rushed from the dark to surround him.

It was over. There was no point in trying to run.

Rough hands grabbed him, pinning him down on his knees. A tall figure strode in front of him and he looked up into the face of Sakir. A smile curled among his black bristles and his eyes moved with the same sullen intensity Piay had seen that night in the fields.

'We have travelled a world to arrive at this moment,' the Red Hawk said, the burns on his taut skin flexing in the torchlight. 'But now we have come to the end.'

Piay strained at the tough hide strips binding his wrists behind his back. As he tested the bonds, he looked around at the Hyksos war band scattered among the trees, resting after the long pursuit. About forty men, he counted. What chance did he have of escaping such a number? But he felt a shimmer of pride that their ranks had been reduced by more than half since they had first set foot on this land. Hannu would be pleased with that.

A circle of light wavered from the torches planted in a wide circle around Piay. A campfire crackled nearby, holding at bay the chill of the mountain night.

Piay searched for Sakir. The Red Hawk had wandered off to organise his men shortly after Piay had been taken captive. There seemed little haste to end Piay's life. Sakir had what he wanted and would take his time drawing out his pleasure.

One of the barbarians lowered a water-hide so Piay could moisten his lips, then snatched it away at the last with a laugh. Those nearby joined in the mockery.

Piay grinned. He thought how weary they all looked, and took some pleasure that he had run them ragged. And the longer they tarried tormenting him, the more distance Hannu, Myssa and Jabilo would be putting between them. When the elephants crashed through their forces in Egypt, justice would come. Their days were as numbered as his. The only difference was, they didn't yet know it.

Sakir strode out of the dark among the trees. A large leather pouch, no doubt containing food, swung in his hand. His unblinking gaze fixed on Piay as he walked. Piay did not look away.

When he entered the circle of torchlight, Sakir pulled out a short-bladed knife and pushed the tip into the red embers of the fire.

'You call us barbarians, but you Egyptians have become skilled in the arts of inflicting pain and punishment.' He turned the knife over, letting the bronze blade heat. 'Stories reached my ears of how men were skinned alive for some crimes while the people gathered to watch. Skinned, fed parts of their own bodies, disembowelled, all while they were aware of their own suffering.'

Leaving the knife in the fire, Sakir wandered over to Piay.

'The Hyksos tie deserters between two horses so they are ripped apart when the beasts are whipped. We lop off the heads of those who have wronged us. But those deaths are quick. We do not revel in the cruelty. Who, then, are the civilised ones, eh, Egyptian?'

'The death matters little,' Piay replied. 'The afterlife awaits.'

Sakir crouched in front of him. 'We will see if you feel the same in a short while.'

Setting down the large leather pouch, the Hyksos captain took a smaller one from his side and reached in. He pulled out the remnants of a blue lotus flower and put it into his mouth. He chewed slowly as he upended the bag and shook it.

'The last of my dream flowers,' he mused. 'I will have to make do without the whispers of the gods until I return to the banks of the Nile to claim some more.'

Piay watched a shadow cross Sakir's face. The absence of the flowers and his communion with his god Seth troubled him.

'Seth is the god of chaos, you know that,' Sakir began, still chewing. 'That is the essence of the Hyksos. Chaos. You Egyptians prefer order, from the earth below to the heavens above. Everything in its place, and everyone in their place. What a dull world you inhabit.' His stare did not waver. 'Chaos cannot abide order. It strives to destroy it. As we have destroyed the Pharaoh's forces. Piece by piece. Whittling you down until there is almost nothing left.'

'You will never defeat us,' Piay said.

'We will. Sooner than you might think.' Sakir jabbed a finger at Piay. 'But you . . . You have challenged me, and I am Seth's messenger upon this world, and so you have challenged Seth. That crime cannot go unpunished. Seth has charged me with destroying you. He told me in a dream. I stood in a cemetery that stretched to the horizon and felt the dry wind on my skin and the dust stinging my eyes. Seth's beast-head loomed over me, blocking out the moon, and he whispered to me the truth of this world.'

Piay stared deep into the Red Hawk's eyes and saw only madness there.

'Seth told me you were more than a mere man,' Sakir continued. 'You were a tool of the gods, too. This is a battle of the gods, played out among men. Your very existence was a poison that could destroy the Hyksos – that's what Seth told me. And you would disrupt Seth's plan unless you were crushed.'

'And Seth guided you to me,' Piay said in a cold tone.

'Seth . . . and other things.' Sakir flicked the tip of his tongue onto his lips. 'You have the slaver to thank for this moment we share.'

'Hanbaal?'

'When your ship first sailed into the delta after crossing the Great Green, he left word with those guarding the waterways that he had valuable information to share with me. For a great reward, of course.'

Piay gaped.

Sakir nodded. 'You were too trusting. You put your faith in a slaver?' He turned up his nose – the first time he had shown any emotion. 'They are lower than the snakes in the swamps.'

'But he never met you.'

'He left signs to show me the way. At Per-Bast. In the stretch of desert between the lake and the Red Sea. In Azania, where I came close to capturing you. And then in the Elephant Kingdom. Which brought me here, to this land, to this night. To your death.'

Piay felt sick to the pit of his stomach. He'd never really trusted Hanbaal, but the slaver had lured him into complacency with his honeyed words. His thoughts flew back across all the moments they'd shared together – the conversations, the discussion of plans, the sharing of knowledge. All those times when he'd felt he had someone beside him whose loyalty had been bought, and from the very first the slaver was looking for ways to turn that trust to his advantage. And now Piay would pay with his life.

'I hope he chokes on his reward,' Piay spat.

Sakir nodded slowly. 'The reward was richly deserved.'

He grasped the large leather pouch and tipped out its contents. A head dropped to the ground and rolled. Piay stared into Hanbaal's eyes one final time.

Piay looked at the emptiness in that glassy gaze. How much suffering had this beast caused? He wished Myssa was here to see this. It would never wipe out the pain she'd experienced seeing the slaughter of the ones she loved and being dragged away from her life and her home to be sold on the block. But she'd know that Hanbaal's whip would never crack on human flesh again, and that others would not suffer at his hand as she had. This ending – brutal and bloody – in some way balanced what had gone before.

It was some pleasure Piay could take to his grave. However small, justice had been served.

'Hanbaal thought he was clever,' Sakir continued. 'If only he had delivered you to me on your voyage south, then his head might yet remain upon his shoulders. But, no. The slaver drew me on, into a contest. Unsure who would be the victor, he played one side against the other until he was certain he would get his riches. He sealed his own fate.'

And now Piay's own time was done. His fate would be the same as Hanbaal's. Piay tried the bonds tying his wrists, but felt no movement. He knew he could not break them, not if he tried all night and all the next day. And even if he did, what then? He looked at the band of Hyksos warriors. He could never defeat them all. Without a weapon, he couldn't kill a single one before he was cut down. The last of his luck had drained away.

Sakir wandered back to the fire and plucked the knife from the embers. The blade glowed red.

Crouching down once more, he levelled the weapon in front of Piay's face. Piay felt his skin bloom from the heat. Sakir twirled the knife in tight circles, no doubt considering where to start to flay.

The glowing tip of the knife inched towards his face.

A low roar shattered the stillness. Almost as if he was surfacing from a deep sleep, Sakir glanced behind him, past the firelight and the torches.

Piay followed his stare. The roar was a familiar sound to him. But he glimpsed something else out there, like a star twinkling far out in the forest.

Another roar came across the plateau, echoed by a second, and then a third. Piay thought he could hear a distant thunder.

Sakir pushed himself to his feet and strode to the edge of the circle of torches. All around, his men stood, taking their lead from the Red Hawk. Piay watched unease leap from face to face like a wildfire.

The rolling thunder of those barks rumbled closer.

The single star had become three. They wandered across the dark expanse, sometimes disappearing behind trees before glowing again, drawing nearer.

'Arm yourselves,' Sakir growled.

Tossing aside the knife, the Red Hawk slipped his crescent sword from his sheath. Blades leaped to the hands of his men. Some backed away.

The first of the great apes exploded from the dark. Black fur gleamed in the torchlight. The beast's dark eyes glittered and its lips pulled back from those jagged fangs as it roared its fury. It bounded through the trees and crashed onto one of the Hyksos warriors. The ape's arms blurred as it tore limbs. The crushing jaws ripped flesh. The victim didn't have a chance to cry out before the ape launched itself at the next warrior.

Sakir's war band was rooted to the spot, as an army of those monstrous apes thundered out of the forest – the entire troop Piay had witnessed the other evening.

Piay stared, both horrified and awed. What could have propelled them to attack?

The Hyksos warriors scrambled in all directions, their cries ringing out into the night, but the apes fell on them mercilessly. Bones cracked and blood sprayed as the beasts tore through that seasoned band of warriors. Swords were useless against such speed and strength. This was slaughter.

Piay pressed himself lower, trying not to draw the attention of the beasts. They seemed to be crashing through the camp to escape whatever lay at their backs. Those warriors only had the misfortune to stand in their way.

Sakir had disappeared. But as Piay pushed himself back from the firelight, his attention was caught again by those stars glimmering in the dark. Only two glowed now, but he could see they were torches streaming through the darkness towards the camp.

Under the roaring flames of the torches, faces flared. Hannu and Myssa hurried on. They must have used fire to anger the apes and to herd them in the direction of the Hyksos warriors.

Piay felt a pang of fear. The apes were stampeding away while there were still surviving Hyksos warriors staggering around in shock.

'Leave me!' he yelled. 'Save yourselves!'

His friends ignored him. As they dashed into the circle of light, they tossed aside their torches. Hannu had his sword drawn and Myssa was gripping Jabilo's spear.

A barbarian lurched towards her. Myssa rammed the spear into his belly, almost lifting him off his feet. Once she'd wrenched her weapon free, she turned to the next assailant. She cut down man after man. She had never been a warrior, but she had the heart of a born fighter.

Hannu carved through his opponents with the cold skill that had earned him such respect in the Blue Crocodile Guards. His blade flashed high, thrusting and parrying. His eyes were black coals among the scars on his emotionless face.

Yet Piay knew those barbarians would soon gather their wits and begin fighting back in earnest. He strained at his bonds until he felt hot breath on his ear.

'Big man.'

It was Jabilo, sawing through the hide strips with Sakir's knife. The strips of leather snapped and Piay jumped to his feet.

'Away, Jabilo,' Piay urged. He beckoned to Hannu and Myssa to come with him.

Suddenly, Piay glimpsed movement beyond the fire. Sakir stepped out of the dark. He was soaked in blood and from his left hand swung the head of one of the apes.

Piay had a moment to take in that sight before Jabilo was dragging him away into the dark. Hannu and Myssa ran beside him.

'To the gorge,' Piay gasped. 'The river . . . That may be our only chance to escape.'

They darted through the trees that offered some cover from the barbarians. Piay could hear Sakir commanding the pursuit. Without torches in that deep darkness, the way ahead was treacherous. Piay had to trust his instincts.

They careered off the edge of the plateau, flying down the steep slope until they were falling and rolling, leaping off trees and tearing through bushes. Piay felt branches rip at the flesh on his face and arms, pain stabbing. They came to a halt on flatter ground, half-dazed and astonished they had not dashed in their skulls on the way down.

'The gods still smile on us,' Hannu croaked, pulling himself to his feet.

'They protect fools,' Piay replied, 'and there are no greater fools than us.'

Jabilo's eyes seemed to see more clearly than their own in that gloom. As he guided them along the track, Piay heard the roaring of the white water of the river.

Piay glanced back. Torches floated through the trees. The barbarians had discovered the trail.

Soon the noise of the river was all they could hear. Jabilo emerged from the trees and raised his arm to halt them. They were teetering on the edge of a void. The gorge plunged down a hand's width from Jabilo's feet into the dark where the rushing water thundered.

'What now?' Myssa said.

'This way,' Jabilo said.

He crept along the edge of the gorge, a narrow path between the clustering trees and the precipitous drop. They eased down a gentle slope, every now and then flailing to keep their balance. One wrong step and they would be plummeting to their deaths.

Piay realised the dawn was coming. In what seemed like no time, thin light crept in, turning the trees to grey ghosts and illuminating the way ahead. They tried to move more quickly.

Then Jabilo looked back, his face creased with concern.

'No way,' he said. 'No way.'

The path had narrowed and disappeared. The trees hung over the edge of the gorge and there was no way forwards.

Behind them, the torches trailed along the cliffside path. Piay could make out the shadowy shapes of the Hyksos warriors in the hazy early morning light. Sakir led the way.

Myssa turned to Piay.

'What do we do?'

Piay looked down the cliffside and he could now make out the white water thundering along the narrow channel.

'No,' Hannu said as if he could read Piay's mind. 'Are you a madman?'

'What choice is there?' Piay replied.

'You *are* a madman,' Hannu replied. 'We will dash out our brains on the way down or shatter every bone at the bottom and drown—'

'We have no choice. There is no way ahead. If we stand and fight, they will cut us down.'

Myssa shook her head. 'I cannot.'

Hannu streamed curses under his breath and growled, 'Piay is right. Pray and put your faith in the gods. And may we see each other again on the other side.'

In that instant, Sakir raced along the last of the path, torch held high in his left hand, sword gripped in his right.

Piay caught a blur of the sword swinging up for a killing blow and Sakir's stony face bearing down on him.

Before Piay could react, Jabilo thrust himself between his comrades and Sakir, with no weapon to defend himself. It was an unconscious act of protection for the ones who had become his closest friends.

Sakir's sword rammed into Jabilo's gut so hard, the tip burst out the other side.

As Sakir struggled to pull his blade free, Piay wrenched the torch from the barbarian's hand. He rammed the burning brand against Sakir's tunic. The flames surged up, crackling and licking, engulfing the Red Hawk. His beard and hair blazed; the skin began to blacken. Soon it would crack and burst, the eyes would boil and Sakir would be consumed.

Yet Sakir did not scream. Perhaps the blue lotus made him immune to pain.

Sakir lurched backwards, teetering on the edge of the abyss, then he staggered into the trees, a ball of fire.

Piay watched as the flames flew into the endless dark. Away Sakir fled until the flames winked out and only the impenetrable gulf remained.

Sakir was gone. He had paid the ultimate price for his crimes.

But further along the track, the other Hyksos were waiting to avenge their master.

'Go!' Piay bellowed to his comrades. 'Go, or die!'

Hannu wrapped his arms around Myssa and hurled himself over the edge. Myssa's scream trailed away and was gone. Piay gripped Jabilo's limp form in an embrace and leaped into the void.

The wind rushed past him. He slammed into the water so hard, all thoughts disintegrated. When his consciousness returned, he was in the blackness of the depths, engulfed in a bone-numbing chill, with his lungs burning and the turbulent river buffeting him madly. How he'd survived that fall, he had no idea, and somehow he'd managed to keep his grasp upon Jabilo. He prayed Hannu and Myssa were still alive.

Piay kicked out, trying to surface to suck air into his depleted lungs. The current was too strong and Jabilo's dead weight dragged him down.

He lunged again, an instinctive, animalistic urge, and broke the surface for an instant, long enough to grab a gulp of air.

But the current sucked him down again, the water so cold he could barely feel his body. He smashed against rocks, sharp edges raking his flesh. He kept one arm tight around Jabilo, hauling him on with prayers for both of them.

The last of his breath choked in his chest. At the moment when he felt death gripping him, the thunderous current eased. He clawed up again and reached the surface once more, this time keeping his head up for longer.

As he bobbed, he saw the river had surged through the gorge and the rapids beyond it and had now broadened out. The dawn sun glinted off the surface and glowed gold among the trees along the banks.

'Oh, Khonsu, preserve this faithful traveller,' he gasped.

With the last of his flagging strength, he swam, dragging Jabilo to the shallows with a hand hooked under his armpit. He glimpsed Hannu and Myssa sprawled on the rocks at the edge of the water, Jabilo's spear beside them. He felt a pang of relief. His two friends levered themselves up as he neared and they pulled Piay and Jabilo onto a broad, flat rock steaming in the morning sun.

The Abantu warrior's eyes flickered. He was still alive. But then Piay looked down his young friend's prone form and saw Sakir's sword still protruding from his belly. The wound was too great. There was no hope of Jabilo surviving.

Myssa kneeled next to him as silent sobs racked her body. Hannu bowed his head in respect.

Jabilo's lips moved. Piay bowed low to hear what the young warrior was trying to say.

'Big man,' Jabilo murmured. 'Big man.'

The last word drifted away; his eyelids stilled and he was no more.

Piay felt anguish well up inside him. He thought of Jabilo's innocence and the trust the young warrior had invested in his new master. This was the bitterest blow of all.

Hannu rested a hand on his shoulder.

'There is no blame here,' he murmured. 'Jabilo chose his own path.'

Piay heaved himself up and pulled the sword out of the young warrior's belly. He hurled the weapon into the waters. Once the ripples had faded, Piay said, 'The road is long. The sooner we start, the sooner we can put all this behind us.'

They buried Jabilo in a sunlit clearing in the forest, dragging rocks from the river's edge to pile across his body. Once they were done, they bowed their heads and Myssa uttered some words in the Abantu tongue. Piay asked what she had said, but she shook her head and walked away.

As they walked back to the river, Myssa began to sob.

'Bast. I have lost Bast,' she cried. 'I set her free before we confronted the great apes, and now I will never see her again.'

Piay slipped an arm around her shoulders and pulled her against him.

'We have lost much, but we have come through this together. We will find our strength in that.'

Myssa looked up at him with gleaming eyes and murmured, 'Together. Let nothing tear us apart.'

Piay waded through the mud on the edge of the swamp. Swatting away insects, he pulled aside a large frond. Ahead, a log-boat had been dragged up onto the riverbank. It was coated with mildew and by the looks of it had not been used in a long time.

'This way,' he called to Hannu and Myssa.

'I can fashion a paddle of some kind from a branch,' Hannu said when he reached Piay's side.

'Thank the gods!' Myssa exclaimed. 'I am sick of fighting my way through these swamps.'

They were ten days into their journey south from the plateau. The rains had lashed down almost from the moment they had walked away from Jabilo's grave, and the going had been hard. The river meandered through the valley, with numerous tributaries and cataracts, and they had been forced on several occasions to leave its banks and struggle through the steaming bogs. They'd seen no sign of other human beings until now.

Once Hannu had made the paddle, they pushed out into the water towards the south.

Navigating by the sun and the stars, they rowed for another seven days, enjoying the opportunity to feast on fish they speared in the shallows after so long on a diet of mushrooms.

But then the river twisted to the west and into a series of falls, leaving them with no choice but to continue on foot.

Every now and then, Hannu would dip into the pouch at his side and pull out the Scarlet Feather to ensure it was still in good shape to trade once they reached their destination. At least the river water had done it no damage.

Piay watched him examine their prize one night as they lay by a fire on the low slopes of a mountain range, with the vault of the heavens sprinkled with stars above them.

'By the time we reach Thebes, two floods of the Nile will have gone,' Piay said. 'What if there is no Egypt left for us?'

Hannu grunted. 'There's no gain in thinking such a thing. We put one foot in front of the other – that's all we can do – and when we reach the end of the road, we'll see what's there and then make our decisions.'

'At least no one will recognise you,' Myssa said, tracing a fingertip along Piay's shoulder.

His hair and beard had grown wild during their sojourn, as had Hannu's. No one would recognise them as civilised Egyptians.

Piay lay back and folded his hands behind his head, searching the constellations until he found the Four Sons of Horus. He took comfort from their unchanging position, just as Hui had done in Lacedaemon.

'I am a changed man in other ways,' he murmured 'If Taita still lives, he will never recognise me even after I bathe.'

'He will be proud to see you have become a better person,' Myssa whispered in his ear, before echoing Jabilo's final words. 'Big man. Big man.'

The boy raced along the rutted track, whooping with excitement, and Piay felt a surge of relief. Myssa had questioned the lad in the Abantu tongue when they'd found him practising with his bow and arrow in a clearing. He'd told them all they needed to know. After two more months of trekking through the forests and the valleys and the mangrove swamps, almost starving to death as they foraged for food, sneaking past suspicious villagers with cold hearts and sharp spears, and sheltering from rain that pounded for days on end, their journey was almost complete. They had reached the Elephant Kingdom. The city of Chemue was only a short walk. Now the boy was rushing ahead to herald their arrival.

While Piay and Myssa hugged, Hannu tramped on. In the tightness of his shoulders and the lowering of his head, Piay knew something was troubling his friend, but he knew this was not the moment to question him.

When they trudged into the city, the people crept out of their homes to scrutinise these strange new arrivals. The boy would have told everyone they were bringing a prize of the greatest value, one that would make this kingdom greater than all others. Piay hoped that would ease their passage into Chemue's presence. He'd long been convinced that the king and his advisor Omari had never thought they would complete their quest and had decided these three travellers were long dead.

Piay felt a simple joy to breathe in the earthy smells of a city – the woodsmoke, the sweat, the dust, even the stink of human waste.

The crowds lined the street from the gate in silence, not sure what they were observing. Piay studied their thin forms and ragged clothes, the babies wailing in their mothers' arms and the hollow-cheeked men. He'd expected them to have grown fat once the civil war had ended and food was not being wasted on endless battle. Yet it seemed that any wealth the king had gained from the end of the conflict had been kept in his own coffers.

The guards were waiting at the palace gate. When Myssa spoke with the captain, the voices became raised and hands gesticulated until Piay feared they were not going to be granted admission. But then the captain swept inside and returned soon after, beckoning them in.

Hannu wavered at the gate.

'What is wrong?' Piay asked.

'I cannot look the king in the face,' Hannu snarled.

Piay nodded. Hannu was remembering the execution of Degba. That cruel act had eaten its way into his friend's heart, rekindling many bitter emotions. Hannu would never forgive or forget. Piay tried to reassure him.

'With any luck this dirty business will soon be done and we can be away from here.'

Hannu handed over the pouch containing the Scarlet Feather.

With the guards accompanying them, Piay and Myssa strode through the gate into the palace grounds. Piay's eyes darted uneasily around him and he told himself to keep his wits about him. If Chemue had betrayed his own brother, the king could not be trusted to treat them fairly. How easy would it be to execute them both and take the feather without having to give up his prized elephants? Piay dropped his fingers to the hilt of his sword, ready to fight his way out if needs be. Myssa, too, gripped Jabilo's spear at the ready. She had barely let the weapon out of her sight since they had left his grave.

The throne room was stuffy in the heat of the day. Chemue sat straight-backed on his chair, grinning, but his eyes were as hard as pebbles. Beside him, Omari leaned on a tall staff. There was a smile there, too.

When Omari spoke, Myssa translated.

'He asks if you have what they desired.'

Piay pulled out the long Scarlet Feather. Balancing it on his palms, he offered it up.

Chemue and Omari's eyes widened.

Transfixed by this prize, Omari edged towards Piay. His face glowed with awe, as if this thing was some gift from the gods themselves, and then he bowed his head and said a few words.

'I . . . I cannot understand,' Myssa whispered. 'Some prayer, I think.'

Omari plucked up the feather with trembling fingers, placed it on his own palms and raised it towards the heavens. His voice rang like a bell.

'Nothing can stand in the way of the great King Chemue,' Myssa translated. 'All that he desires will now be granted. The glory of the kingdom will shine forever.'

Chemue threw his head back and laughed. Piay heard no joy, only a dark desire. Omari called out and a servant ran forwards with a bronze platter. Omari placed the feather upon it and the servant carried it away, no doubt ready to be fixed to the king's headdress.

'Tell him we have done as we were asked,' Piay said. 'Now we claim our reward.'

Myssa uttered the words. Piay watched their eyes narrow.

'Remind them that we are valued servants of the great Pharaoh of Egypt,' he said. 'Our return is eagerly anticipated. The Pharaoh will offer the open hand of friendship to any who would aid his envoys, as much as he would smite down any who betray them.'

Once Myssa had spoken, Chemue and Omari reflected for a moment, their faces darkening, and then the king waved a dismissive hand. He was eager to lay his claim to power.

Omari gave an answer.

'Eight elephants – that is all we are allowed,' Myssa translated.

'It is not much, but it will have to do,' Piay said.

'They are too valuable to offer any more than that,' Myssa continued, 'and the king and his generals will need the rest of the trained beasts for what will come next.'

Piay knew what that would be, just as Hannu had predicted.

'But Chemue demands that in return for his generosity, strong ties will be formed with Egypt and there will be much trade to fill the coffers.' Myssa showed an emotionless face, but her eyes revealed she knew what Piay was thinking. 'A relationship of equals,' she added.

'Equals,' Piay sneered. 'Very well. Tell them we will do what he asks. Then let us claim these great beasts and be away.'

The ground rumbled as the elephants tramped away from their pen. Once again, Piay marvelled at the majesty of these beasts. However many times he saw them, he was no less awed by their power. He could see that their eyes sparkled with the same intelligence he had seen in the horses that Taita had trained in Thebes. They were seemingly as docile as any house-dogs, walking in line, their trunks swaying. After the carnage he had witnessed the bull elephant unleash in Azania, Piay could scarcely believe it.

The Tumisi stepped beside them. A flick of a wooden switch or a raised hand was all it took to prompt the beasts to obey – to change direction, to lower themselves so their human brothers could climb upon them, and to charge into battle and terrify the enemy.

Seats of wood and hide were strapped across the wrinkled grey skin of the elephants' backs so the Tumisi could ride upon them, and harnesses were bound around their heads with ropes attached so their masters could guide them. The Tumisi lined up in front of their mounts. They were young, strong, wearing only leather kilts and a strip of fur tied around their foreheads to signify their status.

Piay nodded to Myssa and she walked along the line, giving the orders with a shake of her spear for emphasis. The Tumisi needed to know that they belonged to Piay now and he demanded absolute loyalty. Anything less would receive a brutal punishment. But for those who stayed true, there would be rewards beyond their wildest dreams.

Piay wasn't about to risk the Tumisi turning on them once they had left the city, killing them and returning home. After Hanbaal's betrayal, he would be more cautious with everyone he encountered.

Myssa performed her task well, showing a hard face. Her voice cracked like a whip.

Once he was sure the Tumisi understood their roles, Piay strode up. He needed to study these great beasts and divine their ways if they were to fight in the forefront of any battle with the Hyksos. To answer any of Piay's questions, Myssa summoned one of the Tumisi, a young man with a shaven head and a gap between his teeth.

'The elephants are not as docile as they appear at first glance,' Myssa translated. 'They each have their own personalities, their moods, which can shift like any man or woman.'

The rider moved along the line, announcing the names of the elephants and describing their traits. Piay marvelled at how the Tumisi saw so many shades of behaviour in these lumbering monsters.

'This one is Raju.' Myssa pointed to one of the beasts.

Piay flinched as he stared into its dark eyes, for he seemed to see a fierce intelligence there. The elephant flicked its trunk, almost caressing the side of Piay's head as it nuzzled him.

'Raju has a gentle nature and loves all men,' Myssa translated. 'Despite the elephants' fear of fire, he broke down the wall of a burning hut so a child inside could be saved.'

'Gentle, you say.' Piay couldn't help but smile at the beast as it playfully tapped him with its trunk. 'But then what use will he be in the thick of battle?'

The young man grinned when Myssa asked him.

'We should have no worry there,' she eventually replied. 'Raju is a happy warrior. Gentle in peacetime, fierce in battle.'

Piay moved along the line until he came to the final elephant. This time the trainer stepped forwards and pressed a hand against Piay's chest to hold him back.

'Do not get too close to this one,' Myssa translated. 'Mero has a temper as foul as a man waking the morning after a night filled with too much beer. He will swat you off your feet if the mood takes him, and one swat can break bones.'

Once again, Piay peered into the eyes, and this time he saw the same sullen warning he glimpsed in a man thinking about drawing a weapon.

'We should all keep away from this one,' he said with a nod.

Nearby, Hannu leaned against a mahogany tree, his arms folded. He couldn't bring himself to show any joy at their success. His heavy-lidded gaze flickered towards the palace rooftop visible beyond the elephant pens.

'We have done it, Hannu,' Piay said as he walked up. 'There were times I thought we would never gain what we desired – this prize always seemed to be disappearing into the distance. But . . . we have done it.' He allowed himself a grin.

'I had no doubts,' Hannu replied. 'If anybody could do this, it would be you.'

Piay furrowed his brow at the surprising compliment.

'We have a long march ahead of us,' he said. 'At least there will be beer and a feast fit for a king at the end of it.'

Hannu grunted.

Myssa strode ahead of a line of slaves carrying bales upon their heads, the provisions for the journey that she had been negotiating with Omari. While the Tumisi fastened the bales to the elephants' backs, Myssa unfurled a roll of papyrus she had been carrying under her arm. It was a map, delicate brushstrokes showing their way in black ink.

'See here,' she said, tracing a finger along the line of their route. 'Omari says we can follow the trade road to the north. It is well travelled and should allow for a fast pace. When we reach Azania we will find a great lake in the highlands, and from there we will follow the waters that become the Nile through Kush and back to Egypt.'

Piay smiled, amazed. 'Every day I watched Mother Nile flow by, and every season I celebrated when the floods came and she offered us her bounty, but never once did I think of her beginnings.' He tapped his finger on the map. 'This lake, you say? What magic must live there. That will be a tale to tell indeed when we are back in Thebes.'

Once the arrangements had been completed, they bathed and Piay shaved off his beard and hair before preparing to fill their bellies from broad leaves covered with fruit that Chemue's servants laid before them. As Piay raised the first bite to his mouth,

Hannu stopped him. Taking a morsel of the fruit, Hannu pushed it into a servant's mouth and watched the man chew. Only then did Hannu nod, satisfied.

'Can't be too careful,' he muttered.

'You are right,' Piay said. 'The king expects us to leave at first light tomorrow. I think it wise to make our departure today, at sunset, should he have any surprises for us. I am told there will be celebrations across the city this evening, and with luck Chemue and all his followers will be distracted.'

'Wise, indeed,' Hannu said.

After that, Hannu grabbed an armful of fruit and wandered away to one side to eat his meal on his own.

'Why is he brooding?' Myssa asked.

'The execution of Degba still preys on his mind. He will be well soon enough.'

Myssa narrowed her eyes as she studied Hannu. 'He seems to be wrestling with some choice. Have you spoken to him?'

'One thing I have learned during my time with Hannu is that when something is on his mind, he doesn't like to be asked about it. I have no doubt he will come to the right conclusion, whatever it is.'

The red sun burned above the treetops in the west. All the preparations had been made and the time had come to depart. As the shadows pooled across the city, Piay wandered to where their caravan waited.

He was happy to leave this place. The throats of sleeping visitors could easily be cut in the dark.

Perhaps he was worrying about nothing. He'd watched the slaves preparing a great feast for a ceremony when the king would be crowned with his new headdress with the Scarlet Feather set firmly in it. The news of Chemue's elevation to godhood had spread across the city. The celebrations had begun. Piay could hear the music and the laughter ringing out. The king's guards were already drunk and soon everyone at the feast would be, too. But even if there was no threat, Piay wanted no part of this merrymaking. The sooner this city was behind them, the better.

Myssa shouted the order to the Tumisi and with a flick of their switches, the elephants lurched along the road and out of the city towards the north.

'We are going home,' Piay said, looking at the darkening sky ahead.

'You are going home.' Myssa's tone was flat. She was remembering what she had lost.

'I hope Egypt will become your home, too,' Piay replied. 'If not at first, then soon. I will do all within my power to show you the joy I feel there.'

Myssa smiled. 'I care not where we are, as long as you are there at my side.'

Piay glanced to the rear of the caravan and glimpsed Hannu with his head still bowed. He marched along the line of elephants to Piay's side.

'I cannot go with you,' Hannu said.

Piay held out a hand. 'If there is something wrong, we can—'

'No!'

Piay recoiled at the vehemence of his friend's response.

'Here is where we part company,' Hannu insisted. 'Do not come after me. Do not wait for me. It will do no good.'

'Hannu,' Myssa protested, 'we need you.'

'I have served you faithfully,' Hannu said to Piay, 'and if you have any kindness in your heart for that – for a friend – then do as I say. I cannot stay with you. I am compelled to go.'

Piay shook his head in disbelief. He did not want to lose his friend. But as he stared into the other man's eyes, he saw the determination there and knew he had no choice. Whatever preyed on his friend's mind, there was no doubt this decision had been a long time coming. He seemed tormented by some inner conflict.

'Why do you feel the need to stay behind?' Piay asked. 'After all we have been through, I cannot begin to fathom this.'

'I cannot say—'

'Will not.'

'Yes. You will only try to talk me out of leaving and my mind is made up. Better not to waste your breath.'

'I beg you to reconsider. Hope lies ahead of us, and victory. A rebirth for all of us. Nothing good lies behind.'

'And therein lies the problem.' Hannu lowered his eyes and said in a quiet voice, 'This may be the last we see of each other. But if I can find my way back to you, I will.'

Before Piay could press him further, Hannu turned and limped back along the road.

The moon turned the road into a strip of beaten silver running through the forest. In the camp at the side of the track, Piay leaned against a trunk with Myssa curled against him. Since Hannu's departure, they had not travelled on much further before they broke their journey. Piay felt too despondent to trudge on, and he could see from Myssa's downcast face that she felt the same. He hoped that after a night's sleep his spirits would improve.

The elephants slumbered, leaning against the trees that lined the road. The Tumisi dozed close to their charges.

'Tell me what Egypt is like,' Myssa said.

'I have never known it at the height of its grandeur. Only stories I have heard, from my master Taita. But his eyes were filled with fire when he told me of the royal barges sailing down the Nile, and the glory of the cities, the feasts and the music and the art, even the simple pleasures of those who toiled in the fields. There was trade from all over the world, and great learning and medicine that healed men and women and children. There was peace. Truly it was a land blessed by the gods.'

'That sounds wondrous indeed.' Myssa paused, choosing her words. 'And you believe your homeland can be that way again?'

'There is no doubt.' Piay's voice rose with defiance. 'Egypt's glory lies in the hearts of its people. That will never be diminished. The Hyksos may have taken us by surprise. They may have been stronger with their bows and chariots and horses. But their time has been like a blink of an eye in the long history of my home. Soon they will be gone and forgotten. Egypt will endure.'

'If your land is to be saved, my love, it will be because of people like you. You are the true treasure of Egypt.'

Piay was moved by her statement. Not long ago he would have said such a thing as an empty boast. Now, to hear those words from another, they shone like gold. He wanted to thank her, but before he could speak he felt the slowing rise of her chest and the steadiness of her breathing and he knew she had fallen asleep.

The shrieking of the birds rang out across the camp. Piay eased himself out from beside Myssa and climbed to his feet. Drawing his sword, he wandered along the road to see what had disturbed them.

The low rays of the sun were streaming through the trees and the cold of the night was fading as fast as the shadows.

He glimpsed a flicker of movement. Something was rounding the bend in the road. The gait was rolling, the shape indistinct in the thin dawn light, but as it took on form, Piay recoiled in horror. Some terrible apparition was lurching along the road towards them, a creature that looked like it had escaped from the very depths of Duat. It had the shape of a man, but it was like no man Piay had ever seen before.

As it lumbered nearer, Piay's gaze settled on its staring eyes, white against the dark mass surrounding them. Closer still it came, and Piay realised it was a man soaked in blood, matting the hair and beard and caking every other part of him. A sword hung from the right hand and the stranger didn't seem to have the strength to lift it.

As the light brightened and the figure lurched to the edge of the camp, Piay saw it was Hannu.

Piay raced forwards and his friend almost fell into his arms. Piay feared that Hannu was dying from a thousand cuts. But as Piay searched the torso, wiping away the blood, he found there were no wounds beneath.

Hannu searched in the pouch at his side. He pulled something out and tossed it on to the dusty road.

At first Piay couldn't grasp what it was. But then he saw it was a feather – the Scarlet Feather, crimson and bloodied.

The sun was high in the sky before they set off again. Hannu cleaned himself in a stagnant pool in the shade beneath the trees. He was so weary, he could barely speak, and Piay decided his friend should ride on the back of one of the elephants until he had gathered his strength. They would need to increase their pace in case vengeance followed at their backs. Hannu would not talk about what had happened that night in the city of the Elephant Kingdom, of the slaughter that must have occurred, and Piay believed he never would.

But of one thing Piay could be certain: justice had been done.

As they trekked on through the heat, Piay strained to listen for any sound of pursuit. After three days, he decided they were safe. Gradually, Hannu's strength returned and he insisted he should walk beside the column like Piay and Myssa. Piay studied him from afar and thought he seemed pleased that a wrong had been righted, as much as it could be.

The days merged into one. On that slow, arduous journey, the routines became everything. Their progress was dictated by the constant search for water to assuage the elephants' seemingly endless thirst, and the relentless feeding to provide them with the strength they needed to move their bulk.

Mero marched at the head of the column. The beast was as bad-tempered as Piay had imagined the first time he had looked in its eyes, snorting and stamping and occasionally threatening to ignore the directions of its rider and tramp off into the depths of the forest. Piay wondered if it could ever be counted on in battle.

Hannu and the gentle Raju took a liking to each other. As they walked side by side, the beast would playfully tap Hannu with its trunk from time to time, teasing him as if it were a child. Hannu had never smiled so much in all the seasons Piay had known him, though he hid it every time he caught Piay looking.

Every now and then, Hannu would slip into the trees to find a treat for Raju, juicy green plants or berries and fruit which the elephant would accept with a gleeful shake of its head.

The other elephants gorged themselves on tree bark, roots and grass, occasionally gouging out holes in the earth with their tusks to munch on whatever succulent morsels lay hidden in the soil.

Six weeks into the trek, Myssa shook Piay awake at first light.

'One of the elephants is sick,' she whispered.

Piay trudged after her to where one of the smaller beasts lay on its side, its breathing shallow and its eyelids fluttering. The Tumisi gathered around it, their faces stern as they muttered together.

'What is wrong with it?' Piay breathed.

'They say it is a sickness carried by one of the flying insects that buzz among the trees,' Myssa replied. 'One single bite can kill a beast this size, so the Tumisi say. Now its life is in the lap of the gods.'

As Piay watched the slow rise and fall of the elephant's chest, he felt a troubling thought settle on him. If these creatures could become sick and die so easily, there may be none left by the time they had covered the vast tracts of land back to Thebes. He had not even considered this. To have fought so hard and still be denied victory by fate.

'We will wait here and keep a vigil,' he said.

And so they did, for three days. Piay felt surprised by the behaviour of the other elephants, who seemed to recognise that one of their own was ailing, and from time to time tried to gather round the stricken beast as if they were mounting their own vigil.

On the fourth day, Piay watched smiles break out across the faces of the Tumisi as they examined the elephant. Not long after, the creature hauled itself to its feet for the first time since it had fallen sick and began to gnaw on the bark of the nearest tree.

Piay felt relief flood him. But as he looked along the road to where it disappeared among the trees, he could only think of how far they still had to go and how many dangers undoubtedly awaited them.

The rains came as they entered the neck of a narrow valley. The downpour crashed down so heavily Piay could barely see more than a spear's throw ahead, the world becoming as night as the light was choked away. Soon the water gushed around their ankles from new-made streams flooding down the steep, heavily forested valley sides.

Piay bowed his head into the deluge and heaved his way up the gently rising track. The elephants splashed on into the gloom, oblivious, the Tumisi hunched upon their backs. No one spoke, for all words were swallowed by the din of the storm.

For what seemed like an age, Piay threw himself on, but every step was an effort. The road underfoot had become sucking mud and the rushing water now reached mid-calf.

He felt a hand grip his arm and he turned to see Hannu.

'I do not like the look of this!' his assistant bellowed.

Barely had the words left his lips when a roaring echoed all around, louder even than the storm. Piay jerked his head up in the direction of the tumult. A moment later he glimpsed trees falling as if they had been knocked aside by an invisible monster, and a moment after that a band of water twice his own height crashed down the valley side to the road.

Myssa struck like a cobra, hurling her arms around Piay and dragging him out of the path of the massive wave. As he crashed off the side of the road, Piay felt a chill wind rush by him. Caught in a tangle of limbs, he unhooked himself from Myssa and jumped to his feet. A black river raced down the road, carrying with it lofty trees torn from the very earth.

Glancing round, he saw the elephants had pounded on to where the road levelled off. They had been just ahead of the flood and escaped by a whisker. His relief stuttered as he realised Myssa was on her feet, screaming, and the Tumisi were sliding from their beasts and running towards him, bellowing and pointing.

Piay whirled and felt a chill as powerful as that torrent rush through him.

Further down the road, in the middle of the roaring river, Hannu's right arm snaked up and his face pushed above the rising water as he fought for breath. An uprooted tree jammed across the track pinned him beneath the water. He was drowning.

Piay threw himself into the flood. The sheer force of the water smashed his legs out from under him and down beneath the churning black water he went. Somehow hands caught him before he was dragged out of reach. The Tumisi hauled him out, gasping for breath.

Piay shoved them away and staggered back to the edge of the river.

'We have to save Hannu!' he howled.

But even as he cried out he could see how hopeless it was. The thunderous water was too deep, too fast. Anyone would be whisked away before they could reach the tree where Hannu was trapped.

The water rose, lapping across his friend's face. Piay felt that despair would break him in two.

A pounding erupted at his back and Raju thundered down the road and into the river. So furious was the torrent, the elephant was swept along in the current until it finally crashed against the tree and righted itself. Once it had braced itself in the flow, Raju curled its trunk around the tree and strained.

On their journey Piay had seen the elephants lift trees before, but in that weight of water this seemed too much. Yet still the elephant struggled.

As he gaped, Piay sensed another great beast lurching past him. This one was Mero. The bad-tempered bull slammed in beside Raju and joined in the labour.

Piay's heart leaped when he saw the tree shudder, then lift. Hannu gripped on to a branch and pulled himself out of the flow, gasping and spluttering. He knew the danger he was still in, Piay could see, and he hauled himself along the trunk until he could leap to safety on the other side of the road.

Cheers rang out from the Tumisi, but Piay was gripped by the battle still taking place in the water. Now freed, the tree spun away and rushed off in the flow. Untethered, Raju drifted away. That elephant was smaller than the others and did not have the bulk to anchor itself. Piay was sure he sensed the panic begin to dawn in the great beast.

Mero must have understood what was happening, too. His trunk snaked out and wound around Raju's, trying to hold him fast.

Piay bunched his fists, silently urging the great bull to succeed. But his heart sank as he watched those linked trunks begin to unfurl under the weight of the water dragging Raju away.

The moment seemed to hang and then the two trunks snapped free and Raju rushed away. Mero pushed his head back and trumpeted into the storm, but it was too late. Raju was gone.

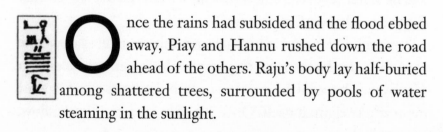 Once the rains had subsided and the flood ebbed away, Piay and Hannu rushed down the road ahead of the others. Raju's body lay half-buried among shattered trees, surrounded by pools of water steaming in the sunlight.

Hannu howled as if he was in agony and stormed away into the trees. Before Piay could follow him, he glimpsed the elephants tramping down the road towards him with the Tumisi hurrying beside them. He watched in astonishment as the great beasts gathered around Raju and, with great tenderness, lowered their trunks upon the still form.

'They are mourning their fallen,' Myssa breathed.

'But they are beasts—' Piay began before he bit off the words. There was no way to deny the truth of Myssa's statement. As he stared, he felt deeply touched by the scene. He would never forget it.

The lake shimmered on the horizon like a polished bronze mirror. Piay shielded his eyes against the glare as he looked across the expanse of water, as big as any sea. He closed his eyes and luxuriated in the cooling wind after the two-month-long trek through the seething heat along the spine of this land.

Since the devastating floods, they'd driven the elephants through rain-lashed forest and up into the rocky higher ground, climbing towards the north. As they crested a ridge, this magnificent sight presented itself, at first as blue as the sky, but now turning to molten gold as the sun slipped down the sky.

According to Omari's chart, this lake was the source of the Nile, to the west of Azania. From here, they would be winding along the banks of the sacred waters until they reached the cataracts in familiar territory.

Exhausted, Piay slumped to the grass. Not far away, the trees spread to the water's edge, and ahead Piay could make out islands dotting the lake's surface. Here they could rest for the night and prepare for what was to come.

In the shallows, the elephants sprayed water over themselves. Mero was among them. Since the death of Raju, the bull seemed changed, less prone to the bad-tempered outbursts it had exhibited so many times before. During the days and weeks, Piay had come to learn all their moods and his respect had turned to something close to love. They felt joy, he could see, and irritation, even anger. They were kind and loving to their brothers, the Tumisi. He had no doubt of their intelligence.

Myssa ran across the grass and splashed in the lake beside them, throwing water on to her face and soaking her hair. Even Hannu ambled down to soak his tired feet.

An abundance of silver fish streaked past in flickering trails of light and by the time the sun had reached the horizon, the Tumisi had speared plenty, throwing them on to the grass. After he'd collected dry wood, Hannu lit a fire. Within no time, the fish had been gutted and scaled, wrapped in large, fibrous leaves and roasted in the embers. They filled their bellies and drank cold water bubbling from a spring.

As they lay on the grass in a balmy night breeze, Myssa said, 'There is magic in the air. Can you feel it?'

Piay thought he could. His gaze drifted to the ivory moon hanging above the lake and he felt a shiver of delight. This could be the last moment of peace before they swept into a conflict that could claim all their lives.

A shooting star streaked across the sky and he felt a notion stir him.

'I must make a prayer,' Piay said in a low voice, 'to Khonsu, for him to watch over us in the days to come.'

At the spring Piay filled his hide with the cool water. Then he slipped into the dark away from the firelight and found a finger of land where he could be alone.

At the water's edge, he raised the hide up high and let the water trickle on to the surface of the lake. The ripples spread glinting with moonlight.

'Great Khonsu,' he murmured, 'protect us on this last stage of our journey as you have guided us on every step we have taken on this long road. Shield us from our enemies. Defend us from those who would do us harm. And lead us to that place of peace and safety where we can find our glorious destiny.'

A sudden gust of wind plucked the words from his lips and swept them out across the water. When it died, a strange silence hung over everything. Piay could no longer hear the crackle of the distant fire or the hum of voices. Two moons glowed, one in the heavens and the other its reflection in the black surface of the lake.

Piay sensed movement, and when he glanced along the shore, he saw a curious sight. The elephants tramped to the water's edge and stood in a line looking out across the lake, almost as if they were waiting for something.

He felt an unusual heaviness in the air, and then the creeping feeling that he was not alone. Far out across the lake, he sensed a presence. Was it his imagination? It seemed that a figure was walking along the strip of light cast by the moon on the surface of the water.

'Khonsu,' he whispered.

Piay thought he could make out the falcon head and the sun disk and moon crescent upon the mummy wrappings. In the blur, the god appeared to reach out the hand of blessing.

In the presence of the god, Piay felt rooted to the earth and his body filled with cold flames. He bowed his head, at once terrified and filled with wonder.

For what seemed like an age, Piay floated in that magical state and then he looked up once more and the moonlight dazzled him.

When his vision cleared, the sanctified atmosphere had passed and the god – if he had ever been there – had vanished. Yet Piay was moved by the experience and overcome by the blessing. He felt protected and guided towards some great destiny.

Along the shore, the elephants trundled away from the water's edge. The spell had been broken.

His legs weakened and Piay crumpled to the cool grass. As the cold fire burned out, he felt the comfort of sleep blanket him.

As dawn broke, Piay returned to the camp. The memory of the waking dream was already fading. Within no time, the Tumisi were flicking their switches and the line of elephants tramped along the track around the edge of the lake.

The lake was so vast, they rested on the shores for another night, and on the following day they came to the river coursing away from it.

'The Nile, Hannu,' Piay whispered. 'There were times when I thought I would never see it again. But look . . .' He pointed into the hazy distance. 'It is taking us home.'

'All well and good,' Hannu said, 'but what is waiting for us when we get there?'

'You are filled to the brim with vinegar. Why I chose you to be my assistant, I will never know.'

'You did not choose me,' Hannu said. 'I chose you.'

Piay laughed. 'What flight of fancy has given wing today?'

'Mock all you want, but it's true. When I saw you walking along the street that day, my first thought was that you looked like a man with no purpose. A man lost. There was a deep sadness in you.'

'You could see this, could you?'

'I told you, if there is one thing I am good at, it is seeing into a man's heart.'

'I had all the success a man could wish for.'

'True. And comforts aplenty, and wine and women. But you were still adrift. It was in your eyes.'

'Let me remind you – I asked *you* to be my assistant.'

'And I would have said no to any other man. My life was hard, but it was simple. I thought, "You've had enough moping around. Here's some direction. A way to spend your days. Show this privileged fool the road he should be on."'

Piay bristled. 'My act of charity was to show you the road you should have been on.'

Myssa stepped between them and hooked her arms in theirs.

'The two of you will find some way to fight over a mouldy piece of bread. Can you both agree that you have each found the right road and it has led to a better place for both of you?'

'I will hear no more sour words,' Piay said. 'Whatever awaits us will be the destiny the gods have chosen for us.'

The Nile widened as it meandered through Nubia. They kept as close to the banks as they could, where it was cooler, but sometimes the way was impassable and they were forced to trek up to the higher ground in the furnace heat. The ochre desert pressed in close and the hot wind blasted clouds of dust.

Beyond the Third Cataract, Hannu pointed to a camp of desert wanderers. Piay broke off from the caravan and strode towards them, hoping to get news of what lay ahead in Egypt. But as he neared, the Habiru raced out from their circle of tents, ululating and whirling their swords above their heads. Piay hurried back to the elephants, and when he glanced again those outlaws were already breaking camp and preparing to move away with a speed that surprised him.

'Don't like the look of that,' Hannu muttered.

'As long as they leave us alone, I am happy,' Piay replied.

Hannu continued to watch. But within no time the desert wanderers had disappeared into the heat haze and the caravan continued in silence.

Only when the First Cataract appeared, did Piay allow himself to accept that he was home. As his gaze drifted down those steep banks of golden sand, topped with slabs of granite, to the river dotted with the jagged teeth of rocks and boulders, he felt an overwhelming sense of relief. Once they had passed through the cataract, the Nile plunged on, unfettered, towards Thebes. The going would be easier. There would be river traffic and farmers in the fields, merchants and masons, the bustle of familiar life.

'Beyond is your home, yes?' Myssa asked.

Piay nodded. 'And destiny.'

'And beer. And rest,' Hannu sighed, limping on. 'Until the fighting starts.'

A band of trees and shrubs edged the rocky banks of the river. The Tumisi guided the elephants along the side of the thorn bushes at the foot of the sweeping sandy bank towering up to the silver sky. With every step, Piay felt his heart lift. He fixed his gaze on the space ahead between the two valley sides, waiting for it to grow wider, the peaks diminishing and the land opening out.

Home, so close he could almost taste it.

Hannu came to a halt ahead and looked around.

'What's wrong?' Piay asked.

'Perhaps nothing.' Hannu peered up to the top of the valley sides. 'A shadow, perhaps.'

A crack of stone echoed and out of the glare of the sun a boulder careered down the sandy slope. Piay cried out a warning. The rock whisked between two elephants and splashed into the river, miraculously touching neither.

An instant later, rocks were raining down from the top of the valley. The Tumisi hooted and swung their switches, whipping the elephants into action. They thundered along the green line of straggly trees and spiky-leaved bushes.

'Take cover!' Piay shouted.

He ran into the trees as the rocks crashed on every side, splintering branches and bursting through bushes. He realised he'd lost sight of Hannu and Myssa, and he shouted their names but could hear no reply. The booming of the projectiles drowned out all other sounds.

Through the leaves, Piay glimpsed movement along the top of the ridge. He made out the familiar sight of the Hyksos in their leather caps and breastplates, with their black beards and hair. He threw himself aside as another boulder ploughed into the sand and crashed through the trees where he had been standing.

He clambered over the rocks and slipped into the cold water, hoping it would provide him with some cover. The barbarians had their swords drawn and some were creeping down the valley sides.

This attack was the same tactic Piay had launched against their enemies as they searched for the Scarlet Feather in those mist-shrouded mountains. Could this be the remnants of Sakir's band carrying out their master's – and Seth's – vision and trying to destroy the elephants, the saviours of Egypt? They must have sailed back much faster than Piay and Hannu. The desert wanderers they'd seen earlier could have been set to spy on the approach along the Nile and raise the alarm if they saw a caravan of elephants.

No more than ten warriors were skidding down the sand. Maybe that was all that was left of the men who had crewed the six warships that first gave pursuit along the Red Sea.

Letting the river current carry him, Piay struck out behind the cover of the trees to where the Tumisi had led the elephants to protect them from the assault. He hauled himself out of the water and ran to one of the men. Without Myssa he couldn't make himself easily understood, but he jabbed his finger towards the advancing Hyksos. The elephant trainer smirked.

The battle cries of the Hyksos rang in the air. Piay turned to face them as the Tumisi mounted their charges. There was still no sign of Hannu and Myssa along the treeline, but he reckoned they'd be biding their time, waiting for the barbarians to pass and then attacking them from behind.

The barbarians scrambled to the foot of the slope and approached Piay. The elephants lumbered forwards, slow at first but then breaking into a run. Piay followed beside them. He knew how fast these great beasts could move. The Hyksos were about to find out.

Some of the barbarians tried to scramble up the slope, sliding in the sand and tumbling back. The lead elephant crushed one man under its feet, and two more warriors fell beneath the feet of the second. Others stumbled towards the trees. Piay was ready for them.

Without breaking step, he thrust his sword into the stomach of one of the Hyksos warriors and hacked into the neck of another. The remaining five men fled. One tripped, screaming as the lead elephant thundered over him. The others managed to claw their way up the slope.

Piay watched them go. They had chosen the perfect place for the ambush, but how hopelessly it had been executed. Had they really thought they'd stood a chance of success? Khonsu had smiled upon them once more.

As the last of the barbarians fled over the ridge, Piay heard groans. He dashed into the trees, calling for Hannu and Myssa. As he searched, he saw Hannu climbing to his feet, a gash across his forehead.

Piay grabbed him. 'Who attacked you?'

Hannu shook his head. Droplets of blood flew.

'He still lives,' he croaked. 'Sakir still lives.'

*How can this be?*

The last Piay had seen of Sakir, he was engulfed in flames. Surely no man could have survived that. But then a terrible cold drained through him.

'Myssa,' he whispered.

Hannu snatched Piay's arm, but his grip was weak.

'He wants you to follow. He is luring you into a trap.'

This was Seth's vision. To isolate Piay, destroy him and thereby destroy any hope of the Hyksos being defeated. If Piay was wise, he would stay with the caravan and ensure the elephants reached Taita.

His heart sank. 'You know I have no choice.'

He felt sick at the thought of Myssa in the Red Hawk's grasp. He lurched away through the trees, leaving Hannu to sink to his knees, dazed.

He scanned along the First Cataract. A line of footprints scarred the sand, leading up the slope – two people, one of them being half-dragged. Piay threw himself up the incline, ignoring Hannu's weakened cries.

At the top of the slope, he looked out across the waste. That ragged line of prints led to the dark smudge of two figures in the distance. The Red Hawk was moving fast for a man who had been half-burned alive. Myssa was struggling. She had a strength that drove her on through all hardship, but Sakir would not tolerate resistance. His punishment would be brutal.

As Piay ran forwards, he felt a moment of clarity: his life meant nothing. He would give it up in an instant if he could save Myssa. He was no longer the man he had been. He was reborn – for better or worse, he did not yet know.

The desert sun seared. The land was a blur of brown dust where mounds of coppery rocks thrust through the surface. The bleak landscape rolled out in billowing waves, the fleeing figures sometimes disappearing beneath the line of ridges. Here and there ravines cut through the sand, with steep granite cliffs dropping down to a carpet of huge boulders.

Piay dribbled water from his hide onto his dry lips – he knew he had to conserve the precious life-giving liquid in the terrible heat.

Dust exploded at his heels as he ran on. He was closing on the two figures. He could just make out Sakir thrusting Myssa forwards, his crescent sword clutched in his hand. The barbarian had tied her wrists to her spear behind her back. She was staggering and seemed dazed.

Piay slid down a bank and lost sight of them, and as he clawed his way up the other side, Sakir and Myssa were nowhere to be seen. He pushed himself onwards, his steps more measured. Sakir must have been planning this for a long time. After the torture Sakir had suffered at his hands, the Red Hawk would want to inflict as much pain as he could dream up in his twisted mind. Myssa was the key to that.

But now a wind was blowing in. A huge cloud of dust whirled along the horizon, darkening the sky. Piay winced as the burning sand blasted into him like shards of glass.

He plunged down another slope and when he rose on the other side, he stumbled across deep gouges in the landscape that looked as if they had been cut by the deluge of watercourses in some long-forgotten time. The footprints ended at the lip of one of the gorges.

Piay crept to the edge and peered over the side. It was possible to pick a path down the rocky side. But at the foot of the incline, the dry water channels became a maze of twisting paths. Sakir had chosen well. Piay would be blind to what waited ahead of him, would not be able to prepare himself when the Red Hawk launched his attack.

Piay knew what Hannu would have advised: it would be reckless to venture into the labyrinth. But he gave no heed to the risks. Myssa was all that mattered.

Piay felt a sudden chill. He was sure he could see a face forming in the dust clouds. Eyes burned and a fanged maw gaped, and around it he could make out the familiar beast-head of Seth. In that moment he had no doubt the god of the desert was present, watching his agent commit an act of slaughter in Seth's name.

Piay shuddered under that terrible vision. It was the dark reflection of his encounter with Khonsu by the lake at the source of the Nile. There, he had experienced love and protection. Here, he sensed only loathing.

Piay drew his sword and crept down the rocks into the depths.

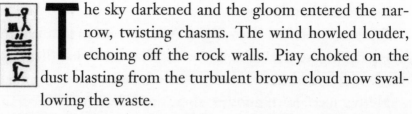The sky darkened and the gloom entered the narrow, twisting chasms. The wind howled louder, echoing off the rock walls. Piay choked on the dust blasting from the turbulent brown cloud now swallowing the waste.

The footprints were no longer visible. Sword in hand, Piay moved along the channels, feeling around the rough rocky sides to guide him. His eyes darted for any hint of Sakir.

A cry rang out.

*Myssa.*

Piay's anger surged and he pushed through the dust towards the sound.

At a point where two chasms crossed, he sensed a sudden movement to his right. Out of the cloud of brown dust, a figure was racing towards him, sword swinging over its head.

Piay felt a wave of horror at the monstrous sight, like some creature from a nightmare. Sakir was blackened by the fire that had only partly consumed him, his beard and hair burned off, the skin of his face charred and blistered. One eye glowed with a milky sheen. How he had not succumbed to death from his injuries, Piay did not know. But there he was, filled with a supernatural power, the power of the god Seth. Vitality coursed through him. His muscles flexed and he thundered with the speed of a fighting man in his prime.

That crescent blade slashed down.

Piay instinctively flung his own blade up, clattering it against the edge of his enemy's weapon. Sparks glittered.

'Where is Myssa?' Piay raged.

'She lives.' Whatever damage the fire had done to Sakir's lips, his voice now had a faint sibilance.

'If you have harmed her—'

The crescent sword flashed towards Piay's gut and he danced back, catching his heel on a rock. Over he went. Before the Red Hawk could seize his advantage, Piay rolled back and thrust himself to his feet. He swept up his sword to parry another strike. The vibrations jolted him to the marrow.

'You have become distracted by the woman,' Sakir hissed. 'Caring for another has weakened you. We were evenly matched before, but you have allowed yourself to bare your own throat. It will be the end of you.'

Piay bounded back again from Sakir's furious onslaught. But he knew what the barbarian meant. His concerns for Myssa intruded into his single-mindedness. If he did not overcome it, all would be lost.

'I would have it no other way.' Piay forced a grin. 'I pity you, Sakir. You have nothing but your hatred to fill the emptiness that is your life.'

'Aye, and life is what I will keep. You have traded that for love, and death.'

Sakir drove on, hacking and slashing with an inhuman strength. Piay felt his arms begin to ache and his chest burn. He leaped around the narrow channel, but there was little room to move freely; all his skills as a swordsman were blunted. Sakir had planned it this way. The Red Hawk's brute strength was now proving enough.

Sakir disappeared into the billowing dust. Piay whirled back and forth, waiting for the moment he would emerge. The crescent sword, flashed. Vanished. Flashed again.

The tip of the blade licked his forehead and he felt the sting. Staggering back, he tripped on the uneven surface once again and crashed down. Sakir loomed over him, the hideous black face impassive. His sword swung up for the killing blow.

Winded, Piay closed his fingers on a rock and hurled it with all his strength. The stone smashed against the Red Hawk's face, ripping open a pink gash. Sakir staggered back, clutching at his features.

Piay jumped to his feet and thrust.

Somehow Sakir twisted at the last moment and the blade merely raked across his side. Blood spattered on to the rocks.

Sakir's good eye flickered, and in its depths Piay could see his opponent knew his advantage had gone. The barbarian curled his ragged lips into a tight smile. He was unafraid.

Dancing back to where the rocky walls were not so steep, Sakir leaped up and heaved himself towards the rim.

Piay felt a burst of panic. In his mind's eye, he pictured Myssa at the top, Sakir hurling her off the edge to gain his revenge, her body broken on the rocks below. He threw himself after the Red Hawk. In his mind he could hear Hannu warning him not to follow, that Sakir would have the advantage of height. But he would not hold back.

*Myssa*, he thought. *Myssa.*

Piay clawed his way over the rocks. Sakir had vanished into the dust storm. Piay's blood-slick fingertips searched for cracks in the rock, his feet scrabbling to gain purchase. But the slope became gentler near the top and then he was heaving himself up with increasing speed.

He pulled himself half over the edge. He glimpsed Myssa sprawled nearby – unconscious, he prayed. Before he could cry out to her, Sakir loomed over him.

'I told you . . . weakness,' the Red Hawk said. 'You have killed yourself.'

Piay sensed the sword flashing towards him. He pushed himself backwards, the tip of the blade missing his face by a finger's width. He twisted and turned as he tumbled, the jagged edges of rocks raking his flesh. His thoughts spun away.

Piay crashed into the jumble of boulders at the foot of the slope. Though pain flared through every part of him, he levered himself up on his elbows.

As he looked up the side of the channel, he glimpsed Sakir staring down at him. When he realised Piay was still alive, the barbarian readied himself to climb down to finish him off.

Piay would not have the strength to resist. Even then, his thought was only for Myssa and the fear he would never see her again.

'Come down here!' a voice rang out. 'See if you have what it takes to defeat two of us.'

Hannu was standing beside Piay, peering along the length of his blade at the barbarian. His friend's face was twisted with rage.

'Two of us?' Piay croaked.

'Quiet,' Hannu breathed. 'Let him think you're as indestructible as he seemingly is.'

Sakir hesitated on the edge. A triumphant smile danced across his lips.

'I will keep the woman alive, for now. Come to me. We will end this on the plains of Thebes before the eyes of our brothers, when Seth will be victorious. Then all will know who is the true power here. But remember this, Piay of Egypt – you have been defeated this day. You have been broken.'

Sakir stepped back into the dust cloud and was gone.

Hannu lowered his sword.

'Thank the gods. I thought I was going to have to fight him.'

Piay pushed himself up. His body was consumed with pain, but miraculously none of his bones seemed broken.

Sakir was right. Piay had fallen for the first time. He'd been defeated. Now, bruised, battered and hollowed out, he had to find the strength to fight the coming battle.

'Fear not,' Hannu encouraged as if he could read Piay's mind, 'you have three days to recover before we get to Thebes.'

**W**ith the First Cataract behind them, the Nile flowed across the fertile valley. Once, Piay's heart would have beaten faster at the thought that he was now back upon the soil of the land he loved.

He would have felt comforted by the song of the land, the rustle of the wind in the papyrus beds, the steady heartbeat of the shadoof irrigating the lush fields, the whisper of the swaying date palms.

Now one thought burned in his mind: do whatever it takes to save Myssa.

Heads turned in the farmlands as the elephants tramped past. Piay imagined how those field-workers must be marvelling at such a sight, one that had never been seen in Egypt before. Would the Hyksos quake in terror when they saw them? The spirits of the Egyptian army would certainly be lifted.

Piay summoned up a vision of the fanfares that would blast out and the soldiers cheering as he led the great beasts towards the front. Would he be proclaimed saviour? Not so long ago that notion would have brought a heady rush, but now he cared little for personal glory. He wanted only Sakir's death, and to drive the Hyksos out of the land he loved. To end this decades-long war.

And to experience peace.

He could barely envisage what that would be like. He hoped – he prayed once again – that it would be another golden age, where he could relinquish his life of struggle and spend his days with Myssa. There could be no better reward for the hardship of the last two years.

He glimpsed Hannu's face hardening. His assistant's eyes sought him out.

'Something is amiss.'

Piay looked along the shimmering river. All seemed well. A boat drifted with the current. Children chased each other along the muddy bank. But then he sensed something in the breeze. Burning.

They marched on, but now he no longer noticed the pleasant scenes of his homeland. The reek of burning grew stronger as they progressed north.

After a while another stench rose: the smell of decomposition. Hannu pointed ahead. Piay saw the dark shapes of vultures circling against the silver sky.

Piay muttered a prayer to Khonsu.

Finally they glimpsed the outline of Thebes wavering in the heat haze. Piay could make out the white walls of the City of a Hundred Gates, and the temple and the great buildings beyond them.

As they crested an area of higher ground, they came across the army of the Pharaoh camped out. He could see the great golden standard from which fluttered the white cloth marked with the yellow orb of Ra. It hung in tatters.

The camp was a fraction of the size it had been when Piay had last seen it. Wounded soldiers limped about or sprawled beside ragged tents. As he scanned the miserable ranks, Piay realised he could barely see any able-bodied soldiers anywhere.

Beyond the remnants of Egypt's once-glorious defenders lay a field of the dead. The birds swooped and feasted, the air thick with their hungry shrieking.

P iay approached the camp. The vision of devastation had summoned up a desperate question: *is Taita still alive?*

Memories of his master flooded back and he realised how much he had missed Taita's wisdom, even his stern condemnations. Taita had been his only family from the moment his mother and father had sent him away.

No one guarded the camp's outer perimeter. There was no challenge as he entered, only the sounds of moaning and the cries of the dying. Piay choked on the reek of blood and the stink of infected wounds. A steady stream of men limped away from the line of tents, heading south. Some were still fit, but they tossed aside their swords and stripped off their armour as they slunk away. They were deserting. Piay was shocked to see it. Where was the courage of the fighting men he knew, the shining spirit of the true Egyptian who would defend his land even unto death?

Had they been so resolutely crushed by the Hyksos?

Could it be that, for all his struggle and suffering, he had arrived too late?

What then for Myssa? If he could not count on an army at his back, there was no hope of victory. His choice would be to flee and abandon Myssa, or give himself up and hope Sakir could be persuaded to free her, and give up his own life in the process.

Piay grabbed the shoulders of a passing soldier and shouted, 'Where is Taita?'

The man pointed into the heart of the camp.

With relief, Piay skirted the line of deserters. Weaving among the ragged tents, he slowed his step as he approached the billowing purple of Taita's shelter. It was larger than all the others, with a trestle covered in charts set up in the front section and a sheet of silk hanging across his master's sleeping quarters at the rear. Piay breathed in sweeter air from herbs smouldering in a silver cup as he stepped across the threshold.

'Taita,' he called. 'I am home.'

The silk curtain was pulled aside and his master stood framed against the sheets of purple. Piay almost fell to his knees before that commanding presence. Not a line had crossed Taita's face in the two years they had been apart; he still looked impossibly young, his beautiful features, his cheekbones, his full lips, all unravaged by the passage of time. His back was straight, his shoulders broad and he glowed with potency. Piay felt humbled by the strength he saw.

Taita stared, as if he was looking at a stranger, and then his eyes widened.

'Piay?'

Piay threw his arms around his master.

'I thought you were dead!' Taita exclaimed. 'For all your skills . . . You have been away so long.'

When Piay stepped back, he bowed his head and said, 'I have travelled the world and seen wonders and terrors that have changed me. But I have completed the mission you set for me. You will be amazed when you see what I have brought back, Taita. Victory will be assured.'

Taita's face was bright with hope. 'You have found an ally who will fight alongside us!'

Piay shook his head. 'No allies. I did what I could but they were afraid of angering the Hyksos. No, see here.'

He beckoned and Taita stepped with him to the entrance of the tent. Piay pointed over the tents in the morning sunshine to where the caravan of elephants had halted on the edge of the camp. A crowd of soldiers had gathered around them, gaping in astonishment.

'Elephants?' Taita said.

'Hear me out . . . there is wisdom here. The Hyksos' success in battle is based upon their mastery of the horse. Those beasts speed their chariots across the battlefield and carve through our defences. But I have learned the horse has one great fear – the elephant. At the sight of these war beasts, the Hyksos chariots will be forced into retreat, allowing our army to drive into the heart of the barbarian horde. They will lose their power in an instant.'

Piay stared at Taita, waiting for praise. Instead, his master nodded his head and said in an even voice, 'You have done well, Piay. I knew you would not let me down.'

Piay frowned. 'What is wrong? Is this not great news?'

Taita walked back to the trestle. His helmet rested on the end of it. One side was dented, no doubt from a Hyksos blade, and the plume had been sheared off. He placed a hand on it and said, almost to himself, 'My servants will be here soon to knock the dent out, ready for what is to come.' He turned to Piay. 'The elephants are a work of wonder indeed, Piay. But there is one thing you have not included in your calculations.'

'Tell me.'

'We have no army. Or rather, what little army we have is next to useless. Once the elephants force the barbarians' horses to retreat, we have nothing to follow through to ensure their might is routed.'

'No army?'

'You saw the scenes across the camp.'

'I saw an army reeling from defeat. But surely they will rally to the Pharaoh's call . . .'

Taita turned and his gaze seemed to carry a terrible weight.

'Even as we speak, Pharaoh Tamose lies in his tent, mortally wounded by a Hyksos arrow. I have done all I can for him, with medicine and spells and pleas to the gods. I fear it is not enough. And while the Pharaoh hangs between life and death, the Egyptian army is melting away.'

Piay's chest felt almost too heavy to stir with breath.

'In my darkest hours, I worried there would be little to return home to, but I still held out hope.'

'Not long after you departed, I even invented a new form of war chariot, one which was far greater than anything the Hyksos had,' Taita said. 'Lighter, more manoeuvrable . . .' He shook his head. 'It was not enough.'

'How did it come to this?' Piay asked.

'During the last year we have lost two great battles. Three thousand men left upon the bloody fields. Those shattering defeats put all of Egypt within the grasp of the Hyksos, and that knowledge seemed to sap the spirit from what remained of our broken and beaten army. They saw how many of their friends and comrades were no longer there. They saw that those who had survived bore wounds that would prevent them being effective in battle. How many of our own horses had been slaughtered, and of those that remained, how many could no longer bear the weight of a chariot.'

'That's why so many are deserting?'

'They have fled in their multitudes. When this mass departure began, I stood on the edge of the camp and pleaded with them to stay. They streamed past me, averting their gaze so they did not have to look me in the eye. Not so long ago they had cheered the very mention of my name as I led them into battle. Now they ignore me.'

Could the Oracle at Delphi have been wrong after all? The gods had sent a message through her that victory could be achieved if the elephants could be brought back to Egypt. Now Piay's great success did not seem so great after all – a distraction while men died and Egypt burned. If only he had convinced the Spartans to become their allies. But he had failed. That was the ultimate truth.

Piay closed his eyes, lost to the crushing wave of despair. But he conjured up one thing: Myssa's face. This war with the Hyksos had consumed him all his life and he hated the invaders more than anything. But now he had a personal stake in this fight and it moved him even more.

'We cannot give up,' he said, his fists bunching. 'There has to be another way—'

Taita's eyes flashed. 'I do not give up. I never give up, not while there is breath within me.'

Piay chose his words carefully. 'The gods have sent me a message that this fight can be won, if only we can find a way.'

'The gods, you say.' Taita stared as if he was looking deep inside him. After a moment, his master nodded slowly. 'If the gods say it, then this must be true. I cannot see this path now, but with some reflection, it may emerge. We must both think about this, Piay. The gods aid us, but rarely do they rain gifts from above. Often they wrap their guidance in mystery and allow us to uncover it ourselves. In that way we learn valuable lessons.'

'How long do we have?'

'The barbarian horde is gathering before the gates of Thebes. Tomorrow the final battle will come. Our last chance to avert a slaughter . . . and disaster.'

'Tomorrow,' Piay said. 'So short a time.'

'When the sun sets, the fate of Egypt will have been decided.'

'We have survived against all the odds so far,' Hannu said as he threw another slab of dung and straw on to the smouldering campfire.

Piay massaged his arms. Every part of him still ached from the fight with Sakir near the First Cataract. He wasn't sure that he was fit for any kind of battle, but he was not about to give in.

'I have discussed various tactics with Taita,' Piay replied. 'Sending the elephants in first like a spearhead. Holding them back and then parting our ranks so they can rush through with the element of surprise. All of it fails without enough men to continue the fight.'

'When the battle comes, you will fight?'

'I'll stand beside Taita.'

'And I will, too.'

'No.' Piay shook his head. 'I would never ask this of you.'

'You do not need to. I am offering my services.'

'No.'

'You need every able hand.'

'You're injured. Your leg—'

'I have able hands.'

Piay knew that when Hannu was in this mood there was no denying him.

'We have walked a long road together,' his friend said. 'And I have guided you—'

'And I you—'

'And if it is to end at dawn tomorrow, then it should end with us together. Side by side.' Hannu looked up and the flames danced in his dark eyes.

'I cannot argue with that. But hear me out. One of us needs to survive to save Myssa.'

'You have a plan?'

'I have a prayer.'

Hannu glanced back at the fire. 'Agreed. If one of us falls, the other should leave the battlefield and do whatever it takes to bring Myssa home. Even if it takes a lifetime.'

Piay stared at Hannu, feeling strange emotions inside him.

'Thank you,' he said. 'You are a good friend.'

Hannu tossed another slab on the fire and the sparks cascaded. Piay thought his friend wanted to say something else, but could not find the words.

'We should get our rest,' Piay said eventually. 'The dawn will come faster than we like.'

Before he could rise, Piay glimpsed a familiar silhouette moving among the tents. Taita must have finished his final meeting with his generals. But where was he going at this hour?

Nodding to Hannu, Piay pushed himself up to follow his master. Taita hurried through the camp until he came to the Pharaoh's grand tent – one almost as large as a house, in white silk, with many rooms inside.

When Taita slipped into the tent, Piay eased in behind him. No guards waited outside. Perhaps they, too, had deserted.

Once Taita had disappeared through a sheet of silk into the heart of the tent, Piay crept to the gap and peered inside. He choked back a gasp when he saw Pharaoh Tamose sprawled on his litter, his eyes shut and his chest rising fitfully. He was an old man, his face a mass of wrinkles dotted with dark spots, but he had taken to dyeing his hair and beard ginger, which only emphasised his ghastly pallor. An arrow jabbed out between his ribs.

Around the Pharaoh, generals and high counsellors bowed their heads while five of his favourite wives attended, choking back sobs.

Taita had been right in his estimation. Tamose would not survive the night. And then his eldest son Utteric Turo would take the throne. Piay felt despair at that thought. The boy was an empty vessel, more ineffectual than the weakest men at court, but his ambition was legendary. What destiny awaited Egypt under his rule? Perhaps this was the gods' way of saying the time of Egypt was moving into the shadows. Soon it would be lost to the sands like the ruins of the ancients.

He felt a surge of defiance. That could not be. Whatever earthly obstacles were laid in their way, they could be overcome. They were being tested, that was all, and they would not be found wanting.

Taita kneeled beside Tamose and brushed his lips against the back of the dying Pharaoh's hand. Piay had seen enough. He doubted sleep would come, but there was no escaping what awaited the rising of the sun.

Sleep did come, but it was fitful and filled with dreams. The soldiers who had been killed in the field trooped up to stand beside Piay, but he could no longer see their faces. Jabilo stood in the dappled light beside his lonely grave, smiling. And there was Myssa staring at him from the shadows, yearning, desperate. Behind her, two figures loomed. One was Sakir, his good eye glowing in the dark of his ruined face. At his left shoulder, the beast-headed god of the desert, Seth, stared with terrible force.

When he woke, Piay was filled with terror that this had been a premonition and that Myssa was dead, like all the others. Haunted, he stalked away from the dying embers of the fire to Taita's tent.

His master stood in a shaft of sunlight breaking through the open flap. He was already dressed in his armour, his face taut.

'The Pharaoh is dead,' he said as Piay entered.

Piay bowed his head. 'I will grieve for him later. But I am sorry for you. I know you have guided him since he was a boy.'

'The curse of a long life,' Taita replied. 'You must watch all the ones you love die.'

'I confess, I have not been able to find any solution to the problem facing us. I discussed the matter with Hannu deep into the night, but if the gods have a plan for us, I cannot see it.'

Taita forced a smile. 'You have not failed me, Piay. You never fail me. The gods reveal their plans for us when they are ready, not when we require it. If the tide of this war is to be turned, it will happen.'

*You never fail me.*

Piay felt warm at his master's kind words – the first time Taita had ever said such a thing to him. That he had chosen to say it now, on the brink of battle, told him all he needed to know about Taita's views on their chances of survival.

'Then let us make ready,' Piay said. 'I am tired of idling my time away here in the camp. We have a fight to win.'

His master would know he was putting on a show, but they would both maintain that illusion to the last.

Taita's chariot rumbled ahead, the sun glinting off the gold coving around the edge. The eunuch stood tall and proud as his horse carried him towards the battle lines – another show, Piay knew, for those cowering men waiting to die. But if anyone could raise their spirits, it was the commanding figure of Taita.

Piay flicked the reins and his own chariot rumbled close behind his master.

'We will leave the chariots at the rear,' he said to Hannu, 'and not waste them in the first rounds of the battle.' He instantly regretted using the word 'waste'.

Hannu gripped the coving, his hair flying in the breeze.

'If the gods had wanted us to fight in chariots, they would have given us wheels.'

'Finish your grumbling now. I won't hear it over the sound of dying barbarians.'

As they neared the battlefield, Piay choked on the reek of rot rising from the bodies remaining after the previous struggle. The vultures still circled; the crows cried and swooped. The jackals and hyenas would be out there now, fighting over the carrion. Was that the end that awaited him? Surely every man was having the same thought.

In the distance, Thebes flared in the rosy light of dawn, the white walls a beacon. Piay thought back to the wonders that lay inside the City of a Hundred Gates – the temple, the palace, those magnificent structures as old as time, the wine and food and gold and jewels brought from the four corners of the earth. Would he sample its delights again? Would he ever achieve his dream of showing that magic to Myssa?

Taita reined in his horse as they approached the neck of the pass through the strip of higher ground that lay in front of the city. Piay peered out at what remained of the shattered army gathered there and his heart sank. So few. They had been in dire straits when he had departed, but now they were an army in name only.

On the other side of the pass, the vast horde of Hyksos barbarians roared their battle cries. Somehow those brave Egyptians had held the invaders at bay for thirty-five days. With each assault, the Pharaoh's defenders had been whittled down a little more. What shreds remained would not survive the day.

Taita rode his chariot around the flanks of the gathered men and steered along the front so that all could see him. Piay was impressed with his master's display. Those soldiers who could still stand staggered to their feet, dragging up their wounded comrades and supporting them. Even so close to disaster, Taita stirred their hearts.

The warriors thrust their swords into the air and cheered. As Taita rolled past, a rhythmic chant broke out: 'Taita! Taita! Taita!'

*Has ever a man been so admired*, Piay wondered? *Even the Pharaoh had not commanded such respect.*

Taita whipped up his arm, urging the men to even greater frenzy. His laughter rang out and he called to many by name, as if he knew every man who stood there. In his heart, Piay's master would be consumed with concern for them, but not a sign of it crossed his face. This was the mark of a true leader. A man who could lock his own doubts and fears away and show only confidence to those who followed, someone who could snatch victory from the jaws of defeat. Piay had so much to learn from Taita.

Once Taita had reached the end of the line, the cheers ebbed away and silence descended on the ranks once again. The men sank to the ground, snatching what little rest they could before the fighting began.

Piay pulled the chariot in next to the others at the rear of the lines. The grooms raced forwards to care for the horses while Piay, Hannu and Taita pulled on their bronze helmets, tightened the belts holding their scabbards and slipped their left hands through the leather straps on their shields.

'You should command from the rear,' Piay said to Taita. 'You are the most valuable man here and we need to keep you safe.'

Taita shook his head. 'I will fight in the shield wall alongside the two of you. That is the right thing to do. The men must see we stand together.'

Trumpeting echoed through the dawn stillness and Piay turned to look along the track to the camp. The elephants were coming. The ground throbbed under their heavy tread and, one by one, the soldiers in the ranks craned their necks to marvel at what was coming. On the backs of the great beasts, the Tumisi were dressed in leather armour, their spears holstered in leather pouches so they could pluck them out and stab with ease while the elephants trampled the enemy underfoot.

Though Piay had spent months beside these creatures, he still felt a shiver at the power rippling beneath that thick grey skin. The Hyksos would quake with fear when confronted with one of these animals bearing down on them.

'Your command is still to hold the elephants back?' Piay asked.

'The first part of this battle will be fought at close quarters. When we break through the barbarians' ranks, then – and only then – will the elephants be brought forwards to disrupt the chariots and archers that wait in front of the city.'

Piay nodded.

*But where will Sakir be waiting?*

That was the question he needed answering.

Taita strode back to the Egyptian ranks and beckoned for his captains to surround him. Piay studied the grim faces as Taita ordered the archers to be sent forwards to retrieve as many arrows as they could from the corpses that littered the tract between the two sides. Their quivers were nearly empty, and any shafts they could reclaim would be invaluable in the battle to come.

The beat of a single drum sounded along the pass. In the ranks, the faces of the soldiers drained of blood. Taita bowed his head, but only for a moment.

'The time has come,' he said. 'Ready yourselves.'

The archers scrambled back with the reclaimed arrows and pushed their way through the ranks. As the captains bellowed orders, the men heaved themselves on to weary legs. Swords drew out of scabbards and shields were rebalanced on forearms.

Piay turned to Hannu. For a moment, they held each other's gaze in a silent acknowledgement of their friendship. No words were necessary.

Then, together, they strode behind Taita into the mass of men.

The tramp of feet boomed through the dusty air. Piay looked over the lip of his shield along the road through the pass, waiting for the first sign of the Hyksos horde. He was surprised at his calm, as if all of his life had been leading up to this point. Whether he lived or died no longer mattered.

The shields of the Egyptian soldiers had locked into place along the front line of the army. Behind the wall, the men pressed together, the air thick with sweat, the heat suffocating with so many bodies in close proximity.

Piay could sense the fear of those around him, but no one made any sound that might unnerve his brothers. To his left, Taita showed an impassive face, his stare unwavering. To his right, Hannu hawked up phlegm and spat between his feet.

Piay nodded. They were as ready as they would ever be.

And yet Piay saw the sword edges were blunted from use, the spearheads chipped. The archers had bound their cracked bows with twine to hold them together, and many of their retrieved arrows lacked fletchings. At close quarters, those shafts would serve their purpose, but beyond that? Piay mouthed a prayer that whatever the gods had planned to save them would come soon enough, for it seemed clear that they could not save themselves.

The thump of feet rang off the steep sides of the pass, growing louder by the moment. Out of the early morning light, the first of the Hyksos horde marched, banging their swords on their shields.

Hannu grunted. 'Not so many.'

They looked like a straggling war band, but Piay's throat tightened as he saw the multitude striding behind the advance guard. The barbarians crushed into the pass from wall to wall, a seemingly never-ending flow.

'Well . . . maybe a few,' Hannu added. He adjusted his grasp on the hilt of his sword.

Piay looked across the vast army, in their leather bucklers and caps, their blades no doubt well sharpened. They must outnumber the Egyptians by four to one, and these were only the foot soldiers. The charioteers that had devastated the Pharaoh's forces in battle after battle over fifty years waited behind for their moment.

'They would not send their chariots through the pass first, for they would have to travel in narrow formation and be vulnerable to our archers,' Taita said as if he could read Piay's thoughts. 'On that front, our strategy holds well.'

'Wait.' Piay jabbed a finger towards the advancing force. 'See? They are not as strong as we feared.'

Taita leaned forwards, observing closely the detail, and a smile spread across his lips.

'You are right, Piay. It seems we have left our mark upon them in the battles we have fought. We were more successful than we knew.'

Many of the barbarian warriors had been wounded. There were bloodstained rags tied around heads and arms. Some limped on crutches. Others lurched, barely able to walk. Their captains moved behind with rawhide whips to drive them into battle.

The Hyksos still had superior numbers. But here was at least an opportunity.

'I will return.'

Taita pushed his way through the ranks behind them and, not long after, his chariot rode along the shield wall once more. He pointed towards the flashing whips and bellowed, 'Men like you never need the whip to convince you of your duty!'

Taita's powerful voice rose above the beating of the war drums and the thunder of the marching feet, and the Egyptians responded by cheering and shouting insults at the Hyksos force.

However old Piay's master was, he had lost none of the fire in his belly.

The time had come for Taita's tactics to come into play. The Hyksos could not use their chariots, but as the barbarians emerged from the pass, that was not a problem for the Egyptians.

Only fifty-two Egyptian chariots remained from the savage battles that had been fought, but that was still a formidable number. Piay thrust his sword into the air as Taita led the squadron out. They raced along the front of the Hyksos army about seventy paces away.

Arrows whined through the air, thumping into the masses of barbarian warriors. Piay counted at least thirty enemy soldiers fall. Their screams rang out, raising more cheers from the Pharaoh's defenders.

The strike whipped the barbarians into fury. Roaring, they surged forwards. There would be no chance to repeat that manoeuvre. As the chariots thundered around the flanks, Taita leaped from the platform of his vehicle, leaving the reins in the hands of a seasoned charioteer. He ran towards the shield wall and Piay turned his shield aside so his master could squeeze in beside him.

'First blood,' Taita said.

The shield wall locked into place. Taita unsheathed his sword and Piay was proud to be fighting alongside his master. He would show Taita all he had learned. He didn't want praise, just for his master to know that all his efforts in tutelage had not gone to waste. Taita was a good man, perhaps the best.

'It's been a long time,' Hannu muttered. 'At least trapped in this foul mass of stinking bodies I can fight without having my ruined leg let me down.'

'A wager,' Piay said. 'The first one to kill ten barbarians gets all his beer brought to him by the other.'

'Get ready to be a slave,' Hannu replied.

The horde swept forwards. The roar of those furious voices swelled until it seemed to be the only sound in all the world. As the thundering army swallowed the ground between them, it seemed that a shadow descended across the Egyptian army, and even in the heat of the day it grew cold.

Piay fixed on those faces twisted with bloodlust, mouths torn wide amid their black bristles, eyes burning like embers. Closer and closer, the storm of sword and spear raged. Piay braced himself.

The barbarians crashed against the shield wall, jolting bones and jarring joints, driving every Egyptian onto their heels. Piay heaved his shoulder against his shield, straining to hold firm. His ears ached from the throat-rending roar of the battle cries. The world crushed in around him on every side until there was only the face in front of him. All the hopes and dreams and loves and fears boiled down to a simple urge: survival. This was life or death and nothing more.

Piay felt something shift in his mind, unbidden. The face bobbing above the rim of his shield blackened and twisted until in his mind's eye it became Sakir staring at him with his one good eye. Piay's lips pulled back from his teeth and he bellowed so that any who knew him would have thought him a madman. Rage bubbled up and boiled his thoughts away. He hammered his sword above the edge of his shield into that charred face. Bone shattered and blood spurted. His enemy fell away without even a dying scream.

Another barbarian thrust his way into the gap in an instant, smashing his shield against Piay's and trying to rake his sword down. Piay twisted aside from the blow and stabbed again. Here was Sakir once more, that visage masking the face of every warrior who confronted him, tormenting him, mocking him that the only thing he had ever truly loved had been snatched away.

His enemy howled as Piay's blade punched into his eye socket. As he, too, fell away, Sakir came again and again. All sense of those around him flooded away, together with any notion of the battle raging. There was only Sakir, whom he hated more than anything. Sakir, whom he would never allow to win.

Barbarian after barbarian died in agony under his sword. Slowly he felt the haze lifting and details begin to intrude from the churning mass of chaos around him. Hannu was still alive, his beard matted with the blood of his enemies. Taita had left his long cavalry blade in its sheath and was stabbing with a dagger no longer than a hand's width. In that crush his knife swooped like a small bird, unencumbered, punching into the faces of the barbarians and finding even the smallest opening in their leather armour.

Egyptians had fallen, too, their bodies trampled underfoot. But every time a man went down, another from the rear pushed his way into the shield wall. Somehow the defences held firm.

Time blurred. Piay felt every fibre of his being burning from exertion. Only the passage of the merciless sun overhead marked the changing moments as he emerged from his delirium to see the shafting light had moved across the line of glinting bronze blades and helms.

Then a cry jolted Piay from his blood-dream: 'They are pulling back!'

Whether it came from his side or the other, he could not tell, but gradually more light flooded in; the din receded and a space opened up between the battle line.

The Hyksos were partially retreating. They had lost many men and their captains had pulled them back to remake their formation. As Piay scanned the barbarians' faces, he glimpsed doubt and fear. This had not gone as easily as they had imagined. Their weary sword-arms hung limply and they sucked in ragged breaths to steady themselves.

Piay staggered, shaking from exhaustion. He dragged the back of his hand across his mouth, wiping away the spittle and the sweat, scarcely able to believe that respite had come. But it would not last long. The Hyksos would come again.

Piay glanced back across the Egyptian army. He guessed that barely twelve hundred men remained. How long could they last in such a furious battle? An hour, little more than that, even if the chariots and the elephants were sent in. And then it would all be over. Everyone he knew would be dead. Egypt would be lost. Myssa would be gone.

Despair welled up until a hand gripped his arm. Hannu leaned in, understanding him better than anyone as he always had.

'While there is life there is hope,' he said. 'Never forget.'

The gods had a dark humour, for in that moment Piay sensed an upheaval in the ranks behind them. Someone was thrusting his way through the jammed soldiers. Piay glimpsed eyes wide with terror and his heart sank.

'My Lord Taita!' the messenger shouted, tugging at the arm of Piay's master.

Taita glared at him, reading the other man's expression, and for the first time Piay saw a shadow cross Taita's face. It felt like the greatest blow of all.

'There is another detachment of the enemy coming up at our rear,' the messenger gasped. 'They have us surrounded. Unless you can think of some way to save the day, then we are done for.'

Piay glanced at the line of barbarians two spear-throws away. Were they waiting for this pincer movement to crush the Egyptian force once and for all?

'Take me and show me, Merab,' Taita said to the messenger.

As his master stepped over the bodies and discarded weapons, Piay fell in behind him, and Hannu followed.

At the rear of the mass of bodies, Taita clambered on to a fresh horse alongside the messenger. Piay raced up to another steed and he reached down to pull Hannu up behind him. The horses galloped away across the ridge of high ground separating the army from the Nile. On the crest, Piay guided his mount beside Taita and felt his stomach sink as he looked down on heaving activity along the riverbank.

From the messenger's words, he'd expected perhaps three hundred fresh Hyksos. But not this! A flotilla of warships trailed into the hazy distance along the east bank of the Nile. Thousands of soldiers swarmed from them, with at least five hundred chariots and an uncountable number of cavalry.

What chance did they now have? His attention drifted to a knot of men on horseback, who had noticed they were being spied on and were pointing and jabbering. They urged their mounts up the slope.

Piay glanced at Taita, waiting for the order to ride back to the relative safety of their army. His master weighed his choice and then he decided to wait.

Hannu whispered to him, 'Do you see?'

Piay tried to see whatever it was Hannu had identified, and then he caught it. As those men rode up the slope, their cloaks billowed behind them, and they were crimson. Those warships were not Hyksos galleys.

Taita must have seen it, too, for he told the messenger to hold his ground. Unhooking his scabbard, he raised it hilt upwards in a sign of peace, then urged his horse down the slope to meet the advancing band. The leader of the new arrivals uttered an order and his men sheathed their swords, holding back in a tight formation behind him.

Piay pushed his own steed down the slope behind Taita.

'Better late than never, I suppose,' Hannu muttered.

Though they were helmeted, Piay recognised two of those Spartans. The leader pulled his helmet off, letting his grey hair tumble down. Hurotas grinned, his leathery face crinkling. The men behind him also tugged off their helmets. Mennias nodded to Piay, his hair still a deep black streaked with silver, his eyes a twinkling blue.

When Taita removed his own helmet, Hurotas laughed and pointed. The two men knew each other well.

'Zaras?' Taita said, frowning. 'It cannot possibly be you, can it?'

'Only the name is somewhat different, but everything else about me is the same, Taita. Except possibly I am a trifle older and a little wiser.'

'You remember me still, after all these years. How long has it been?' Taita demanded.

'It has been a mere thirty years, and yes, I remember you still. I will never forget you, not if I live for ten times longer than I have already.'

The two men exchanged more words, but Piay heard none of them. His heart soared: the gods had answered his prayers. There was hope! He had not failed in his quest. Taita had sent him to find allies and they had answered his call. Yet even as he looked out across the Spartan force, he could see that only a balance had been attained. Victory was not yet guaranteed.

When he glanced back at the two old friends, Taita was saying, 'And so, King Hurotas, why have you returned to Egypt after all these years?'

Hurotas' eyes flickered towards Piay and he nodded. 'I came because at heart I am still an Egyptian. I heard from my spies that you in Egypt were hard-pressed and on the verge of defeat at the hands of the Hyksos. These animals have despoiled our once lovely homeland. They have raped and murdered our women and children. Among their victims were my own mother and my two young sisters. After they had violated them, they threw them still alive on the blazing ruins of our home and laughed as they watched them burn.'

Piay felt Hannu flinch behind him when his friend heard these words.

'I have returned to Egypt to avenge their deaths and to save more of our Egyptian people from a similar fate. If I succeed,

I hope to forge a lasting alliance between our two lands, Egypt and Lacedaemon.'

As the two men spoke, Piay prickled with unease and glanced back. He knew time was running out.

Taita said, 'There will be more time for these reminiscences anon. However, at this moment there are several thousand Hyksos waiting at the head of the pass for our attention. Mine, and yours.'

'Forgive me, old friend,' Hurotas replied. 'I should have known that you would provide me with generous entertainment immediately on my arrival. Let us go up there at once and deal with these Hyksos, shall we?'

Taita leaned in and whispered whatever plan he had in mind, and then he galloped back with Piay and Hannu close behind.

They had not left it a moment too late. The barbarians were once again advancing on the crumbling Egyptian ranks. Piay, Hannu and Taita barged through their comrades to the shield wall. They slotted into place. This time, though, Piay felt his heart swell with hope.

'Stand firm, my brothers!' he called. 'All is not lost. We have allies riding to fight beside us. We will not be defeated!'

At his exhortation, the brutalised men alongside him heaved themselves up and pushed their shoulders back. They glanced at him, seeing the truth in his words, and then the news rushed like the wind through the ranks. Chatter turned to cheers and the reinvigorated army readied itself for the coming battle.

Piay's dream of the dead soldiers and Jabilo standing by his grave flashed through his mind and he pushed it aside. This was not the time to give in to doubt. The odds were still overwhelming, but in that glimmer of hope he could see Myssa so clearly he could almost touch her skin. Never had he wanted something so badly.

The barbarians pounded across the space, their pace increasing with each step, until they crashed against the shield wall. On the last attack the Egyptians had fought out of sheer desperation. Now that ragged army knew they only had to hang on until reinforcements came. All around, Piay glimpsed snarling faces strengthened by belief, arms that had seemed drained of strength now striking as if it was the first time that day they had lifted a sword.

Seeing this transformation, the Hyksos' fury ebbed. Piay hacked harder, slicing into skulls and stabbing the faces of anyone who came into view above the rim of his shield. He no longer saw Sakir there. If the gods were willing, that would come later. For now, the bodies heaped up in front of him, each fallen warrior drawing him closer to that final confrontation.

As he wrenched back his dripping blade, Piay sensed the mood of the battlefield change. The tone of the Hyksos battle cries changed and Piay realised he was hearing screams. The bloody battle slowed; swords fell. The barbarians pulled back a step at a time.

Then, in one fluid movement, the entire line crumbled. Those seasoned warriors fled in all directions, some back towards the pass, others along the Egyptian line. Piay couldn't understand what had caused the confusion. But as the horde broke up, a clear view presented itself.

The Spartan cavalry thundered into the flanks of the barbarian army from both sides, stabbing with their spears and trampling the Hyksos warriors beneath them. Now Piay understood the plan Taita had whispered to Hurotas. The riders had waited at the rear of the Egyptian army, hidden from view until the Hyksos were trapped in an attack formation. Then they'd swept round each side of the Pharaoh's defenders, attacking in a pincer movement.

The Spartan riders seemed to be everywhere, skewering men as they ran. The pitched battle had become a rout. But now that the Hyksos lines had been broken, Piay had a clear view through the pass to Thebes.

He felt chilled by what he saw.

Rank upon rank of Hyksos charioteers waited in front of the city, the archers on each vehicle primed with arrows nocked.

The Egyptian army cheered and a thousand gleaming swords stabbed the air. The men had expected only death before great Ra's orb slipped into the west. How could they have believed otherwise? They were broken, overwhelmed. Now, as the Hyksos foot soldiers fled from the pursuing Spartan cavalry, the Egyptian army was invigorated with a new lease of life.

The shield wall relaxed, the weary men slapping each other on the backs. They knew the job was not yet done, but they could at least draw breath.

Taita turned to Piay and removed his helmet. Sweat dripped from his brow, but his eyes sparkled.

'Now, my trusted agent,' he began, 'it is time for you to play your part.'

'What would you have me do?'

'You brought these Spartan heroes here to aid us and I will tell Hurotas the rest of my battle plan. Yet everything still hangs in the balance here. Now, did one of those gods of the Mycenae not inform the Oracle at Delphi that victory would only come with the elephants?'

Piay nodded, understanding.

'Then bring them!' Taita said. 'Those elephants may well be our only hope of victory. You have earned this opportunity to lead. Without you, Egypt would have fallen. We would all be dead. I would be a feast for the vultures, my eyes and my liver pecked out. If the gods are with us, then it is you who has saved us, Piay. Your name will live on forever in the history of this land.'

Piay was overwhelmed by words he never thought he would hear from the lips of his master.

He felt fingers jab him in the ribs and Hannu hissed, 'Are you going to stand there like a flounder on the riverbank, or are you going to get to work?'

Piay nodded his thanks to Taita and headed off to where he could see the elephants waiting at the rear of the Egyptian army.

Hannu caught up with him and said, 'This is the moment of greatest danger, you know that?'

Piay nodded. He'd been trying not to think of what lay ahead.

'If Sakir sees disaster looming for the Hyksos, what will he do to Myssa?'

'We will find him, and Myssa, even in that multitude waiting in front of the gates of Thebes. Leave that to me.' Hannu's voice was calm, measured, yet Piay heard something in it that chilled him. Piay clapped a hand on his friend's shoulder.

'We do this for Myssa.'

'For Myssa.'

Piay walked along the row of elephants. He felt the power emanating from the magnificent beasts. They dragged their feet and tossed their heads, seemingly eager to be set free to do their work. Mero stood at the end, the bull's mood as dark as Piay had ever seen it, almost as if it knew what waited ahead.

Piay studied the faces of the Tumisi ready to guide their mounts into the thick of the fighting. No man showed fear. Their faces were stony, their eyes narrowed and fixed on the way ahead. They, too, were ready.

Piay raised his hand to the Tumiso seated on the back of Mero. He snapped his hand forward and the Tumiso cupped his hands round his mouth and bellowed. Whatever he said – a command or a battle cry – it was picked up by each Tumiso in turn. Then, in perfect synchronisation, they struck with their switches and the elephants lurched forwards.

The ground throbbed and the air boomed as if a thunderstorm had erupted overhead. Piay glimpsed the faces of the exhausted and wounded Egyptian soldiers nearby, bafflement giving way to awe at the sheer force they witnessed moving towards the enemy – and, perhaps, a hint of fear, too. They would never have seen such a sight in their lives. As one, they scrambled out of the elephants' path.

Piay jogged at their side, but as the great beasts picked up speed, he broke into a run. The ground shook and Mero trumpeted its call, and every man in the Egyptian army turned and cheered. Gripped by the sheer power in those war elephants, they watched the line rumble past them and into the pass.

Ahead, the Spartan chariots rushed down the track to where the Hyksos were waiting. The cavalry pounded ahead of them while the infantry waited for the command of their captains to follow on behind.

The gold on the Hyksos chariots shone like the sun on that plain. They were ready, and what a terrifying sight that was. As the cavalry crashed out of the pass, the order rang out and the chariots slowly heaved forwards as one. Arrows arced through the sky, but only a few. The barbarians were biding their time, trying to lure their enemy into their midst before they unleashed their full force.

If only they knew what was coming.

As the Spartan chariots swept down on to the plain, another command rang out from the barbarians and the Hyksos chariots gathered speed, intending to crush their opponents. Instead of meeting the attack head-on, the Spartan cavalry and chariots veered off to the flanks. To untutored eyes it would look as if they had been overcome with terror at the sight of what awaited them on the approach to Thebes. Piay grinned. Taita was as cunning as he was wise.

While the Hyksos watched their enemy refusing to engage, the war elephants thundered through the pass and on to the plain. The chariots were far enough away now that the Spartan horses would not encounter the elephants. The ferocious beasts were meant only for the Hyksos.

Piay slowed his step as the war elephants drove on faster than he could run. Squinting into the brassy light, he could make out the faces of the advancing enemy as they caught their first sight of the charging elephants. At first there was disbelief as the Hyksos warriors tried to comprehend what they were seeing. Fear began to dawn. But still the chariots advanced at speed. The mounting disquiet must have gripped them, for they did not loose their arrows. That was their first mistake.

The second was to maintain their pace. Mero trumpeted again and the Tumisi guided their mounts into a line without slowing their step. As that huge grey wall rose up, the Hyksos warriors' eyes widened and mouths tore open, but the shrieks they uttered were lost amid the thunder of the great beasts. The barbarians knew it was too late to turn back.

Clouds of dust swirled as the war elephants pounded towards the enemy. The Hyksos charioteers were terrified, and their well-drilled horses, unused to the sight of charging elephants, panicked.

However much the charioteers lashed their whips, the horses tore themselves away from the beasts in their path. Foam flecked their mouths. As its horse veered sharply, the lead chariot flipped over. The barbarian clutching the reins hurtled through the air, crashing to the ground in front of the next chariot. Hooves pounded him and the wheels cut him in two.

The rushing chariots were in packed formation, a tactic that had served the Hyksos well in past battles. But when another terrified horse turned away, the vehicle it was pulling crashed into the one next to it, setting off a mayhem of collisions racing through the force.

Chariots ripped apart, crashing on to their sides, skidding and turning. Wheels flew and shards of wood burst through the air. Horses snorted in fear as they attempted to escape the carnage. Bones shattered. Bodies twisted in pain. The air was thick with screams.

A cloud of dust billowed up and those racing elephants pounded into it. Even though he was used to battle, Piay felt dread at the cries of agony that emanated from the pale shroud.

When the wind blew the dust away, Piay was shocked by the scale of defeat that had been inflicted in moments. The elephants stormed through the wreckage, smashing survivors and chariots underfoot. The chariots at the rear fled from the battlefield, now under the command of their own steeds.

The Spartan infantry advanced through the pass, their crimson capes flying behind them so that they looked like a stream of blood flooding across the battlefield.

The Spartan cavalry and chariots herded the fleeing Hyksos foot soldiers back towards the advancing soldiers. The Spartan soldiers hacked and slashed their way through the disorganised mob. The dust became a sea of gore.

Even when the fighting was over, those seasoned warriors did not slow. They moved among the wounded, slitting their throats.

Piay stared, lost in the delirious nightmare. The elephants had been the deciding factor. The Hyksos had never known a defeat like this, not in Egypt nor in any of the lands they had conquered. All Piay's life, the Hyksos invaders had brutalised the glorious Egypt of antiquity. The citizens had been bent under the yoke to toil for their foreign masters. Good men had been killed, women raped and slain, children's futures cut short. The wonders of Egypt that had been familiar to his fore-fathers were known to him only through tales.

How easy it was to believe that the years of war and suffering would never end. That until his dying day there would only be struggle and strife. But here was a new dawn, fresh hope of a return to the land of peace and plenty and art and joy. And he had played a part in this.

Piay choked back his emotion as the significance of what he was witnessing settled on him. And so many more thoughts bubbled up. Those who had died for him or in his service, like Jabilo, like the soldiers in the field, had not lost their lives in vain. Every step he had taken, every moment for good or ill, had led him to this point. No one could see the plans the gods wove, but when the final moment came all was revealed as if it could have happened no other way.

Piay felt the fog of this furious battle blow away and only then did his fears for Myssa surface once more. He peered across the chaos of the battlefield. How could he possibly find Sakir in that confusion, and if he was already dead, what hope was there of finding Myssa?

He made his way down the track and onto the plain. His heart pounded and his head spun. He glimpsed a familiar figure hunched over the wreckage of a chariot. Hannu must have made his way into the thick of the fight among the Spartan warriors. Now he loomed over a wounded barbarian, his sword jabbing into his prey's throat. He'd tossed aside his shield and with his free hand he waved away any Spartans who wandered up to take the charioteer's life.

Piay rushed over. Hannu glowered at the wounded man writhing beneath him, his lips pulled back from his teeth in a snarl. Piay couldn't remember the last time he had seen such naked emotion on his friend.

'Speak now,' Hannu was saying.

The warrior gurgled, his head lolling back. Blood leaked from his wounds. His end was near, but Hannu was tormenting him.

'Speak, I said!' Hannu dug the tip of his sword deeper.

The barbarian convulsed, then croaked, 'Yes, I know him.'

'The one of your kind with the burned face.'

'Yes.'

'He had a woman with him.'

'A Kushite.' The warrior coughed up bloody phlegm.

'Where is she?'

'I do not know.'

Hannu pushed the tip of the blade deeper still.

'I saw her only once! Never again!'

Piay felt his blood run cold. Had Sakir already killed Myssa?

'One last chance. Did the one called the Red Hawk fight here today? Where is he?'

The barbarian was fading fast. His lips formed words, but what emerged was little more than a faint whisper. Hannu pressed his ear to the man's mouth and strained to hear when he spoke again.

The charioteer summoned the last of his strength and croaked, 'You will not kill me?'

'I gave you my word. *I* will not kill you.' Hannu stood and as he walked away, he beckoned to one of the Spartan soldiers who readied his sword. Hannu did not look back.

'What did he say?' Piay asked, not wanting to hear the answer.

Hannu stared at him, his dark eyes revealing nothing.

**N**ight shrouded the fertile Nile valley and the moon dappled the waters of the river. Piay and Hannu crept alongside the swaying fields of barley, just two more stragglers making their way north.

Cloaks swaddled them, hoods pulled low to hide their identity. No one paid them any attention. After the great battle, the river was empty of traffic and the farmers had long since retreated to their homesteads.

Yet the countryside swarmed with life, like rats fleeing the scythes at harvest time. Bands of Hyksos warriors who had survived the slaughter hurried to safer territory, their meagre possessions strapped to their backs. Horses pounded the tracks and what few charioteers had escaped trundled their vehicles away as fast as they could. Some Egyptians abandoned all they knew to escape retribution from the victorious force. They were the ones who had sold out their fellows for higher status or riches. Now they lived in fear.

Thebes lay far behind them. They'd left the battlefield the moment Hannu had gleaned Sakir's location. Taita and Hurotas would be meeting amid the carnage, celebrating with wine and renewing their old friendship. Piay knew he would have been expected to play his part in those celebrations, but how could he stay?

Looking at the moon, he prayed to Khonsu that Myssa was still alive. He was devastated at the thought that she might be dead and could barely bring himself to think about such a thing. But if that was what had transpired, he would gain his vengeance. Sakir would pay for all he had done.

The wind whispered through the papyrus beds and Piay heard Khonsu's voice: *your destiny is in your hands.*

Hannu pointed ahead. Beyond the sea of barley, at a bend in the river, the light of a fire glimmered. Piay sniffed the wind. Behind the scent of smoke, he caught the fragrance of newly cut cedarwood.

'This must be the place,' he said.

'It wasn't here before we left,' Hannu whispered. 'The Hyksos must have built it to support the attack upon Thebes.'

On they crept until they reached the edge of a makeshift shipyard dug into the rich black earth that lined the river. Several small fires burned across the site, their pale light cast over galleys dragged up the deep sloping trenches where the shipwrights could carry out repairs to the hulls. Further from the water, the timbers of a half-built ship glowed with the pale light of freshly hewn wood. Scattered around were the ship-wrights' mallets and chisels, and bronze axes used to split the great timbers brought from the lands of the East.

Piay recalled the vast Egyptian shipyard opposite Thebes; the old army camp had been set up close by. That once vibrant place had been long abandoned since the barbarians had begun their advance on the City of a Hundred Gates. They'd sent spies to burn the ships and cut the throats of the few skilled shipwrights prepared to risk their necks providing vessels for the Pharaoh. Denied a navy, the Egyptian force had lost their best chance to strike back at the invaders with speed.

This shipyard was smaller. Piay scanned the pools of shadow among the firelight. Guards sat on piles of wood. Others roamed the perimeter. After the battle today and the threat that hung in the air, these men would not be slumbering. Their senses would be attuned to the slightest disturbance.

'How many do you see?' Piay murmured.

'Five . . . no, six. I'd wager there are at least four more out of view.'

'A good number. What say you?'

'Aye. Ten is a good number. We can do that.'

Somewhere in the pit of the shipyard, Sakir waited. He could afford to bide his time with the Egyptians and Spartans enjoying their victory celebrations at Thebes. Was he preparing to flee with the other barbarians? Perhaps he planned to take one of the smaller galleys moored nearby? Why else would he have departed the battlefield to set up camp here once news had reached him that Hurotas had brought reinforcements?

Piay imagined Sakir sitting in the shadows, chewing on the leaves of the blue lotus, hearing the whispers of his dark god. Would Seth have warned him that Piay was coming? Was he waiting to extract his final punishment before leaving?

'You don't need to come with me,' Piay said.

'Now you're talking like you've drunk too much beer.'

'It could be a trap.'

'It could be a walk by the river on a pleasant morning. Let's wait and see, shall we.'

'I was only saying—'

'Well, stop wasting your breath.' Hannu drew his sword. 'Just like old times. You, me, and a band of barbarians who don't yet know they're already dead.'

He started to crawl ahead before Piay could say any more.

As Piay crept to the edge of the field, the air became thick with the rich scent of the loam that had been excavated. A path that offered some cover wound down. That was good. The moon was too bright and he didn't want to be caught out in the open.

Dropping flat, he made his way down the winding slope into the shipyard. Hannu slithered behind him. At the foot, Piay prowled behind a pile of timber where he could gain a good view of the shipyard. Hannu had been right. Four more guards had been hidden from view. If they'd blundered down, they would be dead by now.

Piay nodded to Hannu and they crept in opposite directions. They both knew what had to be done. The fires cracked and spat.

Silently, Piay eased behind the guard, clamping his left hand across the man's mouth and raking his sword across the throat. The guard thrashed, but Piay kept his hand tight to stifle any cries, then dragged his victim to the ground where he wouldn't be seen.

Like a ghost, Piay drifted into the shadows next to one of the ships being repaired. Every fibre of his being was on alert, every lesson Taita had taught him about being a spy clear in his mind. The second guard fell just as easily, the blade stabbing up under the ribcage, the hand across the mouth dragging the man back so he could not gain purchase in his death throes.

The third slid down into one of the channels awash with brown river water. This time there was a faint splash and Piay stiffened, waiting to see if any of the other guards had heard. After a moment, he moved on.

Crawling behind a heap of rotting, discarded sailcloth, Piay glanced around the shipyard. His task had become more difficult. The remaining guards in his line of sight paced around the yard or sat in the glow of the fires. He would have to try to lure them into the dark, one by one.

Piay listened as the soft tread of one of the guards neared. Picking up a small pebble, he tossed it into the dark by the ships behind him. The pebble rattled into the gloom, but only faintly. It could have been one of the river rats foraging for food.

The footsteps came to a halt. Piay held his breath. A moment passed and then the guard stepped forwards, deciding to investigate. Piay watched his shadow fall across the glow of the firelight. As he walked past the sailcloth, he loomed against the sky. He was a big man – broad shoulders, a belt of fat overlying muscle around his waist. He crunched towards the edge of the shadows and peered into the dark, weighing up whether to investigate further.

When the barbarian took another step forwards, Piay eased himself to his feet and stalked behind the guard. He'd taken three steps when a cry of alarm rang out across the shipyard. The body of his first victim had been discovered. Piay silently cursed.

The big guard spun round and stared at Piay creeping up behind him.

'To arms!' he roared.

Piay lunged, but his enemy's sword was already in his hand. The Hyksos warrior heaved the blade down with a force that could have split a man in two. Piay leaped to one side and stabbed, but the heavily built barbarian was faster. With a twist of his weapon, he knocked the strike aside.

All around, cries rang out, accompanied by the sound of running feet.

Ducking, Piay snatched up a chunk of timber and hurled it. The wood clattered off the barbarian's head. Seizing his moment, Piay dashed past the dazed Hyksos warrior and weaved among the maze of cedarwood logs to where the repaired galleys rested in their channels, ready to be launched down the ramps to the river. Hannu came from the dark to intercept him.

'How many?' his friend asked.

'Three,' Piay replied.

'Three,' Hannu said with a nod. 'Six dead, but no sign of Sakir.'

The call and response of the searching barbarians rang out, drawing closer. Piay glanced round and a revelation struck him.

'Sakir must be on one of these galleys. Easy to defend. Ready to launch in the blink of an eye.'

'And a trap for us,' Hannu growled. 'If we are caught on deck with the rest of his men at our backs, we won't stand a chance.'

As the sound of the barbarians drew nearer, Piay hurried away, sweeping from galley to galley. There were five of them. Most had holes in the hulls and were being repaired. Only one looked riverworthy. Piay pointed to a ladder resting on the side.

'This one.'

Hannu glanced round. Those running feet were drawing in on them.

'We can't risk being caught up there,' he said.

'We . . . I . . . have no choice. If we flee now, Sakir will vanish along the river and I will never see Myssa again.'

'If you venture on board, you will die.'

Piay clapped a hand on his friend's shoulder. 'If I do not seize this moment, I will never be able to live with myself.'

Hannu nodded. He understood.

'I have a plan,' Piay said. 'But you won't like it.'

Once he'd outlined the details, Piay scrambled up the ladder. He swung himself over the side and crouched on the moon-lit deck. All was still. The shipwrights hadn't finished their labours and the boards were strewn with pieces of timber and rolls of sailcloth, and tools discarded when the day's work had ended. Instantly Piay knew he had made the right choice. The firepot had been lit for warmth, the red embers glowing like the eyes of a feral beast through the ventilation holes in the side of the pot.

'Egyptian.' The voice rumbled from the shadows beyond the benches where the captain's shelter stood.

Piay drew his sword.

Sakir emerged from under the shelter and stretched the kinks from his muscles. His charred face was lost to the dark.

'I knew you would come.'

'Where is Myssa?'

'Your woman is dead.' The Red Hawk's voice was emotionless. 'I cut off her head and tossed her body into the river for the crocodiles to feast on.'

Piay felt despair consume him. He had refused to consider this outcome, but it was what he had feared all along.

'Why should I keep her alive?' Sakir continued, taking pleasure in the pain he knew he was inflicting. 'She was of no use to me.'

Piay's anger roared like a furnace. He gripped the hilt of his sword with both hands and stalked along the deck. The moonlit world seemed to shatter into a thousand pieces until his vision focused on the form that was the object of all his loathing. The charred black head tipped back, and though he couldn't be sure, Piay thought his enemy was smiling.

Sakir drew his sword and levelled it.

*You will die*, Piay thought, *even if I have to die to end your days.*

As he prowled forwards, Piay felt movement that jerked him from his trance. Beneath his feet, the galley jolted. He knew Hannu had hacked through the hide ropes that held it in place, and was now knocking away the wooden blocks and scaffolding that stabilised the vessel during repairs. Shouts rang out from across the shipyard.

Piay prayed that Hannu would get away. With his injured leg, he couldn't move fast and he had four barbarians on his trail. A part of him knew Hannu was willing to sacrifice his own life so Piay could wreak his vengeance in the same way that Piay was giving up his own for Myssa's memory.

The galley lurched forwards, gathering speed. The ladder crashed away. At least the other men would not be able to clamber on board. This was between him and Sakir alone. It would all end here.

The ship slammed into the water, a fan of spray washing over the prow. Piay crashed onto his back from the impact. Scrambling to his feet, he saw Sakir with one arm curled round the mast. The Red Hawk seemed unmoved. Did nothing trouble him?

The galley slipped out into the current, turning slowly as it drifted downstream. The firepot swung gently, the amber light shifting the shadows across the deck.

Sakir pushed himself back until he was balancing on his toes and then he levelled the sword again.

'Seth is with me,' he said with the strange sibilance. 'Seth is always with me and he has promised me victory.'

'Then the god of the desert whispers lies.' Piay moved his blade from side to side. His rage burned in his heart. 'Those lies have stripped everything from you. Your status, your men, your face, and now this land you conquered. Egypt will be back in the hands of the Pharaoh. Seth has ensured you have lost everything.'

Piay and Sakir leaped forwards in the same moment, bounding from bench to bench with immaculate timing. Sakir swung his blade in an arc as they passed. Piay ducked beneath the flashing weapon and lashed out with his own sword. The Red Hawk danced a whisker away from the tip and crashed on to the boards. He threw himself to his feet in an instant, as calm and relentless as death. He was hurtling back before Piay had even turned.

Piay felt sluggish, his reactions too slow. His head was filled with his fury, the overwhelming compulsion for vengeance for

Myssa's murder. His heart ached for what he had lost. But the strength of his emotions had blunted him, dulling the precision he needed as a skilled swordsman.

In the light of the swinging firepot, Sakir's good eye glowed. His teeth were bared in a victorious grin. He knew what torment raged in his opponent. He knew he had the upper hand.

Piay retreated towards the prow. *Stay calm*, he urged himself, but his fury was out of control.

The Red Hawk advanced once more, thrusting his sword towards Piay's heart. Piay jammed his weapon up in time, deflecting the strike, but the tip of the blade raked across his arm. He choked back a howl as the agony from the wound lanced through him.

As Piay reeled back, he glimpsed the firepot, knowing instantly what he needed to do. Hacking through the leather thong that suspended it, he grasped the frayed end and swung the pot at Sakir. Red-hot embers flew out, sizzling against the barbarian's skin. Sakir did not cry out, but he fell back nonetheless.

The firepot crashed across the deck, shattering. More embers spun out, landing on the rolls of sailcloth and discarded timber. Flames licked up, the river wind whipping them into a roaring spiral. In no time, the fire was raging across the deck.

Sakir pulled himself up to his full height, limned in red against the wall of flames. He raised his sword, unmoved, as if he had decided that his time was done and they would both die together here. He did not seem to fear death. Piay, too, had given up on life, now that there was nothing to keep him in this world.

Piay breathed in a blast of hot air. His lungs seared and his skin bloomed. For a moment, he was back in that burning field, fleeing for his life with Hannu and the captive he had saved. It seemed like an age ago, when he had been a different man.

His skin still smoking from where the embers had burned him, Sakir pounced. Piay clashed his sword against the barbarian's weapon. With the inferno flaring all around, they pressed together in a furious dance, their faces close as their swords locked and ground.

Piay thrust with all his strength and Sakir spun back two steps. At each other again, they came, weapons ringing together as they swept back and forth across the benches. Piay fixed his mind on that blur of bronze while trying not to lose his footing. The burning ship continued to turn in the currents so that the wind blasted the flames in different directions. His skin was scorched and he was sure he was on fire. The flames roared so high he could see nothing of the riverbanks; the sky was a black cloak overhead.

The Red Hawk lowered his shoulders, ready to drive forwards again. Sensing an opportunity, Piay hurled himself, slamming into the barbarian. They careered over the benches, Piay shifting his weight to keep his advantage, until he glimpsed the black square of the open hold.

Thrusting with all his strength, Piay bowled Sakir over the edge and they both crashed down into the belly of the vessel. The barbarian hit the floor, Piay thudding on top of him. He felt some of the Hyksos warrior's ribs shatter beneath him.

Piay lurched to his feet. Here and there, the boards of the deck had burned through and fire rained down from above. Though he desperately tried to suck in air, he found himself choking on smoke.

Piay staggered a few paces, feeling as if he was drowning in the heat. As Sakir lumbered upright, Piay sensed another movement towards the rear of the hold. Half-turning, he felt a wave of shock that cut through the seething furnace.

Myssa was sprawled on a heap of sailcloth, her hands bound behind her back, her ankles tied, a gag across her mouth. Her eyes were wide and she was trying to scream to catch his attention, but the muffled cry was lost beneath the roaring of the fire.

Piay felt his heart leap with joy at the sight of her, but only for an instant. Sakir swept forwards, hacking, his broken ribs barely hampering him. Piay stumbled back, but the barbarian's weapon smashed against his blade, knocking it from his hands.

Piay spun in desperation, crouching beside Myssa. Weaponless, there was nothing he could do but watch the Red Hawk come to them.

He'd failed, at the very last.

Looking at the woman he loved more than life itself, Piay hoped for a final moment of affirmation before this life was stolen from them. Yet as he did, he saw Myssa's eyes were moving to the right. He followed her gaze and glimpsed Jabilo's spear lying on the sailcloth, the one Myssa had armed herself with after the Abantu warrior had sacrificed himself.

Piay snatched the spear and raised it, just as Sakir swung his crescent sword down. The spear tip plunged into the Hyksos captain's belly and Piay heaved it upwards, pushing hard until he almost lifted the barbarian off his feet.

The crescent sword slipped from the barbarian's fingers. Piay rammed one final time, heaving his mortal enemy back and pitching him into the conflagration raging at the other end of the hold.

Piay snatched up the fallen sword and cut through Myssa's bonds. She ripped away the gag and tried to speak, but the air was too hot to breathe, the din of the inferno too loud. Yet he could tell from her eyes all that she wanted to say.

*Please, great Khonsu, do not let us die here*, Piay thought.

As the blistering heat closed in, Piay felt his life ebbing away. But he would not give in, not now he had finally found what he wanted. He threw himself at the hull, kicking as hard as he could. The timbers cracked; the joints of the ship were already weakened by the fire.

Again he kicked, and again, and then one of the planks shattered. Cold river water gushed in. He wrenched at the opening to rip it wider and Myssa threw herself beside him, pulling at the splintering wood. The black water cascaded around their legs and the galley start to keel.

When the hole was bigger, he pushed Myssa forwards. She held his gaze, a look that lifted his spirits to the heavens, and then she plunged through and was gone.

Piay glanced back along the hold, anticipating Sakir rising from the flames. But this time he was certain his tormentor was dead.

**P**iay clawed his way through the papyrus beds and rolled on to his back in the muddy bank next to Myssa. His skin was raw and his lungs ached, but he was alive.

And Myssa was alive, too.

He turned to her, taking in every detail of her features as if she might be snatched away from him in the blink of an eye. Myssa kept staring at the stars. Her hand fumbled across the mud and clasped his, squeezing it.

'I knew you would come,' she breathed, so low it was almost lost beneath the whisper of the wind in the rushes.

Her words echoed Sakir's, though they came from a different place. Piay watched the flames shooting up from the black water in the middle of the river. Myssa slid in next to him. An orange circle spread across the surface of the water around the burning galley. Gradually the circle grew smaller as the ship sank, until it winked out in a hiss and a cloud of steam. Bubbles emerged and disappeared, the ripples ebbed away and Mother Nile returned to serenity.

In the moonlight, dark shapes swam sinuously across the water from the reed beds, then submerged. The river crocodiles were searching for prey.

Footsteps pounded along the track by the river and Piay rested a hand on Myssa's forearm to urge her to stay quiet. Whoever it was stopped running, the only sound the panting of breath.

The person crashed through the vegetation to the water's edge and stared across the river.

'No!' he shouted, his voice cracking. 'Why have you gone? I have failed you!'

Piay glanced at the silhouette against the night sky and recognised a familiar outline. He grinned.

'Silence,' Piay called. 'You will frighten the crocodiles.'

The figure jolted as if it had seen a ghost, then moved through the undergrowth towards Piay. Hannu looked down.

'What foul game is this? You would torment me now?' he snarled.

Piay rose to his feet, wincing from the burns. 'No torment, old friend. I am merely pleased to be alive.'

'I thought you were dead. I followed the burning ship along the river as best I could . . . and then it vanished . . .'

Piay clapped his hands on his friend's arms. 'Enough talk. Now it is time to celebrate victory, and a new dawn in a new world.'

There was laughter and raucous song drifting across the water. The land beyond the city walls of Thebes throbbed with a life Piay had never seen before. The victory celebrations were continuing deep into the night. The Spartan army had pitched a vast, makeshift tent city that sprawled from the Nile to the river gate. Fires blazed and men gathered around them in full voice, dashing their cups together and punching the air. Much wine was being drunk and lavish food was brought in by slaves at the behest of the grateful Egyptian citizens.

Piay looked out across the scene of celebration. He had never dreamed he would see this day. There was still work to do, of course, hunting down the remnants of the Hyksos horde and driving them back through the Sinai so they would know never to attack Egypt again. But for now, after half a century of hardship, bloodshed and death, the Great Liberation had finally arrived.

Turning to the river, Piay looked along the masts stretching into the night. The Spartan navy was moored as far as the eye could see. Piay moved along the quayside, questioning the groups of sailors huddled around their fires until he found the information he wanted.

Climbing the gangplank of the warship as he had done once before, far beyond the Great Green, Piay glanced along the deck to where a lamp flickered. Admiral Hui perched on a stool, sipping from a cup of wine. When he saw Piay, he raised a hand and beckoned to his visitor. Hui looked much as he had the last time Piay had seen him, his grey hair tumbling from his bald pate, his weather-beaten face like old leather, the crinkles of humour spreading around the eyes and mouth.

'Do I have you to thank for answering the prayers of all good Egyptians?' Piay asked.

'You should thank yourself,' Hui replied, his eyes twinkling in the lamplight. He poured Piay a cup of wine. 'If you had not pleaded the case, the call would not have been answered.'

'But Hurotas was adamant that no aid could be offered. He feared retribution from the Hyksos – the damage to trade, even war.'

Hui shrugged. 'Perhaps I had some small part to play. And General Mennias. And the beautiful Serrena.' He winked at Piay. 'You seem to have caught her attention. That rarely happens.'

'You all persuaded the king to change his mind?'

Hui held out a hand. 'It took a good two years. He is not an easy man to convince. But Mennias and I made the strategic case for helping the Egyptians, and Serrena tugged on her father's heartstrings, as only daughters can.'

'Then you have my thanks, all of you. If you had not arrived this day, with such fortuitous timing, Egypt would now be lost and all of us would be buried beneath the shifting sands.'

'I could never abandon the home of my birth,' Hui said. 'And to his credit, neither could Hurotas – or Zaras, as he was known when he lived here in the Land of the Nile. He fought a long battle within himself between the needs of his old home and the needs of the new. But once he made his decision there were no half-measures. He committed the full weight of the Spartan force to come to your aid.' Hui poured more wine in his cup. 'Do not underestimate what Hurotas has done. The risk he has taken. His gamble could have resulted in the destruction of the Spartan army and the loss of all he has fought for in Mycenae – not least the king's throne, and indeed, his head.'

Piay raised his cup. 'Then we will always be in your debt.'

With a sly grin, Hui wagged his cup at Piay. 'I warn you . . . Hurotas will strike a hard bargain in payment for this service Sparta has offered Egypt. Our terms for trade may bring tears to the eyes.'

'A small price to pay,' Piay said. 'I promised the contents of the Pharaoh's coffers to another, but that debt will no longer need to be paid. You can put no value on freedom.'

Hui smiled. 'We will see if the new Pharaoh feels the same.'

Piay looked across the deserted deck. 'Why do you wait here and not join the celebrations?'

'The time for celebration will come. For now, I am waiting for a meeting with my past . . . with the man I used to be . . . when my destiny was still being carved out of the bedrock of this land. A meeting with my old . . . friend? . . . Taita.'

Piay bowed. 'Then I will take my leave. I must speak with Taita first before he is distracted with too much wine.'

A warm wind whistled through the deserted Egyptian camp, billowing the tents and cracking the lines. The soldiers who had survived the battle with the Hyksos had abandoned this place, which had become associated with so much misery, and were now joining the festivities around Thebes.

Piay, Hannu and Myssa strolled past the dead campfires and ragged shelters to Taita's tent.

'You want a peaceful life?' asked Hannu. 'Why?'

'So I can spend my days with Myssa without worrying about having my head removed at every moment.'

'What would you be, then? A farmer?'

'Perhaps.'

Hannu snorted. 'You'd be driven mad by the end of the first planting season.'

Piay sighed. He'd thought long and hard about this and still couldn't find the right answer.

Myssa squeezed Piay's hand, whispering, 'It matters not where we are, as long as we are together.'

'If you become a farmer, I'm not digging ditches,' Hannu said.

Piay slowed his step as he approached Taita's tent. On the long road from the Elephant Kingdom, he'd dreamed of this moment, but now he felt only dread. He pulled aside the flap.

Taita was examining his face in a bronze mirror while smearing some sweet-smelling unguent into his cheek. His armour had been set aside and he resembled the master Piay had always known, in a flowing robe of the finest silk, studded with jewels in the pattern of a bird in flight that glimmered red, blue and green in the lamplight. It seemed the mage was preparing for a new life, too.

When he saw Piay, Hannu and Myssa, Taita beckoned them in. He was beaming, Piay thought, and seemed in high spirits. That was good.

'You are ready for the celebrations?' Piay asked.

'The celebrations and more. There is a new Egypt to build. In the morning I must report our great victory to the new Pharaoh, Utteric Turo, and then there will be much to do as we rekindle the glories of old.'

Taita set aside the mirror and ointment. No one could tell he had fought a wearying battle. He seemed charged with a great power that almost appeared to glow.

'Your part in this will not be forgotten, Piay, nor that of your two friends,' Taita said. 'Your success in the quest I set you has changed the future of Egypt. New trade with the Spartans. And as we rebuild our army, we will keep the war elephants you acquired at the heart of it. You will be rewarded, never fear.'

'That is why I have come to see you, master,' Piay said.

Taita cocked an eyebrow at him.

'I . . . I am hoping you will release me from your service, master.'

Even as he spoke, Piay felt a pang of doubt. This was all he had known since he was a boy.

'It is my intention to marry, and—'

Taita's gaze flickered to Myssa. 'You?'

Myssa bowed her head. 'My lord. If you will allow it.'

Taita smiled. Piay felt relieved. His master was in a better mood than he had ever seen him.

'Tell me about yourself,' Taita continued. 'And how you met and how this love was fashioned on this long journey.'

Between them, Piay and Myssa weaved the tale and Taita listened with interest. There were moments when he seemed to reflect deeply on what was being said, though Piay could not divine those thoughts.

When they were done, Taita said, 'I can scarce believe this man before me is the boy I once taught. I can scarce believe you are the man who came to me that night after the soldiers under your command were killed in the fields. To walk the road of life is a gift granted us by the gods, and we can never tell the ways each step will change us. But change us it does. And in the midst of that change we often believe we want something that we think will bring us joy, but will ultimately bring us misery.' His voice softened. 'I cannot grant your request, Piay.'

Piay winced. 'Have I not served you well?'

'Very well.'

'Then set me free, I beg you.'

Taita shook his head. 'I am afraid that cannot be, at least not for now. You are too valuable to me.'

Piay's eyes drifted to the floor. He couldn't bring himself to look at Myssa.

'You have learned many things on the long road,' Taita said. 'You have learned to be a better spy, a better warrior, a better diplomat. A better man. Would you put all those lessons to waste? We have work to do, Piay. The Hyksos may have been defeated here at Thebes, but they must be driven into the sea so they can never menace Egypt again. This will be your work now.'

'But Myssa . . .'

Taita eyed her, the ghost of a smile on his lips. He nodded and Myssa beamed back, understanding.

'I will accompany you in this work,' she said. 'No one wields a spear better, or a knife.' She looked from Hannu to Piay. 'And if truth be told, you two cannot be trusted on your own. That never goes well. You will need me to guide you.'

Taita nodded, impressed by what he saw in her.

'You may not understand this now, Piay, but this is a kindness. You have been bred for a life of adventure. From the moment your parents left you with me, you have been guided towards a living that stirs the blood. You could never be happy in a simple existence. I know this. I wager Hannu knows this. And I see now Myssa knows this, too, which tells me your heart has chosen wisely. You will spend your days together, and your nights, and you will serve me, and the Pharaoh. And one day you will thank me.'

Piay bowed and left Taita to his preparations for the festivities to come. He wasn't sure he wholly understood what he had heard, but his master was wise and perhaps he would grow to agree with this path.

As they made their way back through the camp, Hannu said, 'Well, it looks like I'll have to shoulder this burden a little longer.'

Piay felt his spirits lift a little. The road ahead would be hard, but who better to share it with?

'It seems your master's decision has been blessed by the gods,' Myssa said.

Puzzled, Piay followed her gaze. A grey cat was winding its way towards them among the tents. Piay blinked, not sure if he could believe what he was seeing.

Kneeling, Myssa reached out and rubbed her fingers.

'Bast!' she exclaimed.

Piay shook his head. 'No, that cannot be the same cat.'

Myssa scrubbed the cat's forehead and it purred, slinking around her.

'See, she has the same white patch under her chin.'

'No, it cannot be. You abandoned her in the land of the Great Apes. No cat could find its way back to you over that distance, or even survive the journey.'

Myssa smiled. 'No earthly cat.'

Hannu folded his arms and said, 'Now there is no backing out. The gods have decided the way ahead. There will be no rest for us. A life of adventure calls.'

# THE STORY CONTINUES. . .

**THE MASTER OF ADVENTURE LEAVES BEHIND HIM A TREASURE TROVE OF NOVELS YET TO BE PUBLISHED, ALONGSIDE CO-AUTHORED PROJECTS AND OUTLINES FOR FUTURE NOVELS INCLUDING:**

**The Courtney adventures continue in *Nemesis*, coming in 2023**

**Two further titles in the exciting new Ancient Egyptian Series**

**Two more thrilling adventures in the epic crossover series featuring the Courtney and Ballantyne families, tracing from *King of Kings* through to *Assegai***

**A brand-new Hector Cross thriller**

**And many more to be announced . . .**

Join the adventure and stay up-to-date with all new announcements at

www.wilbursmithbooks.com

or join the Wilbur Smith Readers' Club

**THE MASTER OF ADVENTURE FICTION
RETURNS TO EGYPT IN**

# THE NEW
# KINGDOM

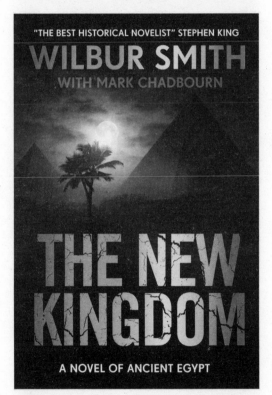

OUT NOW

**FIND OUT MORE AT
WILBURSMITHBOOKS.COM**

# THE COMPLETE ANCIENT EGYPTIAN ADVENTURES

Set in the land of the ancient Pharaohs, Wilbur Smith's bestselling series vividly brings Ancient Egypt to life. Following the beloved Taita, Smith's most iconic hero, this is an unmissable series from the Master of Adventure fiction.

**RIVER GOD**

**THE SEVENTH SCROLL**

**WARLOCK**

**THE QUEST**

**DESERT GOD**

**PHARAOH**

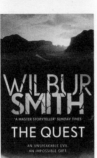
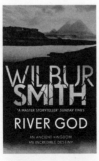
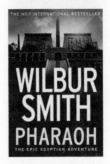
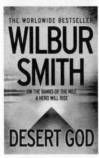
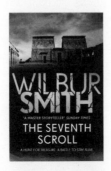
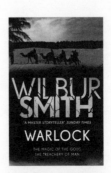

**DISCOVER THE BIRDS OF PREY SEQUENCE
IN WILBUR SMITH'S EPIC COURTNEY SERIES**

# BIRDS OF PREY
# MONSOON
# BLUE HORIZON

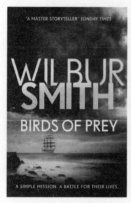
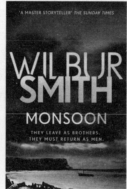
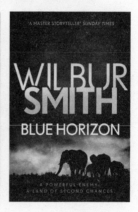

The earliest sequence in the Courtney family adventures starts in 1667, amidst the conflict surrounding the Dutch East India Company. In these action-packed books we follow three generations of Courtney's throughout the decades and across the seas to the stunning cliffs of Nativity Bay in South Africa.

The conclusion to the series, *Blue Horizon*, lays the foundation for the next generation of adventures in *Ghost Fire* and *Storm Tide*.

# AVAILABLE NOW

## A NOVEL OF THE AMERICAN REVOLUTION

# STORM TIDE

**One family is torn apart as three generations fight on opposing sides of a battle that will change the face of the world forever.**

1774. Rob Courtney has spent his whole life in a quiet trading outpost on the east coast of Africa, dreaming of a life of adventure at sea. When his grandfather Jim dies, Rob takes his chance and stows away on a ship as it sails to England, with only the family heirloom, the Neptune Sword, to his name.

Arriving in London, Rob is seduced by the charms of the big city and soon finds himself desperate and penniless. That is until the navy comes calling. Rob is sent across the Atlantic on a ship to join the war against the rebellious American colonists.

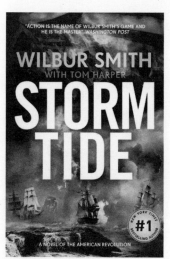

But on the other side of the Atlantic, unbeknownst to Rob, his distant cousins Cal and Aidan Courtney are leading a campaign against the British. Their one desire is American independence, and they are determined to drive the British out of America – by whatever means necessary . . .

**THE THRILLING NEW HISTORICAL EPIC ARRIVES JUNE 2022**

**THE STUNNING CONCLUSION TO THE ASSEGAI
SEQUENCE OF THE COURTNEY SERIES**

# LEGACY OF WAR

The war is over, Hitler is dead – and yet his evil
legacy lives on. Former Special Operations Executive,
Saffron Courtney, and her beloved husband, Gerhard,
only just survived the brutal conflict, but Gerhard's
Nazi brother, Konrad, is still free and determined to
regain power. As a dangerous game of cat-and-
mouse develops, a plot against the couple begins to
stir. One that will have ramifications
throughout Europe. . .

Further afield in Kenya, the last outcrop of the
colonial empire is feeling the stirrings of rebellion.
As the situation becomes violent, and the Courtney
family home is under threat, Saffron's father, Leon
Courtney, finds himself caught between two powerful
sides - and a battle for the freedom of a country.

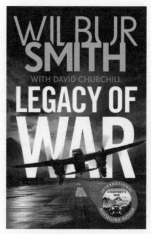

The thrilling conclusion to the
Assegai sequence. *Legacy of
War* is a nail-biting story of
courage, rebellion and war.

**AVAILABLE NOW**

 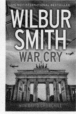 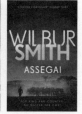

# IF YOU LIKE THE COURTNEYS, YOU'LL LOVE THE BALLANTYNES.

Join the adventure in

# KING OF KINGS

**An epic story of love, betrayal, courage and war.**

Cairo, 1887. A beautiful September day. Penrod Ballantyne and his fiancée, Amber Benbrook, stroll hand in hand. The future is theirs for the taking.

But when Penrod's jealous former lover, Lady Agatha, plants doubt about his character, Amber leaves him and travels to the wilds of Abyssinia with her twin sister, Saffron, and her adventurer husband, Ryder Courtney. On a mission to establish a silver mine, they make the dangerous journey to the new capital of Addis Ababa, where they are welcomed by Menelik, the King of Kings.

Back in Cairo, a devastated Penrod seeks oblivion in the city's opium dens. He is rescued by an old friend,

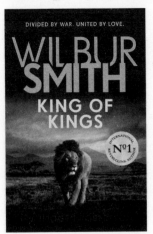

who is now in the Italian army, and offered the chance to join the military efforts. Italy has designs on Abyssinia, and there are rumours of a plan to invade . . .

With storm clouds gathering, and on opposing sides of the invasion, can Penrod and Amber find their way back to one another – against all the odds?

**AVAILABLE NOW**

# WILBUR SMITH
# THE POWER OF ADVENTURE

Visit the brand-new Wilbur Smith website to find out more about all of Wilbur's books, read the latest news, and dive into Wilbur's adventure notebooks on everything from the Boer War to the Skeleton Coast.

And if you want to be the first to know about all the latest releases and announcements, make sure to **subscribe to the Readers' Club mailing list**. Sign up today and get a preview of the next epic Wilbur Smith adventure!

Join the adventure at
# WWW.WILBURSMITHBOOKS.COM